RAINMAKER TRANSLATIONS *supports a series of books meant to encourage a lively reading experience of contemporary world literature drawn from diverse languages and cultures. Publication is assisted by grants from the Black Mountain Institute (blackmountaininstitute.org) at the University of Nevada, Las Vegas, an organization dedicated to promoting literary and cross-cultural dialogue around the world.*

Elias Khoury

As Though
She Were Sleeping

Translated from the Arabic by Marilyn Booth

archipelago books

First Archipelago Books Edition, 2012

Archipelago Books
232 3rd Street #A111
Brooklyn, NY 11215
www.archipelagobooks.org

Library of Congress Cataloging-in-Publication Data
Khuri, Ilyas.
[Ka-annaha na'imah. English]
As though she were sleeping / Elias Khoury ;
translated from the Arabic by Marilyn Booth. – 1st Archipelago Books ed.
p. cm.
ISBN 978-1-935744-02-3
I. Booth, Marilyn. II. Title.
PJ7842.H823K3313 2012
892.7'36—dc23   2012002602

Distributed by Consortium Book Sales and Distribution
www.cbsd.com

Cover art: Edvard Munch

The publication of *As Though She Were Sleeping* was made possible
with support from Black Mountain Institute of UNLV, Lannan Foundation,
the National Endowment for the Arts, and the New York State Council
on the Arts, a state agency.

Death's a long sleep from which one wakes not
And sleep's a short death from which one must rise

Abu el-A'la el-Ma'arri

She is not dead, but is sleeping.

The Gospel of Luke 8:52

The First Night

MILIA'S EYELASHES drew apart over eyes still curtained in drowsiness. She would just close them again, she decided; she would pick up the trail of her dream. She saw a small white candle giving off a wan light that trembled and flickered through the fog. His fist closed tightly around the candle, Mansour walked ahead directly in front of the taxi, the wind buffeting his long overcoat, but she could not make out her husband's features clearly. She reached for the glass of water that she kept habitually on the bedside table but found no glass there. She was thirsty. The dryness diffused along her tongue and broke against the roof of her mouth and down her throat. She dragged her left arm out from beneath her head on the pillow to arrest the numbness creeping from her upper arm toward her neck. She turned over in bed, and over again, and then lay finally still on her back. She put out her hand for the glass of water and found no table there. She shuddered, jerked upright, and suddenly found herself sitting against a wooden headboard. Where had it gone, that familiar white wall against which she propped her head? She could always sense the peeling white paint cracking and splintering beneath her long hair, even commingling with it as she rested her head on the wall. She pressed her arms to her chest, just touching the warm skin of her breasts. Suddenly she was afraid and the coldness of it slunk into her thighs. She placed a hand there to press away the trembling in her legs. Her palm brushed against naked skin, glided upward as far as the top of her thighs went, and she felt blood collecting there. Gone cold, the blood had formed a solid mass at the lowest curve of her belly.

This is marriage, she said, her voice almost a whisper, and closed her eyes again.

Milia's memory preserved the scene at Dahr el-Baydar as though it were a shadow play etched black and solid on the wall. Her husband, Mr. Mansour Hourani, holds a small candle before him as he steps forward in front of the car, still wearing his black wedding suit though a long olive-green overcoat covers it. The young woman in her white bridal finery sits on the backseat, swathed in darkness, staring at the driver's bald head glinting with dandruff. Once they are in Nazareth, she decides, she will tell her husband how his image has been imprinted permanently on her eyes – today, on this evening – as a black wraith fading and disintegrating, appearing and disappearing ahead of the car whose headlights cannot cut through the viscous fog blanketing the heights of Dahr el-Baydar on this snow-mantled night.

At three o'clock, on the afternoon of Saturday the twelfth of January, in the year 1946, Mansour and Milia were married in the Church of the Blessed Archangel Mikhail, their union blessed by Father Boulos Saba. Following the service, the bridal pair stood before the church door surrounded by Milia's family tendering their congratulations. The tears collected in Milia's eyes so heavily that she could not make out even a single well-wisher, as familiar to her as they all were. Her tears overwhelmed her, spurting out as if intending flight before landing heavily on her pale cheeks. Mansour, the thin line of his lips wholly captured and partly transformed by a broad smile that revealed his small lustrous teeth, was oblivious to his bride's weeping until he heard her mother scolding her. Shame on you, dear – Milia, stop it! *Ayb*. For shame – are we burying someone, girl? It's a wedding, after all.

And when all of the guests had gone, carrying away the little silver boxes filled with sweets; and when no one was left in the churchyard apart from members of the family, the mother went to her daughter. She pulled the younger woman to her chest and, their bodies quivering, mother and daughter wept together. Then the mother pushed her daughter away. Even if you *are* breaking my heart, dearest, leave us to do the crying. *You* must show how happy you are! Come, now, we want to see it on your face! The bride smiled, choking back her tears, while the mother went on crying before releasing the joyful trill – *yuuyuuyuu!* – of her celebratory *zaghruda* into the air.

Milia's brothers clustered around the newlyweds. It was Musa who particularly caught the bride's attention, though. The pupils of his eyes seemed to cringe and recede inside their sockets. She sensed danger but could not define where it was coming from. She raised her arm, unconsciously almost, as if to shield her husband's face from her brother's stare.

Milia opened her eyes and saw nothing but the darkness of the night. She made up her mind to keep going. She would follow this odd dream of hers, for even in the face of her fear it reassured her. Finally the dream-spaces had come back to inhabit her nights.

In her dreams Milia had seen herself a small girl of seven, her skin tawny and her hair short and curly. The little girl scampered and darted among the grown-ups, espying everything there was to see. And when Milia got up in the morning she would tell things exactly as she pleased. But the reactions were always unpleasant: everyone stared at her, startled and dismayed, for these dreams of hers were like prophecies that somehow always come to fruition. But here and now, in this unfamiliar bed tucked inside of a murky blackness that thickened to press hard against her eyes, she dreamed of herself, a woman of twenty-four, her naked body lying full length across a bed not her own, her head on an unfamiliar pillow.

Milia opened her eyes to arrange her dream properly before going back to sleep. She saw nothing but a pair of eyes open upon the darkness.

She opened her eyes. She saw her own eyes, open. She was afraid.

The man leaned against the trunk of the lilac tree. He told her about the sky-blue glow that tinted the whiteness of her eyes and gave them a heavenly look. Her pale-white skin and her long neck, he said, had brought him here, not to mention her honey-toned eyes and the chestnut color of her hair streaming down her shoulders. All the way from his distant city her image had carried him. Here, to marry her. And he said he loved her. Where had he said these things? And why, awakening from this dream, did she find the dream still there, and why did it leave her seeing nothing but a pair of eyes open upon the darkness?

Milia decided to get out of bed and fetch a glass of water. She saw her own white nakedness reflected in the twin mirrors of her eyes. She closed her eyes again and made up her mind to ask the man who slept on this bed beside her, his back turned, to come back inside the car because she was worried for his safety. She closed her eyes and saw herself slipping: she was drifting into the white vapor outside. She forgot her thirst at the sight of a woman naked and prone, before her a windshield fogged over with human breath and a man walking in front of the car carrying the trembling flame of a candle as if he would pierce the solid fog in his black wedding suit and his olive-green overcoat.

Silence; a naked woman; a vehicle creeping almost imperceptibly through the dreary fog; a driver hunched close over the steering wheel trying to see the road through a windshield splotched with white; and a man walking before the car draped in white fog and clutching a white candle.

The candle went out or at least it looked that way to her. The man came to a stop, standing in the middle of the road, opening his overcoat as if trying to shelter the candle inside so that he might ignite its flame again. He crooked his back and leaned into the wind; the flaps of his coat flew upward, but the man himself remained motionless, there, outside on the road. The driver's breathing accelerated, coming faster and louder. Every so often he opened the car window, sticking his head out and shouting into the wind, but she could not make out any of his words.

Milia was cold. A sharp pain lanced her belly. She tried to cover herself, wrapping her body as fully as she could in the brown overcoat and pressing her crossed arms to her chest. She could hear her teeth chattering as she enfolded herself in the coat and the darkness. The candle was useless, she thought. She made up her mind to get out of the car. If the headlights weren't able to slice through the fog, she wanted to say to that man, what could a candle possibly do? She would tell him to come back to the car, except she did not dare to leave the car, naked and cold as she was.

Who had put the bed in the car? Why was she naked? After all, when getting ready for bed she always put on her long blue nightgown that covered her body and legs all the way to her ankles. She did not even undo her bra. What had made her resolve never to remove it was the sight, long ago, of her grandmother's elongated, pendulous breasts. She thought of that image of Grandmama as an alarming warning that her own adult breasts might well droop all the way to her belly, and so she had decided to brace them at all times, even when sleeping. But now it appeared she had on neither a nightgown nor a bra. The driver's breathing had grown even louder as he pressed his chest heavily against the steering wheel, his eyes plastered to the windshield. Milia was afraid. The man whom she glimpsed through the fog was moving farther away, almost as though he were flying. His overcoat ballooned with the wind and he looked a lone figure beating his wings against the wind high above the precipitous wadi.

In the dream Milia saw herself a pale-white figure. She did not fully understand where this pallor had come from. The body she inhabited during the day was not hers but rather a reflection from other people's eyes. Her mother had desired a light-skinned daughter with a full figure and so Milia's body had grown lighter in color as it filled out, purely for her mother's sake. At night, though, her body was entirely her own. She was seven years old; her skin was brown and her body lean. Her eyes were big and wide and took over the whole of her face; her hair was black and curly and her nose so small and slender it seemed barely sketched in beneath the long thin sweep of eyebrow. She wore shorts and ran barefoot. Her eyes borrowed a pair of green irises to replace the light brown ones that people saw by day. Those irises floated in a white expanse shot through with a blue so evanescent it was barely perceptible to the eye.

Little Milia is in love with the nighttime through whose narrow lanes she scampers. She lies down on her bed and opens her eyes so that the night comes drawn in dark pencil around her eyelids. When the darkness becomes total she closes her eyes and walks into her dreams. When morning comes she has not swept those dreams from her eyes. She leaves them there, circles sketched in invisible ink so that she can bring them back whenever she wishes. She closes her eyes: this is all she has to do for the voices to dwindle to nothing and the lights to blot out. And then she can go to that place where she sees everything and discovers all the secrets that are there to find.

Milia did not let on to anyone that she was keeping her dreams hidden away, concealed in a deep reservoir beneath the darkness. In the murky blackness she would dig, carving a place to lay down her dreams. She would go to her hollowed-out dreampit whenever she wanted those dreams. There she could extract the dreams she sought and dream them all over again.

This dream, though, comes from no place: in the dreampit this Milia does not exist. Milia of the night is not Milia of the day. Where do the images of daylight come from, then? How are they made? Is it because she has gotten married? Is this what marriage is?

Milia is finding it hard to swallow or to breathe, and she shivers incessantly from the cold. The nighttime is a deep well and she crouches at the very bottom. The driver moans as if with pain and his breathing grows louder and heavier, seeming almost to cuff her lightly on the neck. She tries to ask the driver – whose bald head is all she can see – what the matter with him is, but her voice has dissolved. She tries to raise her head from the pillow but her head has grown too heavy. Suddenly the driver leaves the car. He has disappeared and Mansour has disappeared and the naked woman is alone in bed. The fog swallows her and the snow falls all around. She tries to pick up her left foot, stiff with the cold, but cannot. She has the sensation of falling out of bed. A terrible pain hits her between the thighs, a knife stabs her, and there's blood.

She screams. She means to scream that the driver is violating her. But her voice is gone and her mouth has filled up with cotton.

Alone in the gloom and the cold, Milia decided to open her eyes and pull herself from this particular dream. She saw a white face framed by a pair of white wings. She put her right hand out to it and feathers clung to her fingertips. She cried out, asking the face to save her, but the face did not hear her voice. What she meant to say, what she wanted to say, was that she yearned to go home. That she no longer wanted marriage. But in the end she did not say it. The winged face circled above the car, above the wadi, above the two men. The face floated away, feather-wings dropping from it like the snowflakes falling in front of the pale glow from the car's headlights.

She did not want to spend their honeymoon in Shtoura, Milia said. Snow was falling over the high plains of Dahr el-Baydar and it was very cold. There was no need for the Hotel Massabki, she said, no need for any honey right now. We can stay in Beirut for a couple of days with my family, she said, and then we can go directly to Nazareth.

It was December, after all, said her mother. Kanun, a month when no one could imagine honeymooning *there*. Think again, she said. Change your plans. Come summertime, have all the honey you want.

Sister Milana said it would be better if they did not go to Shtoura in this cold weather; but there was no real danger in going, she supposed. It's a foolish little adventure, she huffed. Much better to postpone it.

But Mansour insisted. *Ma bsir!* he exclaimed. This could not be, he ruled; the journey was not to be postponed. He wanted the honeymoon in Shtoura. Marriage and the honey of it could truly happen only at the Hotel Massabki.

Musa knitted his eyebrows but he told his sister that it was not an issue, really. There was no argument. The man wants Shtoura, so be it, he said. Go with him.

Still wearing her long white bridal gown, Milia climbed into the American-make car and settled herself beside Mansour on the backseat. The shrill joyful *yuuyuuyuus* of the women wishing her well deafened her to her mother's voice. Leaning into the car's open window, her mother was murmuring words of goodbye and whispering women's advice. Musa stepped up to the car and tossed two coats at them: his dark olive-green overcoat and his mother's brown coat. He looked long into Milia's eyes before turning to Mansour.

Congratulations, bridegroom, he said, and walked away.

The car moved through a silence broken only by the fierce onslaught of a Beirut rainstorm, the water coming down in ropes. Milia shut her eyes but reopened them as she felt Mansour's lips kissing her neck. She pushed his mouth away – Later, not now! – and fell back into her sleepy reverie. The car slowed down around the winding mountain roads that would take them to Shtoura. She slept with her head leaning against the car door, opening her eyes only at the sound of Mansour's voice ordering the driver to go on. The car had halted, swathed in a white fog that completely enveloped everything around them. She closed her eyes but Mansour's voice was so loud that they opened again.

He could not go any farther on this road because he could not see it, the driver said. Mansour opened the car door and jumped out into the road. He walked two steps forward until he was directly in front of the car. He twisted around and beckoned to the driver to follow him. He walked a few steps, looking as though he were slipping across ice. When the car did not budge he retraced his steps, pulled Musa's olive-green coat from the backseat and put it on, and told the driver he would walk ahead. All the driver and the car had to do was to follow.

He's gone, Milia said. Gone, for she could not see him at all right then, nor for several seconds after. The cold air struck her face and the snowflakes falling over the interminable fog were coming thickly, spreading across the landscape. Milia lost her husband. Then she saw him through the front windshield, the likeness of a wraith scaling the frosty seething air.

Excuse me, bride, said the driver. But the bridegroom is mad, what can I do?

Milia's body was shivering with the cold and her fear and she did not answer.

Tell me, what am I to do? persisted the driver.

Follow him, said Milia, her voice choked and low.

Khuta! So the bride's a lunatic, too! *Ya* Allah what have I gotten myself into! grumbled the driver. He pressed his foot on the gas and the car began to skate across the ice.

She saw Mansour walking forward, carrying a snuffed-out candle in his right hand. Bent close behind the front windshield the driver drove haltingly behind the olive-green coat that ballooned out as the turbulent outside air found its way underneath.

The driver jerked his head to the rear and Milia could see the black centers of his eyes. They looked like coals, but cold ones, the glow burnt out. His eyes stung her and his raspy voice frightened her. She asked him to keep his eyes on the road and to keep a strong hold on the steering wheel because the car was skidding. But he kept his gaze on her, muttering incoherently as the car continued its slow slide.

Shu amm bit'uul! she shouted. What are you saying, there?

Does anyone go honeymooning in Shtoura at this time of year? Your husband has no brains! groused the driver, his voice reaching her slowly in wisps of sound. Milia stared into the darkness before her and discovered that what she had believed to be eyes were two holes notched into the driver's bald pate, hollows coated with a stinking oily substance. The dark pink tinge that Milia's discomfiture had brought to her cheeks receded. Once again the extreme cold assaulted her bones and her teeth chattered. She pressed her lips together and closed her eyes.

Milia had not understood what the driver said, but she would recall the interminable sound of his mutterings and his grinding oaths. He opened the car door time after time in order to see outside, and each time she could hear the falling snow like a whispering voice as the cold wind from outside hit her face – a bride in her finery, huddled apprehensively in a corner of the backseat.

Milia decided to come out of this dream and speak to the man whom another dream had chosen as her husband. She opened her eyes and rubbed her cheeks with her palms – and found herself in the car. Mansour was not beside her. He was out there, walking in the distance, walking away from her amidst the fierce high winds as the driver kept the black pinpoints of his eyes fixed on her face.

God preserve you, don't you go to sleep now, he snarled.

Milia stared at him, her eyes open to their widest. Seeing those reddened pupils moving in the back of his head, she let out a sudden cry. O Virgin,

Mother of Light, save your servants, O Mother of God! And then immediately she was asleep once again.

Milia did not see what happened nor did she hear the driver exclaim, It's a miracle! She did not notice how her husband turned aside to stand calmly on the verge of the road waiting for the car to draw even with him. For as Milia's cry sliced the air, the clouds outside dissolved and clear skies returned; beams of light carved holes in the fog and the snow stopped falling. The driver braked, and as he waited for Mansour to return to the car, he twisted around to stare into the face of the woman who had worked this extraordinary event with her voice. But Milia had her eyes closed, her hovering dreams forming circles around her eyelids. She was a marvel! the driver told her, and her body twitched. She massaged her eyes and smiled, and Mansour opened the car door and got in next to the driver.

What awful cold! exclaimed Mansour.

And me – how'll I get back to Beirut? asked the driver, as the car careened downward toward the Beqaa Valley.

There was only fog at the top of Dahr el-Baydar, said Mansour. And it's gone now, and everything's going to be fine.

And me, where'll I sleep? asked the driver.

I was afraid to fly, said Mansour, but by God I flew. He swiveled his head to see his wife, a bundle in a brown overcoat that quivered on her body.

The bride–, said the driver.

What about the bride?

She screamed *O Virgin, help me!* and the fog disappeared. She screamed and the snow stopped. The bride made a miracle.

Milia–, said Mansour, and began immediately to sneeze. A fit of shivering swept through him and his teeth began to chatter. Groans erupted from his chest and belly and entrails.

Rub your hands together, said the driver.

Mansour sneezed and moaned as if fighting off an implacable wave of dizziness. His body trembled and shuddered uncontrollably.

It's nothing, said the driver. And anyway you have to get through it. You're the one who wanted to keep going, so just pull yourself together.

Mansour tried to pull himself together, but his reserves deserted him. Tremblings bombarded the muscles of his chest and arms and thighs, and a choking feeling welled up in his throat leaving him barely able to breathe. The driver bellowed at Milia to attend to her husband because his face had gone blue and he could no longer speak.

Milia shifted position, put out her hand and stroked Mansour's hair. Relax, my dear, we'll be at the hotel soon now and we'll warm up there.

The man began to calm down and his breathing grew more regular. He managed to tell his wife not to worry. Don't be afraid, I'm strong, I'm better now, he said, and began to sneeze. When he asked for a handkerchief the driver handed him one but Mansour pulled his own hand back. His wife held out hers. It was the tatted white lawn handkerchief she had inherited from her grandmother, preserving it in her hope chest all this time in anticipation of her wedding day. He bent his head over it and sneezed into it, clearing his throat and spitting out phlegm.

Milia did not know how they reached the hotel, but finally and suddenly they were there. She remembered only the fog, the high winds and snow besieging them on the heights of Dahr el-Baydar. She remembered how she had seen her husband climb out of the car and walk forward, and how the fog had swallowed him whole. She remembered how the driver had pleaded with him when they reached the approach to the village of Sofar, swearing he could not go as far as Shtoura in this snow and ice. Mansour had insisted on continuing the trip whatever the consequences. She remembered the driver appealing to her but when she tried to speak Mansour's eyes bored into her lips and she pressed them together instead. She had a vision of his moustache thick and black and trembling over his upper lip, imagined a red tarbush on his head, and loved him.

There amidst the winds laying siege to the car and the driver's pleading voice insisting he could not go on came the love Milia had awaited for such a long time. Love tumbled into her heart and she felt a stab of pain inside her rib cage as though her heart itself had plummeted. She could hardly keep back a cry of fear but she did not dare make a sound. She kept silent and told herself it was love. In the beginning she had felt no affection, no emotion at all toward this man whom she had seen standing beneath the palm tree in the garden next door. She would stare out the window and see him there, standing absolutely motionless, looking straight at her as he tried to conjure a smile from her lips. He was always smiling and he never lowered his eyes, never took his gaze off her except when she disappeared from sight, bashful and uneasy, her cheeks washed in red.

What does this stranger want? her mother asked her.

Milia knew nothing about the man and she was not disposed to fall in love with him. His hair always glistened as if bathed in oil, and his whitened temples suggested he was already some distance down life's road. She did not see in him the portrait of a long-awaited and much-anticipated lover but rather the image of a father searching for his lost daughter. And when she said yes, she did not tell anyone the true reasons why she was accepting him as her husband.

She told her brother Musa that she had assented because the prospective groom resembled him. She told her mother that she had grown tired of waiting and wanted to get married. She told Sister Milana that she was leaving home to escape the stifling atmosphere that had enveloped the house after her brother Salim had moved to Aleppo and her mother's illnesses had proliferated.

When she spoke to him for the first time she told him he was an old man.

Me?

She pointed a finger at the graying on his temples.

I started going gray when I was twenty! he responded. Do you know what gray hair means? It means we are lions. Among the animals, the only one who goes gray is the lion.

He told her he was thirty-seven. And that he would get married before the age of forty. The first age of prophecy has passed me by, he said. I was not married in time. I'm not going to let the second one slip by. If I do, it's all over for me.

Milia didn't understand what he meant but she smiled. Emboldened, the man said he loved her and wanted her, and then he asked her if she loved him.

How can I love you when I don't even know you?

But look at me – I love you without knowing you. I feel you, who you are, from inside, and that's enough. Do you have a feeling about me?

She nodded, not to say yes but because she didn't know; but Mansour took her nod as a quiet *yes*.

So, it's a possibility? he asked.

She looked into the distance and closed her eyes.

Milia did not understand what Mansour meant by the two ages of prophecy until they were in the Hotel Massabki in Shtoura. On the second night after their wedding, he moved closer to her. He wanted her.

No, she said. I'm tired. She rolled onto her side, turning her back, and slept. He left her to float downward, submerged in her deep breathing. Then he snuck toward her from behind and began to fondle her. He turned her over and then he was on top of her and had her. In the night Milia felt drenched and sensed the wetness of the sheet beneath her and she began to shake with cold. She wanted to get up and go into the bathroom but she felt her knees turn to jelly. She closed her eyes and tried to go back to sleep.

Wake up, wake up! This is no moment for sleeping.

She opened her eyes. She rested her head against the back of the bed. His torso was bare, a cigarette was between his lips and his eyes shone.

Look – how pretty you are! Look at yourself in the mirror. Love makes a woman beautiful.

She shut her eyes and heard him talking about the prophetic ages that so concerned him. The Messiah's age had missed him, he said. But he would not let the same thing happen with Muhammad's age.

Though Milia still had no idea of what he meant, she did not ask. She felt a burning sensation low in her body and she wanted something to drink. But with her nightgown so damp she was too embarrassed to get out of bed.

The Messiah was crucified when he was thirty-three years old. Muhammad's prophethood appeared when he turned forty. Men have to become men at one of those two ages, Mansour said. If a man misses both, then everything will pass him by. I've passed the first age already. But I haven't reached the second age yet, and now I've found you.

The driver was right, Milia whispered. You are mad.

In the car had come love. Milia closed her eyes and searched for the tarbush that her uncle Mitri had worn so that she could put it on Mansour's head. She found it in the hollow that held her dreams. She saw Mansour draping her uncle's white silk *qumbaz* across his shoulders, tipping a red tarbush forward on his head, and chasing after her with a slender reed cane. The cane brushed Milia's brown feet and the man wearing the *qumbaz* shouted at her to eat her *arus el-labneh*. Milia in her short pants leapt and danced under the blows of the cane, fire inflaming her feet. The cane receded and the girl sat on the ground, swallowing her sandwich of labneh and olive oil, tasting the white onion and green mint.

Milia eats but the sandwich lasts and lasts. She turns to her uncle Mitri and invites him to share her food. The man comes nearer and devours the sandwich in one bite. Milia snatches the cane from the man's grasp and runs, and he hurries after her. Milia is in a garden of lush greenery, springing over hollows filled with water. The man's voice pleads with her to stop and give him back the cane. She falls to the ground. Above her, the uncle breathes heavily. She opens her eyes. The uncle fades from view, the tarbush vanishes, and she finds herself in the car encased in the white shroud of fog.

The uncle has disappeared but he has left behind him the play of a smile on the woman's lips and a red tarbush tilting forward on the head of a man she has decided to love. He has left a woman lying on the backseat of an American-make taxi. Milia gives herself up to this woman as she allows herself to sink into a shadowy dream from which she does not awaken until they reach the Hotel Massabki. Nor does she see Mansour's darkly blue face – the blueness brought on by the cold blending into his dark skin color – until they are at the hotel, just before midnight. Mansour shakes her by her upper arm and she hears a voice. *Yallah*, we're here!

Milia comes to as if emerging from a coma. *Shu . . . wayn?* What's . . . where are we? It takes her a moment to remember that she is a bride arriving for her honeymoon. The car door opens and Mansour stands there waiting for her, hoisting the suitcase. He points to the hotel entrance and she walks beside him, then turns back and sees the bald head of the driver, who droops over the steering wheel, his hands slack, as though he is sleeping.

And the chauffeur? she asks.

We'll see about him later, said Mansour, and led her to a high wooden door. He knocked for some time before someone appearing to be the hotel owner opened the door. George Massabki was in white pajamas covered partially by a brown abaya. Khawaja George's small eyes peered at them, marks of astonishment reshaping his face as if it was completely beyond him to believe that this strange pair had landed here at his door, and at this hour of the night, for the purpose of savoring the honey of marriage.

Ahh, you're the newlyweds, said the hotel owner then, trying with the sleeve of his abaya to mute a cough that swallowed half his words.

Mansour nodded before swiveling to indicate the car parked in front of the building.

Welcome, welcome! *Hamdillah a's-salameh*, praise God you're safe and sound after your journey. I told myself you wouldn't be coming in this cold and snow. Please come in, welcome! The room will be ready in a few minutes.

He left them at the door, disappearing inside where they heard him shouting. Wadiia! Wadiia! The bride and groom are here. He rubbed his hands together in front of the glowing stove and said, as though he were speaking to himself, What a night! Then, louder, he called, Where *are* you, Wadiia, light up the stove in the newlyweds' room and come here. You know, monsieur . . . He turned to Mansour but did not find him there. He saw Milia standing before him, still in her brown overcoat, which disguised the white wedding gown almost completely, her big eyes sleepy and color beginning to suffuse her cheeks.

What's your name, bride?

Milia turned her head as if to seek out the person whom the hotel owner was addressing. Raising her hand abruptly and gesturing toward her chest she asked if the question was for her.

So who else would I be asking – aren't you the bride? retorted a startled George Massabki before a wave of coughing engulfed him, doubling him over. He sat down on the sofa and waved his hand at the bride, inviting her to sit down next to him. Milia remained standing, though, waiting for Mansour to come back. She did not know why, but suddenly the thought seized her that Mansour was on the point of fleeing. She could envision him returning to the taxi, climbing in next to the driver, and telling him to drive off to Beirut.

Then what will I do? Milia asked herself in a barely audible voice.

Please, sit down and rest a bit, said Khawaja Massabki. Wadiia will come down now, and you two can go up to the room.

Milia covered her eyes with her hands and heard Mansour asking the hotel owner for a second room.

There were four of them now in the hotel's large deserted reception hall. Near the front entrance a small black table sat in front of a board where the room keys hung. The board was full of keys, Milia noticed; the hotel must be completely vacant. Three couches upholstered in red plush formed a semicircle around the stove. A red-toned Persian carpet worked with animal motifs covered the floor almost entirely. On the facing wall some photos hung haphazardly. The three visitors stood still in the vestibule while Khawaja Massabki remained seated. He called again for Wadiia before getting to his feet and making his way to the stone staircase that led presumably to the rooms on the floor above.

The heat coming from the stove was finally beginning to penetrate the bodies of the two men and one woman who stood waiting for Wadiia. Mansour walked up to one of the pictures hanging on the wall and beckoned to his wife. Come over here, look, here's Faisal, this is King Faisal the First.

Milia walked slowly over to where her husband stood. A gilded frame held a group of men in tarbushes who formed a close circle around a short, frail-looking man. His pale round face was set, and his eyes were fixed rigidly into the distance as if he could not see.

That's Faisal, said Mansour, pointing to the slight figure at the center.

Did he spend his honeymoon in Shtoura, too? asked the driver sarcastically.

You don't understand anything about anything, said Mansour. Soon we can name our little boy Faisal, he said, looking into his wife's eyes. How would you like that?

She did not answer. She had thought Mansour would name his first son Shukri, after his own father. I don't know, she said finally.

And what do you think of the idea? Mansour asked the driver, who rubbed his hands in front of the stove and shoved them into his trouser pockets as if to hide away the warmth they retained.

What's this blasted cold, what a bitch. Your luck, fellow.

The driver glanced at Milia, who stood next to her husband beneath the photograph of the king of Syria, who had been thrown out by the army of the *République Française*, whereupon the English had founded another kingdom for him next door in Iraq. He has all the luck, your husband, the driver said, and collapsed onto a little sofa nearby.

The hotel owner reappeared followed closely by two women, both equally short. The first one was very pale and gave the impression of being half blind. She looked to be in her sixties. The second one had wheat-colored skin and seemed about thirty years old but otherwise they looked as alike as twins.

Wadiia, take the bride and groom to Room Ten, said Khawaja George.

The two women moved docilely as if they were a single person, coming toward the driver. *Yallah*, hurry up, bridegroom, said the first Wadiia, while the eyes of the second Wadiia looked them over, her eyebrows knitted in puzzlement. Which one is the groom? she asked.

It's this one, this one, said Wadiia I, pointing at the driver slumped into the sofa who was half asleep by this time.

Me – I'm the groom, said Mansour.

Pardon me, sir, I thought he was the groom because that's what grooms are always like – ugly and old and bald. And they take the prettiest girls up to the rooms, *ya husrati*, we poor women! said Wadiia I.

Wadiia, shut up! said the hotel owner, yawning.

That's the groom, I knew him right away, said Wadiia II, the darker one, and she grabbed Mansour by the arm to lead him to the room.

And me? asked the driver.

Just who are you? asked Wadiia I.

I'm Hanna Araman, he said.

Pleased to meet you – but still, who are you?

He's the chauffeur who drove us here and he needs to be taken care of, said Mansour.

Wadiia I looked at Wadiia II and then at Khawaja George Massabki, who muttered, Room Six. Light the stove in Room Six. He turned to the married couple and wished them a good night.

Khawaja George bent over the stove, put out the flame, and disappeared through a door at the far end of the reception hall. The three guests followed the two women up a long staircase and were delivered to facing rooms.

Wadiia II opened the door to the first room and beckoned to the newly-weds while Wadiia I stood chatting in a low voice to the driver at the door to Room Six.

Milia entered the spacious room and the first thing she saw was a very large bed. A mirror took up almost the whole of the facing wall. A square table sat in the middle of the room, draped in an orange tablecloth on which sat a bottle of champagne, two large rounds of thin flaky bread, and a plate holding little squares of white cheese. The bathroom was to the left of the bed; the stove close to the table was lit. Mansour locked the door. Milia could still hear the murmurs of the driver and the elder Wadiia, and she could hear their loud cackling as well.

Milia would not retain a clear memory of what happened in that room. She saw Mansour taking off his coat and hanging it behind the door. She saw him walk over to the table, saw him work the cork in the bottle of champagne until it popped and the white foam spilled over into the two glasses he poured. He gave his bride a glass and raised his own.

To you, my bride!

Milia took a sip. She swallowed the white beads floating on the surface of her glass and felt a light dizziness swell up suddenly from her belly. She put the glass down on the table and said she wanted hot tea. But Mansour appeared not to have heard her. He took a bite of cheese on bread and prepared a morsel for his bride. She pushed his hand away and said she was not hungry, so he swallowed it whole. He drank the glass he had poured for himself in one gulp and poured another, and strange phantomlike shapes began to form in his eyes. Milia smiled, remembering her mother's words about the foolishness that afflicts a man on his wedding night.

The man took her by the hand and led her to the bed. She felt her throat dry up. This was the moment one knew was coming, and she must be brave.

They sat on the edge of the bed. Mansour rested his head against her neck and then kissed it. A light shiver went through the body of the young newly married woman and she wanted to lie down. She leaned back a little and saw herself flying, engulfed in Mansour's arms. Now he would pick her up in his arms and fly with her, before setting her down on the bed again and taking her.

Milia leaned back on the bed and waited. The kisses moved away from her neck. The man seemed to be trembling hard. She wanted to hug him close to make this moment easier for him. But he jumped up and began to take off his clothes. That was the last thing Milia had expected. A groom standing in the center of the room taking off his clothes and tossing them onto the floor? His face was contorted as though he wore a mask and the hair on his shoulders and chest grew so thick and black that it seemed to form a second skin.

Now he will pounce on me, Milia thought. He will capture and open me. The most peculiar sensation came over her. She had the feeling she was standing on a very high terrace waiting for someone to come, someone she knew would throw her from this height, and yet she was resigned to the wait. She closed her eyes on the image of a terrifying fall and a pair of hands reaching to throw her down on the bed and strip off her dress before tearing off her underclothes.

The wait went on and on. Drowsiness closed in on her. She leaned back on her right elbow and something like a light and fitful sleep crept over her. The fog of the road began to rise and spread inside her eyes. She shook herself and opened her eyes. Now she did not see Mansour standing naked in the middle of the room. The man had disappeared. She saw his crumpled clothes strewn on the floor and remembered the sight of him trying to pull off his things. His trousers had caught on his shoes, the shirt had twisted around his neck, and his socks seemed to be stuck to his feet. She saw his thick black moustache trembling over his lower lip, and the expectant smile returned to her lips. Then she heard something like a faint moan. She realized it was coming from the bathroom. The groaning grew louder and there were sounds of vomiting and retching. But instead of going to the bathroom to see what had befallen her husband, she lay down on the bed and covered herself in the sheet without taking off her dress.

Honeymoon, *hunh*? Milia raised her voice, believing the bridegroom sitting on the commode in the bathroom would hear her. When he did not answer she was afraid. The image of the man swallowed up by the fog high on Dahr el-Baydar appeared to her, shivering as he ran to the car making sounds like a puppy's yelps overtaken by groans. He opened the car door and sat down next to the driver, trembling and panting. Milia got out of bed. When she went over to the stove she saw that the flame was dying. She added some kindling and waited for the flame to leap. She walked closer to the bathroom door and called to him. Still Mansour did not answer. She knocked on the door several times. She heard only a faint moaning, muffled as though it came from far away. The warmth from the rekindled fire spread across her body and she wanted to take off her dress. She stooped over the suitcase, pulled out her long blue nightgown, and put it on. She heard the man calling for her and she went to the bathroom door.

Open up for me, Mansour, it's Milia.

But the voice calling her had become even fainter, as if whispering. Was he calling for Milia or for Mama?

For God's sake, open the door.

Lower your voice, the driver will hear you, the man said, his voice hoarse now.

Do you want us to get a doctor?

Calm down, please! Just calm down.

His words stopped abruptly and his moans sounded even odder now. Milia was certain the man was going to die and she sank to the floor in front of the door, kneeling there and rapping on it, over and over. She grasped the doorknob as if she would use it to scale the door. She heard Mansour calling for his mother, but in a whisper. She begged him to open the door and she listened to the rattling sounds of his retching. She crouched there, feeling alone and completely helpless, for she could think of nothing to do.

I'm going to go down and ask the owner to send for the nearest doctor.

Lower your voice, the driver'll hear us, he must be laughing at us.

Mansour's voice seemed to be coming from the bottom of a deep well as he told his wife she must not leave the room. There was nothing at all to worry about.

Go on to bed and I'll be there soon.

She did not know how she got to her feet, or went over to lie down on the bed, or pulled the covers over her and went to sleep.

And why is she naked now? And why are these tremors coming over her like blows to her body?

Milia decided to open her eyes because she sensed death. She knew that death comes only as a long dream with no ending. Death is a dream, she said to her brother Musa. Come on, look at your grandmama, see how she's always dreaming. The grandmother lay flat on her bed in a muddle of white sheets and the women sat all around. There was only a faint sound of weeping; no one dared wail out loud for Malakeh Shalhoub when she closed her eyes and passed on. Their grandmother had never liked crying over the dead. When the dead are finished dying, there's no need for anyone to weep! This was what Malakeh screamed at the waiting women when her daughter died. That day after darkness fell, people heard the voice. It was her husband, Nakhleh, howling like an ox under slaughter. Later, rumors would go around the neighborhood that the man died – only two weeks after the death of his daughter – from the pain caused by having to suppress so many tears. His wife had forbidden him to weep over his daughter Salma.

Milia did not tell her brother Musa she had seen her aunt Salma in her dream. Musa was only three then. He could not understand such things.

The night before her aunt's death Milia opened her eyes at the sound of her mother's wailing. She decided to return to her dream where she might save her dying aunt, who was only twenty years old. But even there, Milia's aunt would not emerge from her profound sleep; she would not open her eyes. The dream was a puzzling one. Milia understood its meaning only years later when she began to menstruate and dreamed that she was flying.

When Milia related the dream to her grandmother everything was already over. The elderly woman held back her tears and requested the little girl to tell the others what had happened in her dream. That day Milia learned to speak about the cryptic, perplexing images she saw at night. As she spoke her cheeks would darken to red and her tongue would show in the gap made by her absent front baby teeth. She could not say a single letter without lisping. She told them how she had seen her aunt Salma falling into the pond in the garden and thrashing about amidst a multitude of tiny red fish as she called out frantically for help. In the dream, Milia tossed a rope to her aunt and Salma grabbed it. She tried to get out of the water but the rope slipped from Milia's hands.

Her aunt lies on thick tufts of grass. Milia walks over and tries to awaken her but just then she hears her grandmother's voice: Don't wake her up, my dear, leave her to dream! That was the moment when Milia woke up, shaking with fear. As soon as she went back to sleep, it seemed, she heard her mother's screams, leapt up from her bed in alarm, and understood that her aunt Salma had died.

Actually, Milia was not telling the truth. She lied to everyone, but it was only because she was afraid to tell them the rest of her dream. She was afraid to reveal to them that she had entered her aunt's sleep space. She had dreamed her aunt's dream. Who would believe that anyone could enter the sleep-visions of another human being? Milia herself had not taken in fully what had happened; she would not understand what it meant to enter someone else's sleep space until the moment of her own death. Only then did she see what no one ever sees; and she divulged it only to the infant who entered the world from her body.

Milia lies down next to her aunt on the grass. A filmy white mantle coats Salma's closed eyes. Milia can see herself entering that filmy cloud and then she sees her aunt flying over what looks like a remote and bottomless valley. She hears the heartbeat of the woman who sails across the sky and she sees fear in her eyes. Salma wears a wedding dress; a long white veil ripples and flutters behind her. Suddenly the veil plummets into the round basin below in the garden and rain comes down in sheets. Milia tries to catch up with Aunt Salma but she cannot. Running toward her aunt, she trips and falls. Blood oozes from her right knee. She looks upward and sees Salma drawing farther away until she is no more than a white dot on the horizon. Milia hears her mother crying. She opens her eyes and sees Saadeh huddled in the corner of the room, sobbing. She knows that death has arrived. She understands that death is an unending dream, as her grandmother would say. At the age of seven it dawns on her that she can steal into the sleep-vision of death and savor the watery taste of it.

Salma's death did not come as a surprise. The young woman had contracted the yellow fever that prowled the streets of Beirut. Everyone knew that Salma would die. She had refused all offers of marriage as she waited for Ibrahim Hananiya, who had traveled to Brazil with a promise that he would return wealthy and marry her, and she was still waiting. Malakeh bought a white wedding gown so that her daughter could wear it into her coffin. Milia caught some fragments of the story from her mother, who contributed to the purchase of the gown. But matters became confused in the girl's head. She heard her mother say that Salma's wedding was near; and she saw the grandmother who came to visit them one morning weeping for her daughter's lost youth. But she did not understand the meaning of any of it until she saw it in her dream. When her tongue formed the words to the story, which slipped through the gap made by the missing baby teeth, and she told her grandmother how she had seen what no one else had seen, she was afraid of her grandmother's response. Don't say such things, my dear, Grandmama warned. Only the dead see the sleep-visions of the dead. Her grandmother made the sign of the cross on her granddaughter's brow and asked God's protection for her. May the cross of the Greek Orthodox Church protect you, my girl.

In her dream she saw him, too.

Milia told her mother and her grandmother that she had seen Ibrahim Hananiya walking behind Salma's coffin. She had seen a short, rather roly-poly man in a long green overcoat, his head drooping as if his short neck could not support it. He had been wearing brown and white shoes, she said, and he staggered and reeled as he walked, with no cane to support his body. Ibrahim was alone, Milia told them, and she had spoken to him. No, he was the one who spoke first. He came over to her and remarked that no one had recognized him. He had changed enormously in Brazil, he told her. Before, I wasn't short like this, he said. But I put on weight and fat shortens a person. *Maybe* that's why no one recognizes me. He smiled, showing his yellowish teeth, and asked her if she was Salma.

Salma is dead. Why are you bringing me into it?

I know, I know, he said. But you are Salma, aren't you?

When she tried to answer him her tongue stuck in the baby-tooth gap. She sensed herself powerless to form any words; what came out of her mouth seemed nothing more than a few unintelligible gurgles, and she began to cry.

She wanted to ask him why he had not come back from Brazil before Salma's death. She wanted to know if he had gotten rich like all Lebanese did when they immigrated to those faraway lands. She wanted to say that her aunt had died because of him. But she could not. She felt the words dissolve before they were even formed. She felt herself choking and she could not say a word.

Ibrahim's image remained imprinted in her memory as though he had been her man, indeed her very first man. She sensed a lingering love for him. From the tears welling in his eyes, she knew somehow that he had lost everything by returning to Beirut only to discover that the woman for whose sake he had gone away, and then had come back, was dead.

That was what she would have told Mansour, had she told him anything. Mansour talked all the time. He left no spaces for the silent speech hidden in his wife's pale features. And on those occasions when he did want to listen to her, Milia would find herself unable to speak. Crying in pain, she would call out to the mother who had not saved her from her interminable dream.

When she told her grandmother and her mother about her dream-meeting with Ibrahim Hanania, her mother hastily ordered her to stop.

Enough talking, my dear! We've other things to do. We don't have the time to always be listening to your dreams.

Ibrahim Hanania in Beirut? The bastard, he came here but didn't stop by to see us? He waits until the girl is dead and then he shows himself? exclaimed the grandmother to her daughter, wiping away her tears.

What's wrong with you, Mama? You don't believe Milia's dreams, now, do you? What are you talking about?

Yes, yes, so he's gotten short and round and he can't even talk, but why didn't he come and see the girl before she died? It isn't right! Grandmama went on.

What crazies there are in this family! was her mother's only comment.

You're the one who's crazy. Milia saw the man and I saw him too.

What do you mean, Mama, you saw him? The fellow is in Brazil. His brother came here and told us that Ibrahim is very upset and sorry but he cannot come back to Lebanon.

No, no! He was here in Beirut, but he did not come to see the girl and it broke her heart. Mine, too.

Ibrahim told her he was afraid of death. And aren't you, Salma? he asked her.

No, I'm Milia.

He said he had not dared to visit his fiancée on her deathbed. He began to cry.

Khallaas, ya binti, that's enough, said Saadeh to her daughter.

Milia looked at her mother fearfully and closed her mouth. She went out to the garden, screwed the hose to the water spigot over the pond, turned on the water, and watered the greenery.

Musa was seven when, clutching his sister's hand, he stood by his dead grandmother's bed. The boy did not understand what death meant. He did not know what it meant for his grandmother to journey inside her dreams. He heard the keening of the women gathered around the bed of the chalky-faced woman whose body was covered by white sheets, and his eyelashes filled with something like water although he did not cry out loud or even whimper. He stood waiting for his sister to brush her fingertips across his lashes and lean over to kiss him on the eyes. Whenever she sensed he was afraid, that was what Milia would do. Swabbing his lashes gently like this brought the little boy back to himself and took him out of his nighttime fears. Musa was afraid of the creatures of the night and the nighttime trees. Milia had told him that the trees of the night fill the sky after the sun goes down. Then the dreams come and build their nests on the branches of the night. So the boy was terrified of the night and its nests. When he woke up in the dark his bare feet brought him creeping into his sister's bed. Milia would move slightly without opening her eyes and the boy would curl up against his sister. She would put out her hand and caress his eyelids with her fingertips and then she would give him a kiss on each eye. Only then would Musa fall into an uninterrupted sleep.

Musa was twenty years old when he came to tell his sister that Mansour Hourani wanted to marry her. The young man stood before his sister, who was perched on the edge of her bed, her head bent over a sock she was mending. Before he could say anything she noticed that his eyelashes were damp with tears. He spoke about Mansour and she said nothing. She put the stocking down on the bed, the wooden darning egg still stuffed inside. She stood up to face him. She put out her hand and ran her fingertips along his eyelids. She leaned toward him and kissed his eyes, sensing the taste of his tears. She saw him once again in his boyhood, his eyes alarmed and his lower lip trembling. As she kissed his eyes, she said she would agree to everything he wanted.

This is what you want, isn't it? she asked him.

The little boy regained his height and returned to his manhood. He knitted his brows, looked full at his sister, and said, Yes.

As you wish, she said.

He did not ask her what her relationship was with this man. He did not say that Mansour had said, when he asked for her hand, that Milia had assented and had divulged her love. He felt betrayed but he did not use this word when he asked his sister how she felt about it.

Do you love him?

She gazed at him as if she did not understand what he meant. She smiled and said she had consented because Mansour reminded her of him.

You know, it's as if he is you, she said.

Me! he answered, a hint of disapproval and reproach in his voice.

You're better looking, but he looks enough like you to be your brother.

Musa frowned and muttered something about the wiles of women.

What are you saying? I didn't hear you, Milia said.

Congratulations, sister.

That day Milia sensed she must discover life anew, as though she had been born that very moment, or as though (as she bent over her little brother's eyelashes and then straightened up to stand facing the youth who had reached twenty and whose head already glinted with a few white strands) she had passed through her entire life thus far as though traversing a dream. She pressed her palms to her eyes briefly and then stretched her arms forward, trying to glean the sense of the words coming from her brother's lips.

He told her she would go to Nazareth immediately after the wedding.

As you wish, Milia said, dropping her head slightly. Her steady gaze broke on the floor tiles, tracing their floral pattern on a background of black.

The photographer would come the next day, Musa said. I want you to still be here with us. So I'm going to hang your picture on the wall, just here.

The photograph that was fixed to the white wall in the sitting room would stay there for years. When Musa inherited the house from his mother he left the picture there, as though it had grown into the wall. Printed on a large white sheet of photographic paper and framed in black wood, the image was large enough to display Milia's features clearly and in detail: her long hair and honey-brown almond-shaped eyes, her small nose and full lips, a long neck, hollow cheeks, and fine eyebrows. It was an upper-body shot. Sharif Fakhouri the photographer had stuck his head into a wooden box covered with black cloth. He had made Milia stand in front of the white wall for two entire hours as he tried to find the most attractive pose for her. In the photograph the pale woman with her features etched in black seemed to be coming out of the wall itself, and Milia's eyes emitted a glow of light.

Musa was convinced there was something strange about this photograph. Everything was outlined in black contours except for the pupils of his sister's eyes, which seemed to have been drawn in green.

Musa brought the photograph to the house three days before the wedding. He pounded a nail into the wall and hung it up, stepped back three paces and called out to his sister. Milia hurried into the room to find Musa in front of the picture, his eyes charged with astonishment.

Look, do you see it? he said to her.

Thank you, it's very nice.

Look – the eyes, look at the color – as if there's a green light at the center, coming out of the black. See it?

The girl looked at her photograph and the surprise of it struck her hard. She felt tears coming. The tears covered her eyes and the image broke up into fragments inside a vast watery field. She worried suddenly that her guardian angel had abandoned her. How could the photographer from Zahleh have snapped the secret of her green-tinted eyes? It was only in her dreams that her eyes shone green, only when Milia became the little girl with the brown skin and short curly black hair. How could the photographer have acquired the secret of her eyes? Had they betrayed her? Was this why she no longer saw dreams as she slept? Ever since the moment she had agreed to the marriage, going to sleep had been like tumbling into a deep, pitch-black valley.

Milia had begun to dread sleep. She would lie down on her bed, eyes open, fighting her drowsiness. As sleep began to creep into the tips of her toes her body would jerk awake all at once, chasing it away. But sleep would wrap itself tightly around her and not let go. It came from behind and assaulted her, dragging her downward into its darknesses. Night – the nighttime that had been all hers – was an enemy now, witness to the shuddering and quaking of her body. Her thigh would jerk and go rigid as if receiving a blow. She would feel herself falling and her shoulder muscles would tighten, her body convulse. Trying to lie back and relax her muscles, she would search desperately for a story that could put her to sleep but whatever story she came up with would slide away as the darkness inched in to envelop her.

Milia lost the cavern where she had concealed her dreams. She could not understand why – until the photograph exposed the secret of her eyes.

Now Musa stood rigid with confusion before his sister. Why did she so dislike the beautiful image he had hung on the wall?

Stand directly in front of it, he said to her. See, it's as good as your mirror.

Studying the photograph, Milia saw how the shadows of green had imprinted themselves inside the black ink. She turned her face away and left the sitting room. Standing in front of the picture, Musa sensed it speaking to him. Now, he thought, he could agree well and truly to the marriage of his sister. Milia would not really be going with this Mansour fellow to Nazareth but rather would stay here with them, hanging on the wall. He would not have to pine for her.

Musa turned around. His sister was no longer there. He went out to the garden where she sat on the wooden swing that hung from a branch of the enormous fig tree. He saw his sister's body tremble as she sobbed, but instead of going to her he turned around and returned to the sitting room. He sat down on the sofa facing the photograph.

Milia did not tell Mansour that she had cried bitter tears, sitting on the garden swing. The taste of the tears on her lips did not match the words so often used to portray them. Tears are salty but we describe their tang as bitter. Drinking her salty tears, Milia tasted a bitter essence, but it came to her from a dream that was not hers. The color of bitterness is green, she thought, like the irises that had vanished from the screen where her dreams played.

On a white metal bed set against the white wall where Musa hung his sister's photograph, Milia was born at noon on Monday the second of July in the year 1923. The day was hot and humid. Beirut's metallic sun pounded the streets with cords of fire. The midwife, Nadra Salloum, had hung yellow bedsheets over the sitting-room windows. They burned with the light that beamed through the window and turned the entire room into what seemed a mass of yellow flame. On the bed Saadeh lay moaning. Nadra – stocky and dark and plump faced, with a lit cigarette held eternally between her lips – chided and teased the woman whose torso stretched across the width of the bed, her face covered in heavy sweat and her white chemise spattered with a wetness tinted yellow by the imprint of the sun's blaze.

Shhh, sister, this isn't your first tummyful and there's no need to scream, said Nadra, arms crossed, chewing the butt of her lit cigarette as she waited for the baby to appear.

It was Saadeh's sixth childbirth. Of the previous five three boys remained: her firstborn, Salim; her fourth, Niqula; and the fifth one, Abdallah. Of the two who had died, the second child to be born to Saadeh had gone unnamed, his sobriquet becoming *the Blue Boy* because he had been born with the umbilical cord wrapped around his neck and had choked on his blueness. Number three, Nasib, had contracted jaundice a week after his birth, entering family lore as *Yellow Nasib*.

Saadeh lay across the bed awaiting her fourth boy, whom she had decided to name Musa. After the first two, she had given birth easily, as if the child simply had to slide directly from her womb. As soon as she felt the pains of labor, with Nadra hovering close, Saadeh would sit on the birthing chair, enveloped in the vapor rising from the pan of boiling water on the floor of the *liwan*. The gliding sensation always made her feel a bit dizzy and light-headed; she felt herself slipping downward in sympathy with the tiny being emerging from her entrails. Nadra would pull the child out, lifting him by the feet and slapping his backside to get him to squeal. When she saw the tiny penis between the thighs she would let out a long trill and Yusuf would know that a new boy had joined his family.

On that steaming July morning when the temperature reached 34°C, Saadeh lay flat and still on the bed, pain clubbing her body. She screamed louder and louder as the yellow hue spread across her face and hands. Always before, at the sight of the waters gushing out as the labor pains began, Yusuf had gone running to Nadra's home. Opening her door, the midwife welcomed him with the same words every time: she could see another boy on Yusuf's face. Thick smoke billowed in interlacing circles from the interior and Yusuf could hear Master Camille's cough and his friends' boisterous sounds as they filled the home with the popping and hissing of their narghiles and their noisy card games. He would scurry to the back of the house, pick up the birthing chair, and hurry home, Nadra following him with the inevitable cigarette in her mouth.

That day when the door opened there was no smoke. There were no sounds of narghiles or shouting of card players. Master Camille wasn't there. Nadra was in the kitchen cooking the midday meal. Yusuf bent to pick up the chair but it wasn't where he had always found it before. He froze, not knowing what he ought to do. Nadra tugged at his arm and ordered him to follow her.

The chair broke, she said. From now on we're going to have babies the way those Europeans do it.

He didn't ask her what she meant by this cryptic declaration. He was close behind her as they ascended the long flight of stairs connecting Abu Arbid Street, where Nadra lived, to Zaroub at-Tawil Street, where his wife waited. When Nadra told her to lie down, Saadeh did so, but the midwife scolded her. Sideways across the bed, she ordered. Lift your legs. We have to be able to work.

Saadeh changed position, the pain squeezing her insides. She said only one word – Where's – ? – but could not complete her sentence because she began to convulse with pain.

There's no chair, said Nadra. Today we're gonna do it the *mudirn* way. Lift your legs and push hard. Really hard.

But Saadeh began to cry. Nadra washed her hands with soap and water, came over to Saadeh and told her not to be afraid. Twisting on her mattress, Saadeh did not hear Nadra's words. She needed air; when she pushed, the air seemed to get stuck in her lungs. She opened her mouth in desperate search of oxygen and felt Nadra's hand behind her with a small towel, wiping away the sweat that had collected on Saadeh's neck and brow.

Quiet, Saadeh, relax.

But the child refused to begin the voyage out into the world. Nadra knelt between the thighs of the woman stretched across the bed. She probed for the head, already in the proper position for its descent. Nadra tried to grasp hold of it but could not.

Push, push!

Air, let some air in, I'm choking, said Saadeh, shivering. A powerful tremor seized her and her teeth began to chatter.

I'm dying – air!

Don't be afraid, nothing's going to happen to you! shrieked Nadra.

Saadeh closed her eyes, no longer able to listen. The ringing in her ears got louder. She abandoned herself to the shivering that seemed to have taken over her entire body. The midwife scurried outside to fetch cold water, carrying it into the house in a small basin. She began laying cold compresses on Saadeh's forehead. The trembling lessened and it seemed the pregnant woman had regained her ability to breathe.

I'm going 'neath you, said Nadra, and when you start feeling the labor pains pressing really hard, we're going to push one time and Go' willing that will be all it takes.

The midwife crouched down below Saadeh. The sweat began to spread across her short blue dress and she too felt as though she could not breathe. She wanted to swear – this whole f-ing business! – but she got the better of herself and simply called out, *Push!* Saadeh pushed with all the strength she had. Push, come on, again! But Saadeh's body suddenly went completely limp.

A moment later the tremors once again seized the pregnant woman lying on the bed. The midwife could find nothing to do about it. She stood waiting and then began to notice a peculiar color that seemed to be hovering all around her. Saadeh was floating in the color green. A greenish hue spread over her cheeks and eyes and it seemed to erase everything Saadeh was. Green stains spread across her face and hands, her thighs and feet. Never in her long practice had Nadra seen the likes of this color. When she had entered the room and ordered Yusuf to take a pair of bedsheets and cover the pair of windows that looked out over the Rahhal family's garden next door, the yellow color had convinced her that fire was shooting into the room.

What's this color? Change those sheets!

But Yusuf didn't move. That's all we have, he said.

Out there – go on out, she ordered him.

It's like we're inside an oven, said Nadra to the nun sometime later, as she said goodbye at the front door.

Take that cigarette from your mouth, said Sister Milana as she left the house, raising her palms skyward as if to give witness to the world that she had been the one to handle this birth.

The yellow hue spread across the place like a fire consuming everything in its path. But then came the green: a bright, open green that slowly grew more intense until it was a dark green tint spreading in rings to encircle the hands and feet of the pregnant woman. Her limbs went slack and her tears mingled with the drops of sweat falling from her brow. She looked nothing more than a moaning heap of flesh. Nadra couldn't believe her own eyes. She bent over Saadeh's face, wiped away the sweat and heavy tears with a small white towel, and noticed the smear of yellow left by the sweat.

Nadra was afraid. Her heart dropped into an empty space between her feet. What was there to do now? The nun watched the scene calmly, then she began to issue commands, and suddenly it was over.

Standing before this green pockmarked miasma advancing like rot over everything, Nadra was certain that she could no longer do anything. The one idea remaining in her head was to open the door and escape from this hellfire.

On one occasion, years later, she told Milia that she had been so afraid of Saadeh's color that she had been on the point of running away, leaving the baby girl in her mother's belly.

You mean, I would still be in there? asked the little girl.

No, dear, that isn't what I meant. It's just the way we speak. It's how we say what we mean when we're telling a story to someone.

Milia nodded as though she understood, but she didn't, not really. Long afterward she discovered that *how we say what we mean* is meaningless. When that man left her for a reason she did not know, she understood that speaking had no meaning. People talk to fill the empty spaces that separate them. They fill their spirits with the noise of words to give themselves comfort.

Milia dreamed fragments of her own birth. This dream she refused to conceal in the hollow of her night. She saw the yellow color spread. She leapt up and her eyes flew open when she heard a scream that exploded deep inside her. She found herself getting out of bed and going to lie next to her brother Musa in his bed.

Nadra opened the door to the room and the dusty cloud rose. A tall thin man loomed in the doorway and asked her in a raspy whisper to reassure him that all was well. Nadra answered by ordering him to go quickly to the home of Dr. Karim Naqfour and to bring the doctor back with him immediately.

The woman is not doing well. She's exhausted and she must see a doctor immediately.

What's wrong? asked Yusuf.

Nadra's arm shot out and she shoved her hand over his mouth. He tasted blood mingled with sweat and excrement. He leaned against the door to hide his dizziness.

What's the matter with you, standing there like an idiot! shouted the midwife. *Yallah* – go get the doctor, now!

The man turned and ran to the doctor's home. He knocked on the door but no one opened it. He was in a panic. He did not know what to do, and the taste of blood lingered on his lips as his dizziness grew worse. Loss. That was what he felt. The sense of loss collapsed onto him, falling heavily from all directions, and his legs could no longer carry him. He sat down on the front steps to wait for the doctor. Then he remembered that his wife was dying and it was up to him to do something. He picked himself up and began to run beneath the burning sun, in the direction of the Convent of the Archangel Mikhail. Why the convent he did not know, for he had no love for Haajja Milana. He detested the magic she practiced on his wife. Many times he had cursed her and threatened to abandon the conjugal home if she continued resisting his desire to sleep with her. Repeatedly Saadeh had refused. Haajja Milana told me it is forbidden as long as I am fasting, she said. So he had to wait an entire fifty days: the duration of the sacred forty-day Lenten fast and then through the day of the Messiah's resurrection just so he could lie with his own wife. On Easter morning he came to his wife and took her. She felt like a dried-out dead branch and he savored nothing. The fresh springs washing over him whenever he slept with her were gone. Now his moisture was sucked out without replenishment. He had not been watered; there was no pleasure. It was a sensation that would stay with him for the rest of his life. When Saadeh entered into the rituals of this eccentric nun she shattered his sex life. Now, whenever he approached her, intimations of discomfort and shame inhabited his wife's eyes. She no longer allowed him to put his hands on her breasts and she fidgeted and balked if his mouth so much as came near her lips. Sleeping with her became merely a question of finishing and moving away. She would hurry immediately to the bathroom and wash as if to rid herself of the traces of sin.

It's all the nun, he snarled at his wife, enduring the pain in his sex after their wooden intercourse. She's the devil – she's no saint. I hate that woman! I don't want to see her ugly face around here ever again. Listen to me and listen well. From now on Haajja Milana is forbidden to set foot in this house.

Saadeh turned a deaf ear on Yusuf. She continued her daily visits to the convent and brought the nun home to sprinkle blessed oil over her children. She begged Sister Milana to intercede with God, entreating Him to forgive her husband the sin of failing to have any love for the saintly nun.

Now, and without knowing how it had come to pass, Yusuf found himself in front of the immense iron gate set into the convent wall. He saw his fist pounding on the gate and heard his voice shrieking. Open up, please Haajja Milana, open up!

As the nun opened the door and stepped out, she snapped, It's Saadeh and her girl! Come, follow me to the house.

The shock of it tied Yusuf's tongue. He wanted to remind her that he fathered only boys. But he found himself simply walking silently behind her, seeking shade in the enormous moving shadow that she made over the ground. The sun burned on the dirt lane that linked the Convent of the Archangel Mikhail to his home, and the odor of dry, cracked earth saturated the air. Yusuf breathed heavily. Sweat beaded on his back and rolled downward. His robe stuck to his body. This tall broad-shouldered nun's massive rear waddled along swiftly in front of him in her long black habit. Yusuf kept himself inside the mammoth shadow that swayed and bounced over the unpaved track, broke against the rocks, shot upward to the garden of the Shabbua family, and dropped away to the olive grove below. The air he breathed in was burning the insides of his chest.

Yusuf felt the presence of death and he was afraid. He feared for Saadeh. He told himself he would accept whatever she demanded. He was ready to stop having sex with her if that was what she wanted – and if only she wouldn't die.

He walked on in the nun's shadow as the fear of death possessed him completely. He heard himself murmuring the prayer that his wife repeated every day.

O Lord, why have those who press upon my soul grown so numerous? Lord, many have stood against me. Many have tried to expel me from the salvation of Almighty God. But You, O Lord, You are my succor and my support. It is You who raises my head high . . .

What is it you are saying? asked the nun.

Nothing, nothing at all, responded Yusuf hastily, watching the shadow of the nun swaying before him, her huge body facing the sun, and into his mind came the old-man features traced on her face. Dense eyebrows, bulging half-closed eyes, a broad forehead, thin lips beneath a prominent nose, and swarthy olive-toned skin. A face that seemed to hold nothing but the huge nose with the three hairs sticking out at the center as if this were a cock's crest, and a thin purplish moustache looking as though they had been drawn in with an indelible pencil.

Yusuf told Saadeh that the nun was not a woman but rather a man in disguise, a man in the shape of a woman. He loathed her and found her disgusting, he said. After all, her enormous size was not in keeping with her holiness. Saints, be they men or women, have uniquely attenuated bodies. For the body melts away, that the soul may radiate its light. But this woman's enormous body was extinguishing her meager soul. She was akin to a man with a woman's voice.

In that July heat, though, Yusuf forgot it all. He thought only of death. He found himself walking in this black shadow like a small boy following his mother, sheltering closely in her shade.

When the nun reached their front entrance she turned and raised her eyebrows to signal that Yusuf should go in ahead of her. Yusuf ran up the five wooden stairs and walked through the stand of lilac trees. Opening the front door, he turned back and waved at her to come in. The nun walked quickly toward the sitting room. As she entered the yellow chamber her black shadow climbed over everything. The nun gave Nadra no chance to curse in her usual way. The midwife swallowed her imprecation when it was halfway out: Where is the doctor, that son of a b . . . – as if the vast blackness of the nun's habit swallowed the word before it could leave Nadra's lips. The large room, blazing an excruciating yellow through the sheets hanging over the windows, suddenly lost its hue to the nun's large black shape, as if the sun itself had vanished. Saadeh's trembling body grew still as the blackness flowing from the nun's garment washed over her.

Her color! Please, Haajja, look, the woman has turned green, and I don't know what to do, I don't know, we must fetch the doctor.

The doctor? For what?

Her color. The green!

Where's the green? asked the nun. There's no green here.

On Saadeh's body the green aura had faded to be followed by a thin blue that dimmed in its turn. Saadeh's flesh returned to the pure and bright white it had always been, a whiteness so milky it made one imagine a deep plush velvet covering the body so profoundly that it could conceal the light in its depths, yet one knew that the light was always there. This was the skin color Milia would inherit. It would be the hallmark of her beauty, the light that bewitched Mansour enough to bring him all the way from the Galilee just so his eyes could imbibe the whiteness that shone from the body of his Beiruti darling.

There's no blue, and no green, said the nun. This woman's body was near to gone, but now everything is fine.

Saadeh grew calm and stopped shaking. But never before had Yusuf seen such tears. Saadeh's tears collected on her cheeks, fell heavily onto her nightgown, and soaked her nakedness below. Yusuf stared at that morsel of flesh that through the years he had seen only as a darkened point that he would touch in search of the pleasure that God in His generosity had bestowed on human beings. He was interrupted by Nadra's voice ordering him to leave the room.

No, let him stay here, said the nun in her reedy voice that seemed to issue from her nose. Leave him where he is, so he can see how much the woman suffers.

Yusuf had already turned to leave but the nun's voice rooted him to the spot.

Don't move – stay right here.

The nun ordered Nadra into position, squatting and ready to pull the baby out.

Yallah, Saadeh, my girl. Push hard, *habibti*, my dear, just one push and it's done, said the nun.

Push! echoed Nadra in a low voice, and knelt on the floor, her hands reaching to find the little head in its descent.

There was utter silence in the room, as if Saadeh had suddenly dropped off to sleep. Her facial muscles went lax and a white glow washed over her body. Yusuf saw his wife's face softly stretch and expand, floating in the white light, rinsed by the drops of sweat rolling across it.

Nadra cupped her palms to receive the baby as it dropped and slid into the waiting hands of the midwife. Nadra hugged the child to her chest, forgetting in her astonishment and emotion to grasp it first by the feet and turn it upside down.

Lift her up, bellowed the nun.

The midwife stood up heavily and held the baby by its feet. She could barely wait to cut the umbilical cord, and she had not yet given the baby a slap, when her lips were already moving in a loud and joyous trill.

Saadeh told her daughter that she had not cried at birth like normal babies. Nadra forgot to give you a slap on your behind, she chuckled. So the holy sister picked you up – and no one cries when they're in the hands of saints.

Yusuf had a different view of it. The nun slapped her bottom, he said, and then she wouldn't stop bawling. But you didn't hear it, woman – I don't know how it happens, but when that nun's around it's as if you've been hypnotized.

The nun grabbed hold of the baby, who was wet with blood, and held her high, and away from her own body, as if she were going to plaster the tiny girl high against the wall. *Mabruk* – congratulations! she remarked. Milia has arrived. She ordered Nadra to wash the baby in water and salt.

Salt? Why salt? asked Nadra. We don't wash with salt.

Water and salt, answered the nun firmly.

She turned to Yusuf and ordered him to fetch a jar of olive oil. Nadra washed Milia in water and salt, whereupon Sister Milana rubbed oil into the baby's skin, swaddled her in a length of white cloth, and raised her above the bed with both hands as if – once again – she meant to attach her to the rough-plastered white wall.

Mabruk, Milia has come. May God help her grow, May He preserve and protect her and keep all evil far from her, intoned the nun. She placed the baby girl on her mother's bosom and left the room. Yusuf ran after her and kissed her hands in gratitude, the flavors of salt and oil imprinting themselves on his lips, before returning to bend over Saadeh and give her a kiss on the brow.

Milia has come, said Saadeh, staring at the wall where she saw an image on the white plaster in exactly the spot where the hands of the nun had raised the baby girl.

What's this name – Milia? asked Yusuf. No, no. I want to name her Hélène.

Her name is Milia. She had her name from the moment she was created. You saw what the nun did; you heard her say the name. *Yaani, khallaas*, that's that, Saadeh concluded resolutely.

Precisely twenty-four years after that day Saadeh would stand perplexed before the image that Musa had just hung on the wall in that very room, and in the exact spot where the nun had held Milia's body aloft, cleansed with water and salt and olive oil. The mother would say to her son that she had seen that very image on the day of her daughter's birth. Musa would stare back at her, a look of bafflement in his eyes, and he would lower his eyebrows in an attempt to silence her. But Saadeh would not tell the whole story until a year later, when the photograph was all that remained for her of her daughter.

When the nun raised her high against the wall, the girl became an image. This is the same picture! exclaimed Saadeh. I saw it – I saw it when Milia came into the world, and beneath it I read these words you are writing down now: *but she sleeps*. I saw it all then, just as it is now. *Ya* Allah! Why didn't I understand? Everything was already drawn, already written, in black, and the nun was murmuring the words written beneath the picture.

The photo Musa hung on the wall in the room they called the *liwan* stayed where it was. It did not drop from that wall until Musa decided to raze the old house and erect a new building on its ruins. That house, which looked like two houses side by side, and its big garden: it was the image Milia carried with her, in her waking hours and in her sleep, when she left for the Galilee. She had brought the scent of the place with her, she said to Mansour, and every morning she breathed in the old house, which sat on a rise of ground commanding the slope that led downward to the Convent of the Archangel Mikhail. The lilac trees protected the house from the swarms of gnats that invaded in summertime. Their intensely green leaves sent out a sharp odor that shielded the house from all manner of insect.

But the old house was only half of a house, and the whole structure was not completed until Yusuf married. The original house purchased by Salim Shahin, Yusuf's father, consisted of a spacious open room, or *dar*, separated from the smaller *liwan* off to the side by arches and glass windows. There was a small dark kitchen, and a bathroom at the end of the corridor linking the kitchen to the garden, shaded by a fig tree so old and so large that its enormous trunk was split into three. From it Musa and Milia suspended a long wooden plank, making a swing that could send them soaring upward into the sky.

For the sake of Saadeh's happiness, Yusuf had to add on to the house. He built a bedroom, dining room, and kitchen, constructed of concrete blocks, so that the house looked like two separate properties stuck together – the airy old house, built of yellow sandstone, and the new, smaller quarters of concrete. The roof of the older house was wood layered with earth covered by a thin coating of white plaster, while the new section was roofed in cement. The house really was two distinct structures next to each other: one house through which the breeze played in the summer while in winter the rooms stayed warm; and another house that was hot and close in summertime and ice-cold in the winter. The four boys lived in the new concrete space while Milia stayed with her parents in the old *liwan*, and then shared it with her mother after the father's death. This new family geography took place after the death of the grandmother. Hasiba had lived in the *liwan* with all of her children. After her death, Saadeh decided on major changes. She gave the boys the concrete room and moved with her husband into the spacious *liwan*. No one could find a solution to the dilemma of Milia, though. The mother proposed that the girl sleep in the *liwan* with husband and wife, but Musa was insistent on Milia staying on in his room. So Milia ended up nowhere, her mother summoning her to sleep in her room and Musa calling her to sleep next to him or on a small sofa placed in the boys' room. Milia would have preferred to unroll her bedding on the floor of the dining room but in reality she remained nowhere, sleeping here on the sofa and there on a metal bed her mother had put in the *liwan*, carrying her dreams from here to there, and living her nightly vagabond life. The problem remained unsolved until the father died and she occupied his bed.

Yusuf died when Milia was nine. Niqula and Abdallah took over their father's shop while their elder brother, Salim, went on studying law in the Université Saint-Joseph, and the youngest, Musa, stayed on in the Mar Ilyas-Btina School.

Three days after her father died Milia had the dream of her own birth. Seeing Yusuf stretched out in death, the girl of nine lost her ability to speak.

She heard the women's fierce laments and listened to words that puzzled her deeply.

His beloved has come, one of the women cried.

The girl saw herself standing among the knot of women draped in black and waving their white handkerchiefs over the corpse of the man lying on the bed in the *liwan*. Milia knew instinctively that she was the beloved the woman had announced, but she did not know what a beloved was supposed to do in such circumstances. Suddenly her legs gave out and she saw herself in a heap on the floor. Too many times to count, this dream assailed her: legs collapsing, a little girl falling, and the nun rushing over to pick her up and hold her suspended against the wall. She saw herself wrapped in white swaddling and two cupped hands lifting her high, and then she plummeted.

Milia could not come near her father or look directly at his closed eyes. She could not get there, because she fell, and the taste of fire spread through her insides. The same thing happened when she watched herself approach the man sleeping beside her. She wanted to reach him, cover his body's tremors with the bedsheet, pat him on the shoulder, and tell him not to be afraid. But she fell. She would open her eyes to banish the dream. And she would see the light creeping in through the slits in the yellow curtains over the window. She would turn her head and see Mansour sleeping on his back, his mouth slack and the sound of his snoring rising and falling. She would smile, reassured, and decide to go back to sleep.

Milia got up in the morning, put on her clothes, and sat on the edge of the bed waiting. She looked at her husband and saw Mansour scrunched into a ball. His knees were pulled upward, his legs bent; his left hand stretched beneath his head; he was breathing deeply and from time to time she could hear a sigh released from the depths of his sleep. He seemed a small child to her. She bent over him but then she stepped back and headed outside to the small hotel garden.

You wanted to kiss me, said Mansour.

Me? No, I just wanted to cover you.

All right, then, why don't you let me –

Take your hand away. I want to go to sleep.

But I want to sleep with you.

Please! Don't say those words! I'm so sleepy.

Mansour did not understand why his wife was in such a hurry to sleep. No sooner would she lay her head down on the pillow than she would nod off, her face completely relaxed. He grew accustomed to taking her as she slept. When he sensed her breathing growing louder and deeper, and he thought she had entered her nighttime world, he would come very close to her and begin stroking her. Little by little he would mount her and come into her. Her parted lips would moan but she would not open her eyes. As though she were dreaming. Body and soul, she seemed to float, and Mansour floated over her, as though when he entered her waters he was someone who swam through the dream.

Last night I slept with you, he told her.

What!

You don't remember?

God preserve you! Don't talk like this.

Mansour stood at the threshold about to go to work, holding a demitasse of Turkish coffee. He took a final swallow, set the cup down on the table, looked into Milia's honey-brown eyes, in which played all the colors of the world, and asked her what she had seen as she dreamed.

Go and dream your dream again, he said. I want to see you happy and relaxed today. Sleep a little before I come home tonight, and dream again, and then everything will go well tonight, too.

Mansour believed Milia to be afraid and anxious because of the troubles across Palestine, even though Nazareth was remote from the waves of strikes and clashes that had broken out throughout the country, accompanying ongoing protests against the British Mandate and growing Jewish immigration. She never asked him about politics. And despite his political concerns – as modest as they might be – and his loud debates with friends at the café, and his fear of losing Palestine completely, Mansour did not speak to his wife about any of this more than occasionally and in passing. Worrying about the effect on her, he did not realize that the woman was not particularly taken up with such things, or even aware of their implications. She was living now inside her private experience of pregnancy and her personal bond with the city of Nazareth. The dream that had brought her here, convincing her to marry Mansour, recurred during her nights; the intimation that everything teetered in this city the Messiah had inhabited one thousand and nine hundred years before made her aware that everything in life is ephemeral. She preferred to give herself over to sleep, and so she lived inside a world walled in by the night.

She smiled at her husband when he asked her to dream her dream again, and she said she would do so. He told her that he was very fond of this dream of hers, even though she had not even told it to him, because she had been so sweet and gentle with him in the night. You were like sugar melting at the back of my mouth, he said. Milia remembered nothing, or so she claimed. Every night she dreamed, and redrew her image in the mirrors the darkness held up, that image of Milia as a child of seven: short black hair and wide greenish eyes and the impulse to believe that the night's enticements spill into the daytime – so that, once awake, she would still be living inside her dream. She would intersperse the truth of daily events with the truth of her dreams. This sparked her husband's worry. But the priest from Syria, Father Mikhail Muawwad, who shepherded the flock of the Church of Our Lady of the Tremblings right there in Nazareth, clarified that such things were among the indications of pregnancy and there was no need to work up his mind over it. Milia would emerge finally from this nocturnal existence after giving birth to her first child.

Milia came out of the hotel room into the bright sun of the petite garden.

The snow sat in patches, looking like little white islets amidst the grayness that cloaked the trees. She felt a gust of cold air and saw the sun navigating the clouds scattered across the sky. She washed her dream in the light and the air and strolled in the garden sensing how the cavity inside her body had begun to take on a rounded shape. Every part was rounding out and growing warm. She sat on the edge of the tiny cavity at the center of the garden where the water pooled. She reached her right hand into the cold water and the heat in her fingers vanished. The shiver of the water spread all the way to her shoulders before falling to her breasts, where now she felt the pain of a new mother's milk. She saw milk on those breasts, drops forming little pools and trickling across her skin, making circles, and tears escaped from her eyes, falling over the swollen breasts so that milk and tears mingled.

Milia was four when Hannah came to work as a servant in their home. But the girl did not remain with them for long. The story was that Sister Milana came to give Saadeh cotton immersed in holy oil, and stayed with her in the *liwan* three days and three nights altogether until she was cured. They said the mother was cured, but she was not. She's become another woman, said Yusuf to the nun, who gave him a somber look, cleared her throat, and said, For shame, Mr. Yusuf! And, indeed, the shame sat visibly over the gray head of their father, like a halo that all of his children could see. The nun's words formed into a ring that stuck to the hair of the man and remained there until its erasure at the moment of his death. When his sons bent over their dead father's brow to give him a final kiss, Milia saw the halo fade. The man slept in peace during the last journey he ever made, to the land where his fellow carpenter dwelled.

You and the Messiah, the same work you both did! wailed Saadeh between sobs as they lifted the dead man into his coffin.

Such words – for shame! clucked the nun.

But he was a carpenter, and the Messiah was a carpenter.

Ayb! Shame on you, saying that. The Messiah loved fish, too, and he was a fisherman, said the nun.

But he was a carpenter too, said Saadeh. God forgive you, Yusuf, how could you leave me? But do say hello to my father.

Milia did not actually see her father in that final dream of him. She lied to everyone when she said she had seen him in the dream, carrying carpenters' tools and walking next to a fine-looking bearded youth, the two of them entering together into a black cloud that enveloped them as it dropped a veil over the daylight. When she approached to kiss him, she fell. The nun picked her up and carried her out of the room.

When the nun said it – *For shame, Mr. Yusuf!* – she all but proclaimed Saadeh's eventual recovery from the strange ailment that had sent her to bed.

No one knew the nature of the illness that had fallen upon the mother. She could barely walk. Getting up in the morning, she would do her best to set her feet on the floor but instantly she would feel too dizzy to stand up. She would call out in anguish and one of her sons would hurry over to help her out of bed. She could walk only by supporting herself against the wall and when she reached the kitchen she would start retching, soon to collapse again.

Hannah came to them because of that illness but she did not remain long. Saadeh improved through the nun's miraculous intervention and there was no longer any real need for a maid. But still, Saadeh was not exactly well. True, she was able now to rise from her bed without anyone's help. But she began to abandon the housework. More and more, little Milia was expected to cook and dust and wash clothes and clean house.

The mother's illness entered the family story as if it had begun after the father's death. Or because of it. Yusuf died when Milia was nine. Hannah came when she was four. As for Milia's transformation into the undisputed mistress of the house, that did happen after the father's death. Families invent their stories and then believe them. The story Milia lived placed the illness of her mother after Yusuf's death, and that is what she believed. But Hannah did not seep into her consciousness through the cracks in her memory until she found herself alone beneath rays of sunlight that were vanishing in the white clouds covering the sky. She reached her hand into the cavity of water to extinguish the fire in her fingers, and that is how she saw Hannah exposing her breasts beneath the olive tree, squeezing them as she cried and the milk spurted out. Hannah was short and round, her face broad and pale, her eyes deep set beneath lush eyebrows, and her lips very full. Hannah sat down under the olive tree and shoved her breasts back inside her loose black gown, and saw Milia standing nearby, her eyes scared and confused. Hannah waved Milia closer. The girl came, stumbling over her feet, and heard Hannah say in a broken voice that she longed for her son.

The little girl did not understand much of the fragmented story told by the servant girl who had come from a distant village called Jaj in the region of Jbayl. But she felt the blood leaping to her cheeks as she ran back to the house. Her fingers dipping in the water now and a bemused smile playing on her lips, Milia tried to repair the memory of that woman. She remembered being told of a baby dying three days after his birth, a husband who disappeared from the village, and breasts engorged with milk. Milia heard Hannah's voice as if it came from a hidden niche inside of her. *My breasts are hurting.* She was conscious of the hoarseness in the woman's voice as Hannah asked if she would like to try tasting the milk.

No, it was not like that. Did Hannah really ask her this question? Pondering this, Milia did not know but she did sense the milkiness on her lips and recalled a vague fear propelling her to flee. Had she tasted the milk? If not, why had its sugary taste remained under her tongue so that whenever she was waiting for Najib she would be aware of that savor rising from her breasts to her lips?

After that, Milia no longer dared to leave the house for the garden. Hannah might be standing beneath the olive tree, turning her back on the old house and baring her breasts, their milk dripping onto the grass. What was Hannah's story? And why had the nun thrown her out of the house?

The shadow-shape of the woman with the swollen breasts appeared over and over in Milia's dreams. Yusuf's brown face was there in the background, staring with fierce longing at the welling milk. Was . . . ? She didn't have an inkling but she did know that Hannah had left her village and come to Beirut and worked as a servant in their home, and that her only child had died three days after his birth.

Hannah spoke of a baby with yellow hair who had lived three days. She said that the hair on his head – which reminded her of the fluff on the bodies and heads of tiny birds – went dry and hard like thorns and she knew that he had died.

But why had the nun thrown her out of the house?

Was it because Milia told of the breasts? And was she the only one to see the woman suffering, her breasts swollen and hardened with milk? Here on the edge of the garden basin at the Hotel Massabki, Milia could feel the milk and the painful swelling of those breasts. As a gray stain traveled over the sky, she closed her eyes and remembered.

She was alone, listless in the heavy heat, bare and taking a turn in the house's garden. It was dark but not completely so. Why had she forgotten this intermittent dream amidst all the dreams that had crowded into her first night of marriage?

Little Milia stands naked before the pond in the garden of the old Beirut house, with its large olive tree. Snow is falling, white fluff scattering across the water's surface. Yet Milia feels heat so oppressive she thinks she is suffocating.

Her short orange dress, which does not reach her knees, falls as though a hand has undone the long zipper stretching from the neckline to the lower back. The same hand, reaching for her underclothes, has ripped them off and the little girl sees herself naked out in the pond. The snow is falling on her – hot snow – and she gathers it to her chest. She feels thirsty and puts her tongue out for the snow. Floating on the water, she eats the snow; she consumes it but it does not satisfy her, it will not quench her thirst. Swimming, she feels no cold. Here is a dream that does not end; a thirst that will not end; a never-ending sleep; an endless snowfall; and water. Everything is swimming through the water; and little Milia swims and eats and sleeps and the snow covers her and the heat radiates onto her skin from deep inside.

As a shiver ran from her breasts to her belly Milia withdrew her hand from the water. She saw the face of her father, Yusuf, his eyes half closed. He was moving away from her and then coming closer, and she was trying to say something but her voice would not come out of her throat.

To her breasts swollen with milk, Hannah told the story: how her husband had divorced her and snatched the child from her hands. The child had not died, then, but had been stolen away. Why did Hannah say his hair had gone as hard and dry as thorns? Had his father killed him?

What does she mean, he divorced her? Milia asked her mother.

Don't say that word, we don't have divorce. Divorce is *haraam*.

Hannah disappeared and so did her story. Milia didn't tell the story to anyone. Musa was the only one to whom she could tell things but he was too little. And by the time he was old enough the story had entered the realms of oblivion.

After the death of her husband the mother contracted the chronic illness that obliged her to spend almost all of her time at the Convent of the Archangel Mikhail, in the company of prayers and icons and the nuns. As a grandmother she would become a saint or nearly so, eating nothing but bread and bringing cotton soaked in holy oil for members of the family who were ill. No one could ever claim they had not improved because of Saadeh's sacred oil, because no one else would believe such a claim. All members of the family, big and small, old and young, believed in Saadeh's miraculous presence. After all, the corpulent nun with the thin nasal voice had bestowed a special grace on Saadeh through their relationship.

The water and the morning briskness of Shtoura, creeping into Milia's body, convinced her to return to the room. She went into the reception hall where the breakfast table was set. She saw the driver sitting alone at the table, stuffing himself with fried eggs, labneh, and cheese. When he saw her coming in from outside he rubbed his hands, gave her a sidelong look, and grinned. She saw the words hovering around his lips as if he wanted to talk but he went on chewing his food, exaggerating his lip movements in a show of mockery directed at her. Milia tiptoed up the stone stairs. She opened the door to the room where the drapes were still closed, immersing the place in darkness. She detected an odd smell, something like the smell of the lake in her dream, and felt sleepy. She took off her clothes, put on her nightgown, and got into bed next to Mansour, who was wrapped tightly in the sheets and curled into a half circle. Bringing her face almost to his closed eyes, she felt a rush of tenderness but along with it came an ache that swept from her shoulders to her tailbone.

Milia would not call it love. Here in this bed, and there in the car, she felt something undefinable, something imprecise whose name she would not discover until Nazareth. The word *love* she used only once, returning home from the church, her belly swollen and the fragrance of the incense filling her clothes. Mansour was in the garden smoking a cigarette and sniffing the scent of the earth awakened by the rain. He turned to her and said, You know, Milia, you'll be giving birth on Christmas, at the end of December.

She was in her fifth month. The smell of the rain ushering in the month of September intoxicated her. She knew exactly when she would give birth to her baby, even to the hour. But when Mansour uttered the word *Christmas* she felt a shiver at her lower belly, as if the fetus were moving. She saw a white fog hovering around the eyes of her husband and remembered his closed eyes on that morning in the Hotel Massabki, and she said she loved him.

So, if you love me, great, then why don't you let me sleep with you?

She put her finger on his lips to shush him. Why did he have to talk like that, using that phrase? She had told him a thousand times that she didn't like to hear this sort of talk, and that sex was created for the sake of producing children, and now she was pregnant, and praise be to God.

Mansour began to talk and silence gripped her, as though she had put on a veil that muted her. She would walk through the house on tiptoe, keep everything neat and in order, make food, and wait for her husband. She never asked him questions; he could be out as late as he liked and come home when he liked, always confident that his wife would not complain or ask questions.

He talked to her about love. He told her how her beauty had completely enchanted him when he saw her for the very first time. She smiled and her eyelashes came down to hide her eyes. He said a lot of things, and then he said that marriage makes one thirsty.

Me too, I am always getting thirsty, she said.

He didn't tell her why though. He was thirsty because she was silent, because he had to fill in the empty spaces that the absence of speech created. He didn't ask her why she pretended to be asleep when he had sex with her. He knew that her body arched in pleasure, that her moans were not of pain or refusal. That quiet sound, something between a moan and a sigh, escaping her pressed-together lips, enflamed all of his pores and made him feel like a swimmer in the sea. He would wait until it was dark, close his eyes upon the colors of desire, and sail upward borne on a gentle rippling of waves, warm air enveloping him and inviting him to remain. As he finished, he felt his body sharpen with pleasure, whetting his appetite. He wanted more. But this woman of ever-closed eyes pressed her thighs together, coughed, and rolled away from him in bed, leaving him holding his sex as he crept into the bathroom.

This soft moan that came from her body, shaped and tinted by her dreams, returned him to the first moments of passion. He forgot that he had not succeeded in making love to her properly in Room Ten of that little hotel. His body had broken faith with him and he had felt himself on the edge of death. Walking through the fog for more than an hour; the stinging snow and ice that swirled over him in the storm; his fear that he would lose his footing and fall into the wadi; his awareness of his own manhood – all had overcome him. There inside the shroud of fog his manhood had strutted before him, confident, while he stumbled forward behind it, on the point of falling, his eyes wet and tingling. He wanted to close his eyes to stop the burning caused by the cold wet air. He looked back to see her but saw only the indistinct shape of the car inching forward turtlelike. When the driver got out of the car halfway up the slope of Dahr el-Baydar and said he could not go on and would take them back to Beirut, Mansour shouted at him and said he would drive the car himself. Whipping around to return to the car, he saw the driver scamper ahead to take his seat behind the wheel, gesturing to indicate that he would keep going, following him.

Fine, said Mansour, his words spiraling into the tempestuous wind and getting lost. But in this scene nothing was fine, and the route was full of dangers. He slipped several times and the car behind him was skidding too. As the fog began to break up he returned to the car to find Milia asleep, swathed in her mother's overcoat, shivers running through her body. He tried to start a conversation with her. He wanted to recite poetry to her. He had prepared a good number of lines from his store of ancient Arabic poetry to recite as he drank champagne in the hotel room before taking this woman in his arms. But now he could only locate a few lines of popular verse.

The peaks of Lebanon! How shall one cross them
by winter when their summers are wintry?
Snows clothe their byways blinding my eyes:
A whiteness so pure only black can I see

The woman opened her eyes momentarily and closed them again. Had she not heard? Or perhaps she did not understand what she heard. Mansour felt defeated. For this woman who was his, he had been preparing the surprise gift of poetry. He had decided on love poems of the ancient poets as a fitting beginning. She would realize that indeed he was a poet in his own way, for he had memorized hundreds of lines; and for his wedding night alone he had assembled a lavish banquet of poems. He envisioned himself in the hotel room, drinking champagne as he strewed words across the floor. They would land at the feet of this woman who had stolen his heart and obliged him to spend so much time in transit between Nazareth and Beirut.

Mansour had not known, of course, that the passing encounter in the garden would turn his life upside down and convert him into a perpetual traveler. But, gazing into his hosts' next-door garden, his eyes fixed on the fair-skinned girl, her long hair bound up in a ponytail, whose figure was bent over to water a pot of basil, and he went out of his mind. Mansour had come to Beirut on a buying trip, wanting to stock the dry goods shop he had opened recently in Nazareth. The dispute that had flared between him and his brother, Amin, over how to run the iron foundry in Jaffa they had inherited from their father had settled it: he would become an independent merchant. He was determined to start anew, somewhere else – but that would only be to start.

Here's the plan, he told his wife not long after they settled into their home in Nazareth. I'll put together some money and then we'll return to Jaffa.

Milia hung her head and said she would prefer Bethlehem.

Why Bethlehem?

She did not answer. Through her eyelashes she saw the golden halo flickering. She had not told her dream to anyone. What would she say? That she had agreed to have him as a husband because of the dream? And that she had come to be in this place because she had heard a voice calling her, saying to her, *Go to Nazareth*?

The images that floated in and out of Milia's head plied together and tangled. The woman she saw in the dream was carrying a tiny child. She gave the child to Milia and disappeared, a figure in a long blue gown. Milia watched the blue color of it undulate across the wadi and cover it entirely. The baby whom this woman had left in the little girl's hands was dark skinned. Its eyes were shut and it was wrapped tightly in bunting – or perhaps a shroud. A penumbra of light formed a halo over his little head: a blue light hovering on the knees of a little girl of seven. She sits in front of a stone monument abutting the wadi. Behind her is an ancient crumbling structure half in ruins, perhaps a very old church built of white stone. The woman comes out of nowhere and then disappears just as suddenly, leaving her dress behind to move across the wadi and blanket it. Milia stands up suddenly to reach for and grip the hem of the gown but she senses herself falling. She clutches the baby to her chest and steps backward but her foot catches on a rock. As she begins to fall she opens her eyes and takes a deep slow breath.

The lit oil lamp sitting in front of the wooden icon box suspended in a corner of the *liwan* flickers and all but goes out. The wick glows blue. The blue woman who has left her field of vision – who has abandoned her eyes – enters the icon box, its brown color now a palette of reds and golds. She closes her eyes but the blue woman has already returned. She sets the baby down on Milia's knee and disappears again in her blue gown and the blue fabric covers the wadi. Milia comes out of the wadi carrying the baby boy.

She puts out her hand to take hold of the hem of the blue gown. Afraid, she steps back. And she falls.

The next morning Musa came and informed her of the bridegroom. And he said: Bethlehem. So she hung her head and agreed. And then he said, No, I got that wrong. He is from Nazareth, not from Bethlehem. So she nodded again and said *yes*.

Had she heard the names of both towns in her dream? Had the blue woman told her the name of the town where she would live? Milia does not remember any voices in that dream. But when she smiles at her husband after he asks her, Why Bethlehem? she is certain (without knowing why) that the two towns' names emerged together from the bedrock of her dream and that she cannot answer his question.

Was it true that she had told the Nazarene she loved him?

She saw herself through Mansour's eyes, leaning over the pot of basil and breathing in the fragrance coming from the mixture of soil and water and perfume until she was dizzy. The man saw her figure from behind and decided immediately that he would not finally leave Beirut without her.

When I see you I feel thirsty, he told her.

What does the beautiful moon think of the beautiful moon? he asked her.

I am standing here like this to watch over the basil's perfume, he said.

She heard his voice. She turned around and the face she saw was so very like her brother Musa's face. She felt light-headed: was it the mingling effects of the basil's fragrance and the perfume of this man's words? His words took on the aroma of basil and his footsteps in the garden just across from theirs made a rustling sound that left her trembling. The sensation traveled from her neck to her lower back. But only once did she actually speak to him. It was October and the first rains. Milia stood in her long indigo-blue skirt and white blouse watching the trees lose their leaves when she heard a voice coming from their direction.

It's you. You're the one.

I'm what? she asked.

You know what I'm talking about, he said.

Me!

I love you, he said.

Why? she asked.

I love you, and I want you, he said.

Me!

She shrouded herself in her pallor and went into the house. That is how Mansour would describe her. He would say that she had wrapped herself up in her own paleness; she had gone inside the pure white that was her. She lowered her head and said she agreed.

Disappearing into the old house, she sensed his eyes as nails driven into her body between her shoulders at the very top of her back. Her neck hurt her. When Musa accused her of already knowing the man, of having fallen in love with him without telling her brother, she could find nothing to say. She reached her hand around to her upper back to pull out those nails and said *yes*.

Mansour is sleeping and Milia tries to fall asleep. Closing her eyes, she feels a trembling on the sole of her right foot. She falls onto the stairs. Musa tells her not to be afraid of this long steep flight of wooden stairs. Seashore. Water. Everything is tinted a strong clear blue. Milia is climbing the steep rickety stairs, barely more than a ladder. Sister Milana stands at the bottom gripping the wooden staircase and shaking it. Milia is high on the stairs now but beneath her the wood shudders. Holding on tightly, she attempts to take another step. She looks down to see waves and foam and suddenly she tumbles head over heels like a clown performing a wild acrobatic trick. Her head falls first and her body stretches along the steps as if she had lain down on them. She goes into a somersault. The fall is swift but the staircase seems interminable.

The nun disappeared. Musa was stretching out his arms to catch her. Musa toppled into the water and the sea swallowed him. Milia stood on a rock amidst the waves, her shorts stained with sea grass and salt stinging her eyes. She searched desperately for her brother in the waves but she could not see him anywhere. A hand came out and pushed her into the waters. She was drowning – she knew it – and she felt her throat constrict. She opened her eyes. She licked the salt from her lips and saw only the darkness.

Milia sat on the edge of the bed and pressed her hand to her chest trying to quiet her loud rapid heartbeat. Her heart was erupting, spreading throughout her body. She felt it in her neck and temples and in the soles of her feet. Every part of her shook violently.

Why this fear? Of what was she afraid?

A phantom smile played on the woman's lips in the gloom. The dream came back to her – that old dream which had abandoned her three years before when she met Najib Karam for the first time and sensed that this young man would swab the dreams from her eyes and help her into the world. But Najib had disappeared from her life and the dream of the sea and the wooden stairs had gone with him. And here she was now, sitting on the edge of the bed in Room Ten in the Hotel Massabki in Shtoura, asking questions, knowing the answers, filled with disquiet.

In my dream, I fell, Milia said to her mother, and now my foot hurts. She heard her mother bawl. Stop this foolishness! You're as bad as your grandmama. Well, you're a young woman now and it's high time we find you a man.

The body of the fair-skinned woman shuddered awake. She got up, bent to the floor, picked up her nightgown and slipped it over her head, and sat down again on the edge of the bed. She heard her mother's voice again, that dry raspy voice coming from deep in a throat lined with the smoke of the narghile. This voice would be at Milia's side in Nazareth. It would be the last voice she would hear before she saw that young man sitting beneath her picture trying to copy words written in tiny letters inside the heaviness of the inscription in large Arabic *naskh* script.

Why was the honeymoon chamber like this? The man had his back to her. She opened her eyes on a dream completely at odds with her usual dreams. Where did her old dream go?

Milia lived inside the rhythm of her dreaming. She got up in the morning, washed the dreams from her eyelids, and continued the story. She dreamed that Najib was sitting with another girl in the garden of Milia's home. Standing at a distance, she watched how the man put his hand on the young woman's hair before stooping slightly to plant a kiss on her neck, and how they disappeared beneath the grand fig tree. When he came to visit the next day, she refused to sit with Najib and would not say a word to him. Things returned to what they had been only when a new dream came to erase the previous one.

What was wrong with you yesterday? asked Najib.

She smiled and gave no answer.

I don't understand. What happened?

Ask yourself, she responded, and then burst out laughing. It's not you. I had a dream that wasn't very nice and it put me in a bad mood. Just forget it.

Najib didn't understand. He went on insisting, wanting to know what lay behind it. When he heard accusations of unfaithfulness, hints of the story of his relations with a golden-fleshed girl whose name Milia did not know, he went off in a high dudgeon.

As Najib disappeared from her life – and married that same fleshy woman – she dreamed that he told her he was fleeing from her dreams. How can anyone live with a woman like you? he asked.

What I dreamed turned out to be right. I saw you and I had to leave you so that you wouldn't leave me. So yes, it's my fault.

She saw him standing beside that big woman whose broad shoulders filled the garden. Her brother Salim stood with them.

I hate you, she said to Salim. You make yourself out to be such a good person, so fair, almost a saint – but what shame you should feel! *Ya Ayb ishshoom aleek*.

She saw herself on the steps going into a somersault and crying out. Musa stood beneath, arms spread, waiting for her. She hit the ground hard and felt her bones turn to powder.

Wayn ruht ya Musa? Where did you go and why did you leave me? You're still angry over the money, aren't you?

She had dreamed that Musa stole the few pennies she had hidden under her mattress. She woke up in the morning and didn't find the money and when Musa came home from school she scolded him. The boy's face went red and he tried to deny the accusation before crumbling in front of his sister and admitting his guilt. Milia planted a kiss on his eyelids and forgave him.

Milia played the dream game with herself. When she could not remember her dream she would keep her eyes closed on a pretext, as though she were sleeping; as though she knew she could anticipate seeing something to prop up her day. Her night began when she could sketch out her dreams before falling asleep. Well, no, it was not as clear and straightforward as that. But she did make decisions about where the dream would be located. Most often, her dreams occurred on the seashore or at the edge of the wadi, even if it was a dream set in midwinter. She would go to the seaside having wrapped herself in her bedcovering, closing her eyes to the blueness and suddenly finding herself in the water.

Every day in the summertime, the four brothers went swimming on the rocky Beirut shore. Sometimes she went with them, standing at the edge of the water to watch.

You're a girl, and it's shameful for girls to swim, said her older brother Salim. It would disgrace the family.

Why? Milia asked.

Because you're a girl, Salim answered.

I'm not a girl, she said.

Why do you say that – do you have a *hamama*? asked little Musa innocently.

Shut up, you ass! Salim shrieked. And you, Milia, you stay right here and you just watch us swim.

One time she ordered Musa to take her to the sea. No one else was home. Their mother was at the convent licking the icons – Salim's description of his mother's constant visits there. Salim was at the Jesuit Fathers', and she and Musa were in the house. She was twelve years old. She begged him, and then she ordered him, and off they went. She took off her clothes and pulled on the bathing trunks she had fished out of Salim's wardrobe. She sensed Musa staring at her tiny breasts, which had just begun to round out. She was shivering, naked in front of the unending blue world. She stood there, preparing herself to wade into a small pool that stuck like a rocky tongue into the shore. She felt the sting of her brother's eyes boring into her breasts, two tiny prickly pears planted on her otherwise smooth and unchanging chest. Never before had Milia been truly conscious of them, and she would try to forget them even after they grew into a pair of ripe apples with their tinges of violet, purple exploding across white, erect rosy nipples at the core.

In the dark and in his wife's eternal drowsiness Mansour would discover these breasts and take them. Apples are sweeter than pears, he would tell her.

What are you talking about?

I'm talking about your breasts. I like the shape of apples best. Pears are fine, but apples are round and they fill my hands. *Ya ayni*, what beautiful apples you have!

Stop it, for God's sake!

He would abandon her to her drowsiness when he despaired of convincing her that sex was not shameful or forbidden. The problem was that her refusals merely enflamed him. He would try to take her against her wishes but then, seeing her wet face, he would pull back. He came to fear her sadness, as she sat bent over on the edge of the bed, catching her tears on the hem of the white bedsheet.

Whenever he wanted her she took her time about responding. She warned him away from her bed. She turned over a few times, got out of bed and went to the bathroom, came back and turned out the light, and then asked him to put off that business until tomorrow. So he waited until she fell asleep. When her body was no longer moving at all and she seemed heavily asleep, he would take her. Her water would begin to spill out and spread, and he would drown. He could not stay hard: as if, taking him inside of her, she dissolved him in her world of darkness and closed eyes. Her body began to dwindle away in his hands. He extracted her breasts from her nightgown and began to kiss them, sucking in their taste, which mingled jasmine with the scent of apples. He heard her faint moan and began his journey, slipping inside of her only to dissolve in her waters. Spent, he would make up his mind to keep trying, but with a sharp cough she would expel him from her body, turn over onto her right side, and sink beneath the surface, deep in her universe of sleep.

In the morning he searched her face for any expression of what they had done but he never found a trace of it. Light poured off the pale features that were rounding out with her pregnancy. Had she waited for him to drop off to sleep so that she could go into the bathroom and wash herself, or had she truly been asleep, postponing her ablutions until early in the morning?

Only once did he commit a grievous error. They were sitting in the salon,

Mansour listening to the radio and Milia knitting a woolen jacket for the awaited child. He got up and came over to her. He put his hand on her left breast and bent over, kissing her blouse. When he slipped his hand inside she erupted.

Let me kiss it! he said.

As he lifted her breast from the folds of fabric and took the deep-pink nipple between his lips, the pain showed on her face. Mansour was far away, bathing in the fragrance of apples, when he heard her screech. Enough! The pained look fading, she gulped for a breath of air, repeated it in a mutter – *Enough!* – and stood up.

That evening Mansour did not dare to follow her into the bedroom. She wrapped herself up and slept. That night he did not come near her breasts but when he took her she was very warm and soft. The next morning she told him that his actions of the day before were not to happen again. Breasts are for the child, she said. He must understand that. But three nights later, fondling her breasts, he heard the same quiet moan as before. He let himself go in the sleepy pleasure of love. He would never try again to reveal her breasts to the light. It was enough for him, having the violet color of those breasts overcoming the darkness of the room and opening the gates for his stealthy entrance.

Milia veiled her breasts with her arms and threw herself into the sea. The taste of salt swept over her, a flavor that would return to her lips on that cold winter morning when she found herself in that bed in the room at the Hotel Massabki. She sucked at her lips and went back to sleep. But there she was on the rocky Beirut littoral, dipping her tiny breasts in the salt water and gazing at Musa as he pursued his water games. He dove underwater and she suddenly felt certain that he had drowned and would not return to the surface. But then abruptly he emerged on the other side of the vast open water. She waved to him but he was heading away from her, far away.

She closed her eyes and slipped her head into the water, and then opened her eyes to the intense blue that was turning into a light-suffused green mingling with gray. The depths of the sea have eyes that are green, she thought. These rocks and these colors yielded the greenness that enveloped her night. She raised her head and a light wave of cold swept over her. She felt a pain behind her eyes. She screamed for Musa but he was far away, swimming, paddling with his hands, his head dipping into the water and bobbing through the waves.

When Musa came back he saw her standing motionless in the water, the look in her eyes anxious. He grabbed her by the hand to pull her out of the sea. She shook her hand away and stooped over, covering her breasts. She followed him. She put on her own clothes. She was hungry. A tremor of cold smacked her. The July sun broke hotly over the water but Milia's body shivered beneath her short dress, pulled over the wet bathing trunks that she had not dared to take off. Musa bought a pastry brushed with thyme that he divided with his sister. He tore into his share. She watched him and nibbled at her half.

That night she dreamed of the lamb and felt its wet little kisses. And that night her menstrual blood came. She had become a woman now, her mother told her, and she must act as women do. Milia was afraid of this blood. She did not understand how the egg that had formed inside of her could erupt into this mess of blood. Does that mean the egg has died? she asked her mother. You mean, every month a baby dies inside of me?

Don't talk such nonsense! It isn't death, it's nature, Saadeh told her.

And so Milia understood that nature meant death. Sensations formed inside of her and welled up as her monthly time approached. Her movements grew slower. She sensed something forming ball-like in her belly and it made her queasy. She would press her hands against her lower abdomen as if she were pregnant and wanted to protect the developing baby from slipping out. The blood never appeared until the little lamb did, and not without considerable pain. This sudden panic about the embryo falling out followed her until she was with child. There in the remote little town she no longer saw the little lamb crouching above her. She began to walk daily through the alleys and streets until her feet hurt with exhaustion. Returning home, she would fall sleep immediately and dream of the blue woman coming toward her before disappearing into the wadi after laying the child in her arms. She would bring the baby boy to her breasts, letting him suck at her nipple as though it were an orange. It was ecstasy; her uterus muscles convulsed and water welled up from deep inside.

She never told Mansour about leaving the house to walk through the town. In the morning, feeling stuffed full to the brim like a heavy ball, she would go out for a walk. But Mansour saw her. Nearing the Church of Our Lady of the Tremblings, where the Virgin Maryam had felt the sudden fright of a mother worrying that her son would be sent over the precipice into the deep wadi, Milia sat down on a white stone overlooking a grove of olive trees and let her gaze wander. Mansour saw her by coincidence. He had come out of his shop to smoke his morning narghile in Sulayman's coffeehouse. He saw her shadow from behind and followed her. She was like a rolling ball, a shape impossible to mistake, and so he followed it. When she perched on the small white boulder he hid himself behind a wall. He did not come any closer and he did not speak to her. He stood motionless, hardly daring to breathe. She stood up and began to walk in the direction of home and he went to the café. In the evening he came home and found her asleep, as usual. He woke her up. She made his dinner and went back to sleep without any exchange of words between them.

The next morning as she was making his coffee he came to her wanting to kiss her but she stepped away. He spoke to her but she did not answer, simply giving him a look of rebuke. Mansour was absolutely certain that she had not seen him at the church. He was not prepared to believe her stories about these dreams of hers. He felt sure she was feigning it all, giving herself the freedom to interpret matters however she liked. He asked her what the matter was but she did not answer. He felt smothered. He had gotten used to the silence, to living with a woman who was more like a ghost, but her disgruntlement and sadness were becoming too much to endure.

Tell me – what is the problem?!

You know.

No, I don't know, so tell me.

It's nothing, she said, and turned her back and left the kitchen for the sitting room. He followed her and put his hand on her shoulder. She turned around and said, Take your hand off me, *please*.

What is it – what did I do?

You were following me.

Me?

Yes, you! You stood behind the wall at the church. But I saw you anyway.

When was that? he asked.

I don't know, maybe yesterday, or maybe a few days ago.

How did you see me?

I saw you through my back.

No one sees through their back!

Looking at Mansour, she saw him take the shape of Musa. She saw his lower lip tremble and the tears cling to the underside of his eyelashes. She leaned over, wiped his eyelids with her fingertips, and kissed him there. Don't lie to me anymore. Promise me you won't lie. *Yallah*, tell me.

I promise, Mansour said, penitent.

That was the day on which Mansour realized that he was afraid of this woman. He heard her call him Musa but he said nothing about it. A time or two before he had flared up, raising his voice at her when she called him by her brother's name. My name is Mansour, he said. Why do you pin your brother's name on me?

I don't know, she said. Maybe it's because I miss him.

Miss anyone you want, and yes, I know he's your brother, but my name is Mansour.

Mansour, she said. Fine. You are Mansour.

But Musa did not disappear. One time he heard the name, or thought he heard it, when she was asleep. He was making his usual moves when he heard the name. He retreated and tried to go to sleep. But he couldn't and so he went to her again and took her, deceiving himself into thinking he had heard the name wrongly. But he felt the utter strangeness of it all with a sense of alienation that he could not shake off. This woman was a stranger here. He no longer knew how to talk to her. Her low voice made him wary of voices in general, and her languid eyes seemed focused only on distant points. He had an uncomfortable sensation of never being able to reach them, wherever it was they went.

That morning when she leaned toward him and brushed her fingers along his eyebrows and kissed them, Mansour felt like a child. He had as much as admitted seeing her by chance and following her, and standing behind the wall looking at her as she sat on a rock in front of the church steps.

Now really, how did you see me?

She said she had seen him with her back because she could see everything in her dreaming. She told him how a person sees in all four directions when dreaming. She asked him about his dreams. He never saw dreams in his sleep, he said.

That can't be, she said. You just don't remember your dreams. She explained to him that a person has to train the memory. Dreams are an extension of a person's life. We live as much by night as by day, she declared, and anyone who can't remember his dreams is only living life by halves.

She heard her grandmother's husky voice explaining the importance of dreams in a person's life.

I'm not like that, said Mansour. I never dream, never ever.

Everyone dreams, she said.

For three months now Milia had been growing rounder, with pregnancy and sleepiness and thirst. Her breasts were swelling and her face had grown radiant. He asked her why she walked by herself every day. Why didn't she come with him? They could stroll together in the evenings after he had returned home from work. He asked her if it made her sad to live so far away from her family.

She regarded him without answering at first. Then she said she wanted to acquaint the little boy with the town.

Which little boy? asked Mansour. For us, I hope so! But my heart tells me it's a girl. My mother says that if a pregnant woman gets more beautiful as she gets more pregnant, that means it will be a girl. And you are getting more beautiful all the time.

I said *boy*. He is a boy.

On the day she covered her tiny breasts with her crossed arms, it dawned on Milia that she was on her way to a remote place from which she would never be able to return. In that rocky pool embedded in the sea her bare breasts exposed her. Her breasts betrayed her and it was on that very evening that the lamb appeared to her in a dream that would recur so frequently that Milia would no longer be able to tell it. Waking up, she would simply recall it as if it had happened in fact. In her sleep it came like an anticipated monthly visitor: a small white lamb skipping across an expanse of green grass. Milia sleeps beneath a spreading fig tree, her eyes shut tightly and her small brown body curled into a half circle. The little lamb comes up to her and stands over her. He puts his cheek to hers. The little girl turns over to lie on her back. He steps back, hesitates, and then scampers toward her, leaps atop her, and puts his front legs on her chest. He pokes his head downward as though to eat the grass. The little girl who sleeps sees nothing but the rays of the sun, piercing the lamb's coat as they pour into her open eyes. The lamb's little mouth wanders near her eyes so she closes them. She's afraid he might think her green eyes are of a piece with the grass in the garden and swallow them up. She closes her eyes, feels the tiny lamb's tongue on her neck, and breathes in the smell of the sun. The sun lamb quivers and gives off heat. There is a sharp pain at the pit of her belly, tangled somehow with the intense green all around her and with her closed eyes. Milia wakes up but she does not dare open her eyes. The heat encloses her and hot blood dribbles onto her thighs. She gets up and washes her thighs in cold water. She stuffs a towel between them and goes back to sleep.

Kharuf ish-shams, she named him. The sun lamb. He arrived ringed by a blue halo that gave off a strong light but his appearance took on different aspects. Sometimes he ran over her little body, which expanded to become an unbounded pasture. Or he might perch on her chest and nuzzle her shoulders. Once he buried his head in her neck. She was constantly fearful for her eyes. When the lamb was there, contrary to habit, she would wake up but shut her eyes.

The little lamb vanished when the embryo began to form in her belly. He would not reappear until the end of December 1947 as Milia listened to the doctor's voice telling her to push as she went into her long dreamsleep. That day the little lamb would reappear, leaving her with emotions of longing and fear so strong that they overpowered her caution: she forgot that she must keep her eyes closed to shield them from the lamb's tiny mouth. And so she tried to open them, before the white wool covered them completely, tracing blue halos around them.

The man sleeping at her side was breathing deeply, the sound of it interrupted at intervals by a light whistling in his nose. She rubbed the traces of the journey through the heavy fog from her eyes and tried to collect her memories.

Milia did not know this man. Rather, she knew him but only as her future husband. The tale of passion Mansour lived had skimmed over her without leaving its impress. When, on the evening before the wedding, he related parts of the story to her, she felt she had missed the only story worth living.

He came the evening before the wedding when no one was expecting him. According to custom a bridegroom is not in evidence that day. He spends the evening with his pals at a goodbye-to-bachelorhood party, which is what they call the last sordid fling the groom allows himself before entering the straitjacket of marriage. But Mansour was not like that – not because he was an extraordinarily well-behaved fellow but because he had no such friends in Beirut. Mansour showed up at the Shahin family home on that cold December evening in order to make apologies for his family, who were not able to come to the wedding because of the accumulating troubles in Palestine. He expressed their wish that the bride's family would not postpone the festivities. Musa was sitting in the *dar* with his mother and the unexpected guest while Milia stood in the kitchen making the coffee. Musa's eyebrows knitted and the mother made no response. Bearing the coffee tray, Milia entered a profoundly silent room. She set the tray down on the table before the guest, poured the four cups from the little coffeepot, and said, as if continuing a sentence she had already begun, There's no problem.

There's no problem, repeated Musa.

Ala barakat Allah, said Mansour, his voice quavering, and he stood up to take his leave. The mother yawned and stood up to wish him goodbye.

Sit down, all of you, said Milia. Let the man drink his coffee, she said to her mother, tugging her by the arm until she sat down again.

Mansour sat forward on the edge of the sofa as if keeping himself tensed to leap up at any moment. He took a swallow of coffee. Sitting opposite him, Milia gazed at him as if she expected him to begin telling a story.

You know . . . Mansour's voice trailed off.

I know, Milia responded. Things are not going so well.

That's not what I meant to say, said Mansour.

The silence hung on them, broken only by Musa leaving the room. The oil lamp flickered. Milia wore a yellow dress. She supported her chin in her hands waiting to hear what the man would say. The mother slipped out of the room and one kind of silence blended into another.

She wanted to say to him that he, too, had plans for a last-minute flight in his head but she did not say it. Her lips held the shadow of a melancholy smile as her hand brushed away specters of memories that had crept into her eyes. For the very first time she was sitting alone in a half-dark room with this man who – a few hours from now – would become her husband. She sensed his fear. How could she say to him that she had known he would visit this evening to tell her that his family would not be coming from Nazareth?

The route is blocked. It's the English – their army shut the road three days ago, she said.

The cup of coffee shuddered in Mansour's hand. He imagined something like shadows huddled over the lilac trees. He did not ask her how she knew about what was happening in Palestine, nor how, in the kitchen, she could have heard him say that his family could not come for the wedding. He put the coffee cup down on the little pedestal table. Around its rim were carved Kufic script letters, which he tried to read but could not.

What does it say?

How would I know? You'll have to ask Musa. I think it might be poetry. Musa told me one of his friends brought this table from Syria as a gift.

Mansour stared at the table, trying to decipher the elaborate calligraphy. No, he said finally, this isn't poetry. They are verses from the Qur'an.

He rubbed his hands together against the cold. Milia got up, put some wood in the stove, and sat down again. New warmth surged through the room and the words returned to Mansour's throat. He brushed away his confusion with a wave of his hand, believing that this young woman could not have noticed his fear. He took her hand, kissed the turquoise ring on her finger, cleared his throat, and opened his mouth.

> *She toyed with her ring, a woman as fair*
> *as a full bright moon in a night of stars*
> *But whene'er I tried to slip that circlet*
> *off her soft plump angelical finger*
> *she cast it between her lips! See, I said,*
> *she has hidden the ring in the signet*

And he told her the tale of his love.

Night. Trees leaning into trees, and the winds of December dampen the windowpanes with rain. A man of thirty-seven years sits in the large room that the Shahin family calls the *dar* and rubs his hands together getting ready to declaim. It is a high-ceilinged room and the pleasant wood tones of the ceiling reflect the flames of the stove in the corner. Against the somber colors of four small blue sofas striped in black, a woman of twenty-three glows in her yellow dress. The milkiness of her skin flows all the way to the tips of her slender fingers. The man stares at the floor and imagines those white forearms bare to the shoulders. Out of the corners of his eyes he follows the flicker in the gas lamp hanging from the ceiling and speaks in a low voice. Looking at him seated on the couch, his body leaning forward slightly, one would not notice particularly the modest belly bulging slightly over his leather belt. But one would see his sloping shoulders, his eyes shaded by thick black brows in a dark round face and his black moustache.

When Milia saw him for the first time she truly thought she was looking at her brother Musa and her conviction moved her to accept him as a husband. Or that was what she would say to her brother. The truth was somewhat different. From a distance or in the dark Mansour did look very much like Musa. Even in this pale lamplight the resemblance was strong. But in full daylight the difference between the two men was plain for all to see. Musa's features were gentler and more delicate. True, his eyebrows were thick but they did not descend so closely over his eyes nor did they shadow his eyelashes, across which Milia's fingers had passed so many times. Musa was not overly tall but he had an athletic build and showed no trace of a belly. The contours of his arm muscles were visible, while there was a slackness to Mansour's arms and a slight droop to his shoulders. No one would have noticed it on the thirty-seven-year-old but these omens of roundness would become the last and most definitive marker of his life, for he would come to be called the man with the bowed back. Musa's face was round but the length of his jaw gave it a more rectangular look. His large nose was skewed slightly to the right as if the bone had been broken and not reset properly. His neck was long. Mansour's face, though, was truly round, his nose large and a good match for his lips. But both men had thick black moustaches that were so startlingly, perfectly alike that people who knew both of them or saw them together would look twice.

Studying the two men, one would believe them to be brothers but then would discover gradually that Mansour was a slightly inflated copy of Musa, more or less. The two points of real resemblance, apart from their moustaches, were their voices and their backs. Musa's voice was pleasant and deep and rich, and so was Mansour's. Musa's back was absolutely smooth and his buttocks flat. This was what had arrested Milia's step and drawn her gaze when Mansour turned and left the garden. She saw the fluid plane of his back and told herself that this man was her brother's twin. Milia took note of the points of resemblance, and also the differences, and agreed to the marriage without any hesitation at all.

The mother's view of it was that the girl had suffered a lot already. After two experiences that had not worked out it was high time for her to marry. Musa agreed but only after some hesitation.

Nazareth is a long way from here, sister, he argued. Why would you want to go there? But Musa was convinced about Mansour because he was a right Adam, as he said. A good man.

Milia heard Sister Milana order her out of the room so that she could tend to Saadeh. It's Satan! boomed the nun. I smell the Devil in here. She turned toward the girl who held fast to her mother's hand in an attempt to still her fever-ridden body.

The nun stepped just into the *liwan* and the aroma of incense spread immediately. She held a small brass incense burner from which came a piercing smell surmounted by a white fog. The nun's large body blocked the entire doorway as she carried the scent in. Around the room she stalked, pivoting right and left to reach every corner. She approached the invalid slowly. The sound of her breathing rose in the silent room. She turned to Milia and said, It's the Devil, he's in here. Leave the room, my girl.

Milia stared at her indifferently and said nothing.

Dr. Naqfour had paid a house call. After examining the patient, he called it bronchitis and prescribed medicine. But Saadeh refused to swallow the bitter stuff. The nun forced Saadeh to open her mouth and take the medicine but the sick woman spit it out and retched.

Be patient, *ya* Haajja, the woman's sick, said Milia.

Yes, I know, I know, Niqula came and told me, and that's why I'm here, but you go outside. I can't handle the Devil when you're in here.

What devil?

Ask yourself, ask those dreams of yours, ask those fellows who come looking to marry you and then run away. It'd be much better for you to repent and come into the convent.

Milia started out of her seat, dumbfounded. The nun bent over Saadeh, placed a wad of cotton dipped in oil in her mouth, and ordered her to swallow it.

She can't swallow, said Milia. She doesn't have the strength.

Quiet, you, and get out of here.

Milia said no more but she did not leave the room. She stayed beside her mother; and so it was that she saw how the woman swallowed the cotton, her eyes closed, and how her body settled to the rhythm of the nun's low singsong incantations.

Was it true that her dreams were the work of the Devil?

The nun said that Satan steals into a woman because a female body is beautiful in its perfection. God created woman perfect and complete, she said, but women chose to be deficient. Look at Our Lady Maryam, peace be upon her. Did she need a man in order to fulfill her own existence? Of course not! She was made complete by the Holy Spirit – a perfection she had had from the dawn of her existence.

But not every woman is the Virgin Maryam, said Milia.

Milia! Tell me you haven't noticed how bad you are becoming, how ugly? Me?!

Yes, you, girl – why have you not come to church with your mama, so that we can fight the Devil and chase him out of your body?

What was she to say? That she was afraid of the church? And that when she found herself there with the congregation, beneath the Byzantine icons and inside the cloud-odor of incense, she felt the dread and fear she would feel in a burying ground? People bowed their heads to icon paintings of men and women who had died eons ago, speaking to them as if the distance between the living and the dead had been undone and they all moved now in the world of the dead. Milia feared this open interval between the living and the dead. On Good Friday she would go to church and join all of those weeping for the crucified Messiah. But on all other days of the year she prayed alone at home and asked God to open the gates of life that thus far had remained closed to her.

No. The nun did not tell the truth. Her dreams were not the work of the Devil. How did the nun learn of her dreams, anyway? Saadeh was to blame. Since their father's death Saadeh had become virtually a ring on the nun's finger, there to be twisted and played with exactly as she wanted. All of the family's tales were transmitted to the nun through the ear canal of confession: and in itself, this was an extraordinary tale with no precedent.

The sainted Milana did not stop at exercising control over the nuns of the Convent of the Archangel Mikhail. Her influence extended to the very priest, Father Boulos Saba, whose decision it had been to let her hear confession. The two had agreed that she would receive confession from the women and then would send the penitents to Father Boulos to receive his blessed forgiveness. The priest himself made penance to the nun, in an utter reversal of all the faith's traditions. But the nun's astounding powers and her ability to cure the ill allowed her to exceed the limits in every possible way.

Through the confessional all the stories and secrets of the Shahin clan became Haajja Milana's property. And because of it, no longer could Milia endure the nun's looks with their blend of pity and withering scorn. She realized that the stories she had lived with Najib and Wadiie were known to the nun in all their detail, that her secret lay bare alongside thousands of others filling the holy woman's sainted head.

The mother grew quiet and her body began to perspire as the oil spread across her nightgown.

Once I have gone, said Sister Milana to Milia, rub her body with *spirtu* alcohol. The spell is over and she is fine now.

The nun turned to go out but paused at the door and her reedy voice called out to Milia.

Naam? responded Milia politely.

The nun put her hand on the young woman's shoulder, leaned over her ear, and whispered. The nun told her not to be afraid. The bridegroom will appear, she said. And I see traveling. But you must settle yourself down first. You must pray that God saves you from the worst. Forget Najib, and the second one too, what was his name? The real bridegroom will come, and he'll come soon, don't worry. But what is most important is that you stop this business of dreaming. A believer, my dear, does not dream. Or if he does, he does not remember. Or if by chance he remembers, he does not talk about it. Night is the journey of darkness. It is our practice for death. Only the prophets and the saints see things at night. Ordinary people are submerged in darkness when they sleep, and nothing interrupts it. All praise be to the Almighty who created sleep so that people could prepare themselves for death. The world of night and the world of day do not come together. God is light and the Devil is darkness. My girl, you must forget your dreams and then I am certain that Almighty God will open the gates to your countenance.

But I –

She did not let Milia complete her sentence. She coughed loudly and said that dreams are the Devil's means to land human beings in sin. And anyway, she said, you're a liar. Nobody can remember all their dreams. Every day, every morning, you make your mother tremble with fear listening to you. Every day and the next, hearing your dreams, and that's why she is always coming to the convent. *Haraam*, what has your mother done to deserve this? It's your brother Salim who's to blame, who got that Najib going . . . Enough, Milia! You are like my own daughter. I pulled you out of your mama's belly and I held you high to bring you nearer to God. Enough, now – stop this foolishness of yours!

The nun went out without waiting for any response from Milia. The girl wanted to say that it wasn't true. That she didn't tell her dreams to her mother every day, and that her dreams belonged to her, and that they were not the Devil's whisperings. If they were, how could their predictions always come true? She had told her mother the dream about Najib because she had truly felt humiliated and upset at the time and then afterward she wanted to let on that now the whole affair was a matter of indifference to her. Sister Milana having gone, Milia stood there feeling she had been stripped naked by the nun's words. Suddenly she had discovered that her stories were no longer her own to possess. Her mother had given everything to the nun.

It was nighttime. Trees leaned against other trees in a darkness of their own making, and like whips the rain lashed the rooftops. Milia opened her eyes and wiped the dream from her eyelashes to find herself in water. The ceiling in the *liwan* was leaking and a shiver of cold ran along her arms. But instead of rising from bed to take up the rug and set pots beneath the holes in the ceiling, she closed her eyes again. After all, she did not believe her eyes. The dream returned just as it had appeared to her a few moments before. She saw herself, a little brown-skinned girl sitting on the rocky edge of a deep wadi, at her back a white churchlike building. She was alone and she didn't know where she was. She listened to the rustlings coming out of the wadi and to the sounds made by the wild grasses. From there a woman came toward her, hair concealed beneath a long blue wrap, body encased in a long blue gown.

The blue woman came out of nowhere carrying a suckling babe wrapped in a shroud of white swaddling clothes. She set the child down in Milia's arms and disappeared. Milia is alone, holding a tiny dark-skinned boy child who breathes deeply and soundly. The baby's breath sighs against her neck. She lifts it to hug it close to her chest. She sees large round eyes that seem to take up the whole of his baby face. She watches herself enter the shadows of those pupils and finds herself in a space of vast depth and colossal height.

The child stares at her and takes her inside his eyes where water surrounds and embraces her. She tries to come away from the watery lakes of those eyes. She puts her hands out defensively, certain that she is drowning. She opens her eyes, sees the rain dripping from the ceiling and senses the chill along her arms. She closes her eyes and sinks into the eyes of the dark-skinned boy child. Never has Milia seen eyes like these: the whites so large, black pupils floating at their centers, each eye a black mirror inside of a white mirror. The child takes her to his eyes and the little girl is not strong enough to resist the pull of his pearl-drop tears, ringing the enormous black pupils.

Rousing herself at the sound of her mother crying at her to set pans beneath the holes in the ceiling – And hurry! her mother was shouting – Milia shivered uncontrollably with the sensations her dream had piqued. Cold sweat covered her breasts and thighs and desire swept over her like a terrible storm. It was a longing for which she could locate no equivalent; she had never felt the likes of its force. It bore no resemblance to the desire she had felt for Najib or for that other man called Wadiie, or for the doctor who had treated her broken leg. The three men were simply relics of her tongue and nose and memory. They were the love of storytelling, the love of fragrances, or the deliciousness of love postponed. But this was the desire of the heart.

Three times on a rainy night she saw him. She understood that she must go to him.

The story of the Armenian doctor exhausted that phase of utter exhaustion, her adolescence. A girl of sixteen breaks her right leg after falling from the swing suspended from the fig tree and finds herself in the hands of two Armenian doctors in Bourj Hammoud. Actually, Zaven Hovnanian and his brother Harout were not physicians but "bonesetters" – a *mujabbir arabi*, as were called practitioners of folk medicine learned from their family elders or inherited through blood. Rather than setting broken bones, though, they simply applied a sort of spiritual massage therapy. In a darkened house of closely shut windows and drawn curtains, Milia smelled a strange odor and did not understand the shadowy sensations that infused her.

By this time Milia was well aware that her body had grown and changed quite a lot. Now she could grasp the ropes tightly, shoot her long legs straight forward into space, and climb high as the wind played with her light brown hair. And then, this time, she fell. She would not remember how the parallel ropes eluded her hands, nor how she came to be on the ground with a pain shooting through her right leg. She tried to stand up but she couldn't. The pain mounted from her leg bone to her neck. She collapsed and screamed for Musa. But her brother did not come. She had to get up on her own and hop on her left foot all the way to the four steps that led from the garden up to the kitchen. She managed the steps on two hands and one leg.

Yes, she knew she had changed, but it was only when the swing let fly with her that Milia truly noticed how everything was transformed. In the four years between the day at the seaside when she had hidden her small breasts from the lads' eyes and had dreamed of the lamb, and the day of the swing, Milia had not paid attention to how her chubby preadolescent body had stretched out and how her jaw had given definition to her face, freeing it from that babyish rotundity. Her legs had grown long and slim while her buttocks had filled out delicately. Her eyes were wider in proportion to her face and her neck had lengthened gracefully.

On the swing, as she stretched her legs forward and pulled hard with her arms to give her flight a higher arc, she became a woman. She saw her chestnut-brown hair drink in rich tones from the sun and her pale skin starkly white against the lush green leaves thick on the branches of the fig tree. The plump preadolescent girl whose brothers had made fun of her because she was as round as a ball was now a svelte and lovely silhouette, full without being fat, her eyes honey-toned and large, the crown of her head streaming with luxurious chestnut hair in which surged waves of color mingling the deepest mahogany with red and blond. She did not tell the brown-skinned girl in the dream that today she had become beautiful, because she did not want to abandon the little girl. The little dream-girl who appeared and vanished at will was freer than the roly-poly preteen girl whose breasts had emerged with the salt of the sea under the probing, eager eyes of the boys. The dream-girl had slender legs and the slim straight body of an acrobat, and that body allowed her to claim that she was no different from the boys. She would go wherever she wanted, appear and disappear, viewing the world with her gray-dappled big green eyes.

When Milia fell from the swing the surprise struck her head-on. She discovered that the image of the past was wholly gone – the image that had made her loathe herself, made her refuse to stand in front of the mirror, made her feel disgusted by the tiny pockmarks across her cheeks.

She saw herself on the swing as if she were gazing into water-mirrors. The leaves that flew by her became watery green mirrors reflecting endless faces of a pretty young woman who had torn off childhood's wraps and galloped from the nighttime of her old body to enter her new body. To cling fiercely to her new body. To become it.

Had she fallen from the swing because she had forgotten herself as she gazed into her new image? Or because she had closed her eyes to compare the image she had been with the long and slender image she saw now, pale legs extended forward, exposed by the breeze as the swing rose and fell? Or was it because she jutted her torso forward to halt the swing, ready now to go inside and stand before the mirror and give her new self a good look?

Milia flew and everything in her changed. That is how she would remember herself from this moment on. She would say she became a woman on the swing.

Her mother had told her of the lamb. No . . . her mother knew nothing about the dream of the lamb, but seeing the traces of blood on her young daughter's tubby thighs, she had told Milia that now she had become a woman and must prepare herself for marriage and motherhood. But Milia could not see herself as anything other than a mass of flesh and bone that had now been pierced and marred unkindly by an open wound. Aghast at learning that this monthly gash would be with her all of her life, she was mortified.

Do the boys – do my brothers, does anything like this happen to them? she asked her mother. Seeing her mother's startled expression, she knew it was her injury and hers alone – a girl alone among four boys, living through what the saintly Sister Milana called *that monthly filth*. Swelling up, she had to listen to her brothers' teasing as they called her Drum and Fatty. Only Musa defended her, once in the garden when he told her how pretty she was. She had started to cry after Salim had mounted a vicious party in the garden and had called her over: Hey Drum! Instead, Musa came over to her, seized her hand and told her not to pay any mind to what Salim had said, because she was the prettiest girl in the world. She did not believe him but she kissed him between the eyes anyway and gave him a smile.

Always she felt the blood before it came, and this made her anxious and irritated. The lamb would begin to visit her dreams nightly. But the little animal would never leap onto her chest before the final day when the pain in her lower left side intensified before spreading down her legs, announcing the hour when the anxiety-demon was to emerge from her body. But this day made it better. When Milia tumbled from the swing and broke her right leg, she discovered she was no longer that roly-poly Milia who hated looking at herself in the mirror.

She was perched between the two doctors. Zaven gripped her right foot and massaged the leg with hot oil. Harout stood behind her, holding her shoulders firmly so that they would remain still. Zaven asked her how she had fallen but she did not know how to answer. Had her feet dangled to the ground as she swung her torso forward to stop the swing, causing her foot to catch and the swing propelling her forward so that she fell hard? Or had she fallen from midair, having slipped her hands off the ropes as she had done often before, and there she was on the ground, having been tossed to the right with the whole weight of her body on her right leg?

She tried to remember but the hand of Dr. Zaven, rubbing the oil into her, pulled her mind and spirit downward, giving her the feeling of slipping, before the sharp pain seemed to lift to her upper back, where the other doctor's hands worked the flesh of her shoulders.

Where was her mother? Where was Musa?

She smelled the peculiar odor rising from around her and enveloping the pain washing from her bones. What was that smell called? And why – every time she recalled it – did she feel a mysterious mingling of unspeakable desire and pure disgust?

That day they took the girl to Bourj Hammoud and there she lived something that she could tell no one. But it was always with her in her dreams. It came in the shape of blurred and darkish images cocooned in a mist rising from a vessel that someone had set down next to her. It made her feel dizzy. Only her brother Niqula noticed that she was afraid. Seeing the shadows of fright in his sister's eyes, he accompanied her on her third and final visit to the doctors. He shattered the power of the smell that lingered in the girl's nose, its traces impossible to dispel. On her wedding day, with the cold and the fog enveloping the American car which crept up the rise of Dahr el-Baydar, Mansour sitting in the front seat next to the driver, his body shaking with the chill, she had opened the car window only to hear the driver yell.

Shut the window!

It's the smell, she said.

Smell or no smell, shut that window! We'll die of the cold.

It's the smell of *basturma*, she said, rolling up the window.

Do *you* smell pastrami, bridegroom, sir? asked the driver, guffawing.

Milia did not hear her husband's response. She saw herself edging up the stairs on her arms and one leg. When she reached the kitchen door she shouted for her brother Musa. Just then her mother appeared from behind a large pot that sat steaming on the gas burner. The mother ran toward her daughter, who crouched outside on the steps, and even through the gloom of the kitchen she could see the blood oozing from Milia's knee. She called Musa and ordered him to run to the convent and ask the nun to come.

Why the nun, Mama?

Saadeh bent over the wound and wiped it with a handkerchief she had dipped in water. Her hand probed the broken leg and Milia screamed at the pain of it.

Dakhiilak ya Allah, the mother muttered. She stepped back and asked her daughter to stand up. Milia tried. Rapiers of pain stabbed her leg bone and tore through her all the way to her eyes. Her tears flowed as she collapsed against the wall and slid to the floor. Her voice broken, she told her mother that she could not get up. The nun came, carrying her incense burner. The saintly woman bent over the girl's leg and her short, fat fingers jabbed at it. Broken, she pronounced. Take her to the Armenian, she added, turning her back on them to leave the house.

Saadeh pursued her outside to ask her for the doctor's address. She sought Musa's help in getting his sister up and standing on her one remaining sturdy leg. Milia stooped between her mother and her brother, leaning on the small boy's shoulder, and they made their way to a taxi, which took them to an isolated house on a narrow street in Bourj Hammoud. A short woman whose face was partially covered by a lock of brown hair laced with white received them and asked them to wait.

There Milia breathed in a peculiar smell. She would say that she had not taken in all that happened in that house, because she was in pain. She would say that in her second visit to the clinic she had realized that a strange sensation was sweeping over her, unexplained waves pulsing through her shoulders and chest, the smell of meat cooked with spices mingling with an odor that seemed to come from the bodies of the two men. The first one – tall and broad-shouldered – sat at her feet, probing the sole of her foot and then massaging her leg to the knee, a bar of soap in his hand. Milia felt the down at the tops of her thighs ripple as if awakening from a deep sleep, waiting for a hand that did not arrive. The shorter brother stood behind her, his hands gripping her shoulders, asking her to breathe deeply.

The first doctor had only to raise his eyebrows and stare for her mother and Musa to leave the room. They took seats in the sitting room, where the only light was given by whatever could filter in through the wooden shutters of a closed window. In the other room sat Milia, between two pairs of hands and the mingled odors that she found so strange. The meaning of that smell would remain mysterious to her until she fell in love with Najib Karam. It was his words she fell in love with – his manner of speaking, his ringing laugh, the way he mocked everything. With Najib in the garden, she breathed in that smell – and felt a pain shoot through her right leg. He had come close to her. The evening flung shadows about the garden and the voices of night creatures filled the air. Blind bats knocked into the trees and hovered over the frangipani at the center of the garden. Najib was telling her jokes that made her laugh. He said he would speak to her brother Salim.

This coming week, he said.

What do you mean?

I mean, getting you engaged to me, and then us getting married later on.

Me marrying you?

Of course, you marrying me – what, don't you like me?

Of course, but –

But what?

But Salim might not agree to it.

Salim's my friend, of course he'll agree to it.

What do you mean?

I mean, I love you, he said, and he came very close. He put his hands out, caught her by the waist, and came even closer. At that moment, when Milia was in Najib's arms, that smell assaulted her nose and she felt her right leg go numb. She stepped back to lean against the trunk of the lilac tree. Najib followed and pulled her to him. Her sharp intake of breath did not stop Najib. It simply made him more determined, as if something had caught fire within him. He yanked the girl to him and shoved his lips against her long pale neck. Milia froze, completely unable to move, because now the smell and the pain were twisted together, and because she felt dizzy, and because this youth who was teasing and fondling her began to shake as if he had suddenly contracted a fever. He staggered backward, carrying away the smell, and ran to the bathroom.

The two of them were alone in the house. Her mother was at church for sunset prayers with the nuns and her four brothers were out. When Najib came, she made him a glass of rosewater sherbet and they sat in the garden. He talked and she listened. She stood up to go inside and make him coffee, and that was when he was suddenly there very close to her. Immediately that odor that brought the pain back into her leg enveloped her. As soon as he took her in his arms he began to tremble and then he left her abruptly and loped to the bathroom.

He came back to see her leaning against the trunk of the towering lilac tree. Another embrace in mind, he came to her. She averted her face and said, That's enough.

Do you love me? he asked her.

She said nothing.

Do you know what it means, us getting married?

She said nothing.

It means you want to take your clothes off and sleep next to me, it means I sleep with you.

She put out her hand to press his lips together. He seized the hand, kissed her palm and then her fingers one by one, sucking at them gently. When he licked them, a hot flame blazed through the girl and she thought she would topple over. She pulled her hand away, leaned heavily against the tree trunk, and said, her voice shaking, Please, go, you have to go. My mother will be coming back from church at any moment.

I'll pull off your clothes. I'll bathe you and I'll sleep with you. You'll be like a tiny *samaka*, a cute little fish.

The evening was abruptly pungent with an unfamiliar tang as the breeze dropped and the humid air unrolled a thick blanket of darkness and fog over the city. She felt hot and cold at the same time. The smell of the Armenian doctor assailed her. She felt a sudden light-headedness all of a sudden and was queasy in the pit of her stomach. The desire surging through her fingers held her shoulders rigid. Najib talked; Milia wanted to run away. He said . . . and he said and he said . . . but she no longer listened. She saw herself standing in a pool of water, flies buzzing around her ears. She wanted to come out of the viscous liquid clinging to her feet but Najib's words rooted her in place.

He spoke about a pair of pomegranates. He described how he would pluck a rainbow of fruit from her orchard. Enough! she said. The garden was dark. How had darkness fallen so rapidly? The bats, flying blind, thudded into the trees, and at the sound she raised her hands, wanting to shield her head from the blind creatures and their excrement that thudded onto the walls as loudly as did the bats themselves. She wanted to tell Najib that he must go inside, must protect himself from the darkness and the buzzing and the bat droppings, but she was afraid of him and afraid of herself and fearful of the pond overbrimming with water. She fled inside. She heard his voice demanding to know where she had gone but she did not answer. She went into the house and before closing the door she said goodbye to him.

But I don't want to go, he said. I'll wait in the garden for Salim. You go inside if that's what you want to do.

She vanished inside. She fell onto the sofa, her entire body shaking. The bitter taste beneath her tongue mixed oddly with the strange odor spurting from her broken leg. She closed her eyes and saw him. His laughter bared white teeth gleaming in the nighttime darkness. The trees shook off water as if they had just finished bathing in the dew clinging to their leaves. He came to her. He took her hand and lowered it to his trousers, engorged with desire.

Here, here, put your hand right here, Allah *yikhalliik*, please, see, it's like a bird, a little *hamama*. You've never held a bird in your hands, have you? So you've never felt how a bird trembles.

In her hand the bird quivered. The liquid erupting from his trousers made her dizzy and she sensed herself spiraling into the pond. She felt spider threadings winding about her chest and neck and she was certain she would choke. Then, here was the nun. The Sister dangles the incense burner and the room is lit with candles. Abu Salim Shahin is stretched full length on the bed and around Saadeh's husband the women wail. The nun brings the brass *encensoir* to Milia's face. Embers flare up and the beads of incense melt. The nun blows on the embers and tells Milia to bring her mouth close, to blow on those coals with her. These coals must not go out, my girl, she says. All night long you must keep them going with your breath. The incense must be equal to the deaths it recalls. A person's soul must reach our Lord shrouded in incense. Blow!

Milia blew. The ashes flew up and stung her eyes. She rubbed them but it was no use: the ashes punctured the whites of her eyes. Everything turned the color of ash. The little girl stands before the man with the gleaming white teeth, trying to hold on to a bird that exceeds the span of her hand. The nun has commanded her to blow on the ashes. She hears the dogs barking; she hears the sounds of night. Milia wakes up abruptly and finds herself sitting on the sofa, sweat beading across and down her back. With a shudder of cold she hears her mother saying, as she did before, The nun asked why you didn't come to evening prayers.

Where's Salim? Milia asked her.

I don't know, I came in and there was no one here but you. Haajja Milana sent incense especially for you. She says you must burn incense every day until the engagement takes place.

What engagement?

Yesterday we were talking about Najib, your brother Salim's lawyer friend. He says he intends to make it official. We all know – he loves you and you love him.

Me?!

Ayy, you, and *inshallah* now that he is around, your head isn't busy thinking about Wadiie, that stingy baker! His game was clear pretty quickly. He wanted your share of the house before he would marry you.

The mother went into the *liwan*, leaving Milia behind and alone in the *dar*. Her chin cupped in her right hand, Milia gazed at nowhere in particular. She felt the trembling of the bird in her hand, immediately saw the two Armenian doctors, and smelled that smell again. The memory of the two doctors comes wrapped in black tones, a jumble of specters and indistinct shadows. A tall man, broad shouldered, the one bent over her broken leg who massaged it with his full and powerful fingers. His forefinger found the precise point where the pain was worst. Moaning with the pain of it, Milia felt a pair of firm hands on her shoulders, at the bottom of her neck.

She heard the voice of the taller doctor telling her to lift her other leg to the chair. She extended her leg and felt the firm pressure of fingers. Pain; fingers; a smell; two men. She's aware of the one, standing behind her grasping her shoulders as the other bends over her leg. The oil slinks along her flesh, down there. The fingers of the man standing behind her seem to lift her above herself. As if she has now been suspended between two trees; as if the fragrance of the leaves on the fig tree pierces her flesh. Closing her eyes, she is aware of the pain slowly retreating from her calf; she can feel how it rises on the touch of those fingers. The spicy fragrance rises too, as if they are cooking something or as if the air they are inhaling is composed entirely of spices, producing such a hot sharp scent that her eyes smart. She cannot wipe away her own tears. But the fingers reach for her and pluck the teardrops from her face. The doctor bending over her passes her a handkerchief. She blows her nose and the mountain of pain slides off her.

It feels like a mountain, she had responded when her mother asked what she felt in her leg. She said the same to the nun and repeated it again to the two doctors. The nun turned away and told her mother to take her to the clinic. The tall doctor smiled and told her he would lift the mountain off of her leg.

What happened during those three visits to the clinic?

When Milia tries to collect her memories she has the sensation of being in a very dark room. Why? And why had Niqula accompanied her on the third visit, his face grave? He had entered the room where the two doctors stood. This time, the ruddy-faced doctor standing behind her did not touch her while the broad-shouldered doctor did nothing more than undo the bandage around her calf and rub the flesh with a small towel moistened with oil and giving off the fragrance of saffron. When he told her to stand up, she stood up and walked.

It feels weak, she said.

But there is no more pain, and that's the important thing, said the doctor.

There's no pain, said Niqula tentatively.

Back at home, when Milia stretched her leg out on the bed Musa sat down next to her and massaged it gently. She had the sensation of his fingers holding her lightly on the surface of the sea and that the smell was fading to nothing.

Milia did not believe the tale of the two doctors as her mother, Saadeh, told it. The peculiar smell assailed her again and she saw herself in the gloom. That had been her second visit to the doctors after she had had the bandage on her leg for a week. She felt a hollowness deep in her belly. Her belly button seemed to be submerged in water. She observed the tiny belly button tightly gathered like a flower bud that has yet to open, water enveloping it and everything softening and turning to liquid.

The broad-shouldered doctor massages her leg and the slight doctor whose shadow stretches over her from behind grips her shoulders and holds her upper back rigid. She groans. The doctor smiles as he bends toward her. Moans sweep over her and she cannot hold in the sound; she feels like she must scream. But she claps her hand to her mouth to block the sound. Relax! says the doctor who is bent over her leg. Does it hurt? he asks her. She nods and instead of saying yes a scream escapes her lips. Ple-e-e-a-se, doctor, no! She hears her mother's footfall and the commotion made by her little brother. The current of electricity that gyrates around her and lashes her stops suddenly as she sees her mother standing beside her.

What is it, doctor? her mother asks.

Khallaas, he says, it's all done. He wraps the leg in white bandages. Bring her back in three weeks' time and we will remove the bandage. *Hamdillah a's-salameh*.

With that goodbye Milia returned home to find herself spinning inside a vortex of smells, caught in the sensation of leaning painfully for support on a pair of fused shadows that came to her in her dreams, one man with two heads, one bald and the other's hair thick, entering her bedroom and placing four firm hands on her shoulders and her legs. Waking up she would find sweat rolling down her body from her face to her feet.

In this dream Milia sees herself as smaller than the palm of the hand that reaches for her upper back. She is in the darkness, lying on dry grass near a pond. Thorns push into her back and she smells fire somewhere in the distance. Suddenly the two men appear and as they come closer, and closer still, they become one man with two heads and two necks. One neck is long and the other is short, and the four hands stretch out toward the little body, the frail body asleep on the grass. There is pain; there are voices murmuring. The two men do not speak to her. They crowd close and begin to rub her shoulders. Pain sweeps over her and a scream she tries to keep back comes shooting out anyway. She opens her green eyes and finds herself in her own bed, engulfed in fear and panic.

How will she convince her mother that the story is not true? That it is possible to cast doubt on the words of the saintly Milana?

The saint does not lie, says the mother.

That doctor is a scoundrel! says Niqula.

But the night says things to her that she does not know how to put into words.

It's the secret of life, she said to Mansour when, years later, he asked her why she would sleep when he made love to her.

Why don't you respond to me when I am talking to you?

Because there are no words that say what I want to say.

That was Milia's understanding of speech. It could never claim a hold on her, never work its magic, except when she listened to Mansour recite lines of poetry he had learned by heart. He would set his glass of arak in front of him, keeping his fingers on it, jiggling the glass until a milky cloud rose to fill it.

Now this is arak as it should be! Thrice distilled until it is as pure and clear as the tears in your eyes. Look at that milkiness around the edges, like a beautiful fog. Love, milk, tears!

He stares into his wife's eyes and sees a light blue film tinting the whiteness.

> *What has passed beyond us is ever coming*
> *and what is yet to come has passed and gone*

Mansour takes a sip as if his lips are kissing the rim of the glass, and recommences.

Do you like Mutanabbi's poems? he asks.

> *For your eyes – all my heart's seen and suffers*
> *For love – all I've lost or still have*
> *I was not one whose heart passion entered*
> *But seeing your orbs, one must love*

The lines of ancient poetry well up and flow from his lips – love lyrics upon wine-poems, elegy following panegyrics. He will name his first son Amr, he declares. A-m-r-w . . .

Amrw – that's not a very nice-sounding name.

No, woman, not like that – you don't pronounce the letter *waw*. It's there to soften the *ra*. I'll name my son Amr – say it lightly, Amr! – in honor of the poet Amr son of Kulthum. He was a well-known, well-respected figure in the Banu Taghlib. If it hadn't been for Islam, those "Sons of Taghlib" would have eaten the Arabs alive – they were overrunning the Arab lands! So, we name him Amr, and then you can be Umm Amr and I can really give you some love poems. Listen to this one.

May God forgive you, Umm Amr, and keep you!
Return my heart as it was to remain
Your black eyes ringed in crystal'd white verges
Slayed me and revived not the slain

Me!

Yes of course, you – who else? Here, have a sip.

He brought his glass to her lips. She drank a little and felt a cough coming on but she swallowed it. She turned to Mansour. Me! *Hawal!* Are my eyes crossed?

No, no, not crossed, crystal'd. *Hawar*, not *hawal*. *Hawar* means beauty. It means fair. Meaning, the loveliest thing in the whole world. Dazzling white around a deep black core. Like Daad. Do you remember her? Remember the poem?

Please – I really don't like this kind of talk.

A delicate mound she has, and its touch
is intricate to find, its contour to mount
Pierce it, you enter a warm woolen cloud
Pull away, and it draws closed behind you

Do you know what it means? he asked her.

Let's forget it! *Yallah*, I want to go to sleep.

Hawar, my darling, means paleness. Beauty.

All you think about is this stuff.

When I saw you beneath the almond tree, a fellow with you –

You saw me?

Of course I saw you, and the almond blossoms looked like a crown circling your head. Like a white silk shawl, and you were standing with someone who looks like me. I went a little closer but I couldn't make out any words. I just saw your lips, how they moved. *Asal!* I said to myself. Honey. The sweet jolt of honey. I swallowed my saliva and said to myself, Tomorrow. And then and there I named you Umm Amr. My mother won't like it a bit. She wants to name the boy after my father. Shukri. Mama, I said to her, look here. My brother named his oldest boy Shukri. So? she said. Then we'll have two Shukris. See how her mind works? She's not quite right up there. She didn't love my father until after he was dead. Never mind – did you tell me you liked my mother? She adores you and she told me you're an angel. She said to me, Son, you found an angel come down from the sky. I said, Yes, but, Mama, my angel is always asleep. Milia, do you hear me? Why are your eyes closed? We're out here, we're not in bed.

She pressed her palms over her eyes and felt that all the words were closed. She felt unable to speak. Words were like buttons closing a long wrap covering her body. She had to undo the buttons in order to be in the world and to speak its language. But she could not figure out how to work the buttons. She had an image of herself surrounded by buttons, and Georges Nashif sitting in his little shop yawning, and a cascade of buttons on every side. Holding a button in her hand Milia stands in the shop. The girl puts out her hand and the merchant takes the button, opens a drawer and takes out a handful of buttons, which he mounds on the counter in front of her. The shop is full of colors and the world rains buttons. The little girl stands alone under the pelting shower of buttons. Georges Nashif laughs. Hands come out to pluck away the colors and Milia is beneath those hands. She cannot breathe, she's choking. She opens her eyes and discovers that the coverlet has come off and she is shivering with cold. She covers herself and goes to sleep. She sees the long flight of steps. She falls and her brother Niqula picks her up and carries her to the clinic of the two doctors. The close aroma of spices suffocates her as hot oil glides over her legs and feet.

She opens her eyes again and listens to the snoring of her little brother, Musa, asleep beside her.

Milia did not know how to tell this dream. She did not know how to live with it. She listened to her mother's whispered insinuations, among the neighbor women, about the wickedness of the man, his persistent fishing for women, his generosity to those he found beautiful.

Why did the buttons usher in the story of the two doctors?

She wanted to say to Mansour that words are like the buttons closing a long robe and that she cannot undo them. And that is why she does not talk on and on as he wants her to. She had tried to memorize the poems her husband repeated to her but she would find the metrical patterns stumbling and finally breaking between her lips. It was as though she were walking across broken glass and the words wounded her feet.

Why don't you talk? Mansour asked her.

The taste of blood lay under her tongue and the smell of it lingered in her nose. What do you want me to say? She gazed down at her rotund belly and felt herself dropping off to sleep in the chair so she stood up.

Are you going off to sleep? he asked her.

Sorry, leave everything where it is and tomorrow I will clear up. Right now I am too sleepy.

No, no sleep! Every evening I stay up and you're asleep, and then when I come near you . . .

She went into the bedroom, wriggled into her long blue nightgown, lay down on the bed, and closed her eyes on the image of the buttons.

The shadow-profile of the two Armenian doctors chased Milia until her final moments. The girl never understood exactly what had happened but the story as her mother told it was engraved solidly in her memory and it shaped that memory in a way that was both obscure and familiar.

Was that how it had happened, really? Or had things gotten confused in Milia's memory, assuming the form of a story issuing from the throat of the sainted nun who cursed the two doctors? She said they had betrayed the sacred trust of medicine. They had met a just and well-deserved future in the shape of prison.

Milia sobbed and swore on all the saints that nothing at all had happened. The mother screamed and wailed while the four brothers sat down around Milia in a half circle and began interrogating her. Musa was afraid and confused and perhaps embarrassed. Salim glowered while the faces of Niqula and Abdallah were bleached as white as chalk.

Milia did not say that she did not remember anything, because she remembered everything but she did not know what or how to tell.

Nothing happened, she said. She described how the doctor had massaged her leg while his brother stood behind her, holding her shoulders still.

And then? asked the mother.

And then nothing, said Milia.

How to explain this to them? This *nothing* had so many forms, to which she could not give names because she did not know the words to fit around them.

The problem is that the words are not right, she said to her husband, and said no more. She could not tell him that for her, words were nothing but wraps that hid things. When she listened to people (she could not say to him), she did not understand their words. She would think of the sounds and shapes words made instead of thinking about their meanings. As if the bodies of the words veiled the meanings.

Fine then – listen, he said.

> *No rebuke can you give to the yearner for yearning*
> *If you knew not his depths as you know yours alone*
> *For the slain one's figure stained wet by flooding tears*
> *Is no less than one stained by blood's flow – his own*

Do you love this poetry? Mansour asked. Why don't you answer? She got up and went to bed. She closed her eyes and saw the two doctors, merging into one figure, one man with two heads; and the color white blanketed everything. Whiteness wrapped round the man with two heads as moans sounded through the parted lips of the girl seated under their hands and pain swelled from her leg to her spine.

When the family interrogations were over Musa sat down next to his sister on the sofa. Without a word he took her hand. Darkness spread through the large common *dar*. In the soft gloom the mother came, sat down beside her daughter, murmured words that Milia didn't understand, ordered Musa to leave, and told the story.

It's the nun's fault, said Milia. She is the one who sent us to the doctor.

No, you are wrong, my girl. The nun warned me it could happen, and if it had not been for her, your brother Niqula would not have gone and saved you.

Saved me!

He certainly saved you. Death is preferable to scandal. What a scandal we could have been in!

But, Mama, they didn't do anything. I told you what happened – nothing happened.

They didn't because they couldn't. My God, the story has come out and now they're locked up for it. May the Almighty save us! This is a sign from the other world, my dear. If I didn't have five children to worry about, I would have left this world for good by now and I would be long gone into the convent.

You're always there, always at the convent, you practically live there already! I don't know what you do over there, anyway. Anyway. *Ala ayyi hal*.

Milia went quiet though she did continue muttering under her breath. *Ala ayyi hal* – what does that mean – anyway? Hah, it doesn't mean a thing.

As if I didn't tell my mother anything, as if she doesn't ever talk to me. The story she told me about the doctor – fine, I heard it, and so what, I just said, *Ala ayyi hal*, and I shut my mouth. So that's what life means: we just keep quiet, and we don't understand anything – *ala ayyi hal* – but we act as if we do. So why even talk. So how am I supposed to believe what I hear.

How am I supposed to believe what I hear? she demanded in a louder voice. Her mother turned and asked her what she had said.

Nothing, Mama. Nothing at all. In any case. *Ala ayyi hal*.

When had this conversation taken place?

Was it after the family investigation had ended, when Saadeh sat down next to her daughter on the sofa? And told her the story of the two doctors? Or was it after that surprise that dropped out of the sky onto Milia and poisoned her spirit – when she learned that Najib was going to marry another woman?

It's better this way. I knew that. Anyway, if he hadn't left me I would have left him, she said, and reentered her dream. That day she summoned her dream promptly. She needed to see the birds die in the garden.

The smell of the two doctors hangs in her nose, following her all the way to this faraway town. She closes her eyes and sees her mother sitting next to her, telling her the story in a faint voice. Saadeh is yellow, reflecting the color of the curtains over the windows. The story is an amalgam of interwoven images.

Milia opened her eyes and sat up on the edge of the bed. Mansour was on the balcony, she felt vaguely sick. She did not want to see (even in her mind) the face of the man who massaged her leg, the sweat dripping from him as the sound of his panting rose.

The story goes that her leg slid beneath two bare hands thick with glistening black hairs. The oil was as transparent as water; the sweat beading along the doctor's brow and over his face and neck spumed a strange odor into the room. The hand of the other man, the one who stood behind her, slid along her neck and crept to her cheeks.

Had that happened? Or had the scene planted itself in her memory because that was what her mother had told her? What had her mother told her? And was it true that the two men were all but married to the same woman? And that the police had arrested them because they gave their female patients drugs to put them to sleep and then violated them? What was this talk?

The story sticking in Milia's memory is hazy and uncertain. It was said that the two doctors shared one house – and shared it with that woman. The short and somewhat weak-minded one was not really a doctor but rather served as a doctor's aide to his taller and more robust brother. It was said that the real doctor had studied at the Université Saint-Joseph, specializing in bone surgery, but he refused to follow the European medical procedures and techniques that he had studied at the university. He preferred the traditional ways, and he treated his patients with olive oil plus various other oils that he extracted from wild plants. He rejected the use of plaster casts for setting fractures. He treated broken bones with his hands and with oil, binding them in heavy fabric. He argued that this was much to be preferred, because gypsum eroded the skin and could become worm-infested. He became the most famous bone doctor in Beirut, or this is what Sister Milana believed, anyway. No one raised questions about his perennial bachelorhood or his relationship with his brother's wife until the two brothers were arrested on the heels of the Sayyida Marta incident. She was the wife of Khawaja Nazih Shamaat.

The story goes that Sayyida Marta visited the clinic of the two doctors for a shoulder fracture. She detected something odd about the practices there and then realized that the herbal tea the doctor's wife had offered her in the waiting room tasted strange. She grew suspicious. When no one was there to see, she poured the hot liquid into a flowerpot. She entered the small close room of the piercing odors where the two doctors treated patients. She sat down and feigned sleep. When the massage began to take more circuitous paths, she cried scandal – and that was that. Once the word got out, people began to circulate endless tales about the two doctors and their common wife. No one questioned the validity of Sayyida Marta's accusation. She was a respectable woman. Her husband, Nazih Shamaat, had a successful silk-export business in one of the small streets clustered around Beirut harbor. He was a city father and a member of the Greek Orthodox community council. Her word was not to be doubted.

Stories began to spread about the short woman named Kati. People said her slight husband treated her brutally, forcing her to have sex with the taller brother.

Haraam! breathed the nun.

Did anyone actually hear this story from the woman herself? asked Niqula.

God preserve us! moaned the nun.

Niqula said the two men had fled to Damascus seeking refuge from the stories careening around Beirut. But Saadeh insisted on her version, which was that the wife herself exposed the two brothers and only then was Madame Marta Shamaat summoned as a witness. Kati went to the police station, stood there in front of the officer in charge, and said she had been married off to two men. She could no longer bear this life. She reenacted what had happened. (This was what you had to do in criminal cases, Saadeh explained.) The woman with the unkempt hair stood as tall as she could and represented how her husband's brother slept with her. She said the business would happen on the orders of the husband – before his eyes, in fact. God save her, she could not do it anymore and she wanted to die. She said her husband ruled out having children. It was the tall one who kept me

~ 115 ~

from it, I don't know what he did, Efendi, but now I can't have children, and I don't know anymore whose wife I am, or who I am. He beats me, too. And they're so stingy they won't turn the lights on. I've never seen anyone stingier. Once the patients have gone, it's completely dark in there. They just keep one candle lit and they live like the blind. Everything is black and trembly and ghostlike.

The woman acted out what it was like to live inside the color black. She closed her eyes and repeated her stories. They kept her in the station because she declared herself terrified of returning to the house. The policemen arrested the two doctors and locked them up on the orders of the public prosecutor, who then freed them – it was said – when the French high commissioner intervened. It was rumored also, though, that the woman was not in her right mind, that she imagined things or made them up. No one knew the truth, people murmured.

And then? asked Milia.

How would I know *and then* – I just know that God was our salvation, my girl, and if it weren't for God's mercy, what would have happened to us? This woman, this Kati, came to them in the first place because she was ill, and then who knows what they made her drink, and then they married her, and then they ruined her life and destroyed her honor.

Saadeh stood up, put her handkerchief to her eyes, dabbed at her tears, and stumbled into the kitchen, coming back with a jug of water. She took a drink and handed the vessel to her daughter.

Kati stands before the policeman and informs on the pair of doctors. The woman with tousled hair lies down on the floor of the police station and demonstrates how the two men would have sex with her. Reclining on the patient's chair, Kati flips between the two doctors as if she is a fish on the deck of a boat, just yanked from the water. She opens her mouth, tries to suck in a breath, and goes into a stunned stillness.

Milia told Musa the story was made up. The twelve-year-old boy didn't understand any of this business. He took her hand and asked her to come with him to the sea.

Why don't you ever come with us to the water anymore?

Ask Salim. Your big brother said the sea's off limits because I'm a girl.

I want to become a girl too so I can stay with you in the house and not go to school.

Milia laughed at her brother's naïve words. No, brother, we stay the way we're created, you can't become something else.

Would you like to become a boy so you could come with us to the water?

I'd like to be a boy not just because of the sea, but no . . . I don't know, she said, and then said nothing more. Anyway, that's the way the world is.

When Musa told her of Mansour's wish to marry her and that she would go and live with him in his town, far away, in her brother's eyes she saw that question for which there was no answer. Why did a woman have to follow a man to somewhere she didn't even know the location of? Why was the world like this? After her experiences with Wadiie and Najib, things seemed even more cryptic. Wadiie had taught her that being a man meant carrying many faces around with you, while Najib had shown her the dilemma of a man who must search for something or somewhere to carry him. And a woman has to be the faces, and she has to be the places. She has to be everything – that is, she has to be nothing at all.

It's Salim's fault, said the mother.

No, it's Najib's fault, said Musa. Najib is a coward and he wants someone who's going to carry him all the time because he can't carry himself.

May God pardon him, Milia said, seeing before her how the little air-borne bodies plunged to their deaths. This one she would call the dream of the blind little birds and she would never tell it to anyone. And she never did.

Ever since that encounter in the garden when she had stood close to Najib beneath the lilac tree, she had feared the blind bats who fly into the treetops and whose leavings splatter along the wall. Then the dream of the birds came and she was the first to know the truth.

She comes off the balcony and goes to bed, leaving Mansour on his own. He had asked her why she didn't cook her favorite dish, the one he had come to love the most. There in Palestine, and in the Hourani family with their roots in Jabal el-Arab – as Mansour insisted on calling the Houran region of Syria – they called it *shakiriyya*, while in Lebanon they called it *laban-immuh-wa-ruz*. Mother's milk with rice.

Milia took special pride in two dishes. She called them Beirut's greatest culinary achievements, the city's finest and proudest contributions to the cuisine of greater Syria: *laban immuh* and *kibbeh arnabiyyeh*. When Mansour ate *kibbeh arnabiyyeh* he felt in his gut that it was a true occasion in every sense of the word. One needed serious training to appreciate it fully. Tahini was cooked with seven different citrus fruits, onions were cut to resemble wings, the chick peas all but melted in the tahini mixture with its swirling colors from pale to brown, and finally there were the balls of finely ground meat and – on top of that! – the melt-in-your-mouth chunks of stewed meat. He was utterly bewitched by this dish, which Milia made the central festivity of her Nazarene life.

Mansour could not find his way into this world hedged round with secrets and dreams inside of which Milia lived. He had been lost outside of it ever since their time at the Hotel Massabki in Shtoura. There, dreaming became intertwined with sex, and the images conjured up by the blind flying creatures mingled for Milia with the fragrance of the lilac. All of this left her feeling confused and uncertain of how to behave. What could she do but abandon herself to a drowsiness that pulled her downward, into the deep waters of her spirit, prone, still, and silent?

On that interminable journey through the fog of Dahr el-Baydar Milia retrieved her dreaming and returned to herself. At first her recollection was dubious: the woman whom she saw in her first dream on the night of her wedding was her double. A young woman in her early twenties lying full length on the white expanse of the bed as the whiteness of her skin gave off a translucent glow. Mansour told her that her pale complexion was as clear as water. She was his life's mirror, he told her.

I've begun now to understand Arabic poetry, he said, and I know how to appreciate its beauty. He explained to her that the ancient Arab poets who lived in the desert only wrote love poems to fair-skinned women, as if a woman's pallor was a transparent window that the poets' inner selves could open when they wanted access to the worlds of shadow, cool refuges, and sleep – and perhaps to themselves. A woman has to be pale white, still and somnolent, he said. She must be like an oasis. A woman shrouded in the mystery of half-shut lashes leads a man into the labyrinths of love, he said.

You are a real poet!

I learn poetry by heart but I don't want to be a poet. My love, when you are a child of this language borne on odes that balance ecstasy with wisdom, and that dance to the essential union of still and moving letters, the tempo created by a flux of syllables, then it's more than enough to recite poetry composed by others, to play with it as you like, to immerse yourself joy-fully in its rhythms and cadences at whatever moment suits you. But these poor miserable poets have always stumbled under the weight of the poets who came before them. They cannot figure out how to escape the burdens imposed by crystalline poems composed and recited in earlier eras. So the later poets grow careless, or they shrug off the weight of it, or they imitate, or they kill themselves. Listen, my love, listen!

That day Mansour was saying goodbye to his Beiruti beloved for the last time. He would go to Galilee's capital and make final arrangements about the house to which they would come as a married couple. He would bring his mother to Beirut for the wedding, he said then. But the mother did not come, as it happened, because of the revolt flaring up in Palestine. Mansour would marry without any family members to witness it. And when the family gathering on that stormy night in December broke up, he turned to his beloved and recited his lines on paleness and poetry. He wanted to recite the entire poem but he could only remember its opening lines.

> *Say farewell to Hurayra, for the caravan leaves*
> *Are you man enough to make your final farewells?*

Do you know how el-A'sha finishes the poem? he asked her, but he did not wait for an answer. I swear it's as if he's talking about you, Milia!

About me?

Just about. I want you to feel this poetry as if he composed for you. Listen!

> *Noble, tall and slender, she's a chiseled silhouette*
> *Her gait is most stately, all vigilant and wary*
> *As if her path onward from a neighbor friend's abode*
> *Is a pale cloud passing, to neither hasten nor tarry*

See, Milia, you are the vigilant one, pale and wary. No, she's not wary, she just walks as if she is wary. Paleness, a chiseled neck and face – these aren't meant as similes, they're descriptions of a real person. But a wary gait, that's just a simile. Pale and *looking* wary. So, not really wary.

What's the difference between looking and being wary?

The difference is the poetry. The resemblance. The simile. Like, one thing makes you think of another, and so on.

I don't understand, she said. And then, what's the difference between description and similarity? If someone says *abyad*, white, yes, I get that – it means, his color is white. A noun, isn't it?

No, Milia, sweetheart, it's not a noun. It's a kind of adjective made from a verb, it's called an elative, a form used for comparisons, you know – well, anyway, I swear I don't know why, I just read poetry and then I feel like I'm going to soar into the sky. You fly with the meaning, it's intoxicating, it makes shivers run up and down your spine it's so beautiful. So, I mean, how could I possibly come up with my own poetry?

And he, the poet – what was his name?

El-A'sha. He was half blind and that's why they named him el-A'sha.

Blind, and he could see the beauty of a woman?

He saw with his heart, not with his eyes. He would go all confused and flustered in front of women, just like I am with you!

I came for a visit and Hurayra cried and pined
Woe is me! I fear you and fear for you, man of mine

Milia didn't ask him why he didn't write poetry, because she was afraid. Being afraid was no simile in this case; it was a real adjective. She had made her decision and there was the end of it. It had not really been her decision, though. Najib had decided. He had gone with her brother Salim. The dream told her that her future would be written in a faraway town and she understood that she must let her pallor melt and flow in the hands of this strange man of whom she knew nothing except that he resembled her brother Musa. Milia perceived the swarthiness of this man's skin tinting her own body, penetrating it. She knew instinctively that she must peel off her words as she peeled off her clothes. A woman strips herself naked when she tells things while a man clothes himself in his words. That is how she imagined herself in bed: he would be putting things on while she was taking things off. But she could not find the right words and so she decided not to speak. Not to take anything off. Well, no, she did not decide, after all; her mother had told her in no uncertain terms that she must obey him in bed. Men were of different kinds, her mother lectured her. Some of them, especially these days, demanded that a woman be naked in bed, so she'd be like soft warm dough in a man's hands.

That's the way they like it, and you must do as your husband wants.

What did my father do? asked Milia.

What do you want with your father, God have mercy on his soul? It's wrong to talk about the dead. But no, your papa did not take my clothes off. He took off all of his clothes, but I was too embarrassed. I mean, how are you supposed to take your clothes off when the little ones are right there in the house, sleeping? He didn't care one way or the other. He would get under the sheet and take off everything and say to me, Whatever you want, just stay however you want.

And then?

One of these days soon you'll know how it goes.

The mother explained to her daughter that in bed she must swallow her own pleasure, keeping it to herself and not allowing it to get the better of her. It all must stay inside, she said. You must be absolutely sure of that, my girl. It scares a man to hear a woman breathing heavily or to see her pleasure rising with his. It happened to me, and I learned my lesson right quickly – but why am I telling you all of this? Well, these sorts of things aren't talked about, but . . . there isn't a better man than your papa, God rest his soul, but I couldn't stand it any longer. We had our children, enough is enough. I began to feel I couldn't do it anymore, and I smelled the stink of sin – but maybe I wasn't good enough to him, bless his soul.

It's the nun's fault, she put these ideas in your head.

Don't bring the nun into it, she's a saint! May God permit us to drink of her blessings.

Milia understood things differently. She saw the tiny airborne bodies and went silent. Najib had disappeared from her life and a black curtain had come down over his story. Everyone whispered the news, back and forth it went but quietly, quietly, in the belief that she didn't know. But she knew everything. She saw the truth sketched on Najib's eyeballs when the birds fell dead from the sky. It was not easy for her to recall the dream of the birds. To find it she had to plunge into the darkness and when she did, she was rendered incapable of saying anything about it. She had learned to classify her dreams. They were of three sorts.

The first sort of dream was the one that took place on the surface of things and arrived in the early morning. The shallow dream's role was to motivate her to wake up. These were simple dreams crafted out of the details of daily life. They helped one's eyes stay closed for a while longer but also to face the light of morning. This sort of dream did not concern Milia because the moment she got up it would have already vanished from her mind. Indeed, she could stop its march by opening her eyes and when it faded she would close them again to go to a place that was deeper, wanting to regain her real dream, which had hidden itself away somewhere beneath her eyelids.

The second kind of dream planted a cozy hedge around you. Milia took this sort of dream with her to sleep. Closing her eyes, she felt her head tingle and go numb, and she began to weave stories and images. Bedtime means a person plumps up a pillow on which to lay her head. Milia's pillow was not made from cotton or wool or feathers but from stories. She would lay her head back on the long mound of pillow that also served as a backrest and ply her stories slowly. Images moved before her eyes and she selected those she wanted to use, arranging the elements according to her taste. Najib the lawyer became Wadiie the baker, and Wadiie became the priest at the Church of the Archangel Mikhail, and then the priest was passionately in love with the saintly nun, and so forth . . .

There was another element she could not forget. Ever since her mother's illness, cooking had begun to enter the warp and woof of her dreams. She would be mincing onions for *laban immuh* and suddenly Niqula and Abdallah would appear in front of her, Niqula in his jaunty tarbush and Abdallah wearing the sandals that he never took off, summer or winter. The two young men would be conversing about a visit they had made to the home of an Assyrian wizard called Dr. Shiha. He had come from Iraq and was calling people to a new religion that blended Islam with Christianity. Abdallah talked vividly about the new faith while Niqula made fun of it; the wings of onion turned into little birds; and Milia was fast asleep.

Milia knew that these two kinds of dreams were not particularly important. Even so, many a time she could not keep herself from taking them seriously. This led to her morning problem, which was a matter of persuading her body to acclimatize to moving through air rather than water. Dreams were akin to water; it was as though she swam the waters of her eyes. But she did not dare to tell this to anyone. Moreover, these two dream realms overlapped and ran into each other. An entry-dream that pervaded you with the first spreading numbness of sleep would come back to meet the end-dream that prefaced wakefulness, the door behind which one must shake off the waters of darkness and come out onto dry land. In her waking moment the two worlds fused into a single horizon clouded in fuzzy darkness. The prewaking dream picked up features from the entry-dream of the previous night such that Milia could no longer distinguish between the two. Getting out of bed, she would trace footsteps of the two dreams and behave in a way that those around her could not possibly comprehend.

What does one say to Najib? Should she have told him that she saw him in her dream embracing a plump woman under the lilac tree, while the woman caressed him and flirted with him and rubbed her fleshiness against his chest? Najib told her she was crazy and she believed his innocence. She would stop attaching her dreams to her life, she decided then and there. And then the dead birds came and laid everything bare.

The third sort was the deep dream. In these dreams she saw the dead creatures and knew everything about that woman whom Najib had married. In the first two classes of dreams Milia never saw herself. She would see others, but it was only in the deep dream that she saw her own image reflected in the mirror of the night. This was a dream that did not float to the surface: she had to dive into the depths of herself in search of it. There she would encounter the brown-skinned girl with the greenish eyes who scampered down the alleys of the night and concealed her dreams in a dark and cryptic hollow. Milia became accustomed to not telling this sort of dream to anyone because it was not really in her possession. It belonged to that girl whose form she inhabited, and with whom she flew, traversing the arcs of the night, before everything faded and broke up into fragments.

The birds occupied the deep dream. There, inside a forest of stone pine that rose to the skies, Milia saw herself. The small brown girl stood beneath a towering pine that threw its shade across the scene, though under the hot sun the taste of copper burned her lips and tongue. Without warning she saw him. Najib wore the uniform of a French soldier and darted through the trees as if he were fleeing from her. She waved both hands at him to make him stop. He was running like a blind man, colliding into the trunks of trees. She stood there not daring to move. It was fear that paralyzed her. Flocks of birds filled the vacant sky and eventually blocked out the sun. They looked like sparrows but they flew with a peculiar swiftness, bumping into each other and dropping, folding their wings and falling dead. The earth filled with death. Najib vanished and little Milia stood alone beneath a sun assailed by dark clouds, and the tiny feathered creatures were dying. The girl's feet would not move; she saw herself spreading her arms and falling. She wanted to scream to Najib to come and save her but her voice choked in her throat and he was gone. The heart of the little bird who had folded his wings trembled but he did not plunge hard to the ground. The earth cracked open to make a series of valleys that moved apart, and the little bird was suspended in emptiness.

Milia opened her eyes. She was thirsty. She put out her hand for the glass of water next to her bed. It was empty. She took it to her lips and drank the thirst and the emptiness. She thought about getting up to fetch some water but she was afraid. Her feet were half paralyzed. She put her head down on the pillow and begged sleep to come. It came as waves of tingling and numbness and she saw the birds again. Najib was standing next to her holding her hand. Suddenly he let go of it and went into the tree. The trunk of an enormous sycamore tree split into two and swallowed him. The smell of graves and burials rose to spread across the scene. The little brown girl stood barefoot, pebbles digging painfully into the soles of her feet. The birds came. They spread their wings to fly and dropped, they were falling, and Milia grew smaller and smaller until she was no larger than a mote of dust.

She opened her eyes and heard herself panting with fear and understood that it was the end. Najib's birds had died and it was over. When she heard the news from her mother she felt no surprise. Her almond eyes held a look of repose. It doesn't matter, she said, and ran off to the kitchen to make the *kibbeh nayye* that the family ate every Sunday at midday.

That had happened one year before she met Mansour. It was a difficult year because repeatedly she had to chase away the little airborne bodies that floated surreptitiously from her deep dream into her shallow dream. She began seeing the birds in the morning, but without any trees. Before the birds could retract their wings in anticipation of death, Milia would open her eyes and jump out of bed and head for the garden. She would put her mouth under the water tap in the little pond and drink and drink, getting her chest and nightgown wet. This morning ablution was her way of purifying herself from the filth of death, memories of the trees, and the disappearance of Najib.

How could she talk about these things? How could she strip away her dreams and tell the story to Mansour? How could she make him understand that a person must divest himself of words in order to be capable of divesting himself of clothes? And that dreams cannot be washed away except by water?

Milia's story with marriage could be labeled many things. A lone girl lives with her widowed mother and her four brothers. The mother is afflicted with an obscure, nameless illness. The girl had to transform herself into mistress of a home when she was eleven. Saadeh did not go to the doctor. The sum total of medications she would resort to was a morsel of cotton soaked in the oil she carried home from the Church of the Archangel Mikhail. She would come home from the church and make the cotton into shapes that looked something like pills, which she would swallow after every meal. After Yusuf's death, Saadeh became a nun in all but name – though a nun without a convent. She also timed her prayers to the tolling of the church bell – that never seemed to stop ringing, as it announced the nuns' canonical prayers, which took up a goodly portion of the day. She rose at four o'clock for the morning prayers. She ate her breakfast and crawled back into bed as her illness took over. At eleven o'clock she reverted to prayer, performing that of the Sixth Hour, and when that was over she sat in her room waiting for the lunch Milia would have prepared. Her afternoon nap was over by five o'clock when she prayed Vespers before having her supper and saying her Soothoro prayers before she slept.

Saadeh's favorite ritual, though, was lunch. Sitting in her room, she basked in the fragrance of the stew Milia was preparing, her mouth watering, waiting. When the plateful of food arrived she swallowed it almost at once. Saadeh had discovered the virtues of her daughter's cooking. With exemplary speed the girl had learned to cook all sorts of dishes.

If it weren't for your stomach, you would have become a saint, the nun remarked more than once. Saadeh's appetite for prayer could be compared only to her appetite for food. Between these two desires she lived inside the pain that crawled through all parts of her body. In the end, the aches settled in her feet, which swelled until they could no longer carry her. So her life ended there within that small space, in her bed, praying and eating. She died on a day in July in the year 1960 after wolfing down an entire bowl of *kibbeh arnabiyyeh* that the wife of her son Musa had sent to her with her very young grandson Iskandar. Facing his grandmother's appetite, the little boy stood stunned. *Sitti*, you're going to die! he said to her when she told him she would finish the entire bowl in one sitting.

Then I'll die on a full stomach, she said.

Milia knew her mother would die of overeating and she took it as a fact of nature – simply one of many natural disasters. Milia never did understand her mother's accursed illness. Truth be told, she believed her mother was not ill at all. She had feigned it, Milia was certain, and then had come to believe in her own lies.

Her husband had died suddenly at the age of forty-five. Saadeh felt lost, as the nun said. Saadeh had told the nun that she hated *that business* and could not stand the smell of the man, adhering to her body so obnoxiously whenever he approached her. Immediately after the weekly intercourse that she could not avoid or escape, she would take three baths, trying to rid herself of the feeling that she had sinned, of the fierce notion that she wanted to disappear from the face of the earth.

I wish, *ma soeur*, I wish I could just go through that wall and disappear and make the smell go away, she would moan.

My dear, what are you saying? You smell like bay laurel and soap, the nun would say.

But I can still smell it, said Saadeh.

You were created to be a nun and stay a virgin, Saadeh – if it weren't for that stomach of yours. I've never seen a one who was as fond of the stomach as you are.

This exchange or something like it occurred two years after the death of Yusuf. Saadeh was complaining to the nun of her aches and whining about the smell of the man that still hung in her nose. She remembered Yusuf and cried, and said he had blackened her with the soot of misfortune, she and the children. But what were her tears for?

Shufi ya haraam – al-awlad! The poor children, look what's happened to them. They work from dawn to dusk, through the heat, and if God hadn't opened the gates to my son Niqula and started him making coffins, we would've all dropped dead from hunger by now. Salim the oldest went with the Jesuits, says he's studying law and is going to be a lawyer, and then there's little Musa still in school – it was Niqula's and Abdallah's lot to work from the start and support us all. And then there's Milia, I don't know what demon got into that girl, but one month and she was cooking up a storm. That girl left school though she's always got her nose in a book. She cleans house and does the washing and cooks and gets it all done in a couple of hours, too! When I used to spend the whole day in that kitchen and my cooking still came out *saayit* as the late mister used to say, but she's a different case.

They were devouring a platter of stuffed eggplant cooked in oil. Saadeh couldn't *not* eat with the saintly woman even though she had eaten already at home. This isn't lunch, Saadeh, this is a trial and temptation! the nun exclaimed without missing a bite. Don't you bring any more of your daughter's dishes over here. What an aroma – Lord preserve us from temptation!

Mansour would repeat the story of the aroma that was like making love. He had finished his dinner on the terrace at home in Nazareth. He was getting ready to refill his glass of arak when Milia snatched it from his hand and scurried into the kitchen.

Why are you doing that? he yelled after her.

Enough drink, it's time for something sweet.

She came back from the kitchen carrying a platter of *qatayif* dipped in honey. The tiny sweet pancakes grilled over a very low fire until they were golden gave off the fragrance of pure Hama butter and glistened with pine nuts. Mansour took a bite and cried out at the sweetness of it. *Shuu ha'l-tiib hayda!* Milia explained that she had crushed the pine nuts with sugar and rosewater and orange-flower syrup. He took a second bite with his eyes closed and she heard something very like a moan of pleasure.

This isn't dessert, darling, this is like love. Like I'm making love with you, not like I'm eating! Amazing! And he dove in, and the *qatayif* were gone.

You shouldn't eat so many, you need to really appreciate the taste, she complained. She had invented this sweet by chance, she told him. Making *qatayif*, she discovered she didn't have any almonds or walnuts in the old house, so she hit upon the idea of filling them with pine nuts. But pine nuts are tender and subtle and the taste isn't there on the tip of your tongue right away. To get the flavor you have to wait, and I was afraid my brothers wouldn't like them, especially Niqula, since he's a bit rough and he likes his food that way too. But Musa – when Musa tasted the *qatayif* he closed his eyes and reacted just like you did, and then all of them loved it. Especially the nun. That one's the patron saint of stomachs – I never in my life saw anyone eat the way she does, like her whole body is in a rapture, like the skin on her fingers and hands tastes it along with her mouth.

The nun ordered Saadeh to stop bringing her daughter's cooking to the convent. But Saadeh would show up toting a paper bag in which she had concealed whatever dish she had taken furtively from the kitchen. The nun would become wholly engrossed in the dish Milia had prepared. Making the sign of the cross over the food, she would intone Byzantine hymns adorned with words in praise of the Virgin Mary, just for good measure.

The Convent of the Archangel Mikhail had become Saadeh's refuge long since. There, even her bones eased and the aches retreated. Her spirit was liberated from the burdens of the body. And anyway, the house had become Milia's territory. The three older brothers treated her as the woman she had so quickly become and they were not slow to practice their sense of masculine dominion on her. But her younger brother Musa looked upon her as his mother. She was happy enough with the two roles, which made her a woman and a mother and transformed her into the pivot and core of family life.

Two years after her father's death Milia found herself out of school. Yusuf's death had completely overturned the family's life. Only the eldest son, Salim, preserved the accustomed rhythm of his existence, and that was only because of Niqula's swagger. On the day of his father's death Niqula put Yusuf's tarbush on his head and decided then and there to quit school and go to work in the shop. Niqula was seventeen and had shown no sign whatsoever of academic success, but he did make the most of the talents he had.

If Niqula is going to sacrifice himself, then I will, too. I'll leave school, declared Abdallah. Their mother smiled and said nothing. Everyone in the family knew that this had nothing to do with sacrifice. It had already been established that Abdallah would go to work with his father in the shop, since he had never flourished at school.

It hadn't been in anyone's mind that Milia would be forced to abandon school, though, or that Musa would not enter the university but rather would go to work as an accounts clerk at the Seaside Inn on Lake Tiberias.

But the shop was no longer enough to keep the family going. Milia did not have a choice. After the father's death, Saadeh's illness transformed the house into a living hell. Their mother's right arm was completely paralyzed, the numbness spread across the entire side of her body, and she was in pain from her shoulders to her feet. She was completely disoriented and in a permanent daze, her wailing hemorrhaging the so-called weak letters of the alphabet, with her *aaas* and *aawws* and *aayys*, which Milia was convinced were the letters of pain. Somehow, the girl thought, the Arabic language had been constructed out of groans of pain, creating strength from the weakness that deformed those letters – for after all, these were letters that could connect words and had the power to intensify and condense meanings. That was what she had been taught by her teacher, Ustaz Kamil Samara, who guided her in the worlds of ancient poetry, and made her learn by heart the seven great odes. Their elderly white-haired teacher brought his lunch to the Zahrat el-Ihsan School every day, setting out his repast on his desk in the classroom at midday and letting his tongue go, roaming the universe of literature. His lessons were like a boat bobbing about in an ocean of language. In Milia the elderly teacher saw a writer of the future. She was the only pupil among these girls who memorized the ancient poems and could recite them in others' hearing without stumbling over their words. She would stand up and recite the poem, swaying with the movements of the letters and enabling their ascent when the moment came. The vowels, said the teacher – those sounds that made the consonants move – were like oars in little boats. Three sounds: *aa, wa, ya*. Within them they held the pains of humankind, *aaa* and *aaww* and *aayy*. Weak or deficient they might be – said the ancient grammarians – but they formed the joints between sounds. They were the ligaments that bound words together. They made it possible for words to name things.

Ustaz Kamil Samara was her first story after the death of her father.

When they said goodbye she told him she would take him with her, and she hugged to her chest the notebook she had filled with the ancient Arab odes of the desert. It was the end of the school year. The girls were saying goodbye to their teachers and their schoolmistresses, and they all had armfuls of notebooks, a sure sign that the year was truly over. Milia extracted her notebook of poems from the brown bag in which she had put all of her books and binders and exercise pads. She hugged it closely to her chest when she noticed her elderly teacher's tears. He was saying goodbye to the girls he had taught, for now he was to be put out to pasture.

This is what they want, my children, he said. They want me to retire. He wrote the word *mutaqa'id* on the blackboard and then drew a slash between the *t* and the *q*, just where the *a* would appear if the Arabic script showed vowels. He read the word as if it were two separate words: *mut qa'id*. See? he said. *mut: i have died.* That's what they want. *qa'id. sitting.* Can a man of letters retire? Can any writer suddenly go *mut* and *qa'id*? But that's what they're insisting on! So, instead of my reading the weak deficient letters in the language, I'll be living them with my body.

Tears rolled from his eyes and a murmur went up from the rows of seated students. Milia saw how tears burned their way down his cheeks as the deficient letters spread across his body and covered it in pain.

I'm going to take you with me, she said to him when she said goodbye. But she didn't know that she would leave the school too: that her mother's chronic maladies would sketch out a different life for her.

The mother's medication was the nun and her painkiller consisted of visits to the Convent of the Archangel Mikhail, where mystery mingled with the truth. The nun reduced the world to one word: *sirr*, mystery. The world bounded by Haajja Milana's awareness began with the mystery that brought her to the convent at the age of five. Her mother had died. Her father put her into the nuns' care when he decided to travel to his relatives in the plains of the Houran in order to remarry. It's just a few months and I will be back, said the man whose features Haajja Milana had forgotten. All she had left of him was a memory of his hoarse voice. Just a few months and I'll come back and take the girl home. But he did not come back and his features dissolved into the vapors of the convent's incense.

The vapor that incense makes is the closest substance to a human being because it looks like the spirit: clear air with a wash of viscous white. We are white like this, a thick creamy white that we veil in the blackness of our clothing to remain modest. We wear mourning garb over our sins. People are scented vapors and death returns us to the essence. God can tell sinners apart from the innocent just from the smell of them. It's all incense, my girl, that's all it is.

Milia came to fear people's spirits. When she stared at people she saw not bodies but masses of vaporous incense. In her dreams she began to see spirits – were they souls? – like white smoke appearing and vanishing. She began to fear her mother and the nun and the cures with cotton and oil. The mother picked up her pains and waddled to the church, leaving Milia alone in the house teaching herself how to cook. Suddenly the cooking pot opened before her eyes like the sky opens before the saints. That was the way she felt when she discovered that cooking is nothing more than weighing and balancing relationships between garlic, onion, coriander, and lemon; and that the fragrance comes from the hand that creates the balance. She saw signs of delight on the faces of her brothers. This was the end of the plain, insipid cuisine that Saadeh had produced. Here came Milia's food, laced with innumerable and complicated fragrances. The domestic atmosphere of the Shahin household was transformed. The dinner table, their only daily gathering, became a joyous fête. The poverty in which the family lived had not changed but the fragrance of life entered it with the ministrations of this girl around whose eyes the flavors of words hovered and soared.

When life forced her to leave school, Milia crossed the threshold into the worlds promised by her grandmother's books. According to Saadeh, the grandmother (whose senility she had long had to endure) woke up from her nap one day, summoned her daughter-in-law and pointed to her wooden chest. It's for Milia, she said. All my life I've lived with this chest, my girl – without it, I couldn't have stood to live. This is for Milia. Give it to her but wait until she's a bit older. Tell her, this is from your grandmama Umm Yusuf.

What a woman she was! This was what Milia wanted to tell Mansour about her grandmother, when he started talking about his mother and brother. They lived in the city of Jaffa and they had been demanding that he, Mansour, return there to work in the modest foundry and hardware business that their father had left them. He did not want to go back, Mansour told his wife, because he was no longer willing to put up with his mother's ways. She had always tried to control her sons' lives, ordering them around at work and at home. In Nazareth he had acquired an independent life. Moreover, in this silent woman across whose eyes moved clouds of sleepiness, this man on the verge of turning forty had found his emotional and bodily repose. She was a woman very much like the little town he had chosen as the seat of his trade and the home for the family he would establish.

The woman was eccentric – that was true. She did not finish her sentences. Her speech was fragmented, jumping from one thought to another and one place to the next before coming back to alight on silence. But she gave him a sense of inner peace. His highly strung, ever-demanding mother, who ran the business after his father's death, left him dreading work: going to the foundry seemed daily retribution for something he must have done. The father had died when Mansour was fifteen and Amin, sixteen. At the age of twelve Amin had left school to work alongside his father, and the elder son became his mother's de facto business partner. They treated Mansour like a lowly employee. The younger son expected never to become a partner in the enterprise and decided to move to Nazareth where his aunt Warda lived. It was said that this widowed aunt of his – sister of his father – wanted him as a husband for her only daughter and so she enticed him to Nazareth. But the truth was that Mansour went of his own accord. He would not have ruled out marrying his cousin Samiha but she already had a young man, a scion of the Said family for whose sake she converted to Protestantism. Not wanting to return to Jaffa, Mansour hit upon the idea of opening a fabric shop catering to feminine tastes. It seemed that divine favor was on his side: after seeing some success, he began commuting to Beirut to acquire dry goods from the Souq Tawile, which during the French Mandate had become the premier *souq* for imported fabrics of a feminine sort. Soon the fates would lead him to visit the home of one of his acquaintances among the merchants there, Khawaja Emile Rahhal. It was from the garden of Khawaja Emile and his wife Sitt Sonia, in early spring, that Mansour's eyes lit on the fair-skinned girl standing under the flowering almond tree. It was then and there that he fell a victim to passion. His first gift to his Beiruti fiancée would be an old book printed in Cairo with the title *Masari' el-'ushshaq*. *Lovers' Slayings* would go into the chest that had belonged to Umm Yusuf and Milia would carry it with her to Nazareth alongside the volume of saints' lives and the *Thousand and One Nights*.

In Nazareth, though, Milia did not open the chest to pull out and read her grandmother's stories. Here she needed no reading, for all was written on the stones of the roads and alleys. She had only to walk out of the house to find herself among the lines of script in an enormous book that she read as she was living it.

In Beirut, reading had been her means of bridging the time between kitchen work and waiting for her brothers to return home. She devoured her brothers' books. She solved their math problems and memorized the poems they were instructed to learn. She lived between her grandmother's treasure chest of tales and her brother's schoolbooks, and all the while she was becoming the undisputed queen of the kitchen. And so her brothers dreaded her early marriage. She would leave them prisoners of their mother's food and her incurable illnesses.

But things had taken an unexpected turn. After a short liaison with Wadiie the bakery owner, Milia found herself alone, waiting for Najib, who would also disappear.

Milia did not know why this Wadiie character, this man whose body was dusted in the smell of flour, came to visit every day. The baker became part of the family's evening ritual. This began at six o'clock sharp with the Ottoman-style coffee that gave off its special strong aroma of sugar and orange-blossom water. The evening reached its zenith at half past eight when Milia called everyone to the dinner table. Wadiie would hesitate and fidget and claim he had to return home. The smell of the food coming from the kitchen would gradually bewitch him and he responded to Salim's insistence by clucking uncertainly that he was putting on weight because he was now having dinner twice, once here and then a second time at home so as not to anger his mother.

Milia knew she would not marry Wadiie. But he was real, and he was here, short and pudgy, his belly impossible to ignore. The masses of flesh straining beneath his shirt disgusted her and the smell of flour repelled her. Milia would not remember ever being addressed directly by Wadiie. He sat with her brothers, bringing them bread and petit fours from the bakery he had inherited from his father. In fact, he acted as though he were one of the brothers. Well, no, there was the one time when he followed her into the kitchen on the pretext that he was thirsty. He told her that her cooking was *tayyib*, it was very good, very sweet indeed, and he was waiting for the day when she would cook for him alone.

Everyone said Wadiie would marry Milia. But Wadiie said nothing. And after six months of daily visits, Saadeh asked him when his mother might honor them with a visit. Wadiie's round pudgy face got very red and he cleared his throat before saying, Soon *inshallah*.

Then everything ended.

Milia told Musa firmly that she wasn't angry at Wadiie. Never, not a single day, she declared, had she imagined herself as his wife. She told her mother that she had been horror-stricken when she visited Wadiie in his mother's home. Umm Wadiie took her into the bedroom and jabbed her finger at a wide oak bed at the center of the room. This was my bed, she sighed. Mine and my late lamented husband's. We may be the first newly-weds in Beirut who slept on one bed. That'll be my gift to you and Wadiie when we celebrate the two of you.

You'd want us to sleep in one bed!

When Milia opened the door to the hotel room and saw one bed in the middle of the room, Umm Wadiie's voice clanged in her ears and she smelled old oak. She was nonplussed; where should she sit down? Mansour did not notice her confusion and embarrassment, fully occupied as he was with opening the bottle of champagne. Milia went to sleep alone in the bed and did not sense her husband next to her except through what she would later call the marriage dream. She heard the bathroom door open and decided to go on sleeping. She fell into a rhythm of slow breathing and was soon immersed in the dream. This was a dream without images or words. It was composed only of colors, of intimations that the world was closing in and then opening out, circling and extending, rising and falling. Her face broadened and lengthened and inside her eyes she sensed eyes without end. She was swimming in a world of blue. And then suddenly the dream was broken, the coldness struck her between her thighs, and the man slipped out. She jerked her legs up and curled around herself and felt an explosion of heat from her belly shooting through her body like circles of light; and she was in the car.

In their own bedroom Milia insisted on two beds. Mansour did not understand why she was so determined on this particular issue. But he had purchased twin beds already. In fact, it had not even occurred to him that he might sleep with his wife every night in one bed. The wife's bed, he proclaimed, has to be wide enough to embrace the child who will come, because this is our way. Milia bowed her head in assent and saw a blue halo forming. That was how she saw herself, head bowed in assent. When she became pregnant and began spending a lot of her time among the eucalyptus trees dotted around the house, the blue halo was her constant companion. She did not see the halo reflected in her husband's eyes, and so she knew that she alone saw the blue cloud that hovered over her bowed head and protected the forming baby and his mother. In the shadow of this halo Milia lived for nine full months. The color blue clothed her through the day and at night it became a soft carpet on which she slept and across which her dreams flowed incessantly.

Mansour poured himself a glass. It made his head spin but it also sent him into his poetic state. They were sitting on the balcony in Nazareth. Between sips, Mansour was reciting poetry but there were spaces of silence within and between the lines. Milia was yawning. He had drunk so much, she said, that his recitation destroyed the music of the poetry. Well, no . . . she said his drunkenness slowed the music of the poetry down until it was unrecognizable. Well, no, she didn't say that, maybe she didn't say any of it. Maybe she wanted to say it but said something else. She did tell him to stop drinking, because he was drunk.

Me, drunk!

She stayed silent.

You think I've gotten drunk on the arak but that isn't true. Arak doesn't make me drunk.

She said nothing.

Darling of mine, if I'm drunk, it isn't the arak. It's your eyes. Your eyes intoxicate me and I see a strange color.

You too? she said, and immediately bit her lower lip in regret. Apparently Mansour did not hear her, though. If he had, she would have had no choice but to tell the story of her photograph and the odd green film that Musa had noticed immediately.

One person must know, she muttered, standing in front of the Virgin's image in the Church of the Annunciation. He will. She stared at her rounding belly and begged the Mother of Light to let the boy know the color of his mother's eyes, even if it remained concealed to all others.

That evening Mansour, who did not know this secret, recited the most beautiful poetry Milia had ever heard. The lines he offered told her that only the prophets were privy to the secret cementing the relationship between night and day. He told her of the famous poet Abu el-Tayyib el-Mutanabbi. He was the only prophet whose prophecies emerged in poetry. Prophets before him had been either incapable of composing poetry or afraid of it, though they might make up stories and proverbs. But then came the poet who inscribed his prophethood in incomparable verse. Speakers of Arabic one thousand years ago were captivated by his magic and today they still were. Mutanabbi visited Tiberias, he told her, and even stayed in Palestine for a period of time. That's where he was when he wrote lines describing the lion as no one before him had.

Did he walk on water like the Messiah? asked Milia.

No, he walked on words, Mansour answered.

Meaning, he wasn't a real prophet.

Why not – did all the prophets walk on water?

How would I know?

Listen, Milia, Mansour began insistently, but then stopped, uncertain of how to go on. He wanted to tell her that words were that poet's water and the music of his words the waves. Mutanabbi brought together wisdom and rhythm, and he balanced the two of them. His poetry flung open gates to emotion, and when he died he shut those gates behind him. For an entire thousand years no one could open them again, or at least not as widely.

But if he couldn't walk on water, he wasn't a prophet, she said.

Listen!

> *What mortal has not embraced the earth's passions*
> *but no road to union can one find or keep*
> *Your earthly share of a dearly beloved*
> *Is your grip of a phantom, long as you sleep*

Milia had only to hear the lines of poetry once and she had them memorized. But when reciting them, somehow she reversed the final hemistich and it became something else.

> *Your earthly share of a dearly beloved*
> *Is the grip of sleep phantom dreams let you reap*

Milia was in her third month of pregnancy. As she grew rounder her beauty was almost too much to bear. Mansour did not know how to express the full measure of his love or the weight of his awe. She did not listen to him when he spoke of love. She lowered her head and the blue halo visible above it would veil her as she sank further and further into silence. He resorted to poetry, trying now this poem, now that one, all for her ears. Head still bowed, her eyes sparkled as she listened intently. When he came to the end she remarked that poetry is like prayer.

She saw vapor rising over the table as though the words had turned themselves into incense. Her head spun with the fragrance of incense spreading across them and winding around the words that floated downward from this man's lips.

She had dreamed the incense, she said. When she recounted her dreams to him, it often happened that she halted abruptly midstory and would not go on. She saw fear in his eyes. Only that one dream: she did tell that one to the end. Three months before she had told it, at the moment when Mansour saw his wife's body inscribed with circles, curves upon curves and swirls upon swirls. It was morning then, and he stared, marveling at how her shoulders slipped roundly from the loose neckline of her blue nightgown. He was stunned by how beautiful they were. He followed her into the kitchen, where she had begun to make coffee and set out breakfast. He came up to her and from behind he hugged her tightly to his chest. There was no sound of the uneasy protest that invariably greeted his attempts to embrace her. His body pressed into hers and desire rippled from his pelvis to his shoulders. As he tried to lift her nightgown the dazzling whiteness of her seemed to explode before his eyes, the brilliance knocking him nearly blind. He closed his eyes, his hands pressing in at her hip bones, and he arched forward over her. Her body bending with his, she was soft and warm and her tenderness flowed over him.

Suddenly she cried out and whipped around. She pushed him away gently and told him she was pregnant.

What?!

I dreamed it. I'm pregnant.

He smiled and stepped toward her again but she pushed him back.

I'm pregnant.

Since when?

Since today.

She put the little coffee ewer down on the table and began to talk. She stood in the sunlight streaming through the window, her face growing rounder as he stared and her eyes getting larger. The man felt his legs weaken and he sat down. He let his eyelids drop and darkness swept over him.

Sitti . . .

She told him about her grandmother Malakeh. My grandmama Malakeh came and sat down next to me on the bed, here. I was sleeping. The bed seemed endless, as though I slept on a bed of water, it was everywhere, the water, and Sitti sat with me. She was a young woman – *Ya Latif* she looked so much like my mother! At first I thought she was my mother, and I said, Mama, what are you doing here? She said, I'm not your mama, your mother is in Beirut and I came here to tell you a story. I said, Sitti, is this the time for stories? Don't you see where I am? How I'm living on my own now, and no one is here with me? She said she had come here to awaken me but first I must accept a gift from her. She put her hand into her cloak and took out a tiny icon of the Virgin. It has to stay with you always, she said, to keep you safe. I took the icon from her but I did not know where I should put it. Set it on your belly, she instructed. I laid it on my belly and felt myself sinking. I called to her. Sitti, I'm sinking, I'm going to drown, what should I do? Hold my hand, she replied. I held out my hand but I couldn't reach anything. I tried to scream but my voice wouldn't come. I was drowning. I was underwater and I couldn't breathe. Suddenly a woman in a blue veil was there. She held me. I saw myself on shore. I saw a lot of fish. The fish were poking their heads out of the water, opening their mouths to breathe, and diving under again. The blue woman was beside me. She was whispering to me but I didn't understand a word of it. She talked and talked in a soft voice. I didn't catch any of it except for one word: Tiberias. So then I knew I was at Lake Tiberias. The blue woman closed her eyes and I longed for sleep. If I went to sleep, though, nothing in the world could awaken me, I knew, and I was afraid. I remembered what my grandmama had said about sleep and death. *Khallaas*, I told myself. It's all over for you, Milia. You are going to die in this water. But I was no longer fighting for breath. I was breathing underwater and seeing a rainbow of color. The blue woman was with me. She reached out and placed her hand on my stomach and I felt my belly start to swell and my body grow rounder. She took her hand away. I turned and saw my grandmama, here with me, but now she had no teeth. I used to be afraid of Sitti when she took out her teeth and put them in a glass of water. I didn't understand why her set of teeth looked so strange. It wasn't two sets of dentures, up and down, but four or five. The glass would become something frightful – water all around the dentures and the teeth looking as though they were trying to bite the glass. Why did you take out your teeth, Sitti? I asked. So I can talk with you better. No, no, Sitti, please, go back and put in your teeth so I can understand you. She said she could not, because in a dream one shouldn't fiddle with one's teeth. But you're dead, Grandmama, I told her. It's not important, I don't matter, my dear – the important thing is you, she said. But you've been dead a long time, I protested. She laughed, that mouth of hers wide open, and she began saying things I didn't understand. I caught only one word. She was talking in a very faint voice and I only understood a single word. *Sabiyy*. I said to her, What *sabiyy*? You'll find out later on, she told me. But I'm afraid now, I told her, and I put my hand out to pull her dentures up and out of the glass. She slapped my hand and I started to cry. When my grandmama Malakeh died I cried a lot. Everyone thought I was crying so much because Sitti loved me so much. But that wasn't true. Well, of course I cried because I loved her too, but the truth is that I cried especially because they didn't put the teeth back inside of her mouth where they belonged. I asked my mother where they were and then I ran into the kitchen. She followed me and said, Don't be upset, dear, take it easy. I didn't answer. I just started searching like I'd gone mad. I went under the table, looking everywhere, opening the cupboards. My mother said to me, Stop. They aren't here, we got rid of them.

Where? I asked. In the garbage. Why? Because, it's *haraam*. False teeth mustn't be buried with the dead. A dead person has to return to her Lord exactly as He created her.

In the garbage! I cried. And I went right to the garbage can and began to search. I didn't find them, no. Not then. But yesterday, when I was drowning . . . no, maybe this is another dream, Lord how I've come to confuse things! It has gotten so I don't know the whys and whens and hows anymore. The important thing is that I took the set of dentures and went to my grand-mama but she had vanished. I didn't know where she went. I didn't know what I would do with her teeth. Women were sitting all around me, crying and crying some more. And then I fell. I don't know how. I was hanging on to the akadoniya tree with my feet braced against some heavy branches, and I was eating a hard green fruit I had picked from it, and I was aware of myself only when I began to fall. When I hit the ground I broke my teeth. I put my hand up to my mouth and it's as if they were my grandmama's teeth. I don't know. There was a lot of water, there were eyes and tears. The women's tears were pouring onto the ground and I saw my grandmama drowning and I started crying. I put my hands out to grab my grandmama's hand but I couldn't reach her. I felt like I was drowning too. And then I don't know, everything was blue and I was asleep in bed, and the mattress was like a lake and Sitti sat next to me. She put her hand on my belly and gave me the icon. And I saw the blue woman: it was as though she had risen right out of the icon. I said, Grandmama, this is the woman, it's her, the one who put her hand on my tummy and it started growing. A *sabiyy*, she said. And she told me we must name this boy Mikhail after Sister Milana's convent, since the nun safeguards me, too, with her prayers. But I said to her, no, I'm going to name him Issa. His name is Issa, I'm naming him after the Messiah. Because that's what the blue woman wants. I opened my eyes and got up and went into the bathroom. I washed my face, heated some water, and bathed. You were snoring away. Yesterday I tried to turn you over because the sound of it was so loud. But you were all curled up around yourself, like at the Hotel Massabki. God knows I was afraid for you there. No, not when you were in the bathroom and you weren't answering me. That was easy enough to understand. At the time I felt . . . no, not right then, but later, seeing you asleep in bed, curled up as if you were a little baby boy in his mama's belly, I felt what you wanted was a mother. Now don't misunderstand me, and please, don't interrupt me. I don't like hearing this kind of talk. No, I don't know what all you do and I don't want to know. Did I ever ask you, even once? If I didn't ask you, then why answer me? No, I don't want to understand, these are matters only for you. You told me you don't want to go to Jaffa, and anyhow I don't like it there. What was I saying? Oh yes, I could feel my belly getting big and round, all of me becoming round, and I understood then what the woman had been saying to me, that woman who draped her hair in a blue shawl. I understood that I was pregnant. Me, Mr. Mansour – pregnant since last night. That's what I wanted to tell you. That's all.

Mansour was utterly bewildered, his tongue tied. He tried to puzzle out the way she had of conveying things; to even understand what she had said. He sipped his Turkish coffee slowly, his head bent. But he was exasperated, too. Why didn't she say things in a straightforward manner? Why did the woman wander among words, meandering amidst them as though she were speaking in a dream and not in wide-awake reality? He wanted to wake her up from this ongoing somnolence of hers, and from her insistent refusal to let him express his love. When she said she was pregnant, he tried to interrupt her, to say he had slept with her the night before and that it had been the most beautiful lovemaking ever, the very best they'd had. He said he had seen how it exalts a female when she receives her male and takes him into her. This is the kind of love that makes a woman pregnant, he said, a smile of triumph on his lips.

You don't have anything to do with it, she said.

What do you mean by that?

Yaani . . . well, maybe. How do I know. I don't remember.

You don't remember?

How should I remember, I was asleep and dreaming. The dream I just told you.

You remember the dreams but you forget what was actually happening?

What – what happened?

God give me patience! All right, nothing happened! he said, seething with anger. He must start waking her up at night when he slept with her, he thought. He would wake her up and he would order her to remember everything. He would end this foolish performance that had begun on their very first night in the hotel. True, he had collapsed in the bathroom, but who wouldn't have? What man would have been capable of withstanding the icy cold whistling along Dahr el-Baydar? Mansour alone withstood it. He fought back. He could not bear the idea of returning to Beirut in defeat. He would have been forced to stay in the Shahin family home while waiting to go to Nazareth.

Salim, the eldest brother, did not attend the wedding. When Mansour asked about him, the only answer he got was a cryptic sentence from Musa. Mansour was the only one among the extended family who did not know the story of Salim. From Musa he heard half the story, but still he did not understand why the rupture had happened. Musa told him that Salim had wanted to become a Catholic and enter the Jesuit order. He studied law at their university but then he went a little crazy. Salim had entered the university thanks to a reference letter from Father Eugene, who ran the Sunday school in a cellar vault attached to the Jesuit Fathers' monastery in the quarter. It was not a real school. "Frère" Eugene lured in poor boys by handing out candy. He made them watch religious films and forced them to attend Latin mass. Salim was bewitched by the cinema. He took his brothers along to watch a film about the passion of the Messiah. He was astonished to see them all drop off to sleep. Instead of becoming absorbed in how light became images, instead of letting those images dazzle them, the boys fell asleep. Musa shrieked in fright when he saw the enormous shapes occupying the whole of the huge white screen. Only Milia was an enthusiast when it came to the cinema, but Brother Eugene told Salim that Sunday school was only for boys and Milia could not come in.

I'll go back with you, spoke up Musa. I'm afraid of films and I'm going back with you. But Milia ordered him to go in with everyone else and she returned alone to the house.

Musa said that in Salim, Frère Eugene found a true *iwazza*. Mansour did not understand the expression, but he made as though he did. He always felt disgusted with himself when Milia stared at him, irritated, every time he asked her the meaning of a Beiruti expression that he didn't understand.

It's as though you don't know Arabic, she said.

So he began acting as though he understood everything. When Milia came to live in Nazareth, rather than adopting her husband's dialect and pronunciation – that of the town in which she now lived – she went on speaking in her own Beiruti way, words full and heavy with the flesh of the tongue. Beirut folks worked their lips and their tongues to weight down their words, and the syllables glided downward. Only Milia sang out her letters. She preserved the thickness of her local dialect but instead of pronouncing the sounds from her cheeks and tongue she launched them from her lips so that her words floated out soft and light, as rich and full as they were.

You don't speak like Beirut folk do, he told her.

Inni!

The "I" came out tilted, slipping, reclining in the Beiruti way.

He did not ask what it signified to call Salim a gullible goose. He did not understand why their elder brother's embrace of the Catholic faith had generated so much anger.

They're all alike, he commented.

The mother's eyes scored him as she pronounced the famous line which she said whenever anyone tried to engage her in dialogue about her son's new religious choice. God is Orthodox, she said firmly.

But we are not Greek Orthodox, Mansour wanted to say, relying on what a priest in Jaffa had told him. The exchange had taken place in the thick of the heated protests in Palestine against the Greeks who had held sway over the Jerusalem Orthodox Church. The priest had said that the label Rum, even if it had come to refer to Greeks in general, was coined originally as an insult that the followers of the Syriac rite had flung at the Orthodox Arabs, trying to label the latter as agents of the Byzantine Empire. We were Orthodox Arabs who chose to believe in the two natures, divine and human, of the blessed Messiah, peace be upon him, the priest explained. We adopted the *Greek* part because our small minds somehow accepted our enemies' accusation. They were able to make it stick.

Mansour told Saadeh and her daughter the story of the priest Yuhanna Aazar. Saadeh began to yawn while Milia, her chin cupped in her hand, gave herself up to her mute slumber. The man did not complete his story. He stopped halfway through, getting to his feet to return to the Hotel Amiirka in the carpenters' *souq* where he stayed on his trips to Beirut – now more frequent, ever since he had succumbed to this love.

These feelings that people call passionate love had been alien to his life, Mansour told them. It was true that he was on the threshold of forty, and yes, he had known many women in his life, especially women of the night in Jaffa and Beirut, and he –

Please, please don't use those filthy words.

I didn't use any filthy words! I didn't say anything abusive or insulting, he answered.

Please, that's enough. No more!

Fine, he said. Anyway, we don't use abusive language the way young men in Beirut do! You can't speak to any one of them without their starting to joke with you by tossing out a curse word or two. *Kayfak y'akh ish-sharmuta!* How are you, Brother-Your-Sister's-a-Whore! As if he'll make you love him by saying this. At first I couldn't bear it, and more than once I nearly got into trouble because of it. Then I got accustomed to it and that was that. There's no need to get upset, Milia, my love.

He wanted to say to her that in all his past he had never felt the kind of longings that God put inside men to consume them. All it takes is a lowly matchstick to set a man's entire body alight. He wanted to tell her that, yes, sometimes he had felt a smoldering in his gut that took fire through his body, and then there was not much else a man could do. But after meeting her he was suddenly aware of the emptiness that filled him from his heart to his feet. He felt on fire now, too, but it was different this time, because this was a flame he could not put out. He even wanted to tell her that when thoughts of her had led him to what they called *the secret habit*, the flame still did not go out. It just moved into his hand. But he didn't say anything. He was afraid she would be angry and the wound lines on her neck would appear. Whenever a word or an observation upset her, three horizontal scars, from high on her neck down to her chest, glowed red. When he asked her once about the scars she said the nun was to blame.

She went into the bathroom and washed her neck. When she came out it had returned to a pure, undulating white.

This is the color of love, he said.

Mansour told no one that in the Hotel Amiirka fire and jealousy had burned his tongue. He sensed something mysterious in the unfinished story of Salim, and he had an uneasy feeling that somehow Milia was implicated in the rift that had broken the family's collective spine. But it was only three months after the wedding that he learned the whole story. And then it dawned on him that the red scars on his wife's neck were the remnants of a wound inflicted by a man called Najib Karam on a woman who had waited and waited for him.

You mean – you loved him?

No, not *love*. But something like it.

What does that mean?

I mean, it was as if we were engaged, and then he disappeared. And I realized that it was my brother Salim's fault. Salim was fond of a girl named Angèle. Her father, who gave himself the demeanor of a saintly man, said to her, I won't marry you off until your big sister marries. I don't know exactly what happened but suddenly Salim and Najib were gone. And then we heard they had opened a carpentry shop together in Aleppo. Salim did not dare to tell us anything. My mama said he got married on the run. But my mother knew everything anyway. The nun told her about a grand wedding in Aleppo, two sisters married off on the same day; she said Salim had convinced Najib to leave everything and come with him because the family was rich. I don't know the details. Ask Musa, he knows it all.

When Musa had come home Milia was waiting for him. She had lit a candle and seated herself on the little sofa in the corner of the room to wait. Everything was asleep – everything and everyone but the girl covered in grief and shame. She put her trust in the darkness and waited, a fire burning inside her, feelings of jealousy squeezing her, and a painful emptiness hollowing out her body from her heart to her hip bone. How, she wanted only to know, how and why was it possible for everything to change in this way? And how had Najib managed to love two women at the same time? She told Musa that she was certain Najib loved her. Had he also loved that woman who became his wife?

Milia heard the story in broken fragments dropping from her brother's lips. Everything turned to shadows. Najib became a shadow of Najib. The hand that had reached for her body became a black shadow of a black hand. Even that explosion she had witnessed on her fiancé's face, like a reflection of her white breasts erupting in his eyes, became nothing more than a shadow. She said she no longer remembered anything of the story except for a few remnants which she saw occasionally in her dreams. What could she tell of it, then? Even the encounter in the garden, which left traces of red on her neck she recalled only as a dream. How could she tell Mansour what he wanted to hear that night? And why did he want a story that had died?

There are different kinds of stories, she told him. Two kinds – stories that end and stories that die. A story that has ended we bring back by telling it, and then it lives on with us. But a story that has died goes out like a lamp with no more wicking. How can a person read in the dark? You're asking me to read in the dark and I don't know how to do that.

She tried to tell him that story but it came out confused, lacking any sequence or causal connection. So he understood nothing and he was certain she was lying. He told her she was lying. What she almost said was, Fine, what do you want me to do? You want me to tell it all to you when I have forgotten, you want to know what happened when I don't even know. What do you want me to say? Tell me and I'll say it.

And then she did say it, anyway; she told him a dead story. She did not tell him about what had happened in the garden or about the deep scratches on her legs from the stinging nettles when she had to step back as Najib pressed himself on her. She did tell him about being betrayed.

She tried to explain to him the difference between stories that have ended and stories that have died. All families have at least one buried story that no one dares to unearth, she said. Her story with Najib was one of those, and she remembered it only in the form of muddled and disconnected scenes from old dreams which she could not organize into words. Here she began to recognize that she must stop talking like this, her words like a succession of images before her eyes. Otherwise the poor man would not understand anything at all. More than once he had admitted to her that he could not absorb or comprehend what she said. At first, his inability to follow had surprised her, but gradually it dawned on her that he did not understand because he could not glide with her to that subterranean place where words slipped and dove and circled. Words were Milia's means of sliding effortlessly, from one word to another, or from a single word to a cluster of images. She was no longer capable, when she spoke, of regaining the thread where it first wound off the spool. For her, the thread had no end. She spoke as though wrapping threads over other threads, winding and unwinding spool after spool. Her sequences did not, could not, tie up any loose ends.

I cannot put your words together to make any sense, he complained. Words come in groups, they make sense as a group. I mean, they come together in the head and when they come out as words they form a meaning. But you – is this how you always talk?

In the Hotel Massabki when Mansour opened his eyes the next morning he moved close to the woman lying on her side and put his arms around her. He felt her cold feet and snuggled even closer. Turning his body in toward her he laid his hands on her hips. Milia closed her eyes and went very still inside. Her joints felt limp and she went into something like a trance. She would say that she had dozed off and remembered nothing; but at the time he heard her say something he could not make out because it was only a low murmur. When he got up to go to the bathroom and was ducking the shower as it careened between steaming and icy, he thought suddenly of Najib and the red tracings on Milia's neck. But he decided not to bring it up. It was not very elegant for a man to ask his wife about another man on her wedding day. He whistled in the shower and called to her to come in and join him, but when he came out of the bathroom he found her sleeping. She was lying on her back, as though she were floating atop the pillow in which her face and long hair were submerged. He drew close to awaken her. She opened her eyes as if coming out of a very deep sleep. She smiled at him, turned on her left side, pulled the cover over herself, and went back to sleep. Mansour lit a cigarette, sat down next to her on the bed, and waited for her to reawaken. But she did not. He dressed and went down to the hotel lobby looking for the dining room. The elderly Wadiia scurried toward him and asked if he wanted eggs with his breakfast.

No, that's not necessary.

But eggs are good for newlyweds, Mr. Bridegroom, said Wadiia II, who was suddenly there, as if she had just walked out of the wall.

Whatever, that's fine then, he said, and sat down.

Striding over to him, the bald-headed driver clapped him lightly across the shoulders. The two Wadiias brought coffee, milk, and fried eggs, which they set down on the table, straightening up to stand in wait obediently beside the driver. He said he wanted to return to Beirut immediately. Mansour took some money out of his pocket and held it out with a thank you.

Wallaah inta jada', said the driver admiringly. A real brave man you are! Look, when I think about how you walked through that fog with the snow pelting down, I can feel the cold seizing me from my head to the soles of my feet! Leaves me feeling terrified. How were you not afraid? A lion, not just any young fellow getting married, a true lion!

Mansour said nothing. He noticed the sarcastic smiles pulling at the lips of the two hotel maids. He saw now that they were eerily identical. Yesterday Milia had remarked that they looked so alike it frightened her. That Wadiia II would be the exact image of Wadiia I if it weren't for the sloping shoulders and bowed legs. Mansour hadn't noticed anything yesterday evening. Everything in him had quaked with cold; his bones seemed to be coming apart and he needed a warm bed and the darkness of his closed eyes immediately.

Wadiia I came over to him and asked after the bride. Seconds later the same question echoed from Wadiia II. Same voice, same gesture.

Where is Khawaja George? asked Mansour. He did not know why all of a sudden he should be seeking the aid of the hotel proprietor in concealing his unease about this doubled female image before him.

The Khawaja is asleep. Waiting for you so long yesterday exhausted him, said the first.

The Khawaja is not well, said the second.

Mother and daughter, mused Mansour. Khawaja George Massabki had been very fortunate with these two women, because he had not had to alter anything in his life. The eternal single, as he always called himself. He had found the perfect solution in a woman whose daughter replicated her. It had all worked out so well. The woman was a servitor, which meant no demands, just silence and submission. And she was a widow, meaning she had no independent means of support. And she had a youngish daughter who was just like her, meaning that after he had supported the girl's upbringing, now the two women were like twin rings on his finger and he could live well served and well loved. Now there's a man, Mansour felt like saying, and he attacked the plate of fried eggs. He heard the padding of Milia's feet on the floor. Lifting his eyes he saw her standing between the pair of Wadiias. She seemed taller than before as she spoke in a low voice with the two women. She sat down across from him. She raised her eyebrows and he sensed he ought to stop eating his eggs.

In the bathroom he had felt ashamed and humiliated. He had closed the door and tried to summon his mother because he was certain he would die. Only death destroys bodily desire. When that desire vanishes, death is certainly not far behind.

Nothing makes you cling to life like that does, declared the old man. All Mansour remembered of him was his thick head of very white hair. The man had come to their modest foundry and had bought a heap of iron rods. He said they were for the mujahideen high in the rocky hills. He gazed at Mansour's brother, Amin, and said, If only youth would return one day! He said he knew his hour was near, because that gizmo – and he pointed between his thighs – no longer wanted it. And when it has lost the desire for it, that means it is commanding you to follow it into death. All Mansour could remember of the story were these strands of words. He had arrived as the man was preparing to leave, and so nothing stuck in his mind except this sentence – and now here it was, coming back to him along with the vomiting as his legs turned into jelly and pain blasted his inner organs. Death, he said to himself. This is death, and he cried out for his mother. He saw his mother lying on the ground, her thighbone broken, wailing for her own mother, who was dead. As if life is but a closed circle of mothers and nothing remains but the relationship binding child to mother – that is, to the child's own death. When you call out *Mama!* you are summoning the grave, even if that is not what you think you are doing. A person's life unfolds between two graves: the mother's womb and the soil. Both places shelter you in that stage of becoming, preparing for the enormous transformations that will see you through the tunnel to the next life.

Who told him the tale of the two graves?

Milia? But no – Milia was happy now, with her rounding belly. She slept soundly, drank glass after glass of water, and acted as if her life had only now begun. Sister Milana, then – but Mansour had met the saintly woman only once, when she came to the church for their wedding, and that day he had not seen or heard anything. Had he seen the nun in a dream? But he did not dream. Or he did not remember his dreams.

Mansour would have liked to tell his wife about his experiences with women before getting married. But she did not want to hear. And then, why tell them, anyway? After all, his grand story had begun when his eyes fell on this woman and he attached himself to her without really knowing how. He had not understood what was happening to him or why every time he shut his eyes the curves of her lower body began to chase him. Milia bewitched him with the undulating line that ran from her waist downward. He saw her whiteness erupt beneath a white dress that flowered with a pattern of red cherries. He wanted to go up to her and say something but he did not dare. It took three long months for him to speak to her, when he noticed the dimple in her right cheek and her wide and langorous eyes.

> *Like cream, her beautiful skin dons*
> *a veil of skin to shield her skin*
> *Her chest, two lovely mounds, I see*
> *camphoras capped by ambergris*

What's that you're saying?
I'm saying poetry.
Why – are you a poet?
No. I just love poetry.
And what else?

> *Echoes of Abla arc o'er me in my dream*
> *kissing me thrice on my scarf-enwrapped lips*
> *She bid me farewell and left me aflame*
> *A fire in my bones concealed in my hips*

Were I not alone in this empty place
damping with tears ardor's white-hot coals
I would die of grief but I'd never complain
in my zealous watch – Full Moon that ne'er dips!

So, he would dream her?

Of course – how else to love her?

You mean, you fell in love with me in a dream?

I already told you I'm not a poet.

She noticed immediately how like her brother Musa he looked. It made her heart pound. She smiled, and that was the beginning that brought him eventually to stand up in the Church of the Archangel Mikhail and to walk shrouded in fog on the Shtoura Road. And there in the cold bathroom at the hotel he called out desperately to his mother for he sensed that death was on its way.

Well, no, that was not exactly the way it was. But this was how he told it to his wife three months into their marriage when he knew he wanted to open the file on that already buried story.

He did not say how intensely cold he had been in the bathroom, and yet he had not dared to return to the bedroom because he was afraid that to do so would only make things worse and harder to explain. As he sat on the toilet seat, the bathroom's red tiles began to look and feel like blocks of ice burning his bare feet. Milia was knocking on the door and saying that she was going to call the doctor. No, Milia, no – I'm fine. Go to sleep, dear, it's all fine, really.

He had no idea how his violently trembling lips actually produced the words but he heard her moving away from the door. His joints went completely limp and the shiver that his rib cage had kept imprisoned now leapt out and swept over him. Walking on tiptoe, he headed back to bed, his whole body shaking and his mind in despair. He stopped to warm himself in front of the stove before feeling his way into bed, where he would curl up around himself like a snail.

Milia was already asleep. He lay down, careful to leave a space between them. He pulled the covers over his body and head and heat began to penetrate his joints. He dozed off and then suddenly his eyelids flew open as though in fright, and he thought, I am a bridegroom on my wedding night and a just-married man must not go to sleep before taking the bride who lies next to him into his arms.

He told her he had not been able to sleep. His desire was so implacable. The image of her waist as she stood beneath the almond tree . . . the curve of her abdomen and hips . . . With each touch, every kiss, he began to regain the flavor of things. He began to collect the straying fragments of his spirit, scattered in the cold and the fear.

Today he saw her growing round and she told him she was pregnant, as if she were being born anew; as if the child in her belly would give Milia her ultimate shape. Seeing the red lines on her neck he remembered the story they had not told him. He wanted to know.

As for her – she had not cared. Her fixedly downward gaze, which had suggested to Mansour that bashfulness was this young woman's hallmark, seemed now to take on another meaning. The gazes of this woman traveled only inside the world of arcs and circles in which she existed. Looking down, she saw the circle complete. She was closed upon herself and she would go where no one else might follow her.

He felt jealous. No, it wasn't jealousy exactly. Distance – as if, with these circles of hers, the woman encloses a space, draws a line between herself and him, and leaves him powerless to break through it.

She said she was going to sleep and stood up.

Sit down.

As you like. And fine, you name him. I don't know why you're acting like this, I thought you would be happy the way any man is when he knows his wife is pregnant.

No, it's not the name, he said. What I'm concerned about is something else. And he asked her about Najib.

It was the first time in two years she had heard this man's name. Everyone in the family had stopped mentioning his name. If they needed to refer to him they would say *that one there*. The pronoun replaced the man, and so Najib had become a mere jumble of letters empty of flesh or sense.

Najib had disappeared as had his image and his name. Now here he was suddenly coming back at the very moment Milia was freeing herself of her past, and of the memories of those days. She wanted to say to Mansour that she didn't know. Or, she wanted to say: No, it isn't that I don't know, but the story died and has been buried, and there's no call for reviving it.

It was her grandmama Malakeh above all who taught her how necessary it was to distinguish between stories. She would scold her daughter Saadeh whenever she mentioned the name of her husband's father and the story of the house he had bought.

The story that goes rotten has to be buried, said Grandmama. Stories carry odors.

This grandfather, Saadeh's father-in-law, had caused the women of the family deep and chronic pain. It was imperative to forget the story of the house. The woman who had lived there had to be buried along with the story. No one spoke now of the Egyptian woman, or of Khawaja Efthymios, or of the scandal that flared up when the grandfather bought the house after the death of his lover who had been the mistress of another man. So why, now, would Mansour want to resurrect a story that Milia had buried?

At least for Saadeh, finally the nightmarish business of the priesthood and the monks seemed over. Wherever had that naughty boy gotten his ideas about the Jesuit monks and this Catholic business? He was the only one among his brothers to finish his education, saying he wanted to become a lawyer, but then he had started his interminable chant about joining the Jesuits, stirring up a veritable storm in the household.

His brother Haajj Niqula swore he would kill Salim after hearing the screaming match between mother and firstborn son. Niqula went into the *liwan* and returned to the *dar* wearing his father's red tarbush. In a deep fierce voice he told his brother that he would kill him.

Does a brother kill his own brother? Salim shouted.

That's how killing came into the world – brother killing brother. Cain killed Abel. Now Abel wants revenge. No one can mess around with me. These idiotic behaviors have no place in this house. It wouldn't cost me anything more than a single bullet. And I can furnish the coffin easy, from my shop – with pleasure.

From that day on Niqula never, ever removed the tarbush from his brow. Through the tendons of the family ran shivers of fear. Saadeh did not know what to do. She went to her holy woman for advice. I have two boys, she said. The first wants to become a Jesuit monk and if he does, the second will be a criminal. What am I going to do?

A Jesuit! cried the nun. I take refuge in God from evil Satan! As though he is not even the grandson of Salim who first rang the bell of the Church of Mar Girgis in Beirut. That Salim was a true man! And now comes Salim the Younger who inherited his grandpapa's name, but so what? He's leaving the true faith – he's leaving the Orthodox to go join the French! I spit on the Devil!

She made Saadeh spit on Satan, too, and then Saadeh asked what she ought to do to avoid this mess.

Is this brother serious about killing his brother? asked Sister Milana.

Saadeh confirmed it.

What a man! said the nun. He ought to have been your firstborn son. If Salim really wants to be a monk, he should go to Mount Athos in Greece. The monks there are the real thing – true Orthodox monks, praise the Lord!

So you want to send my son off to Greece, God forgive you!

Wouldn't that be better than seeing him die?

Why would he die?

Didn't you tell me his brother Niqula means to kill him? Niqula should give him a bit of a scare to get him to change his mind, and meanwhile I'll see to what we need to do.

What if he doesn't change his mind? asked Saadeh.

Then he dies, said the nun.

He dies!

What can we do about it?

You mean, you'd approve?

No, I didn't say that, but these things are the will of God.

And I lose my boys!

You won't have lost more than you've lost already – is there anything more fearsome than unbelief like this? Leave Niqula alone to say what he wants and don't put any pressure on him.

You mean, you don't have any problems if a brother kills his brother?

Of course I do – Thou shalt not kill, says the Commandment. But that doesn't mean a person knows how God's will is going to work out. The Commandment says: Thou shalt not kill, and the Commandment said it a very long time ago, but people did not stop killing each another. Anyway, all people are brothers. Saadeh, that means when people kill, they are always killing brothers. But of course I'm against killing.

The nun pulled Saadeh forward by the hand and they knelt before the icon of Mar Ilyas. The nun murmured her prayers in the presence of the saint who stood erect in a fiery chariot holding up a flaming sword.

He is the one who will deliver your children to safety, Saadeh. Don't be afraid.

Saadeh cried for most of the day. This woman whose solace was to spend almost all of her waking hours in the Convent of the Archangel Mikhail felt profoundly shaken and lost. Yes, in her prayers and her fasting and her devout hope for brotherly love, she believed in the power of true faith. But she despised the Jesuits because they spoke in Jesuit-speak and prayed in the Latin language, which she did not understand.

But it's just like you, Mama – you pray in Greek and you don't understand what the words mean, Salim protested.

No, we do understand, or even if we don't understand the words, Greek touches the heart as it is spoken, and the heart is where we understand everything.

It's not necessary that we understand the words of the prayer, said Salim. The Pope is the only one who truly understands. That's why someone has to know seven languages – at least – to become Pope.

Shut your mouth and don't say a word about that man! She made the sign of the cross as if seeking Satan's protection from the fellow.

The storm Salim had set off dispelled quickly enough. After Niqula announced his intention to kill his brother, Salim never returned to the topic of entering the monastery. Milia was convinced that one day her eldest brother would simply disappear without a trace, having been swallowed up in a black robe in one of the Jesuit monasteries somewhere outside of Lebanon. That way the original sin would not really be committed and so Abel would not seek revenge on his brother Cain. For what was the meaning of the story if it became mere revenge? Had it been a matter of simple revenge, and had it worked, then no one would remember Abel and the story would have died a swift clean death.

No one knew why Salim changed. Was it the relationship with Frère Eugene or was it failing to pass his courses at the law school, or was it something else entirely?

Salim's relationship with the Jesuit brother began with the Sunday school and the films and continued for a very long time. Salim started going to the summer camps which Eugene organized for the youth of the area. And then suddenly Salim came and announced that he had gotten a scholarship to study law at the Jesuits' university and it would not cost his family a penny. But Salim seemed unable to bring his study of the law to a conclusion. He remained at the university for years, and whenever he was asked when he would become an *avocato* he would respond by saying that he was working and studying at the same time, and that had delayed his graduation. As for what he worked at and where, no one knew. It seems he failed at the law or was distracted by other activities. And then when he came to them with his Jesuit bombshell, everyone realized instantly that he had not been simply studying law after all. Probably he had even joined study sessions in Catholic theology. He told Musa that Frère Eugene had promised to get him a travel bursary to Rome so that he could continue his studies there, but only on condition that he would enter the monastic life.

Ten years had gone wasted, while Niqula and Abdallah worked in the father's shop and then switched to the coffin business, and Musa went on with his studies, and Milia left school to become a homemaker. Salim just went on playing around with theology, as their mother said. Then he had the goodness to come and inform us he was going to become a monk! she groused. Thank God Haajj Niqula threatened him, said Milia – and she heard her mother's voice coming out of her own throat, as if she had had no part in forming those words. There's no doubt Frère Eugene was the root of this disaster, but we rid ourselves of one calamity only to fall into a new disaster.

The *new disaster* was the buried tale. Mansour listened carefully to the unfamiliar fragments that came his way. He became convinced that he had been in the wrong. Now he must give the story another burial out of fear for Milia's neck, which had filled up with razor-thin red lines.

It didn't bother me all that much, said Milia. A bridegroom, they said to me. Oh, a bridegroom, I said, and I accepted because what they said to me was *accept*. Then he disappeared and we understood that Salim had dragged him off so that he could marry Angèle. Exactly how it all happened no one seems to know. What did I have to do with whether Salim could marry his girl? I certainly don't know! All I know is that Angèle had a sister, an older sister, named Odette, and that their father wouldn't hear of Angèle marrying until her older sister was married. So, Salim convinced my fiancé to agree to the scheme, and the two men disappeared and went to live in Aleppo and got work in the woodworking shop owned by the girls' uncle Jacques Estefan. So, instead of a brother killing his brother, a brother killed his sister. In a word, it seems the blame for it all falls on my brother – everyone said so. I said, No, maybe it is Najib's fault. Maybe he's the one who made it all happen. Najib was smarter than Salim and he didn't fear his Lord. My brother's just a poor simple fellow trying to get along, I'm sure of that. But no one believed me and all of them went on saying it was Salim who was to blame. So I believed them – what could I do? And I started saying the same thing they said. Then the nun came and said, It's time to put this business to rest – one scandal but it's the size of two. The girl's exposed and so is her brother. The scandal over the girl is nothing unusual. She was engaged and the engagement was broken off.

So, Milia went on, at this point the nun raised her voice loud enough for the neighbors to hear her next words: And she's as much a virgin as Our

Lady Maryam, peace be on her name! And that won't change. Then the nun lowered her voice again to say that Salim had gone and married into the Roman Catholics and he'd become one of them. Well, with him, out of the frying pan into the fire, she commented.

Lower your voice, shrieked Saadeh.

It was the only time Saadeh ever raised her voice to the nun. In fact, no one had ever even heard Saadeh's voice in the presence of the nun. Saadeh always made herself as inconsequential and obsequious as she could before the nun, slumping over, swallowing her voice as though she had developed laryngitis, and speaking only when necessary and in a nearly inaudible murmur. But on that disastrous day Saadeh's emotions were fixed on her daughter, dreading to think what Milia's future might be. The business of Salim was not so earthshaking, after all, nor the two women whom he had married. That's what she said – that he had married two women – and then she hastily retracted it. See – look what I'm saying! But it's my heart talking, it's as if he kidnapped his sister and killed her. People are despicable!

Milia told her little brother about the two look-alike sisters – two girls of medium height, round faces and fair skin, long noses and lips so thin they seemed to have been erased and teeth so tiny the gums seemed to swallow them up. Salim had taken the thinner one and given Najib the plumper one, and that was that.

Where did you see them? asked Musa.

They were with Salim at Bourj Square. I was dropping in on my brothers in the shop at the Souq of the Carpenters, and then I walked toward Souq Tawile and saw them. Salim was trying to hide behind the women. No – that wasn't it. I was walking down the street in the dark. It was raining. I slipped and fell and my dress got completely soaked. I got up and began shaking off as much water as I could, trying to recover, and that's when I saw them. Najib was strutting along arm in arm with the fat one, and Salim was scampering along behind as if he were trying to catch up with them but couldn't. And then Salim slipped. They looked back and saw him, but they just left him there. He was lying on the ground completely soaked. I started to go over to him – I wanted to help my own brother. And then Najib did turn back. I jumped and then I ran. I looked back and saw Najib kiss the fat one and they started laughing, and I started crying.

Musa closed his eyes and said he didn't understand anymore. As far as my brother Salim goes, he said, he has died and that's that, I have to forget him. And you as well – you have to forget.

Milia's tears slipped down her cheeks. Musa bent over his sister, touching his fingers to her eyes. He saw a little girl and saw himself kissing eyes wet with tears. He stepped back and heard his sister asking him not to cry. It's not worth it, she said. Anyway, it is better this way. It never would have worked. But if he and my brother were failing at university and wanted to become carpenters, fine, then why didn't Salim get work in the shop here with his brothers? And what does that other one have to do with being a carpenter anyway? Salim we can understand – he is the son of a carpenter, after all. But Najib? Since when is he carpenter material? And then, who is this father who wants to marry off his daughters at any price? And what are they doing in Aleppo, anyway – soon enough they'll regret it.

Did Milia tell the story the way it happened? Of course not, because no one can know how to tell a story exactly the way it happened and in the order it happened. If that were possible, people would spend their whole lives telling a single story. Milia passed over a number of things. She said nothing about her love for Najib, the way his anecdotes and experiences attracted her, the obscure feelings that took over her spirit and her body, the like of which she had never felt before. Not, at least, until finding out yesterday that she was with child.

But she told him, and she said it had nothing at all to do with her.

But, *yaani*, you loved him? You were in love with him? Mansour asked her.

I've not been in love with anyone.

And me?

You're something else.

What does that mean – something else?

It means, you're my husband.

And so I'm asking you if you love me?

Can you be married to someone and not love him? Of course I do!

On that day when she became pregnant and gave her body the freedom to become as big and as round as it wanted, Milia began to feel that she no longer had any need for anyone else. There was a new soul inhabiting her, and she no longer felt like one lone human being.

I didn't mislead anyone, she said. He misled me – he deceived me. My brother deceived me, and so did my mother, and I didn't understand any of what was going on. What do you think I could have done?

In the third month, when Milia entered the sovereign realm of the dual, she regained little Milia through her dreams. She discovered then that the melancholy solitude she had been living through had not been a question of longing for her mother or for her brother Musa. No, she had been aching for the tawny-skinned little girl who had filled her nights with movement and her life with light. She allowed Milia to see the world through the brilliance that shone from her eyes.

Milia did not cease falling asleep whenever Mansour came near, but she did begin to have dizzy spells, and somehow inside the dizziness the waters inside of her would flood over her surfaces. Mansour claimed once to have seen her smile but she did not believe him. The room had been dark; there was not moonlight enough to filter through the windowpanes near her bed. She had chosen this bed for the window. She could not sleep without a window nearby, she said. Mansour was left with the farther bed, parallel to hers. She closed her eyes upon the colors of the darkness, having refusing to hang curtains over the window. Curtains blot out the hues and tones of darkness and she wanted to have them there with her. Mansour didn't mind.

Whenever they entered the bedroom at the same time, invariably she told him that she was exhausted. In quick succession she pulled on her long nightgown, dove into her bed, pulled the covers up to her neck, and fell asleep. He waited. Mostly he dozed off and reawakened sometime later. Slipping out of his bed, he tiptoed over to hers. Milia would be plastered against the wall, her back to her husband's bed. He would lie down beside her and one hand would begin its slow voyage upward to her shoulders and then down her back, wrapping itself finally around each of her breasts in turn. He would listen for a first moan and when he heard it, he turned her over, so she was lying on her back. He pushed her gown up and entered her. Her breathing would grow deeper and it was interrupted by short, half-suppressed sighs. Her hands dangled loosely and her head was submerged in the long chestnut hair covering the pillow, though he could see her closed eyes and the half-parted lips from which he managed to glean an occasional kiss. Those little sighs and the soft relinquishing contours that this woman's body gave, as it floated on the darkness, drove Mansour a bit wild. Even after finishing, he contended with the flames of his desire. He would come out of her quietly, go into the bathroom and wash himself, but he would feel as though he had not yet slept with her, his loins still on fire. Returning to the bedroom he saw immediately that she had turned her back. Trying to lie down again next to her, he found no room. He would push her gently but she did not budge. In disappointment, he went back to his own bed.

Not once after his lovemaking did Milia go into the bathroom to wash herself. But in the morning she would get up looking fresh and bright and smelling of soap. When he reminded her of what had transpired during the night her eyes would widen in an astonished stare as though this could not have been her. It could not have really happened.

When did she bathe, then? Did she wait him out, and then once he went to sleep hurry into the bathroom? Did she wake up very early and take a bath and then go back to sleep? Mansour got up at seven o'clock as his wife still slept. He made his coffee and sat at the kitchen table, lighting his first cigarette, and by this time he would see her coming. The few moments between his rising from bed and her arrival in the kitchen were not enough to dispel that fragrance of soap and laurel floating off her hair. She would come in glistening with water and he would ask her when she had bathed. She never answered.

I've thought about how much I'd like to watch you taking a bath.

She picked up the coffeepot from the table in front of him, added a touch of orange-blossom water, and put breakfast on the table: labneh, cheese, thyme paste, honey, and quince jelly.

What do you say – tonight before we go to sleep?

What do I say about what?

About taking a bath. About you bathing and me watching.

Watching!

He said he wanted to see her in the bath because of Abu Nuwas's poem.

Yallah, get yourself up and go to work! I have a lot of work to do today, too.

He didn't ask her what she meant by *a lot of work*. He knew she took walks alone through town. Mansour was certain the fault was his. After two short excursions through the streets of Nazareth he had stopped going out with her. Even on Sundays he left her to go on her own to mass in the Church of the Annunciation while he would lounge about, alone in the house. He didn't quite understand the meaning of this expression – lounge about – but he figured that it was probably a fair description of the way he frittered away time on a Sunday morning at home, waiting for noon to arrive. When it finally came, he promptly poured himself a glass of arak and began grilling the meat in preparation for a vigorous drinking session that usually ended in an argument between husband and wife. It started with Mansour insisting on sex in full daylight and ended when Milia left the house, returning two hours later when Mansour would be asleep and she could clean and straighten up.

How did she bathe and when? Mansour imagined his wife as the silhouette of the bathing woman in Abu Nuwas's poem. He saw her, a form as delicate as the water, like water falling softly onto water. He would bring his glass of arak to his lips, sip the cloudy whiteness, and launch into his performance.

> She faced the breeze, her body bare
>   a dainty figure, wind or air
> Her hand reached rippling, water-soft
>   to nectar in a bowl unquaffed
> She saw the watcher's eye rove nigh . . .

Mansour interrupted himself. No, no! It doesn't go exactly like that.

> Her wish attained, she made to leave,
>   So swift her cloak she would retrieve
> She saw the watcher's eye rove nigh:
>   she let fall darkness over light

No, the line with *naddat* comes first – that means *she took off*, or something like it.

Her gown she dropped, let water pour,
a bashful pink her features wore
She faced the breeze, her body bare –

and then (said Mansour) comes the rest of it. And this is how it ends:

Her morning dwindles after night
Water on water falls like light

He cavorted among the lines, returning to the first one and then skidding all the way to the final line, skipping ahead, jumping back, rising above the water and plunging into it as if he were swimming. Poetry is water, he said, and a woman's body is water. Love is water and God sits on a throne of water. And – Mansour would add – He made us from water, every living thing.

He would jump ahead to steal from the woman of the parted lips a kiss she was concealing or a word she was about to say. Suddenly he would find himself at the end of his forces. I am the bearer of passion, like in the poem, he would say. It's exhausting to be a bearer of passion. At that point, Milia got up and went to the kitchen, where he followed her. This is arak, woman, real arak, *ya Latif* what arak does to a man! White upon white. Ten out of ten. That's what arak is, ten out of ten.

Milia did not understand why her husband was so consumed by a single thought, leaving him oblivious to all else. Why could he not see how much of a stranger she felt herself to be here, and how alone she was? Sometimes, she felt truly afraid. . . but no, Mansour was not like that, he was not like certain other men. But fathers do kill their sons, she had always believed. Well, no, not always: she had believed it because her father told her so. Well, no, actually, her father did not tell her anything of the sort, perhaps he did not tell her anything at all. But it was the family story, after all, and this story had not been buried along with her father at his death. For the image of Salim the Elder, the grandfather, lingered: indeed, it occupied center stage – even when their father grew to be so like his father. As Saadeh said to her children, though, the image of the victim never disappeared from Yusuf's face, with its deep dark clefts and the half-closed eye.

Can the father really kill his son? she asked her grandmother.

No, my girl. He didn't mean to kill him. He hit him with the rock because he didn't recognize him.

How can that be? How can a father not know his son?

His father thought he was someone else. He thought it was a thief and so he threw a rock at him. It isn't the fault of either the father or the son. It was the circumstances. Those days were tough ones, my dear, and most likely it was the woman's fault. She created the problem and we inherited it after she died. Your grandfather Salim bought the house. That was the real problem – the house. Your papa tried first to sell it but he couldn't. To sell it, he had to find someone to buy it, but in those days there was no money around. So Yusuf – and all of you with him – were stuck with the house. Your grandpapa didn't intend to kill his son – that's just chatter from that nun your mama follows around and repeats as if she's a parrot. No, that sort of twaddle! Can't possibly be right. Enough talk.

On the night when pregnancy filled her and she entered that sovereign realm of the dual, Milia decided to begin her life all over again. But then, all of a sudden, where had the specter of Najib come from, and why? Why had Mansour yanked it out of the cave of memory?

Mansour had married this young woman for love, and he tried to explain to her the meanings of love. He had believed she was as much a lover as he was but simply could not find the words to express her love. And so, he borrowed poetry and rolled it out like a lush carpet before her feet. He said that far back in the eighth century Bashshar b. Burd described love when he wrote his body into his lines of poetry.

Take my hand, lift my robe, and you will see:
spent is the body my wrappings enclose
What runs now from my eyes are not my tears
but a soul that melts and in melting, flows

He was wolfing down the plate of eggs in the hotel dining room when she came over to him. She lifted the plate away from his hands and passed it to one of the Wadiias, saying it was bad for his health.

I'm fine now, and that's all over and done with, he said.

No, you aren't fine yet, she said.

Fine, but didn't you see what a tiger I was last night?

Last night!

I hope you're just pretending you don't understand.

What I do understand is that you must pay attention to your health. We must go back to Beirut – where's the chauffeur?

He told her he had paid the fare and the driver had eaten his breakfast and left for Beirut.

And us?

We're going to stay another two nights and then we'll make our way down to Beirut and from there to Nazareth.

No, we have to go today, it's very cold.

She sat down across from him, ate a little cheese, drank a glass of tea, and saw how the man devoured everything on the table in front of him. Milia was hungry but she knew that faced with her husband's exhaustive appetite she would eat only sparingly, satisfying herself by observing him as he exclaimed over her stunning cooking. A day would come when he would call himself the first man in the world to prefer his wife's cooking to his mother's. Listening to him, she would wonder about her three brothers in the ancient house in Beirut who were having to get reaccustomed to their mother's bland dishes. She would think of them, but the disturbances in Palestine had closed the roads and letters did not arrive. That is why she decided to talk with her brother Musa in her own special way. When Mansour left for work and the house was empty, she would call for Musa and he always came. She asked him questions and he always answered; she saw him there in front of her. She complained to him, too. She was so alone, she said, and so afraid, and she longed for the scent of the lilac trees in their family garden.

Milia spent three days with her husband in the empty hotel. The only people there were Khawaja Massabki and those two women of his. There was the tiny pond in the hotel garden, mounded with snow, and Mansour's voice reciting poetry to her as he gripped her hand, pointing out certain photographs on the wall of the empty reception hall.

This one's the king, and next to him is the prince of poets Ahmad Shawqi, said Mansour. The king fled when the French attacked Syria, and he set himself up as king over Iraq. What a joke – did you ever in your life hear of a king who betrayed his kingdom and got a second kingdom? But that's us for you! Ahmad Shawqi stood weeping over Syria, which the French army had bombarded with heavy guns.

> *Greetings softer than Barada's east wind*
> *to you, my Damascus, with love I send*
> *and tears and tears that never end*

Milia lies between wakefulness and sleep. She feels fire in her bones. She goes out into the garden and thrusts her hand into the snow and brings it up to her mouth and swallows the soft white stuff. The snow melts against her burning lips and thirst stalks her. She sleeps next to Mansour in one bed. The man takes her with his powerful hands. She dozes in fire, and dreams. But little Milia will not return until three months have passed. Her place is taken by a woman of twenty-four stretched out over the fog of Dahr el-Baydar, going into a shadowy world, led to its gates by a blue woman whom she does not know.

The Second Night

ND THERE WAS DARKNESS.

Milia was in bed and in pain. The pain pincered her lower body and shot upward. She could not breathe. A fisted hand plunged into her lower parts and tugged. Her body seemed paralyzed and her head was heavy. She opened her eyes but saw nothing. The pain ebbed, as though diffusing and spreading along her belly before it melted away to leave behind an evanescent memory.

The nine months had passed. The time was come.

The pain returns. Her belly convulses and with that appears her grandmother Umm Yusuf. Why has this grandmother dropped from her memory? And why, today, does she return?

White hair in a tight bun clustered against the nape of the old woman's neck. She reclines in bed, mute and paralyzed. An ancient cat hovers nearby but dares not jump up to snuggle next to her in bed. It is Umm Yusuf – by her premotherhood name, Hasiba Haddad – who died when Milia was three years old and was erased from the girl's memory, or perhaps she never actually entered Milia's memory in the first place. Why does she return today? And why the cat?

Milia awakened, her eyes flashing open to the morning rays. She swung her feet out of bed, setting them down into her slippers as usual. The cat jumped between her legs and the slippers turned into a bounding cat. She chased after it, cornered it, crept toward it, and put her feet on it, hearing a meow that was more like a rattle. She saw her grandmother, Hasiba, whose name originally had been Habisa. Preferring not to be known as "Imprisoned One," she had switched two letters around and called herself Hasiba. Much better to be thought of as one respected!

Saadeh did not understand why Abu Said had given this name, Habisa, to his daughter. Perhaps it had been the name of the daughter's own grandmother, but then why had that grandmother gotten the name? In any case, the woman had changed her own name and everyone began calling her by the new one – everyone except her daughter-in-law. Even after Hasiba's death Saadeh went on calling her by her original given name. Distressed by it, Yusuf would beg his wife in a shaking voice to stop, but Saadeh was Saadeh.

I want to call her Sitti Hasiba, Milia said to her mother.

Call her whatever you want, my dear, but her name is Habisa. God has released her, and released us, and released the cat, too, and in one fell swoop!

What was the story of the cat of whom it was rumored that Saadeh had poisoned twenty-four hours after the death of her mother-in-law? Milia did not remember her father's tears but Saadeh did. He cried over that cat more than he did over his own mother, she said.

Grandmother had given the cat the name Pasha because she said he looked like the Turkish pashas: light yellow hair, brown eyes, long whiskers, and a body as fat as a sheep's. He was old and had an eye problem – glaucoma, most likely, for he was nearly blind. But Saadeh said his stumbling walk wasn't because of his blindness. It was because he was senile and couldn't tell the difference between one object and another. Instead of behaving with typical feline modesty, he did his business everywhere and filled the house with the smell of shit. Saadeh wanted to throw him out but Yusuf felt sorry for his invalid mother and gave the cat his patriarchal protection, ordering that Pasha be allowed to stay in the house.

He pleaded with Saadeh. Mother is going mad, he said.

She's already mad.

God be kind in your afterlife, woman, don't say that! I'll clean up after the cat.

And your mother – who cleans up after her?

Lower your voice! She'll hear you.

Grandmother sat in bed listening to everything and saying nothing. She had already entered the desert of silence and would never find her way out. Milia did not know where the expression had originated; it must have been the nun's. The saintly woman labeled Hasiba's silence *the desert*. All saints chose the desert at the end, she said. And the only person who showed reverence and respect to Hasiba was Sister Milana. Arriving at the house, she would go directly to the old woman's bed, sponge her brow with a cotton wad that had been immersed in blessed oil, give her a kiss on the top of her head, and refrain from showing any disgust at the smell coming out of the old woman's cracked skin.

Was Sitti born paralyzed? asked Milia.

No, my dear. When she was born, your grandmother had nothing wrong with her. She slept on this bed right here, next to the one you were born on. But she didn't sit at home much. She was always going about. When you were about five months old, one day they brought her in and said she had fallen, out on the road. She was never the same again, until she died.

And when she died, where was I sleeping?

You were with her, sleeping in the very same room, but we didn't let you know anything, you and your brothers. Except Salim, who came into our room and said his grandmama was frozen. I ran to her – your father stayed

~ 181 ~

in bed, unable to move, until I screamed and he came after me. We sent all of you children to my mother and you didn't come back home until after everything was over and we had buried the cat as well.

Milia did not remember her grandmother. Whatever images of the elderly woman did come to her came from the memory of words heard from her mother, fragments of stories gathered from a scattering of words to become images that had their place in her dreams.

I must let go of this dream, Milia said. She stood up, opened the door to her room, and begged the cat to come, but the cat ran and crouched under the bed and began to meow. Milia knelt down and made kissing sounds. The old cat lifted his head but his body shrank back as if he were getting ready to pounce. Her fear pushed little Milia into retreat. He was beneath her bed in the *liwan*. The grandmother watched, her head bowed forward onto pillows set on her thighs, her eyes open. The woman was bent almost double; she could not straighten her body.

Why does she sleep like that? Milia wondered. Now she could see only the old woman's back, her pale cheek turned sideways on the pillow, white froth around her lips that were always shut, always silent. That is how she spent her final three years.

The story goes that Yusuf got up one morning to find his mother asleep in this odd position. His mother told him she had decided to sleep bent over to keep death at a distance. If I sleep on my back, she warned, the Angel of Death will come and steal my soul from inside me.

Hasiba believed she would likely die if she lay on her back. If she was curled up, she could face death. Death could not enter a circle, for life is round. That is what Yusuf said his mother said, but no one believed him. How could a senile woman whose ravings ranged far and wide and made no distinction among things speak in this wise, philosophical way?

When she died she was wooden and cold, a rigid back nearly snapped in half, bent over itself, face supported on two raised pillows, feet twisted into an odd position, and a thread of dried blood that had trickled downward along one ear. Had Saadeh not been so quick to realize what this meant, and had she not gotten her husband to help her pull the old woman's corpse into proper shape, it would have hardened to the point where they would have found it nearly impossible to fit it into the coffin.

Milia makes sucking noises at the cat, who tenses to pounce. But then, suddenly the cat walks out from under the bed, staggering crookedly, and dives into the slipper.

No! screams Milia. And sees Mansour standing by her bed. The clock shows that it is five o'clock in the afternoon, not yet dark. Milia had gone to bed because she felt an unusual weight in her belly. She thought she would lie down for a bit before making supper in anticipation of her husband's return. The numbness which would take her to sleep swept over her and the pain came in one wave after another before fading away. The cat appeared in the guise of a slipper and she heard moaning.

She opens her eyes and waves to Mansour to leave her alone for a few minutes. Five minutes and I'll be up, she says. Then everything goes and she is submerged in dusky light. Her stomach contracts. She folds double to lighten the pain and once again sinks into the story. She sees that the cat has died and hears her father sobbing as he carries the dead cat wrapped in brown paper outside, for burial in the garden. The cat had eaten poisoned food; without a sound it crept to the foot of the bed in which Hasiba had slept. It collapsed on the floor and died.

The cat – or Pasha – was the final chapter in the life of Hasiba, who had met her end crouching in a white metal bed, sitting because she was afraid of sleep; waking startled, eluding death in terror.

The elderly woman lived her final days in utter silence undisturbed by anything more than indistinct phantoms that crept into her room through the window. She listened to strange voices and felt ringing in her ears. Ghosts assuming shapes like black smoke surrounded the woman in her bed and told her stories of a past that had not wholly disappeared but had turned into images coming in rapid sequence and all wrapped in a gray light, and into an interminable tolling of bells. Help, it's the voices! she would cry out from time to time, but when Saadeh came running into the room the woman would have already returned to her desert of silence.

Habisa was the second daughter of Nasif Haddad, who had fled the killing fields of Mount Lebanon in 1860 with his wife, four daughters, and one son. He abandoned the house and the silk loom inherited from his father, as well as the small plot of land where he planted vegetables in the growing season, to escape with his skin and not much more from the village of Kfar Qatra in the Shouf. In those savage days when blood ran down the slopes of Mount Lebanon, Nasif did manage to save his family, though twelve-year-old Said, his only son, was lost on the way. Nasif lived his entire life waiting for the return of a son who would never return. The father sat in the garden of his home in the Mousaitbeh quarter of Beirut. He would never go out to visit anyone because he was waiting. Every morning he told of smelling his son's fragrance in his dream. The son never returned, the three other girls married, and the only one left at home was Habisa, who refused all suitors. Then – to the bewilderment of her father – she agreed to marry Salim Shahin the carpenter, who was a *kashtabanji* – a cardplayer of the wiliest sort, spending most of his time in the courtyard of the Church of the Archangel Mikhail, a fierce shuffler of those crucial three cards. Or he was drinking arak in a tiny tavern adjacent to the church.

Habisa surprised not only her father but everyone else when she agreed. By the age of twenty she had endured her father's and sisters' incredulous gazes for some time, as she rejected one prospective bridegroom after another. In their eyes she saw mirrored the threatening idea that she was on the dangerous threshold of spinsterhood. But this young woman who never wore anything but a long black gown with seven buttons down the bodice had continued to refuse marriage stubbornly and persistently and she protected herself with a silence that became her guardian veil. It was said that Habisa wore black for her brother, whose unexplained disappearance she could not accept, nor could she acquiesce in her father's wishful view that the son had fled in disgust as the troubles in Lebanon worsened. He must have found a French steamer to take him to the New World – as their father speculated endlessly – and eventually he would return, surely. The father composed an elaborate story about his son's emigration, which he believed fully and fiercely. His patience, as he waited on and on for his son, became legendary, and was universally respected. His wife had died only seven months after their descent from the Mount to Beirut, a victim of the exile fever that decimated the populace of nineteenth-century Lebanon, attendant upon unabated emigrations, massacres, and a general state of disaster. For three days she lay prone in a tiny hut that her husband had erected hastily on land belonging to the church. With her death, her daughters worried themselves sick over the possibility of their father's remarriage, but he did not seem interested. Women in Beirut who had migrated from elsewhere and were available, he remarked, draped themselves on the backs of whomever they could find to carry them.

In a silk-weaving shop belonging to Abdallah Abd el-Nour, Nasif found work, plying an ancient loom which the Beiruti merchant had moved to a narrow passage giving on to the shop. Nasif returned to the work he knew and his life returned to him. He erased his natal village from his memory.

Habisa stayed on alone at home with her father. He would come home late at night, drunk, eat a bite that his daughter had prepared for him, and bury himself in sleep. Habisa remained awake in the black gown she never took off.

No one knew what the story really was. Saadeh would say she heard the old woman, as she descended into senility, speaking French with an imaginary man whose name was Ferdinand. Saadeh fired up her imagination with a story of Habisa's love for a French officer who promised her marriage and then disappeared as all soldiers do. Was she wearing mourning for her lost love and her wasted virginity? Had the young man bewitched her with the white color of his skin and his blue eyes, and carried her off to the kingdom of fantasy dreams before he moved on?

Saadeh consulted the nun but Sister Milana simply scolded her, telling her not to interfere with what did not concern her. God alone knows the unknowable; God alone holds the secrets of hearts.

What was the story, then?

When Saadeh broached the story of Ferdinand with her husband, Yusuf's thick eyebrows came together and he called his wife a liar. Woman, that is not my mother! he barked. Would you want me to talk that way about your mother?

That evening, though, Yusuf spoke to his mother, trying to elicit a response. But the woman remained silent. Staring into the distance, she appeared not even to listen as her son asked questions. Then suddenly she began to blurt out foreign-sounding words – the name Ferdinand among them. Thus was revealed a fragment of the momentous secret concealed within the ribs of the elderly woman who had entered the desert of oblivion.

The story that Yusuf did know was the one about his parents' nocturnal wedding. The girl had insisted on one thing only: that she would marry Salim Shahin after dark. She emerged from the house swathed in her long black gown, surrounded by her father, her three sisters, and their husbands. The nighttime gloom mantled the funereal bridal procession. At the church door Salim stood waiting, decked out in a gold-embroidered silk abaya and red tarbush. He waited alone as the bride had requested. They stood before the candle-lit altar and Father Andraos blessed their marriage. They went to his house on foot, although the groom had arranged for a carriage pulled by four horses. The bride refused and said she preferred to walk. Her arm tucked into her husband's arm, they disappeared silent into the surrounding night.

Did Salim learn the story of Ferdinand and plot revenge on his wife? Or was what Yusuf believed to be revenge simply Salim's response when it became clear that he would not beget more than one child, after he contracted the mumps that descended as far as his testicles?

How can this story be? Milia asked her mother. Someone dawdles away his life waiting to get married and then as soon as he's married, he starts feeling he has to look for something else?

That's men for you, my girl – when a man has nothing left, nothing to fill his life, this is what happens. You see, a man who isn't capable of giving life feels empty. He starts talking bull and he's full of ridiculous mischief. May God protect us all!

From his wife Salim learned to turn the darkness into a curtain veiling his life. That was Hasiba for you. She never really woke up or got up except at night. She cooked to the flame of the oil lantern and when her husband left for his shop in the morning she snuffed out the light and went to sleep.

It was Yusuf who convinced her finally about the new house. Mama, open your mind up a little – it's just a house like any other. When Hasiba discovered that her husband had bought the house that Khawaja Sergios Efthymios had built for his Egyptian lover, who had then become Salim's mistress – which everyone more or less knew about – she went out of her mind, screaming and raving at her husband.

It was only then – during the time that witnessed the woman's fierce sadnesses, her sobs and her sense of betrayal and shame – that Hasiba came to know the story of the rock that had nearly taken out her only son's eye.

It was around this time that the family moved into the house Salim had bought from the heirs of Khawaja Efthymios after the Egyptian lover's death. Hasiba was not so angry about a straying husband: she felt pity for the man – for all men, as she told her only son. But for things to reach the point where she would live in this hovel surrounded on every side by trees and infested with freely roaming snakes and spiders, for the sake of Salim's fidelity to his Egyptian mistress – it was too much to bear, even for Hasiba.

No one asked Hasiba how she knew of her husband's relationship with his Egyptian paramour. She learned of it after the story had become generally known. And stories that are known have no need of a storyteller: they are like smells that mount and expand and penetrate everything around them. The reek of this scandal rose and spread, and the woman wrapped herself in blackness once again.

What floored and upset her was his treachery. That gutless cringing son of a bitch! she called her husband. And that's what he was. No man known to anyone ever feared his wife as the carpenter feared Black Hasiba. And then suddenly the woman discovers that behind this pusillanimous exterior hid a sneaky weasel bent on getting revenge.

But what would he avenge, someone in Salim's condition? His predicament was not to be envied. After the birth of his son, Yusuf, Salim got a bad case of mumps. Normally it was children who came down with Abu Ku'Ayb's Sickness, as it was called – a reference to swelling in the glands. When adult men got mumps it was far more serious: Abu Ku'Ayb could make a man sterile. If the disease sank all the way to the testicles, it was all over.

And that is what happened to Salim. The man had a bad case of it and he suffered long and hard from the malign disease. The physician who treated ailments according to old Arab practices came more than once. He prescribed various bitter herbs that Salim was to steep and drink. Once he was finally pronounced well, the doctor told him that all recompense is God's and he would not be able to sire any more children. He must be content with the one son who was God's precious gift. The news affected Salim radically and events took a new turn: he was no longer capable of fulfilling his marital obligations, for suddenly everything in him went limp. He considered suicide. He consulted the doctor, who confirmed that the illness had destroyed his seed but would have no effect on his sexual prowess. The physician prescribed a strengthening medicine and advised him to breakfast on honey and pine nuts. But nothing could return the man to his masculine vigor. Nevertheless, pine nuts became an essential element in the family legacy. Yusuf had grown accustomed to eating them as a child, and the practice was passed on to his children. When Milia took over the kitchen, she made pine nuts into a staple, used in almost every dish she concocted. She added pine nuts to *burghul*, used them in stuffed vegetables, and garnished sweets with them. She even made her sweet pancakes with pine nuts, a practice unheard of in Beirut then and likely now. Only the "Milia Clan" ate this, a family extended through the brothers' marriages and their success in convincing their wives to prepare the sweet in this fashion.

Though for the Lebanese, *sunuubar* was practically a synonym for Beirut, in truth pine nuts were an Egyptian accomplishment. It was Ibrahim Pasha – subjugator of Lebanon and Syria in the nineteenth century – who planted the pine-nut forest in Beirut, or perhaps replanted it, God alone knows. Salim breakfasted and dined on Ibrahim Pasha's pine nuts dipped in honey but with no obvious outcome. Whenever he approached his wife at night, feeling life stirring within him, without warning he would collapse. Hasiba never said a word about it. She felt the heaviness of his chest above her as he tried, and then pulled back to turn away, claiming he was tired and needed to go to sleep. Salim tasted bricks of pure dirt and mud, as the Egyptians say, and nothing could save him: nothing except the Egyptian woman. Surely that was where he had dug up this expression, and how he found himself

through a new dialect, in which he began to converse with his only son, relying on the lingo spoken by the grandsons of pharaohs. She said her name
was Maryam and Salim was never able to verify the truth of it. She hailed
from the unacknowledged childbirth bulges that Ibrahim Pasha's military
campaigns along the Syrian coastline had left behind. Now came the question that stymied young Yusuf. Who was this woman, really, and how had
she entered the life of the family? The question cost him his right eye and
implanted a sentiment that dogged Yusuf all his life, and that he passed on to
his children: it was the uneasy feeling that a father could kill his son. When
what had remained hidden and sheltered from view was revealed finally,
Salim explained that he had believed Yusuf to be a thief who had stolen into
the ancient house. The man threw a stone at the intruder, it never entering
his mind that it might be his only son, trying only to steal puzzled glances
at his father's activities. The rock struck the boy in his eye and left it half
closed for the rest of his life. Salim turned and strode back into his Egyptian
lover's home full of swagger.

But Maryam was not Salim's lover, not really; she was another man's
lover. The tale was like a mass of tangled threads. Grandfather Salim never
told anyone of his abiding relationship with the Egyptian woman. In his
final days, when asked about it he would wax eloquent over the beauty of
the almond tree for the sake of which he had bought the house, a foolish
little grin on his lips. The true and original lover, Khawaja Sergios Efthymios, was not a married man. He had been among the first Lebanese to
pull off his abaya and tarbush and put on European-style garb. A confirmed
bachelor, he had studied architecture in Paris and was one of the generation of Lebanese architects who introduced Italian columns to the spacious
Beirut homes being commissioned by the city's wealthy silk merchants.
Why would a bachelor embark on a surreptitious relationship which he was
fierce about keeping under wraps? It was one of the secrets that the wealthy

stratum of Beirut families harbored: families established only to collapse when men of the younger generation avoided marriage and honed a social tradition founded on the principle of a divided life – on the surface all piety and dedication to worship at church, while beneath the surface flourished illicit relationships with secret belles who could claim one of two genealogical strains. Either they were Egyptians, born out of Ibrahim Pasha's military operations, and thus a much newer subspecies than the local Greeks. Or they were Greeks, a community said to have started with Alexander the Macedonian which was more recently embodied in a certain lady named Marika Spyridon – and that was another story.

Enough! said Hasiba. I'm not living for a single minute in this house of sin. But which of the two sins was she talking about? A husband striking up a relationship with a woman whose life was not exactly suspicion-free, or a father attempting to kill his son, precisely here in front of this house of sin, when he threw the rock and came into his lover's chamber puffed up with pride?

What Hasiba did know was that she had returned to the state of a virgin exactly as she had been before giving birth to her only child, Yusuf. She hid behind her long black gown where the closed buttons down the front testified to her closed body. She was an unusually tall woman and her body was beautifully slender. Her striking eyes bulged slightly and her large nose commanded her face. She carried a dignity not to be resisted, crafted by the silence in which she lived and the black color that cloaked her to the outside world. Her son claimed that she could see in the dark; her gleaming eyes, he said, could pierce the very thickest gloom. He entreated his wife to act kindly toward his mother, who, frail and broken, now faced her end. He enumerated the woman's virtues and reprised her sufferings. See how the pain is carved into her face? he exclaimed to his wife. This was her whole life, pain on top of pain. Be kind, Saadeh, please be kind!

But the stink! she would snap. Your mama won't use a pot to do her business, and if she does, she doesn't do anything there. The minute we go to bed the smell gets so bad I can't bear it. Lord, what did I do to You to deserve this?

The odor of which Saadeh complained was the last thing one would have expected from a woman like Hasiba, who seemed evanescent with soap and exuded perfumes. Hasiba made her own scents. She steeped damask rose blossoms in water and blended them with jasmine and sweet basil. From this concoction she made the preparation she used to wash her face. Its fragrance would spill across the room to cascade over everyone. She was a woman enclosed in black garments who gave off nothing but perfumed scents, who behaved like a silent phantom and, when she moved among people, evoked sentiments of astonishment and fear. Even so, her husband's behavior was enough to expose her to ridicule and disorder, and it passed on to her progeny when Salim bought the house after the death of Maryam the Egyptian. Milia knew the story because her mother recounted it to her, and her mother knew it from Yusuf her husband, and Yusuf knew it from the rock that had struck him in his right eye.

Why did Yusuf not say anything when his father bought the house? When Salim arrived to announce that he had purchased the house, Hasiba remained silent. The joy she had anticipated when the decision was made to move from the two small rooms with a toilet in the outer courtyard into a true house never arrived. Her husband summoned her to see the new house but she refused. He asked for her advice on buying suitable furnishings and she said it didn't matter what he got. She spent her time making certain their belongings were secured and preparing to move. Everything happened in a perfectly ordinary way. The family moved into the new home. Husband and wife established themselves in the *liwan* overlooking the spacious central room while Yusuf's mattress was placed in an out-of-the-way nook in the *dar*. Everything went very smoothly and naturally until she learned of it – and when she did, Hasiba exploded. Now all the silences that had been shut inside her closely done-up black garments spurted out and she poured her anger out and fully onto the head of her son, Yusuf. She would not forgive him for having hidden the house's secret from her. How she learned of it and who told her were not issues of particular importance. No secrets are truly concealed, Saadeh said to her daughter. Everyone knew about Salim except his wife, and I didn't really believe that she didn't know. I think she knew from the beginning but acted as though she didn't have a clue. But I wonder what took her over the edge? And anyway, what frightened her so much? Men! From the moment he picked up the disease, it was all over, but when she discovered that the house had been the Egyptian woman's home, and that the bed had been hers, she began wailing and screaming and insisting she wanted to die. She poured kerosene over her robe and tried to light it. Yusuf threw himself on her burning body. He saved her and God kept the matter veiled from others.

But what happened to Salim after he found out he was impotent? That is the question for which there is no straightforward answer. He ate bricks of pure dirt and mud, as Maryam the Egyptian always said. He consulted every doctor he could find but without any luck. When his feet led him where they led him, though, the problem was resolved so perfectly and easily that it might as well never have existed. Khawaja Sergios Efthymios ordered an almond-wood bed frame from his workshop. Salim crafted it and delivered it to the house in person, with the help of his son, Yusuf. There he saw her; and his world became bright. The man had been living in total misery. Every night a desire he could not speak engulfed him but the moment he approached his wife, who was shrouded in the inevitable long nightgown, he was a block of ice. But now, standing before this short, deliciously plump and dark-skinned woman of forty or so, he felt simply and clearly that he was a man and that was more than enough. He made up the bed in the *liwan*, acknowledging the woman's presence with a nod. He had gripped his son's hand, ready to leave, when he heard her lilting Egyptian dialect and felt a tremor through his spine.

We'd like to try out the bed, M'allim, please don't rush off! She sat down on the bed, leaned back as if to stretch out fully, and – Allah! – proclaimed it wonderful. She arose to thank him with a handshake. She squeezed his large rough hand, he was certain of that; and he would claim that he heard her say, Let us see you, M'allim. He got the message. He would indeed return, he decided; she would see him again.

Much later, when he told her he had fathomed what she was letting him know with her hand and her words, she nearly collapsed laughing. No, she said, she had not said anything like that; he had made up the story; nothing like *that* had even occurred to her.

No . . . and in fact Milia invented this dialogue out of pure thin air. After all, no one knew, not even Yusuf, how it all had happened. Milia said she had dreamed of her grandfather running and skipping among grassy hillocks. He had become another man, she said, at least in her dreams. The fresh vigor of youth had come back; the old fierce grandpa they had known once had returned and his laugh rang out as it once had, no longer kept silent by the suffering he had endured. Apparently the man promised marriage to the Egyptian woman. Word was bandied about, even, that he considered embracing Islam, but the hand of God alone saved his wife from such an outrage. The Egyptian woman died suddenly and between a day and a night all that remained of the story was the house over which she would cast her shadow until Hasiba's death.

When he broached the subject of marriage she said no, but she strung him along fleetingly with the teasing way she had. She could not help feeling ever so slightly, ever so dizzily, happy with the idea. It was the first time ever that Maryam had heard such a proposal addressed to her. Khawaja Efthymios had treated her strictly as a mistress. He had picked her out, taken her off the street, and made her into a lady. He had built this fine house among the trees just for her. He visited once a month. But he never proposed marriage, and in any case it would never have occurred to her that he might do so. He was seventy-five years old. On the first Wednesday of every month he came to her, paid her what had somehow been agreed on as her monthly salary, and reminisced with her about love in the past tense. And then he would leave. The man stayed loyal to this woman with whom he had fallen in love when she was twenty and had rescued from a likely future imposed by Ottoman law. The Ottoman Turks had grown fiercely interested in regulating and organizing those who professed prostitution by compelling women of error to live in a sealed-off quarter that would come to be named after the great Arab poet el-Mutanabbi. Efthymios took Maryam under his protective wing and treated her like the respected mistress of a man of the Beiruti aristocracy.

The story goes that Maryam died suddenly, the heirs of Khawaja Efthymios put the house up for sale, and in the end they settled on Salim Shahin, who bought the house for cash. It was perhaps as much as a year after her move to the new house that Hasiba became aware of the double life her husband had been living. But the only tactic she had at her disposal was to blend her scream with the gas she needed to burn her body after *that dog son of a bitch had burned her heart*. And then she submitted herself to God. To her passion for walking alone at night she added a passion for cats. The garden rapidly became a refuge for stray cats from all over town. From among them she would choose her favorite, bringing it into the house and insisting that her son and husband treat it exactly like a member of the family.

The pain thrashed Milia in her lower belly until she could barely suppress her screams. She cried out Mansour's name. She knew he was not at home but there was no one else to whom she could resort. It was at this moment that she heard her grandmother's voice, a voice she had not heard before; and here was the cat, and then suddenly she saw her grandfather Salim standing in the garden and tossing a pebble upward toward the window to tell his Egyptian lover that he was here. He would crouch beneath the eucalyptus, waiting for the woman to appear, her shadow already etched behind the window, half hidden by the thick interlacing of jasmine tree leaves. She could see it all and, seeing it, she was mortally afraid. No, this was not a dream. That cat was a dream – the cat that had nipped at her feet and whose meowing had lacerated her heart. All the rest consisted of circles rippling out from the dream, spherical waves of memories, images of all of the deceased who visited Milia in her dreams. She seemed always to be witnessing a story that was not hers, as if she was reading a book or as if the lid on the ancient chest her grandmother had given her was opening and instead of removing books and papers and letters of the alphabet she was taking out a man and a woman and their only son. In the distance stood the mistress, the lover waiting under the window while Khawaja Sergios Efthymios stood motionless in a corner, in his red tarbush and his carefully pressed European suit, the rasp of his coughing unmistakable.

Milia knows that Mansour is not here. For three months now he has been disappearing for days at a time and when he returns, his face is governed by a sadness that shows especially mournfully in his eyes.

Where has the poetry gone? she asks him.

She knows well that poetry's greatest enemy is death. Poetry cannot conquer death, contrary to what Mansour would argue. Poetry's greatest function is to help us accept death, and to make our peace with it, to the point perhaps where we are able to believe it has been victorious over death when in truth poetry is the mere progeny of death: its secret voice.

When Mansour's brother, Amin, died, the world was turned upside down. Though she would never have believed it could happen, immediately Milia saw another man born inside of her husband. The man she knew – and about whom she knew everything, she was certain – simply had disappeared. That open book she had known so well was no longer. As the childbirth pangs squeezed her and wrung her out, now, she would say that, yes, she had loved him, on that night when they had finally reached the hotel. She had fallen in love with the man who entered her sleep and her wakefulness, who could fill up her silence with words and who awed and bewildered her with the poetry he declaimed. He was a man whose love of life – and the particular route it had taken – revealed itself in his insatiable adoration of the food his wife prepared and the myriad of excuses he found, a new one every day, to drink arak. Good food demands arak. *Haraam!* that a man would eat this stunningly delicious food without drinking arak! he would exclaim. He would plunge into Milia's various ragouts and float on the bliss of her *laban immuh*, then laugh and say that the ancient Arabs composed odes on sweets. He would remember Ibn el-Rumi and his relationship with that sweet of sweets, *zalabiya*. Sweet pastries are gold, woman, he'd declare. Listen!

The dough flows swift and silvery
off graceful fingertips
and puffs and swells all buttery
into latticework of gold

But no one ever wrote in praise of stews and other ordinary dishes, alas! And then, what about this food to end all foods, *laban immuh* with rice?

That is not its true name, interjected Milia. Yes, Beirut folks call it that, but it is from Syria and there it is called *shakiriyya*.

It doesn't matter! What does matter is – God forgive us – its very name is a bit of a fierce warning. Listen to what's written in the Torah: Do not eat the calf in its own mother's milk. Our cousins the Jews do not eat meat cooked in butter, and that's why.

They're right, said Milia, and she announced then and there that she would stop cooking calf in its own mother's milk. Because it's a savage thing to do, she said.

Not savage, not silly! This *laban immuh* is the mother of all foods and we will all be cooking it come Judgment Day!

He sipped his arak and then took a taste of *laban*, and enjoyed saying that no one had ever quite approached it like this before. Milk and milk; lion's milk (arak's other name, Mansour told her) and cow's milk. We're mixing milk and milk. A man can be a child nursing at the breasts of heaven.

Such a moment would spur Mansour to begin reciting poetry. From where had his memory gathered in so many stored-up poetic treasures that his stock never seemed to run dry? Where did it all come from, this daily infusion of a new fund of poetry to add to his never-ending verbal effervescence? She loved him. She had fallen in love with his words and with his love for her. She began to grow accustomed to the triadic life she lived here in Nazareth: the house, the street, and her dreams in her sleep. Then came the news that shook her life to the core and forced her into a relationship with a completely different person. She had to make an entirely new attempt to love him, at a time when she was no longer prepared for such a trial.

Her husband suggested she go to Beirut to have her mother at her bedside for the birth. Even before hearing his wife's thoughts on the matter, though, he withdrew the idea. Everything is ransomed to its own time, he said, and the security situation is very unsettled. He did not want to expose her life or that of the baby to danger and so he proposed instead that she invite her mother to come to Nazareth. But Milia rejected both suggestions. She would not go to Beirut because she had come to Nazareth to give birth here, and she would not summon her mother for the mother was chronically ill. Such a visit would impose an added burden on Milia, who would have to take care of her.

From the start – that is, ever since the girl's memory had taken form – she had seen herself as a mother to her own mother and had thought of herself as an orphan. No indeed, she did not want Beirut and she did not want her mother. She wanted to have the baby here because that was what the child wanted. All she wanted from the world now was fulfillment of a single and singular desire: to meet this child whom she saw in her dreams, his immense eyes open so wide that they seemed to have no eyelashes, staring at her from within the waters in which he floated, and telling her the story that no one had ever heard.

Then that news came and everything changed. She recognized finally and fully that if Mansour had once fled from his brother to her, now Amin had succeeded in regaining his brother, and she had no power to change any of it. In the end, there was no choice but to go to Jaffa.

Jaffa is not Beirut. Nor was Manshiyya the Bourj Square she knew so well. The rough humidity here was not like that of Beirut with its scent of gently rotting trees. She went to Jaffa to attend the brother's funeral and there she saw the country called Palestine. In Beirut she had not sensed herself as part of a country despite living through the headiness of independence from the French Mandate. She had remained mostly oblivious. She had not heard about Faisal I and the story of the kingdom he had founded in Damascus, which was to extend all the way to Beirut, until her husband told her about it in the Hotel Massabki, when he called her to stand beneath the image of a man with distracted eyes who was said to be king of the Syrian lands.

In Nazareth she lived outside of time. The city was boiling over but she did not really notice anything out of the ordinary. The only person in town with whom she had spent any time was Mansour's aunt Malvina Surouji, whose only topic of conversation was the man who had married her daughter,

Nadiya. People had comforted her with the words that he would be a reasonable substitute for Mansour, she said. Ahh, my poor girl, you were meant to marry your cousin Mansour, but what can we do with Fate? The bride from Beirut had to show her sympathetic solidarity with this woman who still dreamed of Mansour as the rightful husband for her daughter.

Then there appeared that aged man who claimed descent from that eminent Lebanese warrior of another age, the Emir Fakhr el-Din el-Ma'ani II. At first the man frightened her, but she grew accustomed to him soon enough. She asked Aunt Malvina about him. He was called Mad Tanyous and he had left Nazareth long ago. But he was not really mad. Milia did not know how one might accurately describe this odd man who wore the black vestments of a priest but with a felt skullcap in the way of the peasants of Jabal Lubnan, wrapping his middle with a white and black striped Palestinian Kaffiyeh. I am all alone, he said to Milia in his Palestinian accent, skewing some of the letters and sounds in an attempt to give it a Lebanese twist. Appearing before her window by night only to vanish, he would reappear in the mornings to shadow her through the streets of the city.

The woman lived her Nazareth story in walking its narrow streets and uncovering this place to which she had come. This town was in essence the solemn and dreadful anticipation that it inspired. That is what she came to understand about the Messiah's town as she lived there. In these wanderings around town she would see him now and then, and she gave him a few pennies because she believed him to be a beggar. He took them without thanking her as though she were simply doing her duty. She began to bring him loaves of bread and other food. To be more accurate, several times she invited him to the house so that he could eat but she did not dare bring him inside. She brought the food to him in the garden and observed him as he ate, though he did not give the appearance of eating. He did not look at the food but simply swallowed it rapidly and perfunctorily as if he found it beneath him, wiped his moustache and beard with his chapped palm, and melted away. She did not tell Mansour that she had invited him. She said he had shown up. She told a story that had not come to pass but she was certain that in some way or other it must have come to pass.

And where was I? asked Mansour.

You were asleep, here in the house, Milia said. I tried to wake you up but I couldn't. I found him standing in front of the window. He said he was hungry. That is how he began coming here.

Milia was not speaking the exact truth. She heard a knock on the window. It was nighttime and Mansour was out. Everything had changed since Mansour had started going regularly to Jaffa and had decided to take up the hardware manufacturing business that his brother's murder had left untended. Mansour was not there and Milia slept alone in the house. She was not afraid but she was uneasily aware of the dreadful solemnity of the night, of her solitude, and of the baby in her belly. She heard a knocking at the window. She got up and saw the dark outline of a man just disappearing behind the trees. She went back to bed, covered herself up, and waited. The next night the same scene occurred but the third night was different. It was about ten o'clock. Everything was silent in the Greek Orthodox quarter where Mansour had bought the newlyweds a home. This time she heard a violent knocking on the window. Going over to the window she saw the ghostly form of a man.

Who is it? she asked, her voice quavering with fright.

Me, answered the shape standing behind the window. Open it, I have brought you a gift.

She did not know where the strength to open the window came from – as though she were not herself, as though she were sleeping. As though someone gave orders and she obeyed. She opened the window and noticed a goblet of wine in the man's hand. He gave it to her and said he would come back.

It is the water of life, he said, and disappeared.

She did not see him leave; she did not see the back of him. He had been facing her when a darkness fell suddenly and covered him. The little girl found herself standing alone with her swelling belly in front of the window holding a glass of red liquid near to overflowing. She brought it to her nose and smelled aged wine. She touched the glass to her lips but did not drink. She returned to the window to close it and saw that it was already closed. She shouted for Mansour but no one answered. She saw Musa coming toward her. She wanted to ask him what had brought him here. Musa took the glass from her hand and drained it. He held the empty glass out for his sister as a darkness fell over him and erased his form. The girl saw herself holding an empty glass and standing alone. She stepped back and was suddenly submerged in darkness pierced by a single bold light. She picked up the light in her hands. The goblet shone. Suddenly and without her realizing what was happening, the goblet slipped and shards of glass scattered everywhere. She bent over the glass slivers intermingled with points of light, wanting to pick them up, but every time she touched a shred of light it went out and blood dripped from her finger, as though she were replacing scraps of light with blood. But she had to pick up the fragments somehow. She waited for Mansour but he did not come. She was afraid he might step on the shreds of glass and hurt himself. She picked up the glass chips and saw their shine suddenly extinguished between her wounded fingers and saw how they were coated in dark, dark blood. She carried the bits of glass with her wounded fingers and slipped to the ground and saw the blood. She opened her eyes to find herself in her bed, her heart pounding so hard that she could feel it throughout her body. She made the sign of the cross and decided that she would forget this particular dream, and closed her eyes once again.

In the morning when Mansour stopped in, having just returned from

Jaffa, and woke her up, his face as pallid as ever since the assassination of his brother, Amin, she jumped out of bed barefoot to make his coffee and breakfast. She remembered the glass and felt something pricking the sole of her foot. She searched for her slippers beneath the bed and found them covered in white-blond feathers. She had no idea where the feathers had come from, but she brushed them off and put the slippers on her feet. She went to the kitchen and put the coffeepot on the flame. She reached toward the small wood cabinet to get coffee cups out and saw it there. Among the coffee cups, the goblet shone with light. Where had the wine goblet come from? In her house there were no wineglasses. Mansour drank arak exclusively and if she drank, it was to drink arak along with him.

She asked him where the wine goblet had come from. He was in the bathroom and did not hear her question. She picked up the goblet with two shaking hands and set it down on the table. She saw the gleaming flashes of light and scattered fragments of glass. When the coffee boiled over on the stove she did not notice. She saw Mansour hurry over to turn off the flame. Setting the coffeepot down on the table, he asked her why she was standing so still.

The goblet? she asked him.

What goblet?

On the table, she said.

This glass, he said, picking it up, and it slipped from his hand to fall to the floor, covering the kitchen tiles in splinters of glass.

You broke it! she shrieked.

It's nothing. Broken glass, broken bad luck. We have plenty more glasses just like it.

O Lord, what am I going to do now? She squatted to pick up the bits of glass. The shards sank into her palms and blood appeared.

What are you doing! he yelled at her. Get the broom.

She did not change position. She picked up all the glass splinters, put them in a tray and washed her hands in the sink. The water swirled down the drain dark red.

Blood, she said, and staggered as if about to faint. Help me, please!

He seized hold of her and half carried her to bed. He brought some cotton and antiseptic ointment that he dabbed along her fingers. He told her to go to sleep.

I'll be back at midday. Don't be afraid. Don't make lunch, I'll bring something from the *souq*.

Later, when she got out of bed, she found no trace of the glass shards in the tray. She cried hard and bitterly, weighted with the sense that she had committed a grave sin.

Without any advance warning Milia's world had turned upside down. The news came and she found herself in Jaffa. She said she did not want to live in this city on the coast. She said she hated the house in Ajami which the widow shared with her two sons and mother-in-law. She said she was afraid of the roar of the sea. She said when she left Beirut she left behind the sea and she did not want to return to it. She said many things but all to no avail.

There in the church Amin's coffin was cloaked in a four-colored flag. Everywhere, laments, weeping, and expressions of anger prevailed. Milia had never seen anything like the place in which she now found herself: a city roiling in fury, and specters of fear and hatred etched on people's faces everywhere. Milia saw faces contorted by grief and a city sliding into its own death. She was afraid for her womb, apprehensive about the effects this city would have on her baby, whom – she feared – would drop into the tumultuous froth of Jaffa's waves and disappear forever. On the face of her mother-in-law Najiba she saw permanently carved lineaments of despair.

You killed him, said Najiba to her son Mansour. The mother did not mean what she said – or she didn't mean to let these words slip out – but she spoke as though for the moment she had appropriated the voice of the young widow, who did believe that Mansour was responsible for his brother's death. Or she believed that his brother had died in his stead; not only had she lost everything but now she must live with the two young children and the old woman at the mercy of this Mansour who had fled Jaffa, leaving its death sentence for his brother.

There on the dust-swirled rise overlooking the sea Milia observed the change that had come over Mansour. Her husband stood motionless with the rest in the seaside cemetery where the Hourani family had buried their dead for a thousand years. When the coffin was lowered into the ground, a single sad ululation, a salute to the martyr, rose hoarse from the mother's raw throat. In that moment Milia saw Mansour completely altered. The man seemed suddenly to shrink in size, his limbs contracting. Milia could not describe what she saw but it was as though she felt her husband's joints congeal and collapse into an indistinguishable mass of flesh. And Mansour wept. From his insides erupted a peculiar howl as if the man were exploding, yielding a whole world of tears that poured from his eyes. Entering the home and seeing the women clustered around the corpse of his brother pierced by bullets, Mansour had not cried. His face had been contorted into a dreadful frown. Bending over his brother to kiss the dead man's brow, he felt himself collapsing forward. His head met the pillow and he put his cheek next to his dead brother's as the women's sobbing and moaning grew louder and wilder. The mother said she saw tears rolling down the cheeks of the dead man. My Lord, he is still weeping for himself! she moaned. But these were Mansour's tears, the widow said. And he must not cry these tears onto his brother's cheeks – that's taboo! she fretted. Milia recalled the tale of the poet Dik el-Jinn of Homs who killed his lover Ward. His tears welled across her cheeks as his poem soared.

O face on which the white dove lit
To pluck the self-sown fruits of ruin
I watered earth with her blood and saw
her lips water mine with passion
My sword ran firmly through her sash
And now my tears run o'er her cheek
No sole has trod the earth, I swear,
more dear than the slippers upon her feet

Milia did not understand the story's import. What was this love about? A poet from Homs has two loves: a Nazareth woman named Ward and a boy called Bakr. She was not convinced by what Mansour had said about the practices and morals of the Abbasid age: that there was no harm in a man loving another man on condition that he be too young to have yet grown a beard as well as being of a sweet and comely appearance. The poet married Ward and installed Bakr in the same dwelling. When the poet was told that Bakr had fallen in love with Ward, had flirted with her, and had even slept with her during one of the poet's journeys away, Dik el-Jinn – "rooster of the demons" – went devilishly mad and killed them both at once, together.

But the story has not really begun yet, not with this, said Mansour. The story begins when the poet discovers that the story he was told was one lie piled upon another and that Ward had not betrayed him after all. He went directly to the grave and scooped up two handfuls of soil, one from where Ward lay and the other from Bakr's grave. He stirred them into two goblets and began to drink from each, weeping for his two beloveds and composing poetry. That is when he uttered the line *And now my tears run o'er her cheek*. Meaning, yes, he had killed her, but equally he wept over her out of love. That is true passion, my darling. True love.

That's love!

Of course it is.

You mean, something that you kill for?

Of course I would kill for it. There is not a lover in the world who is not ready to kill or at the very least would not want his beloved's death if she deceived him in love.

You mean, you could kill me?

It's just a story, my love! As we say, it is the story of Dik el-Jinn. Everyone must live his own story. Dik el-Jinn killed Ward because that is what his story demanded. After all, people are stories. What is life, my dear? We live a story whose author we do not know. That is why I am afraid to read novels. Every time I read a novel I have the uneasy feeling that the writer is a brute. To entertain their readers, authors put their heroes in tragic circumstances. I feel my whole self squeezed and pressed inside a telling that goes on and on, as though at any moment I am liable to fall headlong out of life, lose my foothold, and pitch forward into the midst of a book. No . . . poetry is better. Among the ancient Arabs poetry was the ultimate art because it is all description and no story. And to make stories attractive to listeners, story-tellers used to insert a bit of poetry. Poetry was the sense and the story was the structure, and that's the way it went.

You mean, you kill because the story says to kill?

Now your story begins, Mansour . . . whispered Milia to herself. You tell me that a story begins only with murder and death: We tend to believe that a person's story begins at birth, Mansour said. But that is not the case, my dear. The story begins when we die or when we kill.

And so now Mansour enters his own story, beside the deathbed as a brother's tears run across a brother's cheeks.

Mansour did not cry. Milia does not know where the story of the tears on the brother's cheeks came from. She was there and saw no tears. But there had to be some beginning to the story. She told him she was becoming afraid of his story. She told him she had seen how everything in him had altered. Mansour had come to look like his brother: it was not so much that the man had changed but that he had stripped himself away and donned a wholly new image. The poetry disappeared. Erased as well was the giddy passion that had captured his eyes whenever he gazed at the soft pale angelic face that filled out with bashfulness and went pink with desire – that vision of which he never got his fill. But now, everything went dry. Even that thing of which Milia had never spoken, never in all her life, vanished; the flow of it dried up. He would sleep with her, and as usual she would not be awake, but still she did not sense the quiet eruption of waters from deep inside the earth that resided quietly inside of her. As though he were not himself.

When they returned from Jaffa she discovered that the man who had come to her in Beirut in flight from his own story had fallen into the story written for him by the hand of fate. The fisher of tales had triumphed in impaling him. His brother was dead and there remained no alternative before the trader in cloth who had dreamt of transforming himself into a silk merchant, because, as the proverb goes, If it's a lover you are, the silk trade takes you far. The eternal lover who sips from the water of his beloved's eyes day after day (as Mansour called himself) fled to cloth and to Beirut because he sensed there was no future for this miserable country where the prophets' presences had led to so many disasters. He knew that his brother had done his utmost but that Jaffa could not sustain it. I know them, and I told Amin. We cannot do it, Mansour told his wife. But Amin said, simply, It is our homeland. Mansour knew that Amin had right on his side; he knew that the business the two of them had inherited from their father must be at the service of those defending the threatened city.

How can you say that? Amin had continued, challenging his brother. At least we make cartridges and repair rifles. Are you saying we should just let the Jews take the place and push us out?

This issue had provoked Mansour's departure. No, I'm not a coward but I don't like weapons. You and Mother are right about this – but personally, I can't do it.

But then how are we to fight the English and the Jews? With words and stories, or by making things we can really use?

He told his brother he could not do it, and he went off to Beirut. There he fell in love with the Lebanese woman. The thought did pass through his head that staying in Beirut might mean an easier life. That proved impossible, though, and so he opened the little boutique in Nazareth. Traveling to Beirut to procure the new European fabrics became an essential part of his life, and that's how it all unfolded. His heart fell into captivity at the Shahin family garden. This, he said, was the beginning.

But the true beginning awaited him in Nazareth. There – and as he contemplated the apple of life, which was the name he had given to his wife's swollen belly – the news came that overturned everything, announcing the end of life in Nazareth and the imperative of moving the little family to Jaffa.

But – the dream, said Milia.

Instead of smiling at her dream as he had always done, Mansour's face was all frowns. She did not understand the meaning of what was happening, he snapped.

But, the dream, it was the dream, she told him. She reminded him of the goblet he had broken. He said it had not been as she said. You were talking about a wine goblet, he said, but all I saw was an ordinary glass. It fell and broke. Now please, let's get on with packing our bags and getting out of here – no more of these silly tales!

Milia persisted. Musa drank the wine, she told him, and the splinters from the shattered goblet, strewn across the floor, were shot through with light. But when she knelt down to –

Enough! Mansour barked. Milia froze. That word – Enough! – was more than enough for her; it rendered her speechless. She recognized immediately that henceforth she must reckon with a new and wholly unknown man.

A woman does not marry one man alone in her life, Hasiba had said. If anyone tells you she does, they're lying. The Salim whom Hasiba had married was not the Salim who came down with the mumps. And then, Salim the invalid was still another man. Nor was he the Salim who recovered and then became obsessed with the problems in his "little brother," which occupied his wandering eye. That Salim of the wandering eye was not the Salim who was the lover of Maryam. The lover of the Egyptian whore was not the man who bought the house and dragged the family there after the late lamented's death. The latter Salim was not the same man who had intended to kill his son with a rock. And then, the supposed killer of his son was someone other than the man lying on the ground who was carried off somewhere unknown by the coma that felled him. I married a whole gang of men, she said, and every so often I've had to get used to a new one. I'm tired out. Son, let me die. That would be so much easier.

These were Hasiba's words to Yusuf when he found her sitting alone in the dirt lane beneath the carob tree. Hasiba had left the house, in her long black gown, as she always did in the evening, to stride the nighttime streets. But she did not come back. Yusuf went in search of her. He circled all the streets near the house before fatigue took over and he nearly went home, but then he found himself in front of his mother under the carob tree. He launched immediately into a scolding but her faint voice stopped him. She seemed unable to rise from the ground. She told him she could not get up and when he took her hand he realized how weak and trembly her muscles were.

What's the matter, Mama? Come on now, get up.

What Hasiba had to say about her husband, about how many times she had married him or how many husbands she had married, were the last words she ever said that made any sense. Yusuf tugged at her arm to get her up but she dwindled away in his arms.

What's happened, Mama? Will you tell me?

Yusuf saw tears on the white face shadowed by so many wrinkles. He bent over the woman, folded her carefully at her middle, and hoisted her onto his shoulder. She was as light as a feather. Tall beautiful fierce Hasiba was no more now than a collection of bones held loosely together. Her body had withered away, and now the woman was like a tiny light sparrow without wings.

He hoisted her and walked. He knew he was taking her to her death. He heard her scream in his father's face. He saw her wrench away her body in anger as she declared that she would not stay in this house an instant longer. She demanded he find her another dwelling place. This was the moment when she turned to her son and asked him why he had not told her the plain truth about his eye. The young man's hand went up to his scarred split eyelid as he gave his mother a look pleading for her silence, but she went on nevertheless.

Tell me who put out the boy's eye? For once in your life act like a man and speak up.

You'll shut your mouth, woman, if you know what's good for you. Anyway, the boy's eye wasn't put out by anyone. He was just horsing around with the other boys and thank the Lord it ended there.

I never in my life saw a papa try to kill his son! You wanted to kill the boy to cover up for yourself and the Egyptian whore. I don't know how you can be so pitiful, you're half a man, I've seen enough of you, I know you. I'm not staying a moment longer in this house.

Yusuf spoke, or tried to speak, but his father commanded him to be silent. You! Not a word from you – get out of here and leave me to make the woman understand what the real story is. You want to know the story, woman, fine. The one that everyone knows? The one about the French soldier you've been wearing black for all your life? I'm the one who secured your honor and maintained the dignity of your family. Don't make me say any more than this!

Salim broke speech with speech; he said what is not said; he undid the buttons on the long black gown and stripped naked the spirit of the woman standing before him. Hasiba's knees gave out and she collapsed. Her young son sank down to crouch next to her like a faithful dog. On that day Yusuf decided to forever treat his father with contempt. He had endured the cleft chiseled in his eyelid by the rock with long and silent patience. His mother's cry of agony offered him the prospect of revenge and a stab at the truth. He even felt himself capable of striking this man who had transformed his impotence into a notorious love story with an Egyptian woman who had taken up prostitution as a profession. But his mother's collapse and her exposure, through her husband's words, kept him sitting next to her like a dog who did not even dare to bark.

Yusuf thought his father was an idiot – enough of an idiot, perhaps, to not even realize the truth. Maryam had not really been his, after all. Khawaja Efthymios gave her the house as a means of income. He had had his fill of her and giving the house to her meant regaining himself. He did not actually even give it to her, for it was never recorded in her name. He gave her the use of it for life. That is how Salim was able to buy the house from Efthymios's heirs after her death. The woman turned this house in Daaboul Street, off the Street of the Archangel Mikhail, into a den of prostitution. There, behind a thick screen of trees, the man who had bought a house and allowed his mistress to live in it had also given her the means to live from it.

You're an ass, Papa, said Yusuf. She was just a whore who wasn't worth a penny.

Shut up, you – you son of a bitch! Salim screamed at his son before turning toward his wife and shaming her by hurling the story at her that she had believed buried within her ribs. For the blond youth with eyes the hue of the sky she had carved out a tomb in her heart and buried him there. It had been love but there had been no story. She saw him twice and he spoke to her once. No, in fact he had not said a thing. He had smiled at her and disappeared. That was the whole of it. But it had been love. She had felt her senses collapse into singularity, seeing nothing and no one except the blond young man and smelling only a white fragrance given off by the body of a man as white as snow. Hasiba did not know how her sisters learned of the story. She had wrapped herself in black to erase all traces of the white angel. Then she married Salim Shahin the carpenter, who barely got any work, in order to quiet the pounding of her heart. The marriage extinguished both heart and body. And now Salim – whose impotence and infidelity she had endured – was opening the wound, pulling from her guts the corpse of the blue-eyed young man.

Hasiba was broken. Her lips, pressed together, began to tremble and she sat in a corner, weeping without tears. Yusuf felt smothered. He wanted to understand. He imagined himself as the son of a Frenchman whose name he did not know and about whom he could ask no one.

After her son's marriage Hasiba consented to the project of adding a wing constructed of concrete to the house – just as it was Hasiba who had encouraged him to remove his abaya forever and adopt European clothing, another tale that entered the history of the Shahin clan as a staple in their day-to-day storytelling. Yusuf was always acting out the story in front of his children, though Saadeh would order him to shut his mouth, for now the girl was becoming a young lady and for shame, telling that story! But this man (who, home from his shop, peeled off his trousers immediately and put on his long dishdasha, refusing to buy pajamas because he feared restricting his testicles at night) paid no attention to his wife's rebuke. Instead, he described yet again how cramped and squashed, even unable to breathe, he had felt when he tried on trousers for the very first time. He did not know how to arrange his parts; a leaden pain dragged through his lower body and he could barely walk. Reaching the church door with his bride on his arm, he was certain he would collapse onto the ground. The truly awful difficulty he recalled was emerging from the church with the terrible realization that his trousers were about to split from the load that pressed insistently against the seam.

Yusuf never tired of telling the story that worked up Beirut in the 1920s. Very quickly, after the fall of the Ottoman Empire and the occupation of Syria and Lebanon, people adopted their new monarchs' religion. Wearing trousers became a common sight among the middling classes. The upper classes – Mr. Efthymios's social world – had grown accustomed to trousers at the start of the century under the influence of the men who had led the Ottoman Empire's reforms and believed that going European would solve their society's problems. Wearers of European fashion were exposed to the mockery of ordinary people: even Maryam the Egyptian could not help but laugh with Salim at the apparatus Mr. Efthymios displayed, his trousers as tight as could be, whereas the moment the seventyish man took them off the reality was as clear as daylight.

In essence, Beirut experienced its phase of European fashion as though it were a carnival of laughs: men walking with their feet unnaturally far apart, as if every male in the city had suddenly gone lame; endless jokes; and a devastating sense of professional impotence among the traditional tailors who could not accustom themselves to the new style of apparcl.

Later on, Yusuf said, he figured out the consequence of trousers: they demonstrated the sanctity of manhood, putting it on display for all to see. But, he admitted, he had not always been so comfortable. In the beginning, he said, I would always be so conscious of what God gave me, but that is shameful. I would always stand up when I was wearing trousers, feeling I could not sit down. Then I got used to it. And now – God help us! – they say women are wearing trousers. Look what we've come to – women showing themselves off, and men as well, what a world we live in! We thought when we put on trousers it would mean facing the Day of Judgment, and then we found out that it didn't mean a thing.

So why don't you shave your moustache and take off your tarbush? Salim asked him.

You're talking like a Frenchman, son. Where you get that from, I simply don't know!

What do they have to do with each other?

A man without a moustache! What's left of him? And the tarbush – not a chance. Ask your mother. You'll never see me without a tarbush – it only comes off when I go to bed. Even when I'm asleep – when I dream about myself, I'm wearing that tarbush. A bare head is uglier and more disgusting than a naked body. I don't know how you can do it, Salim. Yes, I know the world has changed and everything changes – not for me, though. When I'm dead, bury me in that tarbush.

After Yusuf's death Saadeh dressed him in a long traditional robe and mantle and his tarbush. The holy sister said it was not right; people must face their Maker with heads bared. They tugged the tarbush off his head and laid it beside him on his deathbed. When they carried the bier to the gravesite the tarbush sat atop the coffin, its black tassel dancing in time with the wooden box as it swayed and tipped on the shoulders that bore it – as if the man's final communication was ensconced in that thin black shadow. Then the tarbush disappeared. Milia believed they had buried it alongside Yusuf but three days after his death she saw her father's tarbush on her brother Niqula's head – tantamount to a proclamation that the new head of the family had been born.

Milia stands among the mourners revering Amin's shrouded bier. No tarbush graces it but rather a four-colored flag drapes over it; later on Milia would learn that this was the flag of Palestine, the flag born in the great Arab Revolt against the Ottomans, led by King Faisal, whom Milia had dubbed King of the Hotel Massabki. Green and white, red and black: Mansour explained to her that the four colors were those of the ancient Arab states that had ruled this land one after another. The colors of the flag gave material reality to a poetic couplet in which the medieval poet Safi el-Din el-Hilli expressed the manner in which these colors became the emblem of the Arabs' wakefulness, a legacy of the ancient Arabs' boldness and persistence.

> *White are our works, and black are our battles*
> *Green are our fields, and red, every blade*
> *Their boldest claims the world saw as true*
> *At their summons, "Thus it is!" History bade*

Milia did not like this one. It's a long way from true poetry, she said to Mansour.

At the church she noticed a cluster of blue-eyed, light-complexioned men standing at the front with the family as they received condolences. They were Husaynis, Milia realized, relatives of Haajj Amin, the mufti of Jerusalem, and a leader among Palestinians. Their presence announced to all that Amin Hourani had died a martyr to the homeland. For he had put the foundry and hardware business inherited from his father at the service of the uprising, ready to resist the British Mandate and the Zionists. She sensed the odor of death at hand. For the entire week she spent at the family home in Jaffa, not once did Milia remove her protective hand from her belly, as though she was determined to protect the baby from the dangers threatening it. At church, the short, light-haired man who was said to be a cousin of Haajj Amin's stood next to Mansour and, even at home, would not leave his side. Why did these men look the way they looked? Milia wanted to ask. They seemed so like the French, or at least as she imagined the French to look. But she asked no questions. She sensed a misfit of things and images, and said nothing. What kind of sense did it make, that a grandson of Crusaders was resisting the new crusaders who had occupied Palestine and were trying to hand it over to the Jews? Later, Milia understood that the Husaini family had ancient Arab roots; pale complexions and blue eyes were not the monopoly of the Europeans. Remembering how the poetry of the ancient Arabs extolled cream-complexioned women in one seductive line after another, she smiled at her own naiveté.

When Milia married she did not think about what awaited her in a country plummeting into an infernal abyss.

I didn't think about it because I didn't know, she would say. But my brothers – why didn't it occur to them? Perhaps it did, but they saw this as the only way to marry me off and be rid of me.

After the tale of Najib and his little birds, Milia had felt increasingly that her presence was becoming heavy at home, that she was taking up too much space. The tempest over Salim and his two wives – as Saadeh persisted in calling Salim's wife and her sister – had died down. All mention of Salim vanished, as if he had never existed, and Niqula assumed full responsibility for the household. He ruled with a fiery-red fist, the shadow-image of the red tarbush he had claimed and seized after the death of his father, which would not budge from his head until his own death. Milia – mother and sister, as they called her – had to go. Her own mother's eyes said so as did the looks her brothers gave her. Even Musa began to distance himself from his older sister; he no longer knew what to say to her. Life is simply like that: it changes, and its channels narrow, into weariness and anxiety. Milia felt confined, and as wretched as could be. Her dreams had turned into suffocating moments when she felt herself lost in darkness and cringing as little birds flew past. Her rib cage felt compressed and she felt herself moving through airless space. She was a lost young woman plunging into the void. Walking along the edge of the wadi, she watched herself pitch forward and fall, as if the little Milia who appeared in her dreams had forgotten how to walk. More and more, her dreams were a succession of painful falls, until one morning she was unable to rise from her bed, so stricken was she by the pain shooting through her back and legs brought on by repeatedly falling as she walked down the dusty unpaved track. Milia decided to take a cane along into her dreams, and she laughed at the possibility of it.

I wish life were like this, she said to her husband.

Like this – meaning what?

Meaning, like I dream it to be. Like, something comes into my head that I want to take with me into the dream, and there it is.

She told him about the dream of the cane that saved her from falling on the pathways of the night and gave her the ability to endure a cramped and anxiety-ridden existence – for life did not reopen its doors to her until Mansour and the blue woman appeared on her horizon.

I wish we could go back to our time at the Hotel Massabki, she said.

Why?

Because then your brother would not have died, and we would not have to go to Jaffa.

Mansour got her to understand that the decision about Jaffa was irrevocable. He could not alter it, he said. All his life he had fled from the reality of things; his brother had faced it alone. Now he has died, said Mansour, and I must do what has to be done.

And then? What will happen then?

And then – it's impossible for it to happen, he said. The Jews want to throw us out of our own country. Can you believe that?

It's unbelievable, she said. But what can we do about it?

We can fight.

And if we fight, can we really change anything? Because it's . . .

Because it's what? he asked her. Don't tell me you dreamed the Jews took the country and threw us out!

No, I didn't dream it, she said, and was silent.

Milia did not want to leave Nazareth. She had tried and tried to win over Mansour but it was no longer possible to talk with him. He put an end to words by slipping into his brother's skin. And the end of words meant the end of everything. Logic said he could not abandon the foundry; that the mother could not run it on her own. But an opposing logic said Mansour could not work with his mother because she was so domineering and also because his brother had kept the entire business to himself without clueing Mansour in. Milia could not say that Mansour had been a coward or had claimed to flee Jaffa out of fear. He told her that he had preferred to get away from the atmosphere there, to avoid headaches, but those headaches had pursued him all the way to their home in Nazareth.

Yet Amin's story remained obscure for Milia. Well, not exactly: she *had* dreamed something that night but told no one her dream. She was afraid; she believed the figure she had seen might be Musa. Her eyes were swollen and sore when she awoke. She had dreamed herself crying, she said. She did not get up to make coffee. She told Mansour she did not feel well and was tired. She pretended to sleep until he left the house and only then she got up. She rinsed her puffy eyes and did not leave the house. She was too afraid of encountering that elderly man and bursting into tears once again. She had cried seeing Tanyous lying full length on the ground, his belly inflated and flies swarming around his body. She tried to stop people on the incline that led to the Church of Our Lady of the Tremblings to tell them that the man had died and must be carried to the cemetery. No one paid any attention to the stiff and motionless little girl with the huge wide-open eyes that suggested she was waiting hopelessly for her mother. Men filled the narrow street, marching shoulder to shoulder; no one stopped. Then suddenly out stretched a hand holding a pair of scissors and clutched a handful of her short hair. Blackness began to rain into her eyes and she no longer saw anything, then she began to cry.

That morning Mansour came back at noon to say that they had to go to Jaffa immediately. There was bad news. She did not ask what the news was. She dressed and said she was ready. He asked her to pack their suitcase because they would be staying for about a week, and his brother . . . and Mansour began to cry, his flooding tears tinting his face darkly. Ever since that moment, this new dark color had not left the man's face. Musa's face disappeared. Milia didn't know what had happened to the resemblance between the two men that had stayed resolutely in her memory. Mansour became a Jaffawi, his skin dark and his gaze coming through the glinting eyes of his brother, as he worked to conceal his weeping behind loud and prolonged yawns.

She smelled the fragrance of oranges. This was not Beirut's particular aroma, though, that blend of seductively swaying pines (and the perfume of pine nuts) with acacia blossoms. Jaffa was another story: the scent of lemon trees, of spacious houses, of fear. When she visited Jaffa for the first time – a month after her wedding – she told Mansour she would never go there again because she saw fear carved into the thick fragrance of orange trees. She was no longer fond of oranges, she said. The smell of oranges would send her into a fear she could not pinpoint, but it spread throughout her body all the way to her toes and fingertips and paralyzed her. She could not face the smell of oranges, she said. She must cover her face.

It's the cravings of pregnancy, or it's morning sickness, said her mother-in-law. Just be patient.

No, that was not it. This was a feeling that crept into the bones and stayed there, there was no antidote for it. All she wanted was to cover her face, to put on the Jaffa niqab that she saw draped over the faces of the city's women.

And now here she was, in the City of Perfume as Jaffa people called it. It was so sweet smelling, they claimed, because the scent of bitter orange permeated the air. They did not know that this perfume skirting the heavens would become the city's shroud, the emblem of its death.

The woman who arrived from Nazareth carrying a seven-month-old baby in her belly would find herself lashed by a profound sorrow that bore no relation to the grief that spread across Ajami and pervaded the Hourani household after the tragic loss of their eldest son. The woman's despair swelled because she saw what no one else could see. In the scent of Jaffa she smelled the sign of its demise. It was not because she had seen Amin dead. It was because of the scent, which had begun to turn yellow on people's faces, transforming mourners into phantoms. A crowd came to the home to mourn the martyr who had left behind two children, the eldest seven years of age and the second one only five years old, and a young wife from near Beit Sahour, and had deposited a hoarse scream of revenge in the throats of the mourning crowd which turned Mansour utterly speechless. Amin's killing took place as a fierce wave of explosions sliced through Jaffa in 1947, and it seemed that the young man's talkative ways had led him to his death. Mansour was convinced that his brother died from telling people too much. A person who puts the shot into English guns and figures out how to turn ordinary automobiles into armored cars so that the Palestinians would possess some sort of heavy weapon with which to square off against the superior Zionist matériel does not talk about it. But Amin was a voluble man who enjoyed making a spectacle of himself, and this was the main reason behind the brothers' rift and Mansour's flight to Nazareth. Well, no . . . the chief cause was their mother. The mother was not only partial to her eldest son but indeed completely wrapped up in her fondness for him. Since the father's death she had treated her eldest as though she were his wife. She asked him to come and sleep in her room, in the dear departed's bed, because she was afraid to sleep alone.

Amin was active in the ranks of the city's Orthodox lay association and was a member of the League of National Action formed by the Arab Higher Committee. In the Grand Mufti he saw a savior, and he dreamed of traveling to Iraq to aid the revolution mounted there by Rashid Ali el-Gaylani against the English. It was whispered that he had undergone training in the use of weapons and that he kept an English gun at home.

His mother did not love him, Mansour said. He did not know why. Perhaps it was because he looked like her. Since his early childhood he knew the story firsthand and heard it repeatedly from his mother: she had expected God to give her a daughter. When a second son was bestowed upon her she treated her son as though he were a little girl. She grew his hair long and braided it, and added a feminine ending to his name. Amin played along, treating his brother in the same way. He even tried to carry the game into their school and Mansour found himself hearing his classmates calling him Mansoura as if he were truly a girl. He responded aggressively, acting out like any feisty boy and thus laying himself open to beatings at the hands of classmates on a daily basis. He often came home covered in blood, a taste he knew very well, he told Milia. He had gone through adolescence drinking the blood that poured from his nose; and when he grew a bit older he sensed the oddness of his family, run by an ironfisted mother who showed no mercy.

I am nothing like her, said Mansour. She is an overbearing, dominating woman who thinks of nothing but amassing money and property. So I left her with everything. I don't want to go back to Jaffa or to the smell of blood that runs across the city. Yes, resistance is a duty, but I just don't know . . .

Seeing Mansour change before her eyes, Milia remembered snatches of this family story. Putting on his brother's face, he would declare his intention to return to Jaffa. On their very first day back from Jaffa, after the funeral, he spoke to her of returning there to live. She replied that she could not do it, not right now. She must have the baby first. And she could not give birth in that city.

But my mother is there, he said. She will help you.

No, I don't want your mother. And my mother isn't well enough to come here. But I'm staying. You go if you want to.

He said he had considered sending her to Lebanon but it was not an easy matter because the roads were not secure. He said he was ready to agree to what she wanted on condition that they move to Jaffa a mere week after the baby's arrival. He would have to sell off his Nazareth shop and his merchandise now, he said, because he must start spending most of his time in Jaffa, to put the foundry in order and resume his original line of work.

Milia's nights filled now with oranges that looked like bombs, the color red everywhere, covering faces and objects. Mansour was away for three days of every week and Milia began to spend her nights alone. The man was no longer able to pierce the veil of solitude behind which this woman lived. He no longer came near her at night. The poems vanished. Speech became a repetition of speech. Mansour became another man and Milia, another woman. Her dreams took on other shapes, new ones. Everything she saw was floundering, or drowning.

Milia's nights were long and sorrowful. There in the hollows of her darkness she saw the short men with blue eyes gathering around the bier, hoisting it onto their shoulders, and marching to the seaside grave. On a hill facing the sea where the waves swelled high, the coffin dipped precariously over hands attempting to hold on to it. The waves came up, the sea roared near, and like a blue animal with an unending body it leapt atop the rise and swept over it, pulling the coffin outward as it receded, and swallowing the men.

The little girl stands next to Mansour, terrified. She does not know how to escape the waves. She grips his hand but the hand slides out of hers. She runs but the waves gallop after her. She climbs and the waves mount behind her. She falls and finds herself in the water. All of them have disappeared. The waves have swallowed everyone and have taken them to a place she does not know and cannot find. The waves stalk people. The little girl is alone, her hands slipping, water all but swallowing her, water and her tears. The water slithers into her lungs; her chest swells and there is no air. Water and salt. Her throat is salt, her lips are cracked, her hand jerks back and forth along the horizon. The coffin lid is open. A blond man is holding his hands out to her. Where did this French officer come from? He was standing alone in the street at night as an autumn breeze swished raindrops through the sky. The woman who always wears black awaits him in the garden. But the man does not move. He stands at a distance as if spying on her, and then he comes forward, stumbling as if he is slightly dizzy. His body juts forward. He falls. Blood spins from holes high on his back. Blood fills up all the spaces. The street is flooded. Blood. The coffin floats on the red-black flow.

Milia knew she was the only one to know the story. She knew it because she saw the blond officer whom her grandmother had buried deep and invisible in her breast. She saw him more than once, even, walking and stumbling just before he fell, clutching at a cushion there on the ground, becoming like Hasiba was in her final days, a mass of skin and bones practically severed at the middle and unable to move, her cough keeping her from breathing and curlicues of dried orange and lemon peel hanging on the opposite window.

The woman preserved lemon and orange peel, spreading it over the line hanging in the garden until it dried and then used it for its fragrance. She let it glow in the oven and the house filled with the aroma of citrus. She put a flame to it and let it burn with the wood heating the bathwater, which turned the scent of orange. She would put it next to her pillow to breathe in the smell of life. When she became ill, all she wanted was dried fruit peel. She demanded it be hung on the iron bars of the window that faced her bed. After she lost speech, and after someone took down the peel from the window, three days passed and she began to moan and refused food until her son discovered the secret of her woe and returned the peel to the window.

Saadeh came to despise the smell of dried peel, especially in her mother-in-law's final days when its aroma mingled with the odors of urine and feces. But she was helpless before her husband's fierce wishes and Hasiba's moans. In the end, burning all of the citrus peel she could find was not enough to satisfy Saadeh. From then on, having pickled lemons and the like in the house was a problem for her. No doubt that is why Milia perfected the art of cooking *kibbeh arnabiyyeh* – which required lots of pickled citrus – at the age of ten, transforming herself rather prematurely into mistress of the kitchen and doyenne of the sensual aromas of fine cuisine. She took her skills and her love of cooking with her to Nazareth only to find herself, ten months after marrying, forced to submit to the decision to leave. Milia was not granted the time necessary to become attached to Nazareth, the White City, or the Flower of Galilee as it was also called, with its three distinct parts all overlooking the fertile plains of Ibn Amir: the Greek Quarter, that of the Maronites, and the Latin Quarter. The entire town was perfumed with incense and poetry. No town, other than Beirut, was really known to Milia. Even in Beirut she knew only the area where they lived, the street where her grandmother Malakeh lived, the bakery that kneaded a tale of transient love, and the sea which frightened her before ever it entered her dreams as a route to faraway worlds.

Had she not felt so apprehensive, so fearful for the baby inside, Milia would not have opposed the move to Jaffa as strenuously as this. True, she had formed a strong and intimate bond between her pregnancy and the place: it was partly Nazareth's sacred associations, partly those frequent dream-images of the blue woman, and partly the tang of discovering secret places that she savored in her meetings with Tanyous. But in the end, she knew, a woman must follow her husband to wherever it is that he wants her to go. Yet in Jaffa there was the fear, there were undertones of death, the faces of those blond men in the church. And there was the smell of oranges replete with intimations of dying. She wanted to tell Mansour the coffin dream in hopes it would deter him from the move. But the man no longer believed her dreams. She wrapped herself in her sadness, yielded to his fierce insistence, abided his anger, and lived her two final months of pregnancy more or less alone.

She saw Grandmama Hasiba in a dream. It happened in Nazareth. She saw Hasiba and there was the French officer standing to one side. His hands reached for the woman wrapped in black but the woman stayed where she was, standing at a distance, coming no nearer. Milia went up to the officer to tell him Hasiba had married and forgotten him. His beloved could not come to him now, anyway, because she lay in bed unable to move and incapable of speech. But the officer did not hear her, thought Milia, or perhaps he didn't understand the words she said to him. In Beirut, Milia had never dreamed about her grandmother or the French officer. What had brought the two of them to Nazareth? Milia had been convinced that the officer had never existed and was merely a story that Hasiba had concocted to justify her slowness to marry, her rejection of suitors, and her withdrawal into her own solitary world. Milia dreamed of herself as a small girl in her room in

Nazareth. The grandmother slept on Milia's bed and the girl gazed out of the window, seeing Ferdinand in the distance, his hands out, leaning forward and then falling, and she was afraid. Mansour was not there to protect her from the creatures of the night.

When they married, Mansour described Palestine to her as a land governed by curses and sin. The fault is God's, he said. No, he said. I'm wrong – and God forgive me if I've blasphemed. But human beings have never truly taken to heart the Almighty's proclamation that one city out of the thousands that exist would be His, and that one tiny region – no bigger than a grain of wheat – would be the territory of His only son. All the wars have erupted here, and they still do – ever since Akhenaten the Egyptian realized that there is only one God. All eyes were turned to the land of Canaan because it was God's land, and the wars began. Unending war, war after war. War will not stop until God decides either to let go of His city or to enter it. But this He will not do. Don't be afraid – I am with you and I will not allow anything to touch you or harm you. This land is going to know many more wars but we will live far away from war. No one will dare spark off a war in Nazareth. We will live in Nazareth and peace will shade our lives.

Milia did not believe this story of peace but the man enfolded her in his words. Listening to him, she felt as though he were bearing her aloft, taking her with him as the poems he recited floated in front of her eyes tantalizingly, bringing together the two of them in a land of enchantment crafted by the man's voice. She loved his voice, she told him, with its husky tinge evincing a brew of tobacco and coffee, its waves of tenderness swelling upward on the high seas of the ancient Arabic poetic meters, and its soft depth, which made her think of velvet. The voice carried her along, swimming through its worlds that drew her far away. And then suddenly she was discovering that this man concealed a momentous secret and had come to her to seek the refuge he believed she could provide. He promised her protection but in reality what he wanted was to travel inside the worlds she had made, so that he could skirt the dangers hovering darkly over Jaffa.

I am not objecting to going to Jaffa or anywhere else – wherever you want to go – but because of my pregnancy I cannot go right now.

Milia could appreciate the importance of keeping the iron foundry going in service to the city's defense – this little city on whose bowed shoulders was growing a new city trying to swallow up the old one. Tel Aviv was an attempt to legitimize the Jews' quest to occupy the whole country. She understood all of this. But she hated the violence and the blood and she was afraid for her son.

Had her grandfather not killed her father?

Why was she saying this when she knew full well that he hadn't killed his son?

But he intended to kill him, Saadeh told her daughter. If it had not been for God's mercy and the purity of his mother's heart, the boy would have departed this world.

Did the man kill his son, or at least throw stones at him, because he did not know who it was, as he claimed? Anyway, this was not so important. The real question was: what was Milia's link to her grandmother and to this foolish legendary tale that had transformed itself somehow into a memory wrapped in nebulous indistinct dreams? For after the death of Amin, the tale returned, as Jaffa's phantoms invaded and occupied Milia's life during the two final months of her pregnancy.

It doesn't matter to me, she had told him. Instead of Mansour returning from Jaffa the next day as he had promised her, he returned three days later. He said he had been forced to stay and could not find a way to get word to her. He read the doubt in her eyes, swallowed, and his voice stumbled as he said he had been forced.

It doesn't matter to me – just no more words, please.

She heard fragments of the words her mother-in-law had said to Mansour about his marriage. The mother had told him he would have been better off not rushing into marriage. What are we going to do with the woman and her children? his mother demanded to know. She realized then that her mother-in-law had wished Mansour could marry his brother's widow as customarily happened in the case of a brother's death. But it was not possible now, of course.

The die is cast, what's gone is past, murmured Milia, invoking her Lebanese idiom.

What are you saying? Mansour asked her.

I told you, it doesn't matter to me, you can go wherever you want to go but don't worry me like this. I am not my grandmama. I will not scream or yell or do anything. This child is enough for me.

No . . . Milia did not say these things. Nor did the mother-in-law wish out loud that her second son had remained single so that he could marry his brother's widow. No, it was simply that Milia imagined all of these possibilities as she waited for her absent husband. Coming in, he gave her a kiss and said he was tired and needed to sleep.

What I really wish is that I could fall asleep quickly and not wake up, he said.

May such an evil not happen! his wife replied. She bit her lower lip and sensed the taste of blood.

Milia turned restlessly in bed. She heard Mansour's voice but he seemed to be calling her from far away. She tried to open her eyes. Enough! she wanted to say as the glass bit her lips. She was sitting on the swing, the wind gusting around her. She was flying on a long wooden plank swing that was attached to the tree by two long ropes. She looked overhead and did not see the fig tree. Where was it? Here was a swing but no tree, and the garden looked more like the garden of her new home in Nazareth. Who had brought the swing here? She decided to get off and bring the thing to a standstill. She gripped the ropes tightly, rose on her delicate legs and bent her knees to give herself leverage. She paused, pulled herself forward, and flew. She sailed upward, where there was nothing but further upward. The sky was gray and overcast with fear. Her heart dropped. Searching, she saw nothing but a gray sky splotched with fog. Suddenly her fists relaxed on the cords and let go as if an outside force propelled her upward. Her body took the form of a crucifix, arms sticking out rigidly, fists finding nothing to grasp. She plummeted. She heard screaming and the tang of blood spread over her tongue.

She opened her eyes but found no one in the room with her. Her heart was fluttering and a ringing filled her ears. She decided to get out of bed and then discovered the pain that spread across her belly as it came and went in small waves, one lapping over the previous one. She chewed on her lips and wanted a drink of water but she did not find the glass of water next to her bed. She closed her eyes and saw him. Najib stood there, covered with dust. He came toward her and sat down next to her on the bed and wept.

Why are you crying? What did you come here to do? *Yallah!* Get up and go to your wife. I am here now, and that's the way it is, and you are there.

He put out his hand and took hers and in her fingertips she felt the man's heartbeat. She wanted to cry but she did not ask him why he had done what he had done. She did not say to him that her heart was broken. How could she explain to him that, yes, a heart can be broken, and then to repair it is more difficult than mending a shattered pane of glass. She said she had left her broken heart there in Beirut but here she had found a new heart. No, no, you cannot break more than one heart for me – God forbid! She withdrew her hand from his and opened her eyes to see Mansour drawing the blanket up to cover her.

When did you get here? she asked him.

Just now.

I'll set dinner out for you.

No, no, you must rest. I will go call for Nadra.

But Nadra died, said Milia.

Now there's a woman! her father, Yusuf, would exclaim.

Whenever Yusuf spotted Nadra in the short dress that showed off her full brown thighs, he would go completely still and stare, his eyes hungry. In her father Milia saw how a man's eyes could become tiny balls of fire, and how a man's body could become the enunciation of an inscrutable desire that possessed him. In the end Yusuf died in the hands of none other than the plump midwife whom he desired until the end of his life.

The man simply toppled to the ground and could not move. Nurse Nadra described how he fell and died, even though she was not there, and her story of his death became the story of his death. He had come home very tired, she said. No one else was there. The children were at school and Saadeh was at the church. The man had come home early with a stinging headache. He drank a glass of hot sweetened orange-blossom water – what the Beirutis call white coffee. He dragged himself into the *liwan*, where he collapsed and lost consciousness. The children came home to find their father crumpled up on the floor. Salim ran to Nadra's house and Niqula ran to the church. Nadra arrived before Saadeh did and she, Salim, and Niqula succeeded together in lifting Yusuf into bed. It was hemoplegia, she said, and there was no hope. When Saadeh arrived Nadra told her how the man had come home fatigued, drunk some white coffee, and then fell unconscious. Saadeh asked her eldest son to summon the doctor and Salim ran off while Niqula ran back to the church. Doctor and nun arrived together. The doctor examined Yusuf, felt for his pulse, took his blood pressure, and tried to awaken him but had no luck. He looked hard at Saadeh and then at the nun and said, Hemoplegia. *Inshallah* it won't go on for very long. Then he won't suffer and you won't suffer. The doctor left without taking his fee. The nun said she would bring the priest to their home to perform last rites. The house filled with the fragrance of incense. But the man did not die. For four days he lay in bed. Nadra came every morning, moistening her finger with water and putting it to his lips. On the fourth day when she arrived, Nadra said, It's over. And that is how he died.

He died on your finger, said Saadeh.

God be merciful to him and to us, said the nurse, weeping.

She loved him, said Saadeh.

No, that sort of woman doesn't even know what love means, snapped the nun. All these women know is this business.

Now what had brought Nadra here?

Milia told Musa she had begun to fear the midwife. Nadra brought death with her, said Milia to her brother.

Nadra carried a vesselful of water from which steam poured. She pushed up her sleeves and began to cough. Her cigarette end fell from her mouth into the basin and Milia heard the sound of it sizzling as it went out and the place filled with smoke.

I don't want to! she screamed, and opened her eyes.

She saw Mansour standing by her bed with his aunt. *Yallah*, my dear, we must get to the hospital. The aunt seized her hand firmly and helped her up.

Not today, said Milia. Let me go back to sleep.

Absolutely today, said the aunt.

What day of the month is it? asked Milia.

It's the twenty-first, said Mansour.

No, it won't be today, then. I am not having the baby today. The doctor said it would come during the night of the twenty-fourth.

Mansour dragged a small case into the room and asked his aunt to help in packing Milia's things. Milia stared at herself in the mirror. Her entire face was puffy and her usually pale cheeks were almost saffron. She saw black circles under her eyes. The stomach pains came again and she moaned. Mansour hurried over to her and helped her sit down on the edge of the bed. *Yallah*, we must go! he said, turning to his aunt, who seemed lost among drawerfuls of clothes. Aunt, we're not putting together a trousseau. Just a nightgown and two sets of things, that's enough. I can bring more if we need it.

Milia found herself in the car. Mansour sat next to the driver and she sat in the backseat next to his aunt. Passing through a narrow, choked street, the car turned right and began to climb the hill toward the Italian Hospital. A flash of light lit the sky and heavy rain began to fall. Shivering, Milia complained of the cold. The aunt removed her coat and covered Milia with it. The car seemed unable to mount the steep incline. It bellowed as if calling desperately for help and the tires spun, unable to gain purchase on the asphalt.

It's the tires, said the driver. Not catching the road.

The driver pulled up on the hand brake and put the car into low gear. He pressed the accelerator pedal to the floor and the car emitted a strange sound as though it were a wounded animal groaning. It started to climb, juddering violently.

What is it? asked Milia.

Nothing, said the driver.

When the car reached the top of the slope and began to slither over the puddles, the motor died and all they could hear was the patter of rain.

What do we do now? asked Mansour.

We can't do anything, said the driver.

Mansour opened the door and heard Milia scream, No, don't get out! He closed the car door and began to plead with the driver to do something. The woman will have her baby right here! Please, get us moving somehow. Both front doors opened and Mansour and the driver got out simultaneously. Milia saw the two men disappear behind the car trunk, which was now open. She turned to the aunt sitting next to her but the aunt was not there. She closed her eyes on the first streaks of darkness that were creeping in between the splashes of rain. She heard her father saying, Snow. It's starting to snow.

Where did you go, Mansour? she screamed. Mansour is not here and she is alone in the car wrapped in a brown overcoat, shivering with cold.

The two men returned to the car. The aunt's hand went to her brow as if she needed to check her body temperature. Mansour twisted around in his seat and asked her to hold herself together. She said she did not feel the pain anymore but she was afraid, seeing the thickness of the fog.

There's no fog, he said. But she saw fog and she saw the snow coming down hard and she saw a man in the distance carrying a tiny girl, running with her beneath the falling snow. What had brought her father here, into this storm? Why was he carrying her and running through the driving snow? Cradling his daughter, Yusuf was running to Dr. Naqfour's clinic. He had snatched her out of bed while the nun recited prayers over her and swung incense across her body. The nun told her to open her mouth and swallow the oil-imbued cotton. Yusuf snatched his daughter from the nun, wrapped her in their brown woolen blanket, and ran to the doctor's clinic. That year the snow came down hard in Beirut. Milia did not remember the snow, but she remembered the woolen blanket and her father's hard breathing. The girl was four years old. She remembered hearing crying around her bed and having the sensation of floating above her fiery body. Did she hear the word death? She did not know. No, perhaps not then, perhaps only later, when her grandmother told her the story and she sensed how close death had passed, in the form of a fever that consumed her tiny body for ten days. Malakeh said she was reassured when she awoke the feverish girl to ask what she was dreaming and Milia's reddened eyes opened to answer her grandmother that she wasn't dreaming. Malakeh was relieved because – as she said – death requires a long, long dream. She told her daughter Saadeh not to worry, and she went home.

No, Papa, I don't want to! shouted Milia trying to wriggle out of her father's grip. She waved her hands about and the blanket slipped down, snowflakes wetting her skin and causing her to shout as if the falling snow were stinging her. Papa, let's go back home! But Yusuf paid no attention. He ran on and on, tears streaming from his eyes. You are my darling, *ya habibti*, he babbled. He ran beneath the pounding snow until they reached an enormous black door. At his rapping the door opened. The snow stopped falling and darkness covered the girl's eyes. At that point memories snapped out like a light.

The driver lit a cigarette and began puffing nervously. No smoking, please! said Mansour. Can't you see the woman is pregnant and having difficulties? The driver opened the car window to toss the cigarette outside and the cold wind hurtling in flapped open the aunt's overcoat covering Milia. She whimpered, feeling the baby shiver in her belly. Sacred Virgin! she cried out. She heard the sound of the car engine starting up and found herself at the hospital entrance.

The Italian doctor who examined Milia said, No, nothing today, perhaps tomorrow. He asked Mansour to take his wife home and observe her condition. When the pains in her belly come one right after another, he said, and the pain is getting stronger, bring her back to the hospital. There's no need for her to be here right now.

Yes, that's right, she said, and stood up immediately. *Yallah*, home, she said to her husband, who could not believe his eyes, seeing how the thread of pain slid away from her eyes as if the doctor's words were a magic remedy that wiped the contractions from her pale face so that the black lines ringing her eyes vanished and the milky limpidity of her cheeks returned.

Yallah, home, she said, and walked out. The rain had stopped. Rays of sun cut through the gray cloud cover dusting the city.

Where're you going? Wait, I will call the driver.

No, I want to walk, she said, and walked on.

Is it all right for her to walk, doctor? asked Mansour. But the doctor had disappeared and there remained in the room only two nurses who looked exactly alike except that one was young and the other old, the first one lighter and the second one darker. Mansour assumed the paler one was Italian, so he tried to ask her the question in English. The nurse smiled and gestured to indicate that she did not understand anything that was being said. He turned to the dark one and asked her in Arabic. She smiled too, as if she too didn't understand, and raised her eyebrows to suggest that he would find an answer only upstairs. Mansour left the hospital to find that Milia was not outside. He stood in front of the Italian Hospital like a man lost before the city's many alleyways and twists, not knowing which way to turn in order to find his wife. He saw his aunt and the driver waiting for him in front of the American car. He got into the front passenger seat and asked his aunt to get into the back.

We want to go home, he said to the driver.

What about Milia? asked his aunt.

Later, said Mansour.

Milia walked on, as if the pain and the scene of her father carrying her in his arms as she begged him to put her down because she wanted to walk had generated in her a desire to find him now, to tell him she had reached the end of the road and was preparing to depart for a distant city.

Milia said she remembered the very first time she had walked. Her father was carrying her in his arms, she said, and she was crying. I started pulling and wriggling to get down but my papa didn't understand what I wanted. I heard my mama tell him to put me down. I didn't know how to speak but I did understand and I watched myself being lowered to the floor, on my belly. He thought I wanted to crawl but I grabbed on to a chair leg and pulled myself up, and began walking. Everything began turning around me and I heard my mother saying, The girl is walking! and she started ululating to let everyone know the happy news. And from that moment I never stopped walking. I was always walking round the house as if I had just discovered the world. It looks so different from above!

Do you really remember all of this? asked Mansour.

Of course I remember it all.

But a person doesn't remember anything that happened before the age of three.

Well, I do.

Fine, fine, he said, and didn't go on. Ever since the incident of the broken goblet, the expression *tayyib tayyib* had become his polite way of letting her know he believed she was lying. Listening to her stories, suddenly he would realize that his mind was incandescent with the thought that she was lying.

You're lying to me, Milia, he would say, his voice sweeping the specters of her words from his eyes as he gave her a tight smile. She would never answer. Milia had long been accustomed to these words, which her mother used to say, and which the nun said, and which her brothers said. Only Musa believed her – and believed in her. Once he told her he believed in her. No, she said. A person must not believe in people. A person believes only in God.

But my mama believes in the nun.

I don't like nuns at all.

But she is holy.

When had this conversation happened? Had Musa really said he believed in her, or was she confusing her dreams with what had truly happened?

She told Musa he didn't know her. No, she hadn't said that. She believed Musa had not really seen her, not the real Milia, not even once. How could he have seen her since he had not gone inside her dreams? He had never seen the tawny-skinned girl who ran through thorns and felt no pain. But on the day he brought the photograph home and hung it on the wall she felt afraid of the light that radiated outward from the eyes. He saw her then but did not really attend to the truth that the image on the wall revealed to him, without any effort on his part to seek it.

Why this photograph? she asked, stepping back. Take it away.

It's so you'll stay here with us, said Musa. When I miss you I know where to come to see you. When I'm longing for you I can say so to your face.

Milia walks alone, the baby nearly ready to emerge from her belly, sorrow encasing her, and fear. Nine months of fear, Milia told Tanyous. But whence had this strange obscure old man come, this figure who so resembled the prophets of old?

The goblet, Milia remembers. He had brought her a wineglass poured to the brim with a slightly yellowish liquid. No. . . he had not actually given her the glass. He left it on the windowsill. Milia had been alone in the house; Mansour was in Jaffa. She heard a knock at the window. She wrapped herself up hurriedly in the coverlet and told herself out loud that she would not open her eyes. Her fear of the dream mingled with her fear of the night. She squeezed her eyes even more tightly shut, turned onto her right side, and focused on the ringing in her ears. She went limp, acceding to the power of the ringing and her drowsiness. With that sound from outside she felt the baby churning in her womb, kicks battering her intestinal wall.

She opened the window to see him creeping among the trees. Amm Tanyous! she shouted. She wrapped her fingers around the glass set on the windowsill. The liquid inside was like gold. She brought the glass to her lips and drank a single drop, enough to send her into a floating reverie. She set the goblet down on the table next to the bed and fell immediately into a deep sleep.

How did the white wine turn into red wine by morning? And why had Mansour not seen the wine? Why this blood-red stain tinting her fingertips, which she couldn't remove with soap and water?

Tanyous was the sign. He was an old man: who knew how many years he had lived? He wore a black robe as monks did, and his beard was white and long and bushy. His eyes were sunk deeply into his face, sharp points of light, and his voice gurgled and rattled as if coming from deep in his belly.

He had never seen this man in his life, Mansour told her.

But he's a monk, said Milia.

A monk would not be wandering around the streets like this, said Mansour. I've never seen him, not even once, and my aunt, who has lived in these parts for twenty years, has never heard anyone speak of him. Anyway, there's no one from Beirut in this town. If Beirutis work around here, they're in Tiberias or Haifa. Enough, woman. Tomorrow or the next day, *inshallah*, you'll have your baby and that will be the end of these infernal dreams.

Mansour was convinced that the strange things his wife saw in her dreams were brought on by her pregnancy and her sense of loneliness. His mother had told him that when a woman gets pregnant she goes a bit eccentric. Some women even sleep all day long. Some eat dirt, and some . . . well, God help them! When she had been pregnant with him, his mother told Mansour, she couldn't stop eating tiny pickled lemons even though they turned her insides into flames.

No need to worry, son, she comforted him. These are just the symptoms of pregnancy. Even though Mansour was persuaded by his mother's view and held to his hope that after the birth Milia would stop her odd behaviors – no longer going out for her daily dreamlike wanderings through the town's alleyways – Mansour was certain that the true problem was Nazareth. It's an insane place, he said to his wife. He had discovered this truth the very moment they set foot in the new house. Something had shifted in Milia's gaze to the point where he could no longer read her feelings through the shadows hovering over her eyes. It's what love means, he had told her, trying to explain how he would know her feelings. I read your eyes and I know. Only the lover can read eyes. It is the sign of love, and it means I love you.

But I don't know how to read eyes, she answered. Does this mean you love me more than I love you?

Definitely, he said. Come on, now, look into my eyes and learn how to read them!

They were in the garden of the old house. Mansour put his hand out to take hers but she gave him no more than her fingertips, and her cheeks went red. She dropped her lashes. She said she was reading.

But your eyes are closed.

I read when they're closed.

Milia was not lying to Mansour. She read other people with her eyes closed. What baffled her, though, after they married, was that she never saw Mansour in her dreams. It had worried her at first; it felt as though she was being unfaithful to the man she had married. She didn't tell him this, although she felt guilty. Can a woman tell her husband she's betraying him? Of course he would react with anger – but only until he knew what this peculiar betrayal consisted of, and then he would laugh and say he knew all about it and had no need to hear her confession.

Milia did know somehow that the time when she would find Mansour inside her dreaming had not yet arrived. When Tanyous told her that he was waiting for her newborn to arrive before he could pass on, and that he had come to love her very much and wanted to take her with him, she felt the soles of her feet turn icy with fear.

No, she said. She did not want to go with him. What she wanted to do, she told him, was stay in Nazareth. After all, she was the daughter of a carpenter. She would open a shop for her son here so that he could learn the blessed Messiah's craft. The old man smiled. Her son, he said, would live in a faraway place, and she was consecrated to see what no one before her had seen. And she would discover who Mansour was all at once. For time has no meaning except for those who have not been granted the blessing of vision.

But I do know him – he is my husband.

No, no. You will come to know things about him that even he does not know, Tanyous replied.

But those things don't concern me, she said.

Everything in its time, the old monk answered her.

When she came to this town her first question had been about the location of the Messiah's home. And then Mansour saw everything in this woman change. Her eyes clouded over and seemed encircled by little halos that were nothing like the shadowy circles around her eyes that he used to notice in Beirut. He cursed the hour in which he had decided to make this town his home.

Mansour sensed Milia slipping from his hands into unknown territories. But he did not know how to follow her or how to take hold of her and bring her back. Her wanderings among the town's churches and her insistent search for the house in which the Messiah had lived frightened him.

No one knows the house, and anyway it might well be just a legend. Maybe he did not even live here. Or perhaps ancient Nazareth was not exactly where modern Nazareth is.

Since marrying, Mansour discovered, he had begun to loathe this land in which he lived. Can anyone truly live in a country saturated with legends and miracles and prophets? This is a country that drives anyone who lives here insane, he would think. A country means a country, and that should be that. A person cannot tread the same path as the saints; he will simply grow more and more terrified, afraid even of his own shadow. This woman has put fear into my heart. These strange dealings aren't for those of us here. They are for tourists and lunatic worshippers, the rest of us just live here as if there's nothing at all out of the ordinary.

But there is a lot out of the ordinary here, said Tanyous when she made him listen to what her husband had said.

Who was Tanyous, anyway? And what was this Lebanese story she had heard from him?

When she told her husband that the people who founded the modern city of Nazareth were Lebanese sent by Emir Fakhreddin in the sixteenth century to work as sharecroppers in the lands belonging to the Franciscan monastery, and that those monks were the first to build anything here, over what was at the time merely some empty ground and ruins, he laughed at her.

Lebanese, hah! No one here was Lebanese, or non-Lebanese, for that matter. *Lebanese* didn't exist. It was all the Syrian lands. God's mercy on your soul, King Faisal! He reminded her of the portrait of the king's slight figure in the Hotel Massabki. He began to describe the Battle of Maysalun and how Yusuf el-Azmeh the Syrian minister of defense had died hugging his rifle to his chest as he tried single-handedly to block the French army's advance on Damascus. And . . . and . . . and . . .

But I'm not talking about politics, she said. I'm telling you that half the people of Nazareth are Lebanese – Maronites and Catholics, whom Emir Fakhreddin sent to work with the monks, and then a little later came the Greeks from the Houran region and the area around Ramallah Town. Everyone who came looked and looked for that house but they could not find anything. The only one who knows the location of the house is Brother Tanyous.

Who told you these silly tales?

Brother Tanyous.

Where does this brother come from, anyway? I've never seen him, not even once. No one in this town has seen him.

I've seen him.

When Mansour Hourani came to live in Nazareth it never occurred to him to think that he was coming to the city of the Messiah. The people of Nazareth had marked out their distinction – from very beginning of the holy narrative – by calling themselves *Nasrawiyyin*, Nazarenes, rather than by the plural noun *Nassara* by which the Qur'an would refer to all of the followers of Jesus the Nazarene. They were Nazareth natives, and they wanted that to be clear. Now where had this woman with her religious tall tales come from, making his life hell?

Of course, Mansour had been introduced to the religious atmosphere governing the Shahin family home in Beirut, but he had not grasped its seriousness; indeed, he did not take it seriously at all. He attributed it to Saadeh's hysteria, which he had heard about from Milia. He explained the mother's religiosity and her almost childish dependence on the nun as a symptom of menopause, which always made women go a bit crazy when their menses ended and they had to endure the bouts of heat rising from the depths of their dessicated wombs. Saadeh's state was better than his mother's, he told Milia. Saadeh released her tensions by kissing icons and swallowing cotton balls dipped in holy oil. His mother vented hers in an increasingly demented state of tyranny over the foundry and her sons. Because she could see to repairing a few rusty guns, she believed herself to be more important than even Haajj Amin el-Husayni! But now what was happening? Why did he feel that the ghost of the saintly nun was living with him right here in this house? How had this man called Tanyous – who claimed to be of Lebanese origin and who had told Mansour's wife that his ancestors came from the village of Beiteddin in the Shouf to work as farmers with the French monks – managed to become such a haunting presence, hovering constantly over his wife's existence and his own?

You want to flee from Nazareth, Milia said. But I want to stay here. I don't know why you're so determined. Your work is going well, *alhamdulillah*, and your mother can manage her own business. Didn't you tell me that your mother prefers to run things herself? I get the feeling you are fleeing something and I don't know what it is. Maybe you're right, maybe it is some sort of vision. That was what Yusuf did, after all. He escaped, leaving here to go to Egypt, and he was right, too.

Yusuf who?

Yusuf the Carpenter.

So now this – where do you get this from?

This – he was the Messiah's father.

You're talking about Saint Yusuf as if he's some friend of ours! I never did like Yusuf the Carpenter – he was just a man whose wife cheated on him and he put up with it. Anyway, all the prophets loved women, from Ibrahim to Nuh to Daoud and all the rest. Adam – now tell me why Adam was thrown out of paradise, wasn't it because of the Tree of Knowledge? And what do you think *knowledge* is? It's Eve – in other words, it is fu –

Don't say that word!

Don't act so clueless.

But Mar Yusuf wasn't like you say he was. He saw the angel in his dream, and the dream told him everything.

So now we're back with the dreams! Milia, my dearest love, I don't have anything against Mar Yusuf, but tell me now, how could he have gone along with it?

Gone along with what?

Being told he was the father of the boy when he knew he was not, and no one knew who the true father was.

Because he was a saint. He was Mar Yusuf.

May God feed us saintliness!

You mean, you would not have accepted it?

Of course not! The boy would either be my son or he wouldn't be. Stay away from these stories – they make one start thinking like a blasphemer.

How had the old man believed the story his young wife told him? Was it she who told him the story or did the angel come to him in the dream as the Gospels say? How could a person believe his dreams like that?

That's the way of all prophets, said the saintly nun. But of course it could be the Devil, too. Saying this, Sister Milana began to mutter her prayers rapidly and Saadeh pressed little Milia's brow with a handkerchief dipped in cold water. Milia did not remember the story but she had not forgotten the dream.

Whenever the mother told the story to her daughter Milia felt estranged from herself. She was ten when she came down with the fever for the second time. Everyone, including the nun, was convinced that the girl would die. The doctor came and said that the only hope he held out for her was in God. To Saadeh, God meant one thing, and that was the nun. Saadeh ran head-long to the Convent of the Archangel Mikhail and tugged at the hem of the nun's long habit. But the nun did not turn to her, because she was praying.

When Milana stands behind the open Triodion and begins to recite the prayers and invocations in the book, particularly at Vespers as she prays in the twilight, melancholy descends on all who are gathered in the church; they are overcome by a sense of humility and submission almost like a trance. The voice of the nun is like a rocker cradling the ears of the worshippers, like gentle hands drawing the listeners onto the twisting paths of the cosmos. They listen to strange voices and they see how the bodies of the saints are etched delicately on these Byzantine icons as though with a feather. Sister Milana does not permit the use of electricity in church. This threw her into an ongoing, never-resolved argument with Father Gerasimos, who insisted that the nuns turn on the electric chandeliers when they performed their collective prayers. The saintly nun thought this heretical, for she believed that the angels do not like electricity and that their own light was more than sufficient. But our master the bishop insisted on his version of things. He made fun of the nun's silly tales and mocked her claim to sanctity. He ridiculed her in front of the nuns and her throng of adherents.

Well, no – it was not the electricity that led to their difference. Milana found a solution to that problem when she ordered the nuns to close their eyes whenever the electricity came on. We will close our eyes and so will the angels, she assured them. Nothing will change.

The real issue was that woman of devilish beauty called Marika Spyridon.

Marika – here was the story that gave rise to so much gossip in Beirut in those days; it caused quite an uproar, in fact. Had she been the lover of the bishop as was whispered around? Or was she a modern version of Saint Maryam of Egypt, who had begun her life as a prostitute before repenting at the hands of the great Saint Anthony? She came to the church every Sunday morning in the company of three Greek women. They came for mass and then returned to the street of sin, which had come to be known as Mutanabbi Street, where they resumed their usual business.

What sent the nun's ire soaring was not this fact which everyone knew – for God alone knows what is in our hearts and He is the Reckoner, as she would always remark whenever asked about the goddamned whore who followed Monsignor and donated regularly and frequently to the church and bought the most enormous chandelier in Beirut to give to the Church of Mar Girgis. The sainted nun did not allow anyone to use the word *whore* in her hearing. She preferred to use the term *daughter of sin* as she prayed to God to cast His protective veil over all of His servants. But now things had gone too far and she could endure no more. It was said (and God alone knows) that Monsignor had gotten the authorities to issue extraordinary permission for Marika and her girls to circulate freely in Beirut on Sundays, even though such had been prohibited ever since promulgation of the Ottoman decree prohibiting prostitutes to leave the vicinity of the main *souq*. It seems that the governor of Beirut (appointed by the French mandatory authorities, and a scion of the Greek Orthodox Boustrus family) granted this, perhaps being of the same mind as the bishop. Maybe he was a customer of the lady's. In any case, the special dispensation made it possible for Marika to attend any of the churches where the bishop conducted mass on Sundays. It was true that His Eminence Gerasimos held mass most Sundays in the Cathedral of Mar Girgis, where Marika could go anyway since it abutted on the market area. But to fulfill his pastoral duties he also conducted mass in churches throughout the city, from Museitbah to Ashrafiyya, Mazraa and Ras Beirut. And now, on Sundays, no longer did Marika have to distance herself from the bishop. And that is why the saintly nun could not but see this woman of the Devil who caused Milana to lose her equilibrium and, in front of a whole crowd of people, to say the word she had barred everyone else from using.

Monsignor is coming and he's bringing the whore with him! I will not attend mass today, she said to the nuns, stalking out of the church sanctuary and into her cell.

What exactly transpired, though, when the bishop entered that cell and ordered Milana to come down to church? No one knows. But plenty of people were there to witness as Marika knelt before the nun, and as the nun did the same, matching the Greek woman gesture for gesture, and as the nun wept loud enough for all to hear, throughout the entire mass.

The story would be told forty years later but no one dared to publish it in a newspaper. Iskandar Shahin, eldest son of Musa Shahin, afflicted with the wretched mania of literary ambition, got a job at the famous newspaper *el-Ahrar*, founded by a group of men led by Said el-Sabbagheh. They wanted to found a newspaper that would circulate the ideas of the Freemasons, who had instigated an active movement throughout the Syrian lands, including Lebanon, drawing adherents with their calls for secularism and lashing out with bitter humor at the region's men of religion.

Iskandar stumbled on an extraordinary journalistic coup. By coincidence he got to know an old woman who lived in the neighborhood of Furn el-Shabbak, adjacent to the Church of Mar Ilyas, and was treated with particular fondness by the priest Samir Abu Hanna. The young, twentyish aspiring journalist was always stopping by at the priest's home, for he was in love with his only daughter, Futin, who would reject his love and turn his heart to ashes when she decided to follow her vocation as a nun. That is another story, though. This old woman, the young man discovered, was none other than Marika Spyridon, the mistress of the market, who spent her last days in prayer and repentance.

When the young man visited the elderly woman armed with information on her relationship with Bishop Gerasimos, given him by Monsieur Said el-Sabbagheh, he found himself confronting the story of his paternal aunt Milia. He heard interminable details he could not believe, about the nun's miracle in rescuing Milia when she was at death's door at the age of ten.

Marika was not stingy with details. She told the young man everything he wanted. Her relationship with the bishop, she said, was not like any relationship she had ever had with any other man.

I am a Greek, she said. We are a people who are everywhere. The Spyridon family is Greek through and through, with our origins in Istanbul. I did not choose my line of work – it is something I inherited. My mother was in the same profession, and so were my grandmother and my grandmother's mother. In those days it was not a big issue. My mother married like any woman anywhere in the world would. I don't know what's gone wrong, why people think the way they do, how *whores* have become outcasts. Son, if only you knew what I have been through and what I've done! If it were not for us, how would there be so many healthy families in the world? You must know that men are dogs, they cannot do anything to fight it – that's how God created them, after all. Adam, peace be upon him, betrayed his wife, Eve, even though there were absolutely no other women in existence! Don't ask me how he managed it or what he did. Ask His Eminence the Bishop, he's the one who told me. Actually, who sent you to me, son?

He told her about Monsieur Said and she collapsed in a fit of laughter. Said! That's Neama's son. God be generous to him – such a bighearted man but he was a such a coward, too! I was something like forty-five years old when I took his virginity. You think it's just women who are deflowered, as they say? No, honey! It's young men just as much. God, how can I describe it so you'll understand. First time and he went completely mad. When it's a young fellow's first time he only needs a little push and I gave him that – I was very fond of that boy! But he would finish too fast. I'd say, no – the first is for the Devil, come on, now, try again – and the second the same – too bad, he didn't get it. Such a nice boy, from a good family I think, and the third time he did it like a man, and I said to him, you're there, you know now – and come back anytime. I'll tell you, I felt like I'd never felt before, maybe because he was so young and it was his first time. Why are you laughing? Yes, I can say *virgin* of a man. Ahh! It doesn't usually happen to me. And yes, it was the same with His Eminence. God's mercy upon him, he would exhaust me. He was old, at least sixty-five, long white beard – you know the sort. Maybe he was shy, I don't know. He would never take off his clothes. I would always say fine, and take mine off and come to him, but he could never get it up, and he would blush to the ends of his white beard, as red as a tomato, and would say, It's my medications. And I'd say, Forget those medications and your babbling, I'm Marika, sir – and I'd throw myself on him, and I'd get his clothes off and I'd get to work. Don't ask me what I did – I tried every trick in the book, and he started moving. I'd hear him shout, Hallelujah! I would tell him to lower his voice – Sir, we're in a cell and there are people close by – but he didn't care, and he began calling me Marika the Marvelous. No, I wasn't in love with him but I had a lot of sympathy. And that's one way to love. How love happens is a secret, and there are a million ways to get there. If someone tells you they know what love is, you can be certain they don't know what they're talking about. No one can know what happens between women and men – and between men and men, and women and women. When Sister Milana knelt down in front of me in the church and then I knelt down, I felt the strangeness of it! Oh God, Satan be cursed! I didn't like it, but that woman was a true saint, son, I don't want to make too much of it but I know what she did with your mama Milia, when she was little, and that was enough to convince me.

Milia was my aunt, she wasn't my mama.

Your aunt, your mama, whatever. Where were we? Yes, we were with the bishop. So with a lot of hard work he got to be a man, and like men he would pounce on me with his hallelujahs something fearful. No, he really frightened me. He called me his *dinner table* and he devoured me. What can I tell you, he smelled like incense and a little honey and he thought he was God. That's how he acted, and anyway he was a big man and I was like you see me now, thin, but when I'd undress he would stagger back and ask me where I could hide all of this? My thighs are full but that doesn't show under my dress. Maybe it was because I was afraid of him. No, I wasn't – I was afraid for him and maybe that is why I felt so good with him. I went to him to confess; I knelt on the ground. He covered my head. I talked. I had never gone to give confession before. At Easter I went to church, but I was there with everyone; the priest would raise his hand and just bless us all at once. I don't know what came over me on this day; I went very early, at dawn. I went straight to the bishop's seat. He put his hand out thinking perhaps that I wanted to kiss it as worshippers do. I took his hand and kissed it. And then I came right to him and whispered that I wanted to confess. He gave me a very strange and full look, and I understood. I heard how his voice trembled as he said, You! He asked me to kneel to the left of the altar – and, well, then it went from there.

Iskandar Shahin wrote down everything Marika said about the bishop and Said el-Sabbagheh (with a judicious change of names, of course) and about the sainted nun who cured diseases, and how Marika had become infatuated with the nun and the bishop had gone over the edge and ordered Milana's banishment to a remote convent away in Koura. And there in a half-savage place the nun had transformed herself into the patroness saint of the village of Bkeftayn. At first she had lived alone; and then three nuns from the Convent of the Archangel Mikhail joined her so that they could serve her needs. There the nun lost her sight and her miraculous powers began to show themselves. When she prayed the vapor of incense came from her mouth. She no longer had any need for cotton dipped in blessed oil to cure the sick, for the touch of her hand was enough to conjure the oil's healing aroma and expel the demons from the invalids, as much as those devils shrieked in anger. In her final days, her miracles doubled. Though nearly paralyzed, she would move from one corner to another in the convent without need of anyone's help. Three days before her death she agreed to accept the repentance of Bishop Gerasimos, who came to her in tears, seeking forgiveness and asking her to absolve him of his sins.

Marika told the young man that his grandmother Saadeh had gone faithfully to visit the nun in the Convent of Mar Yuhanna the Baptist in the village of Bkeftayn in the Koura region on a regular basis until her death. These visits were Saadeh's sole consolation as she faced the calamity that had befallen the family.

Iskandar was stunned when Monsieur Said el-Sabbagheh took his article, slid it into a desk drawer, and said to the young journalist that he respected the immense effort he had made in writing his fine piece but that he would not be able to publish it since that would sully the memory of the bishop and thus might encourage sectarian rifts in a country like Lebanon. When Iskandar asked later to have the manuscript back he found out that that Monsieur Said had lost it – or that is what the editor claimed. So all that remained of Marika's story was the echo of her name in people's memories, whipping up desires and pleasant images of the past, especially in the bewitching relationship the memory of her created between the letters *kaf* and *alif* at the end of her name, so far apart in the alphabet but collapsing into each other when written together. Between them they could gesture to desires repressed inside and offer through their linguistic embrace a stark and lovely image of how disconnected forms might intertwine to love one another.

When the young man asked his father, Musa, about his aunt Milia and the stories of the nun and the bishop, tears sprang from the elderly father's eyes. The dark-skinned old man, whose head was covered in the whiteness of old age, did not utter a word. Perhaps he had not heard his son's question? But no – for his tears poured silently and his voice choked when he heard his sister's name.

Saadeh gripped the hem of the nun's robe as the saint prayed to the evening light. O Mother of God, Saadeh shrieked, deliver us! It's Milia, O Mother of Light, please! Milia is dying.

The nun turned toward the source of the voice. She yanked the hem of her garment from Saadeh's clutch and told her to go home. Milia's time has not come yet, she declared. Woe is you, Saadeh, when the hour does come. Go home and I will come soon, and *inshallah* there is no cause for worry.

The nun's words could be trusted. Milia crossed over the valley of death borne on that strange dream carved into her heart. Milia forgot the days she passed through, so ill that her mother and the neighbor women gathered around her bed weeping for the girl who was dying. She forgot the delirious words and the body that vanished to nothing and seemed a mere apparition. But the dream by which death passed her by remained suspended in her memory as though she had dreamt it only yesterday or had seen it times without number. This was the dream that now rose before her eyes as she listened to Mansour talking about Yusuf the Carpenter. Perhaps Mansour was right. This hallowed man who gave the Messiah his royal lineage – the line of King Daoud – had been marginalized completely by the Catholic Church. He had no feast day of his own, no miracles ascribed to him, and even the date of his death remains unknown. Did he die before the Messiah was crucified, and if so, when? If he died after the crucifixion, then why was he not there with Maryam beneath the cross? It was as though he were a mere implement – and a marginal one, at that – of the divine will. He was not a prophet or a true saint, but all the same Milia loved him because he had fled with his son to Egypt when he sensed danger, and he refused to sacrifice his son as Ibrahim had done – may peace be upon that holy man's name. Most likely, had Yusuf the Carpenter been alive, he would have prevented Jesus from entering Jerusalem on the back of a donkey and announcing himself king, in that escapade that led him to the cross.

She found herself in a place she did not know, and alone, lying on her back in a meadow of green grass. When she conjured up the memory of this dream she did not see her own image in it. Probably she did not recognize herself in that little girl's shape, even though when she saw the little girl in her dreams, Milia did believe the figure was her. It was only in this odd dream that she saw everything else, but without seeing herself. Perhaps this was why she was so terrified, why she screamed and raved, causing the women clustered around her bed to believe that these were the girl's death agonies and that she was seeing the phantoms of the world of the dead, covered in soil. Milia screamed out that it was soil. She would not remember her scream or her fear; she remembered only that child covered in dirt who lay by her side. Her lips were cracked with thirst and the grass that had gone yellowish crept over her eyes. Grass began to grow all over her. The baby needed water, she cried. And suddenly here was that man. Who was this man wearing an overcoat, jumping over Milia to pick up the child and throw him into the flames?

Why did you kill him? she wanted to scream, but her voice wasn't there. The fire swallowed the mother's voice before it consumed the baby boy's body.

She saw herself flying without wings. She was on a rocky incline leading down steeply to a crevice-like valley filled with dry brush, brambles, and squat shrubs. She could see the man below, holding the baby before tossing him into the wadi. The child stretched out his arms like wings to become like a bird, but bird feathers did not sprout. Where are his feathers? screamed Milia.

She stands at the summit. The heat stifles her and the smell of fires whirls around her. She wants to hold on to something and, seeing a rope, grabs it, but it turns out to be nothing more than a dessicated woody stem and it crumbles in her hand. She sees herself pitch forward into the very pit of the ravine and she sees the child open his crushed splintered arms as if he is awaiting her. She screams.

At that instant Milia opened her eyes to see the nun embracing her and patting her dessicated hair gently and requesting the mother who hovered there to bring a glass of water for her daughter.

The girl is cured, with God's leave, the nun said. To the women who stood there, stunned, she said, Bring her a glass of water and make her some lemonade. Keep her on liquids for three days and you'll see her back to normal.

The nun's miracle, as she stretched out her arms and rescued Milia from falling into the valley, was the last thing the nun did for the girl's sake. I saw her, the nun would say later. She was falling. I interrupted my prayers and ran to you at home and if it were not for God's mercy, I might not have gotten there in time. I reached for her, and as I held her she opened her eyes and was pulled from death. It is the second time. The first was when she came into the world. I ran to you and I pulled her from the womb. The womb stands in for the grave. When one is born, one is simply practicing for rebirth; when one is baptized, submerged in water from head to heels, it is a watery burial which allows the old person to die so that the new one may rise. I heard the voice of Mar Ilyas the Ever-Living. I was standing and praying and suddenly I heard a voice coming out of the icon. It was Mar Ilyas perched in a chariot of fire circling in the sky. He said to me, Run, Milana, run to the home of Saadeh and pick up the girl before she falls into the valley! And tell her mother that this is the last time. For when the third time comes, you will not be here nor will she. There will be no one to intercede for her except the son.

Had the nun said these words? Did she say them after hearing Saadeh relate her daughter's dream?

The nun is a liar, said Milia to her mother. I don't believe a word of this. She was just sitting next to me and she heard me say, I am falling! And then I woke up because it was my heart that fell. When you fall, your heart falls first of all. I told her it was my heart that fell because I was falling in the valley, and then she made up the whole thing. Anyway, who said the womb is a tomb? This is unbelief. Heresy. Your friend the nun hates me. Mama, didn't she say that my dreams come from Satan? And that I must come to church with you and pray until I could forget my dreams?

Milia did not forget her dreams. But she did forget the nun's warning that there would be no intercessor for her but this baby son. And now today here was this man who had become her husband cursing the monk who had recounted Nazareth's stories and had led her to the ruins at the Church of the Annunciation, getting her to bow almost to the ground before entering because that man of pure goodness had lived with his mother and father in this secret place that no human foot had trod. Here he learned how to walk and here happened the vision that announced him as God's only son.

He led her toward the dry dead trunk of an ancient olive tree. It had dried up, he told her, after the Romans had imprisoned Yusuf the Carpenter. It seems the man disappeared and was killed before his son was crucified – perhaps a decade before. Had he remained alive, surely he would never have allowed the crucifixion of his son.

Here beneath this tree, at the age of twelve, that vision came to the Messiah telling him he was God's only son. How could a child take in the meaning of the angel's words, heard in a dream? Lying beneath this tree he heard a fluttering of wings and saw a six-winged angel whose blinding whiteness drove his sight from him. He heard a voice saying he was the awaited Messiah and that since the beginning of time God had chosen him as a son to bestow upon him the throne of his ancestor David and to make him eternal king.

The child awoke in a state of fear and thirst; for three days he remained utterly without speech. He seemed completely aghast and confused, drinking water obsessively without assuaging his thirst. His mother suspected that a vision had overpowered her son. She remembered how Zakariya had gone dumb when the angel told him the news of his wife's pregnancy; but to her husband she said nothing. For, ever since the journey to Egypt, and indeed ever since her pregnancy and her repeated attempts to tell her husband the truth, she had lived with this man in silence. Whenever she opened her mouth to tell him, he would stop her with a wave of his hand and a shake of his head as if to say that there was no need for words, for he knew everything already. When he returned home from the olive tree with his son, she tried to talk with him but he averted his face. She went to her son to ask what had transpired there but all he would say to her was, Get away from me, woman! The Gospels erred, saying that he upbraided his mother at the wedding at Qana in Galilee, the site of his first miracle, when he turned the water into wine. To the contrary, in Qana he kissed his mother's hand and embraced her before embarking on the miracle, for he knew that the hour to make himself known had arrived. But coming home from the olive tree in fear, he did not relish speaking to this woman who had suppressed the secret of her son from that son himself.

He had accompanied Yusuf the Carpenter to the olive tree and there he had told him of the vision that came to him in his sleep. The aged father cried like a child, took his son in his arms and kissed him, and told him that only now could he walk with his head held high. Only now did he know that his dreams had not been mere delusions, and that God had put him through a trial that none of the prophets had experienced. God tested his dignity as a man and for twelve years he had waited steadfastly for this blessed moment. Yusuf prostrated himself and asked his son to kneel beside him. Blessed be the beast You sent, O God, he murmured. For You have allowed me to avoid the trial of Ibrahim, prepared to slay his son for the sake of Your holy name. Blessed be You, O God of Ibrahim and Ishaq and Yaqub, for this is my son who will become king in Your eyes, and will bear Your name and will be holy for ever and ever. Blessed are you, God of all creatures, for You have made me Your partner in the fathering of this child. From this moment I am the brother of the Lord and I will sit in the embrace of Ibrahim, Your faithful friend and dear companion.

The old monk told Milia that his priestly grandfather had owned a secret manuscript filched from the Italian Abbot Bougi, Father Superior of the Franciscan monastery, which told the full story of Yusuf the Carpenter. He told her of the existence of an underground sect that sanctified this man whom they considered the avatar of the Prophet Ilyas the Ever-Living. God had elevated Yusuf to His holy presence ten years before his son died on the cross.

Yusuf the Carpenter, asserted the old monk, had been erased from the story because the Apostle Paul, who had written it down, did not understand the relationship between father and son, and did not understand Yusuf's weeping as he was borne heavenward, for he saw with his own eyes what would happen to his only son.

Tanyous took her to every quarter in Nazareth Town. He drew a line separating Nazareth of the Messiah from Nazareth of the Franciscans who had founded the city in the sixteenth century. He narrated stories from his near ancestor who had possessed the strange and astounding manuscript that revealed the secret of Yusuf the Carpenter.

You read the manuscript? she asked him.

No. The manuscript is written in Syriac, and I don't know Syriac, but my grandfather spoke and read the language of the Messiah, and he told me everything.

So why did your grandfather abandon the Latin rites for the Greek?

Because he fell in love with a woman from the Houran region. He discovered that God reveals His truths only through love. When he went to the abbot and told him this, the fellow went mad with anger and began cursing women. He forced my grandfather to spend a month in detention, that he be purified of sin. But my grandfather did not sin. All he did was to see the girl by the spring across from the monastery gates and his heart was stolen. He could no longer think about anything else. He went to the Father to seek his advice and the response he got was imprisonment, torture, and flagellation. In that cell of imprisonment, he heard the voice of the angel and Mar Yusuf appeared to him. At first he thought it was Yusuf son of Yaqub, the handsome youth whom his brothers tried to kill and with whom every woman fell in love at first sight. This is God guiding me, he told himself. He knelt before Mar Yusuf to ask his pardon for the sin he had committed in his heart and mind, and he heard the saint whisper. The saint told him of the manuscript in the abbot's treasury. If he read the manuscript, he would understand all.

A month later my grandfather came out of the detention cell and found a way to steal the manuscript. In that hour the truth was revealed to him. He decided to abandon his monastic habit and marry. He became Greek Orthodox.

But Mar Yusuf wasn't –

What are you getting at? You can't believe those outrageous tall tales certain repressed men of religion have invented! Hah – Mar Yusuf was impotent, because he had some sort of accident in his carpenter shop and lost his manhood? It's a bunch of nonsense, there's not a single saint who couldn't perform, especially not the Messiah, glory be to him. Beware of this sort of stuff, my girl. Remember, the fellow was a widow and had five children. The story of his marriage to our Lady Maryam is beyond belief! Listen, my dear, listen.

The old man began to recite as though he read a text in front of him: Maryam was the daughter of Joachim and Hannah and had been consecrated to temple service since birth. She lived in piety, sewing the porphyry tent and performing her devotions. She grew in stature and grace. When she reached puberty the temple Elders deliberated, settling on the view that she must leave the temple and marry. Among the men of the temple was an old and pious man named Yusuf and called the Carpenter. Yusuf proposed to the men gathered in the temple that they pray to God and ask for a sign from Him. Emerging in the evening to take their canes from in front of the entrance, they saw that out of Yusuf's cane had grown a lavender bloom. In unison they proclaimed, Him!

Me? said Yusuf, startled. How can I take this young virgin girl? How can I marry her when she is the age of my children and I am an old widower living my final days? He is wise who knows that a human's life wilts like the flowers in the field, and the body dissolves into dust. Life is naught but the losses that follow upon one another as we await the great and final loss.

But seeing the cane's miraculous flowering, the wise men of the temple would not rescind their words. So Yusuf took the woman and was betrothed to her. Before he consummated the marriage he discovered that she was pregnant and he broke down in tears. And then – well, I have told you the rest of the story.

What does porphyry mean? Milia asked.

Red, the monk said.

But why do you talk as if you are reading, you told me the book was in Syriac, so how could you memorize it in Arabic?

Instead of fingering his beard, eyes shut, before responding, he gave her a long and direct look. Blessed is the one who believes without seeing. Milia, I am afraid for you. Come with me, I am counting the days, waiting for you. I shall take you by the hand and you will cross that valley and no harm shall come to you. What do you say?

Before she could say anything the man vanished from sight as if lifted by a cloud of dust that whirled him away.

Milia told the Italian doctor she was afraid. The elderly man in a white medical coat was bent over between Milia's legs that were held high on a medical bed where the nurse had ordered her to lie down. The doctor went out of the room and the woman was alone. The pain seemed to have lessened to the point of vanishing and she breathed deeply, as though she was no longer pregnant. Her light spirit returned to her and the black shadows faded from her eyes. She had just let her eyelids drop and was sinking into a doze when she saw him. But how had the monk gotten into the hospital room?

He was covered in dust as though he had just now arrived from a distant place. He came up to her holding an incense burner on a long chain that gave off a white smoke thick and acrid enough to blind one. Behind the smoke she could make out the shape of a little girl shimmying up through the air and dissolving into the whiteness. No, this is not my daughter, she said. I am going to have a boy, not a girl. But then she realized that the girl she saw there was herself. *Ya Latif*, Merciful God, this is not easy! Giving birth, O Mother of Light – now I understand how you suffered. A woman no longer knows herself. The girl dwindled to nothing inside the smoke and the white cloud of incense grew more opaque and only the old monk stood there now.

Get away from me, please go away! Allah *yikhalliik*. I want to have the baby now, I beg you. You should not be here.

She heard a voice coming out of the smoke.

O Virgin, please, I beg of you, tell him it's enough.

But he went on with his words. The Blessed Virgin refused to intervene and Milia was left to her fate. She heard the story. This was not the first time she had listened to this story. Who had told her the story of Eve? She remembered scoffing at it but she no longer remembered when or where that had been. Yes – oh yes, Sister Milana. What brought her here, and why did the beggar monk appear to have taken on her image?

Was it? No. It could not be. But he was a beggar. The first time she saw him he left the goblet on her windowsill and vanished. But on the many occasions since then when they had met, she had fed him and given him coins – after all, he was only a beggar who claimed to be Lebanese so that he would have an excuse to approach her.

Go, please! Now! I will see you after I have had the baby and I will cook some truly delicious food for you. But I want to be by myself right now.

Her husband had been convinced that he was nothing but a swindler who was hoodwinking Milia in order to get her money. No one in Nazareth had heard of a monk of Lebanese origin calling himself Tanyous who lived alone in the city. Woman, use your brain, there's no monastery for the Greek Orthodox in this area! There is the Muscovite monastery but the monks there are all Russians. How could this be – a monk living alone who knows where the Messiah's home is? Take me to that house and I'll strike it rich – it would be the most visited tourist site in the entire world. Come on, *yallah*! Show me where the house is.

She wanted to tell him that it was a secret the monk had trusted her to keep, and she couldn't reveal it to anyone at all. But she found herself walking through the narrow lanes in search of the olive tree and the adjacent ruins. She didn't find either one. And where was Mansour? They had left the house together but now he had vanished and she was walking alone, stumbling as she searched for the dead olive-tree trunk where she would rest her tired head. But she had lost the place.

Milana told her that Yusuf the Carpenter had been stunned by how quickly the midwife was there, and how quickly she worked in that tiny shelter they had stumbled on in Bethlehem. The woman whom Yusuf found at the door was waiting for him, the nun explained. She knelt beneath Maryam and put out her hand, and the baby boy simply came out seconds later. The Blessed Virgin did suffer pain, added the nun, for no woman could give birth without pain – and that was because of Eve's original sin. But the pain was light, hardly worth a mention. For the newborn was not the son of sin. He was the new Adam, who had not been cast out of paradise. That was why the old Eve had to come and kneel before the new Eve – our Lady Maryam was the new Eve – to whom all of God's creation prostrated. When the boy spoke in the cradle he gave thanks to the midwife who pulled him from the belly of his mother and he called her Eve. Maryam heard him say the name but did not dare repeat it to her husband. She was afraid he would believe she was raving, or simply he would not believe her. She told him of her vision but the man frowned and would not allow her to finish the story, insinuating that he knew it all already. But in fact he did not know anything, and he would not know anything until the boy recounted his dream and the elderly father threw himself flat on the ground. He prostrated himself before his wife the Virgin, whom he had not come near because he had doubted her fidelity to him. He would come to her as a husband comes to his wife but only after time had passed, only when age had erased those carnal desires, replacing them with a gentle affection and a tender hand.

This is not how the nun told the story, however. What she said was that when she came running to the home of the Shahin family she saw the yellow hues smothering Saadeh and ordered the midwife to pull the baby girl from her mother's belly immediately. In that moment she saw two women, the first bending over and drawing the child from its mother's body while the second woman stood next to her, a shape draped entirely in purple and blue. She was the ancient Eve, the figure said, and from that blessed moment she had been the intercessor of midwives; indeed, she was the midwife whom the Holy Spirit sends to save women from dying in childbirth. Milana said that when she saw these women converge she was certain that God wanted this baby girl to live and be a witness unto Him.

But Tanyous scoffed at Milia when she told him that Mother Eve had attended her birth. This is nonsense, my girl! God sent Eve to observe, that she might see how the pains of birth can disappear if sin disappears. Fine, all right, I don't want to argue with her version; maybe the nun was a saint and maybe she had a vision. But in the grotto at Bethlehem it did not happen like that. Eve herself – Eve in person – appeared and knelt down and pulled Jesus from his mother's body. This was the decision taken by the father of Issa Himself, and it was this that forced Yusuf to say nothing for twelve long years. Eve herself uttered only one sentence. Who are you? Yusuf asked her, and he tried to give her money. She refused the money with a brush of her hand and said to him, I am Eve, and then she disappeared. But the real story isn't here. The real story is the one about the Messiah and the fish. When the Messiah, peace be upon him, walked on the face of the water the fish swam to him bearing a message from Mar Yusuf. People call the tilapia in Lake Tiberias the Mar Butrus after Saint Peter, but its true name is really Mar Yusuf. No one, however, knows this name except the fish, Mar Yusuf, and God. The fish hovered next to him and said, Do not go to Jerusalem, they will kill you there. The Messiah blessed the fish and told it, Have no fear. He said the fishes need not bother with this issue any longer. His father was going to send a sheep.

And this fish? asked Milia. All these words – did the fish really know how to say all of this in Syriac?

Of course. After all, fish do speak, but human beings have forgotten the language of the animals ever since the story with Ibrahim, peace be upon his soul.

What story?

. . .

You mean the story of the sacrifice, don't you?

. . .

You mean, he would have slain his own son. Is there anyone who would kill his son?

. . .

True, he had to do it. God commanded him to kill his son, and he had no other solution at hand. Not without some anger . . . but what else could he do? It was either eat his son or the animal.

. . .

Do you mean to tell me that Ishaq sat there with his father and they ate the sheep? No, I am not going to believe this story.

. . .

Why do you say this? Do you not fear God?

. . .

Yes, two sons, that is what he had. The older one he cast into the desert along with the boy's mother, Hagar, and the second he took to the mount to offer as a sacrifice.

. . .

My God, what am I saying? God forgive me! Maybe the story today has nothing to do with the past, yes, you are right. But then why was Amin killed in Jaffa? And what am I going to do there? Please, please, tell Mansour that Milia is sad and she wants to live by the olive tree here and she can't bear this.

. . .

I don't like these stories. Let's go back to the story of the fish. Tell me, now, when the fish carried Yusuf's message to the Messiah, what response did he give?

. . .

Allah *yikhalliik*, I want to go back to the house now. I've lost the way home. And now Mansour is worried, with me in this condition. Take me to the house.

When Mansour listened to her wail that she wanted to go home he felt utterly, devastatingly helpless. Milia had begun to cry out this way, in her sleep, ever since his brother's murder in Jaffa. It seemed as though this woman had broken the customary rules of her sleep-time and entered into a baffling struggle with all of existence. The first time it happened, he wakened her to tell her that the route to Lebanon was rife with danger but he was prepared to contact the Red Cross to assure a safe passage to Beirut so that she could give birth there. I can't come with you, though, he added. The situation is difficult and I cannot leave my mother alone. What do you think, my love?

Her drowsy eyes gazed at him, she turned over in bed, rolled onto her right side, and fell asleep again.

Mansour no longer knew how to deal with this woman, for her habits had changed since his brother's slaying. She no longer got up early. When he left for work she would still be asleep; when he returned home from work he would not find her at home. He learned not to search for her in the town's streets because if he found her, she would be furious at him. She would accuse him of treating her like a little girl. His new routine was to come home from work and sit waiting for her, anxiety gnawing at him. When she came in she behaved as if nothing had happened. She would go to the kitchen and warm up his meal and as he ate she sat silently by, neither eating nor talking. Whenever he tried to ask her a question her eyes filled with tears and she would say she was worn out and needed to go to bed.

But where do you go every day, God be pleased with you, Milia! This is not good for the child. You are in your final month and the doctor ordered you to rest.

But I'm walking for the child's sake.

How is that?

How can I make you understand, when it really is not your affair. I don't want to go to Jaffa, I want to stay here.

But you know why we have to go.

I know and I don't know, but I'm afraid for my son.

This is crazy talk. You must see a doctor who can talk some sense into you.

He lifted his glass and looked into her eyes and began to recite.

A regard that is drowsy, should it gaze,
or weak and ill and yet to awaken

~ 266 ~

Lashes line eyes holding nothing impure:
a beauty to cure all eyes forsaken

You are right, Milia, and I'm in the wrong. I have changed and you don't bear any blame for that. But, look, *we have walked a destined road, and what is destined to be, had to be where we strode.* Let's go back to the good old days. Where's the *laban immuh*? I am longing to have it – tomorrow, make me *laban immuh*! We'll have a glass and recite poetry like we used to do.

He put out his hand to feel for the baby in her belly and she jumped back. No – please, no, she said.

But I want to hear his voice with my hands, Mansour said.

Mansour did not understand her fear. Hearing her wail in the night that she wanted to go home, he promised to arrange to send her to Beirut. But she started, as if that frightened her even more, and said no. She did not want to go to Beirut. She had come to Nazareth to stay. And, she told him, she had begun to fear *him* because he was hearing her dreams, and when a person can listen to another's dreams the listener can control the dreamer.

Since the death of his brother, their mother, Umm Amin, had become a different woman. Suddenly and without any advance warning she became terribly attached to Mansour. In him, she declared, she saw the image of his brother; she had never really paid attention to how alike they were; why, they were as alike as two tears from the same eye!

Is this exactly the way Umm Amin had put it? Most likely not, for this was Milia's manner of speaking. In the morning, when Milia had just risen from sleep, her speech was soft and pliable. Speech was like dew, Milia told Mansour. Dew appears in the moment that connects nighttime to day; getting up, her mouth held the fresh aroma of this moment. He said he loved to kiss her in the morning because her lips tasted like fresh basil. When she spoke in the morning she used words that were sweet and fresh, words through which the breeze blew, words the like of which Mansour had never heard except in ancient Arabic poetry.

Why did Mansour mix up his mother's speech with his wife's? Was it because a man loves only one woman in his life – his mother – and then spends his entire life searching for her? Mansour was not any such man. He told Milia he despised his mother's immoderate affection for his brother. He did not understand how the mother had been able to organize all of life to revolve around her, so that she was the pivot of the household and the engine behind the family business. Asma – Amin's wife – was like a mere visitor in her own home. She could not do anything on her own, and if God had not made a woman's breasts a fountain for the nourishment of children, then the woman would have found herself without anything to do at all.

With her beloved son dead, the older woman wandered aimlessly like a lost soul. The once-imperious eyes were broken and an uncharacteristic timidity came over her. The wife was another story, though. The woman who had kept to herself and had made her body and personality practically invisible, as if she were secluded from all eyes and veiled in bashfulness, became a new woman. The beauty of her black eyes was revealed and that beauty shone; and Lady Asma became the household's presiding mistress. Between night and day roles were reversed. Mansour told Milia he had been taken completely unawares by Asma's beauty. Where was all this loveliness hiding? he exclaimed. I mean, is it reasonable for a woman to become beautiful when her husband dies? They used to bury women with their husbands because a man's death meant the end of her life, too. See how things have changed?

Now Mansour said to her firmly: I cannot leave my mother on her own.

So now it's your love for your mother, is it? Fine, I don't have anything to say about this and everything will happen just as you want. But I am afraid for you – and for my son, too. I mean, we don't have to put ourselves in the paths of death as your brother did.

Where had Mansour found this new language? He stood in the kitchen and spoke of the Persian poet Abd el-Rahiim Mahmoud, and quoted a verse of his:

> *I will cradle my soul in the palm of my hand*
> > *Yet I'll hurtle it down ruin's dank pit below:*
> *I will lead my own life to give my friends joy*
> > *or I'll die me a death to curdle my foe*

That isn't poetry, Milia said. I mean, would you ever claim that this can compare to the verse of Mutanabbi?

> *Should you hazard an honor for which you yearn,*
> > *aim not for any less than the stars!*
> *Death's essence can be but one flavor, one fate*
> > *whether faced for ideals or mere scars*

No, no – this one's even finer – listen!

> *Knowing death meets the foot soldier, you stood your ground*
> > *As though ruin's eyelid held you bound as it slept*
> *Heroes tread past you though in wounded defeat*
> > *and your face is alight, your mouth smiles: you accept!*

But I love *these* two lines:

A sole departure left us apart:
      now death is a true leave-taking
Has this night not seen your eyes through my vision:
      wasting to nothing in abject forsaking?

Now isn't the time for love poetry, said Mansour. Listen again!

Think not of glory as wineskin and songstress:
      it is naught but the sword that kills at first slash,
to strike off kings' necks, and glory is to see
      the black swirls of dust as the fierce soldiers clash

Bring me poetry like this! Bring me a poet like Mutanabbi, and then I'll go anywhere! Then the taste of war becomes the tang of poetry, and poetry's flavor is the deliciousness of love. But this fellow who carries his soul in his palm, well . . .

He was a great poet, and it wasn't enough for him to compose verse: he bore weapons into war and he died in glory and he named his son Tayyib so people would call him Abu'l-Tayyib, Father of the Good One – a father of goodness, if you like.

Martyrs are to be kept with reverence in our hearts, but a poet of this land has not yet been born. When his time comes all of you Palestinians will know immediately that this land has been created out of poetry. This land is not soil. This land is words kneaded patiently into stories, from the very time the Messiah walked on earth. The dirt here was a compost of letters and words. *In the beginning was the Word, and the Word was God's, and the Word was God.* He was the word; and poetry is the ultimate word. Tomorrow, my love – well, after something like fifty years when this soil, our soil, gives birth to a great poet, you all – you Palestinians – will know that struggle yields victory only through the word, for it is stronger than weapons.

First, Milia, you are saying *you all*, why *you*? Aren't you part of this?

You're right, my dear, I'm sorry. Yes, I have become *us* and when I talk about *all of you* I'm really speaking of *all of us*.

Secondly, I don't think we can wait fifty years to see the poet you speak of appear – and I don't think we need to wait. We have to fight with the poetry we know how to compose now, and with that poetry we'll win the fight.

I don't know about that, she said.

Thirdly, you know, you don't know – whatever. All I know is that my brother died and I cannot leave my mother on her own.

Can you see yourself? Do you realize how like your mother you are, in the way your hands move and the twist of your mouth and the things you say? You yawn like her and you suck your lips when you are angry, just like her, and you stuff the pillow under your head when you sleep, even that's like her, too. *Ya Latif*, God of grace, why have you changed like this!

I've always been like this.

Fine, perhaps you were. Perhaps – but I didn't see it. You really are your mother's son. I don't know how I didn't see that from the start.

Of course I'm her son but I'm not so much like her as you say, I'm only doing my duty toward my mother and toward my brother's children and his wife.

Let's thank God that you are not a Muslim, maybe you would have married your brother's wife and bestowed on me a co-wife! Especially since you've discovered that she's so beautiful.

. . .

Don't get upset, I was joking, and besides, how would I know about these things!

She said *how would I know* so that she wouldn't have to tell him that she had seen him in a dream with that woman. It looked like Najib, but nevertheless it was Mansour.

Never, not even once, had her dreams confused her husband with the image of the man who had dropped out of her life as if he had never existed. Usually, Mansour's image blended into that of Musa. Seeing Musa in her dreams, Milia would realize that the message concerned Mansour but came by means of someone else. Mansour never entered her dreams; not until the very final dream, when this dreamer would discover that the endings of all things are so very like their beginnings.

This dream takes place in a space that resembles the garden of the old house but that's not situated in Beirut. No, it is Jaffa. The smell of the sea mingles with the aroma of oranges. Najib peels an orange as he stands next to a woman of medium height whose figure is full but not fat. Are you really Najib? the girl wants to ask this man. And who is the woman? Yes – why is Asma here?

Milia hides behind a jasmine bush whose proliferating trunks entwine, thin and fierce. She does not sense the fragrance of jasmine, though. Oranges, sea salt, damp: these assault the pores of her skin. The man who looks like Najib tosses the orange from hand to hand before his right hand goes to the woman's chest and grasps another orange. The woman moans.

The knife shows in his right hand. Najib sends his left hand to the woman's breasts, extracts an orange and begins to peel it. The woman cries in pain and the man swallows the orange. He has tossed aside the knife. He comes closer to Asma, or to this woman who looks like Asma, and presses his lips to her chest, now only half an orange, and he begins to kiss her there.

What are you doing here, Najib? Didn't I tell you that I don't want to see you anymore? This is what the little girl says, emerging from behind the bushy jasmine, knife in hand.

Who are you? the man asks, his features changing sharply, suddenly.

. . .

No, sorry, you cannot be Milia. Where are Milia's green eyes?

How did this man who looked so much like Najib know the color of her eyes?

Go back to your own land, girl, and leave me alone.

Again the man bent over that woman's chest and an orange liquid dripped from his mouth. At that moment, the two of them disappeared. Milia did not know where the man had taken the woman. She lay down on the grass, and saw that man as Mansour.

The woman was crying as if this man who carried a knife in his hand was assaulting her. She heard the woman begging him for something but she could not make out those low-pitched words – or perhaps, she thought, the woman spoke a language she did not know. Was she speaking German? but no, German doesn't sound like this. But I don't know German, thought Milia. In Lebanon they taught us French at school. No, not German, it sounds like Arabic but I don't understand a single word. Arabic that's clear as mud.

Yesterday you were speaking Hebrew – how come you know Hebrew?

Me?!

Yes, you – who else?

Where?

Doesn't matter where, but I'd like to know why.

No, I don't speak Hebrew. Well, I know two or three words. My brother knew it.

Hmmm, maybe it was your brother, then.

What about my brother, God have mercy on him!

Nothing, forget it.

What matters right now is for you to get some rest. And start packing. The plan is that we'll move to Jaffa immediately after you have the baby.

No, we are going to baptize the boy here and then we'll go if you wish.

Bless your heart! Right, forty days after – that's why we need to start getting ourselves ready now.

Doesn't matter, she said.

The woman cried. She disappeared into Najib's arms, or into the arms of this person who looked so much like him, submerged in her own tears. Concealing herself behind the jasmine, Milia saw and yet did not see. Trying to remember this dream, she managed only an indistinct image of a man with disheveled hair carrying an orange and a knife, and a woman petrified and sobbing. Then that second woman appeared. Shears in hand, Mansour's mother began to trim the jasmine. Milia, a little girl hiding behind the blossoms, under the tree, began to tremble as the shears came nearer and nearer to her hair.

She did not tell this dream to Mansour because she couldn't find the words for it. What had brought Asma to the old house in Beirut? What did Najib want now, after all of this time? Long ago the book had closed on that story and the hollowness that had engulfed her after Najib's flight and his marriage was gone. The rupture in her life had mended slowly with time's passing. Mansour had been the messenger of its final disappearance; why, then, was he cracking open a new abyss deep inside of her, leaving her incapable of distinguishing between the move to Jaffa and her profound fear of the specter of loss that Najib had planted in her heart? What did her mother-in-law mean with the scissors? They want to kill me, Milia screamed, and started up from the bed to find Mansour sitting next to her, lighting a cigarette, his face screwed up in pain.

She said no to Mansour's proposal that they settle into the family's home in the Ajami quarter of the city.

This is the home of your father and your grandfather, Mansour's mother had reminded her son. There are only two of us here, two women, plus the two children. Where else would you want to go, anyway, and what would you do with us? You and your wife will come and live here. It is a big house and there's no problem at all. And once you are here you can take care of your brother's children as you ought to. You are the man of the family, after all.

When he told Milia that he was the head of the family and he must act like a man, she gave him her look. This was the look that invariably flustered and silenced Mansour. She would let fall her eyelids and then that look would come, first from the tiny niches in her eyes formed by her large, honey-brown irises and mounting slowly to settle on Mansour's eyes. In the very beginning, this was the look that had bewitched him, a magical blend of bashfulness that sent a pink tinge across the young woman's cheeks mingled with a desire obliquely expressed. As the days and weeks passed, though, the meanings of things shifted, and Milia's look now imprinted dread on the man's heart.

He listened to what her gaze said. He took it in. This was just a temporary arrangement, he told her. Darling, it's impossible for me to spend the rest of my life with three women – I have my hands full with one woman.

. . .

Of course, of course, my dear, but we need a bit of time, and then once the business is up and running again and God grants us a measure of success, we can move, or we'll figure something out. What I am planning on is that I'll buy a house for my mother and the children. They'll live there, on their own, and we will take over the family home.

. . .

No, I don't like the family home. Remember, I fled that home for Nazareth. All right, look, we can buy a house in the nicest part of town. You'll pick it out and I'll make good and certain that we get it. Just let's move to Jaffa first, and once we're there, nothing's simpler. You'll decide and I'll be happy with whatever you choose.

. . .

No, we need a little time, two years I think – what do you say to that?

. . .

All right, then, give me nine months. Let's figure that the house won't take any more time than the baby. And anyway, don't worry, we'll have our own life, and we'll have no one telling us what to do. Look, in the beginning anyway you'll have your hands full with the child. My mother and Asma will do the cooking and housework and you'll be living like a queen. And then we'll go to our own house. See, houses are a bit difficult in Jaffa. It's a big city, like Beirut, and it isn't easy to find a decent house. I mean, it takes a little patience, and then it will all be fine.

Ever since she had met the Lebanese monk everything had changed. Before, when irritation had gotten the better of her voice, she would hear her mother's voice issuing from her throat and she couldn't stand it. It was the voice of a young girl who had suddenly found herself responsible for an entire family made up of four men and a nun in lay clothing: their invalid mother, whom everyone was obliged to make their chief concern every moment of the day. When Milia snapped at her oldest brother, Salim, saying that she was not a servant and heard her mother's voice coming out of her mouth, the words got caught at the back of her throat and threatened to choke her. Milia did not remember exactly what had happened that day. She did not even remember the cause of the argument with her brother or what precisely she was saying when she choked on her own voice and no longer could speak. Then and there she had decided – in her own mind – that never again would she imitate her mother's voice or gestures. She truly did calm down and become more accepting. But when she had first come to live in Nazareth she began to listen to her mother's voice as it welled up from her memory. The memory of voices, she thought, was very frightening. In dreams you do not listen to the voice of the speaker. Words come without a voice; this is the secret of dreams, their bewitching nature. But when the voice of someone far away or dead erupts from your memory, and you listen to it with your own ears, it is bewildering and disorienting. Milia's bafflement as she spoke to her mother and listened to her mother's answers had congealed into fear.

Now this woman who embodied absence for her only daughter – and the awful sense of being left an orphan – revealed a presence that was wholly unexpected. In Nazareth her mother's appearance did not create self-loathing. Milia found that even the absent mother was a linguistic necessity. You scream *Mama!* not because you are thinking of the woman who gave you life but because your lips need the sound of it, the letters blending warmly into each other. Milia, who in her moment of most intense pain in the Italian Hospital in Nazareth would scream out this magic word, before Mansour would hear the crying of the infant emerging from his mother's body, did not then see her mother or feel her presence. What she saw was a world of white so total and profound that it had to be the brilliance of light.

Milia sensed how Mansour's voice had lost itself inside the voice of his mother. She told him as much. He shrugged it off, saying he had been this way all his life, but he did begin attending more closely to his own gestures and avoided imitating his mother's. He stopped yawning loudly with his mouth open, as his mother did with her repeated *Ya Allahs*.

But he did not notice his wife's loss of voice, obscured by the Lebanese monk's way of speaking. Now, whenever she spoke, she felt as though her voice was clothed in that of the strange man whom Mansour had tried to convince her did not exist except in her own mind.

On that day, when Milia had returned home exhausted, the pains of childbirth outlined on her face, Mansour sat alone in the large room with a handful of roasted chickpeas in front of him.

You must be hungry, she said, and hurried into the kitchen.

No, I'm not hungry. Come here and sit down next to me, let's talk. That's what I want.

She sat down beside him and he began talking – and relating the story of Tanyous the monk. He said he wanted to apologize to her, but at the same time he remained astounded that she had met the monk in the flesh. Apparently the man had been thrown out of the Franciscan monastery twenty years before and he lived in open country on his own. From time to time he was spotted in Marj Abu Amer. Only very rarely did he come to Nazareth, intending to pray in a grotto where he believed the holy family had lived. Whenever the monks saw him they chased him away with a shower of stones.

He had been afraid for her, he said, and had gone to the monastery in search of her. He knocked and knocked on the door before it was opened by an elderly monk who spoke Arabic with difficulty.

I asked him about you, explained Mansour. He was shocked, and said, Women do not come in here. He wanted to shut the door in my face but I begged him to listen to me. I asked him about the Lebanese monk; he was very reluctant to answer me. He crossed himself several times and asked if I was a relative, so I lied and said yes. He said he had thought so, from my Lebanese accent. I don't know how he could have thought I speak like a Lebanese! It must be your influence, Mistress Milia. So now you can't tell me anymore that I sound like my mother! Was he right, do I speak Lebanese?

How would I know!

And you sound more like a Palestinian now, anyway. We speak the same way. Then the man told me the whole story. This monk was thrown out of the monastery because he claimed he had found a gospel written by a disciple of Yusuf the Carpenter. And that this gospel written in Syriac tells the story of the Messiah differently than the four Greek gospels do. Supposedly it claims that Yusuf rejected the idea of the Messiah's crucifixion, and wanted to do what Ibrahim did when God asked him to offer his only son as a sacrifice. It contains all sorts of heretical ideas, and if these were true, they would put Yusuf the Carpenter on the same footing as the Prophet Ilyas. The old monk called Tanyous a madman invaded by devils. That's why they threw him out. He went back to his hometown in Lebanon. It's said that he tried to preach his views in the holy valley where the Maronite monks live. He believed the Maronites have remained loyal to the faith's covenant and its earliest days, because they use Syriac in their prayers and that is what the Messiah spoke. But it did not work: the monks in the Wadi Qadisha mocked him and even tried to drag him to Wadi el-Majanin – valley of the insane – where they put him in irons and threw him into a windowless grotto without water or food. He claimed that God sent him food dispatched on a huge eagle whose wings were so enormous that they veiled the skies. And that God sent him an angel in the guise of a lion who undid his chains. But it's all lies – the man is crazy. The abbot explained to us that this sort of madness is very common in these lands that gave birth to all of the prophets. As he put it, this patch of ground witnesses a continuing struggle between God and the forces of Satan that is difficult for human beings to withstand. It becomes confusing, and some are unable to distinguish between the voice of God and the Devil's voice. That Lebanese monk was the victim of his own lack of judgment; he could not tell one voice from the other and so he became Satan's plaything.

And you believed all of this about him?

That's not so important. What does matter is that I'm convinced where it concerns you. At first, I thought this monk was one of your hallucinations. Perhaps not, but, dearest, you need not believe him. This fellow is a devil, not a saint as you've been thinking.

How do I know, one way or the other?

The woman doesn't know what to tell her husband about her first sighting of the Lebanese monk. Did she dream about him before meeting him or was it the other way around? The world of dreams flings all of its gates wide open only in that terrifying hour when the world disappears and everything melts into everything else, just as her grandmother had cried, repeating the words of Solomon the Wise, *Vanity of vanities!* And then, added Grandmama, everything enters the light. We see what no eye has seen. We meet again the people we know, and we meet those we don't know, too.

Was the glass that the man set down on the windowsill a dream or did it really happen? How had she recognized this man when she saw him on the street at the Virgin's Spring? He had come up to her and told her to follow him. I am asking you one thing, Marta, he said. Come, follow me. And she did.

She told Mansour now that she wanted to go to sleep because things were confused in her memory. Mansour had changed and so had she. A single year had been enough for her to see life unrolling ahead of her; to sense inside herself an implacable aging that left her fatigued – tired of life and the upsets and reversals of time. *For a thousand years in your sight, Lord, are but a yesterday now gone or like a mere watch of the night.*

When she catches sight of the photographs of her mother-in-law or those of Asma, she is left feeling wearily sad. How has the house filled up with portraits like this? When they were married the photographer was there in the house and at the church, looming up in front of the bride and groom to snap pictures and asking Milia – tears clinging to her eyelashes – to smile. The camera's aperture and that black cloth behind which the photographer hid stayed in Milia's memory. She was apprehensive lest the photographer steal the color of her eyes from her, as had the photographer from Zahleh whom Musa had brought to the house, and so she kept them closed. The photographer begged her to open them, at first with gentle phrases and then in growing irritation, to create some light in the photo.

When they passed through Beirut again on their way to Nazareth, Mansour refused to wait. The man had said, only two more days, no more, and the photographs would be ready. He asked Musa to send the photographs to Nazareth. But since the roads between Lebanon and Palestine had been closed, Milia had never seen her wedding photographs.

Actually, no one had seen those photographs. In a fit of anger the photographer tore them up. When Musa came to his little studio he told him he had ripped the pictures to shreds because they would not uphold his reputation. The bride did not open her eyes, he said, not even once! As though she were sleeping.

Saadeh was angry. Then she asked her son to write to his sister and to tell her to bring her wedding dress with her when she next visited Beirut with her husband. They can be photographed again, Saadeh said. What difference would it make? Everyone has to have a wedding photo.

Milia had no idea what had happened to her wedding photos. Mansour never asked about them. He put mirrors throughout the house, a big one in the sitting room and smaller ones in the dining room and bedroom. Milia did not object until he tried to put a mirror in the kitchen. She said no to that. It doesn't make any sense! she fumed. Have you ever heard of anyone putting a mirror in the kitchen?

Mansour said he wanted the house to fill with a single image that he could see everywhere. I want to see you, my love, that's all. He made an obsessive project out of convincing Milia to stand in front of the mirror, first thing in the morning, so that he could prove to her that nothing radiates a woman's beauty like love.

See how beautiful you've gotten? That's from love. You were asleep, and you were as warm as bread out of the oven – you were gorgeous this time! I turned you over on your back . . . it was so-o-o sweet. The most beautiful it's ever been.

Stop talking like that!

So, you don't agree with me? That this was the best ever?

Mansour made up for pictures with mirrors. Otherwise he left the walls entirely bare. One time when his mother had upbraided him for not hanging a portrait of his late father in the sitting room – after all, that is what everyone does – he told her he hated photographs. Those pictures freeze people! he said. They look dead. I would rather keep the image of my father that I have in my head.

But your father is dead and gone, his mother said.

Dismissing her words with a brush of his hand, Mansour said, No, a person does not die – but we kill him when we hang his likeness on the wall. In his memory, his father lived on, he wanted her to understand. And he did not want to assassinate that papa who lived in his mind by hanging a photo on the wall.

Why did you kill her, Musa?

Suddenly the house was crowded with pictures. First, Mansour hung an enormous photograph of his brother swathed in black. Then he added one of his father, and then portraits of his brother's children. Finally, he brought a picture of his mother and along with it a photo of the widow in her wedding dress, standing next to her husband. He even stuck photographs into the mirror frames that were now nearly everywhere in the house. Little photos, enlargements – Mansour even came back from Jaffa one day with a long-faded photograph. He said he would search for a portraitist who could reapply the oils because it was a rare picture of the late lamented with his mujahideen companions.

Why did you kill her, Musa?

Milia felt no jealousy at all. Me?? I don't think I've ever been jealous, not even with Najib. No, I never felt any jealousy.

You'd be right to feel some. Tomorrow the photographer is coming to take a picture of you so we can put it in here.

I don't want my picture taken!

I want a picture like the one in your family's home.

Why did you kill her, Musa?

Little Milia stands alone amidst the mirrors, looking at herself in the descending early evening. She sees the lane outside in the large mirror in the *dar*, and then, in the mirror, she sees Musa striding into the house hoisting a large black-and-white photograph of a woman on a yellowing background. Seeing her brother, she hurries to hide under the sofa, waiting for him to come in search of her as he invariably does. But the swarthy young man in a white shirt does not turn toward his sister. He fishes in a small toolbox and takes out a hammer and a few nails, and begins pounding the picture onto the large mirror that his image has just passed across. Milia puts her hands over her ears so that she will not have to hear the mirror shatter beneath the heavy nails, which transform the light beaming from the mirror into splinters.

Milia wants to come out from beneath the sofa to prevent this man from shattering the mirror any more. In a dream, she knows well, shattered mirrors signal disastrous luck. She crawls farther under the sofa to find herself in open air. She is in the dark; she senses danger. She does not know where she is but she does know that the wadi is directly in front of her and that she dares not budge, fearing that the darkness will swallow her up. The pounding knocks an unbearable ache into her head. She wants to scream – Musa! She hears herself scream – Mansour! She covers her mouth with both hands, afraid that her husband, asleep next to her curled into a ball, will awaken.

Where are you, brother?

The girl's voice goes astray in the darkness and she decides to open her eyes. She will not allow this dream to continue; she will not see the shattered mirror in her home. O Lord, is the meaning of this that Mansour will follow his brother into death? We will be two widows in this house, with the old biddy, and what will I do here alone, and then the little boy – perhaps they will kill him, now that they have killed his papa. Isn't that what they did to the Messiah? They killed his father Yusuf the Carpenter, or perhaps they just took him away – how would I know? And then they crucified *him*.

God save you, stop pounding those nails, brother!

She sees herself getting out of bed and walking barefoot into the *dar*. The gloom is barely touched by a pale nighttime glow that creeps into the house through the window. Little Milia walks across splinters of glass, and her blood makes butterfly shapes on the tiles.

But the mirror was there, hanging on the wall. She almost whispered *thank God* because the dream had not been able to break the mirror. But her heart fell sickeningly and she felt faint. She saw her portrait there, suspended inside of a swaying beam of light coming out of the mirror. The photograph Musa had hung on the wall of the *liwan* in the large house – precisely over the bed in which she had been born – was here. The white background blurred into the black. Only the open eyes escaped the black patches spreading across nose and lips and chin and brow. She did not see the long hair extending down this silhouette's back like a river dyed in black and brown tints that curl round each other.

Where's her hair? she asked, her voice low.

She looked around to find Musa sitting on the sofa beneath which the little girl had hidden herself. He had on his father's tarbush and he held a black rosary.

Where did those beads come from, Papa?

That's what she called him but she didn't anticipate a response, for she knew well that this person sitting on the sofa gazing steadily at the picture in the mirror was not her father. It was her little brother, whose fear of the dark she had once dispelled with a touch of her fingers.

What brought you to Nazareth? she asked.

I've come to take the boy.

No, this is my son! No, you can't do what your father did to you when you followed him to the Egyptian woman's place and he threw a rock at you, trying to kill you.

Why, when she thinks of them, do people get confused with each other? This is not her father, she knows, because this man's olive coloring is nothing like the pallor of Yusuf's skin. But why did he come to take the boy who has not yet been born? Why does he pound nails into the mirror? She hears the pounding of that day at the cross. The Lebanese monk had told her that the greatest suffering the Messiah endured in his final moments was that of hearing the sounds of his own crucifixion. As they pounded the nails into his hands and feet the sounds grew louder and louder, unbearably loud, and his whole body seemed a pair of enormous ears transmitting the tiniest sound. Everything rang and pounded. Can you imagine what heartbeats sound like when they escape the rib cage? The crucifixion, my daughter, is the sound of this violent pounding which turns the body into nothing more than an echo. Stand above the wadi and shout and then listen. Imagine that your body is the valley and there are hundreds of pounding nails screaming into it.

Musa had become a little boy again. Milia had to stoop to wipe away his tears with her fingers; to raise him from childhood to manhood. But when she bent over and put her hand out to his eyes, he pushed her away roughly and stood stiffly silent before the photograph.

She looked where he was looking. She saw an image of Mansour reflected next to the image of Milia that was now fixed onto the mirror. Instead of calling her husband by his name she screamed. Why did you kill her, Musa?

On the day when she got up and walked out of the Italian Hospital, leaving her husband there with the Italian doctor and following whatever path her feet led her down, Milia searched through the streets and alleys for the Lebanese monk but she found no traces of him. She sat down on the stone edging at the Virgin's Wellspring, closed her eyes, and saw.

Do not ask her – none of you, no one ask her – what she saw for she will not be able to tell you. This was the miracle she had awaited ever since the puzzling dream that had seemed more like a vision and that led her to her future fate in Nazareth. Did Tanyous not tell her that the Carpenter had lost his speech when he went in to his virgin wife and found her pregnant? He tried to ask her and his tongue turned to wood in his mouth. Rather than expressing anger or pain he went into a comalike state and that brought the angel. There he heard the beginning of the story which he would only fully understand beneath the olive tree, when the boy told it to him, years later.

Tanyous said that they used to call Yusuf the Carpenter the mute saint. True, he did utter words when his son told him the story but then he lived out the days of his life permitted to him on this earth in a more or less silent state, uttering the fewest possible words, as though he understood that whatever he had to say would be said only at the very end, when he would go in search of the boy before he was snatched away and taken above.

Was it true that Milia saw the sainted nun?

She sits, tired and faint, bent over her pain. She tries to speak but she cannot. The Italian doctor does not know what to do with this woman. And then he turns to the nurse and says something in Italian which the patient does not understand and she embarks on the voyage inside the secret world of childbirth.

Human voices faded and the nun appeared. She spoke in Tanyous's voice and told this woman she must prevent Mansour from taking his son to Jaffa. Milia wanted to say, *I beg of you, Haajja Milana*, and she heard her mother's voice edged with fear. What choice did the woman sitting on the brink of the Virgin's Wellspring have other than to pursue her entreaties. *I beseech you, Haajja Milana, I don't want to become like my mother*, she said in the same voice that she seemed to hear.

I beseech you, my sister, why is your voice like his? Where is our Father Tanyous? He said he wanted to tell me the secret and then he disappeared, and now you have come to me instead. I am afraid of you, ever since I was little I have been afraid of you, and I don't want to live this whole story. I am not my mother. Mama was halfway to being a nun and that is not what I am. My fears are for the boy and all I want from God is to be left alone. I am going to Jaffa, fine, and I am so tired, but tell Tanyous that I want to see his face before I have the baby. I just want his blessing, that's all, and then, *khallaas*, fine, whatever he wants can happen. Where is Tanyous?

I am Tanyous.

Milia heard Tanyous's voice coming from the nun's body. Had this all been a delusion of some sort? Then why would Mansour have told her he had gone to the monastery; why would he make up an entire story, start to finish, about the Lebanese monk? Who, then, had told her about Yusuf the Carpenter? Had it been nothing more than a very long dream?

She got up heavily and walked home. She kept her head bent so that she would see no one and be visible to no one, and when she reached the *dar* she saw her image suspended upon the mirror. She wanted to ask Mansour why he had brought the photograph here and from where he had gotten it. She discovered, though, that she had lost her voice. She laid her head on the pillow and fell into a deep sleep.

Musa came because she wanted him to come.

She was alone in the house. December darkness spread over the room, settling onto the coldness of the house. She put on her blue nightgown and slipped between the whiteness of the sheets and closed her eyes. And she told Musa to come.

She needed him, she said, and she wanted to tell him the story. She did not dare tell him she had heard the story from the Lebanese monk. She was not certain of anything now, anyway. The monk had disappeared into Milana's long black robe. She did not like the nun. She did not want Sister Milana.

Mansour sits alone in the *dar* waiting to see the first signs, those the doctor has described. Milia lies on her left side. She told Musa her belly had become as big as the whole world. It was not really Musa; she wished he were there. She wanted to tell the story and there was no one to listen. It was no longer a question of proving that what she had seen was true and really there. She was so tired out, and she needed her little brother, and so she asked him to come. Musa believed everything she told him. He always stared at her with an expression that blended melancholy with love, and he drank in her words. Even in those difficult moments when Najib had disappeared and the family split apart, Musa was the one who saw the grief in his sister's eyes and believed every word she said or didn't say. At the time Milia had not shared the mysterious story of her love with anyone. The mother told her she had been in the wrong. Why did you let him slip out of your hand? It's the second time, my girl! Wadiie . . . well, we realized how cheap and grasping he was, and how greedy, but this one – what's the complaint about him? And now what? How will I ever find you a husband?

Milia had become ill. She came down with an inexplicable headache which no one could diagnose. Everyone was stymied and anxious. She bound her temples with a handkerchief soaked in water to lighten the pain. She peeled raw yams and put slices against her forehead tied in the damp cloth. Why did she forget the story of the voices that nested in her ears and made her incapable of speech? Why did she erase from memory the brief coma that, unbelievably, God had saved her from?

The story goes that Milia was alone in the house when she fell. She was standing in the kitchen stirring curdled milk in a large pot over the gas flame. Musa was the first to come home and he saw his sister lying flat on her back on the floor, as the smells of yogurt and simmering *kibbeh* filled the place. He tried to wake her up by throwing some orange-blossom water into her face. But she seemed too deeply asleep to awaken. He picked her up in his arms and carried her to bed and went out at a run to get the doctor. He came back with Dr. Naqfour to find that his sister had regained consciousness and the nun with her brass censer in hand was stalking around the girl's bed muttering prayers.

The doctor did nothing at all. He simply kissed the nun's hand when she told him all was well, and left. The nun bent over Milia's ear and whispered something. Two days later Mansour appeared and that was the beginning of the love story that conducted Milia all the way to marriage.

That night, the story goes, Milia dreamed the dream that determined the future course of her life. Did she see the blue woman when she fell in the kitchen? Or did she see her amidst the cloud of incense? Or did the whole business occur through the machinations of the nun?

It was a story of love at first sight, Mansour would tell his mother and brother. As for the question of what Sonia Rahhal had to do with it, this was a mere trifle. After a tiring day spent in Souq Tawile choosing the right fabrics for his new shop in Nazareth, Mansour accepted a dinner invitation from his friend the merchant Samir Rahhal. Over dinner, the merchant's wife, Sonia, drew him into conversation, urging him to get married. He must go out to the garden and see the prettiest girl in Beirut, she said.

That is how the story began. Milia stood canopied in the branches of the flowering almond tree. Her cream-white complexion mingled into the almond blossoms and enflamed the heart of the man who had come from Nazareth.

It doesn't matter if Sonia was the nun's friend. The sister had nothing to do with it. I didn't even see her until the wedding. No, the nun wasn't involved. I loved you from the first glance, and that's all there is to it.

Milia closed her eyes and didn't open them again until she felt herself submerged in water. She turned toward Mansour but he was not beside her in bed.

She screamed, here was the water, and she was aware of Mansour getting her up and helping her to dress and taking her to the hospital.

The Third Night

M ILIA CLOSED HER EYES AND SAW.

Everything was white. Coming to her, the doctor's voice was muffled in cotton.

She saw two nurses. One held her right hand and the other stood at the end, beneath her spread-apart legs. The first was older, the second one young, but otherwise, two unassuming women as alike as two drops of rainwater. The first was short and so was the second; the first was stooped and had bowed legs, and the second equally so. What had brought Wadiia here?

Twinlike, mother and daughter circled round Milia and issued orders in voices indistinguishable from each other. Now a voice coming from her right, now the same voice from below. The pregnant woman listens to a sound like waves swelling from deep in her belly, as if the child who has dropped his head ready to tumble into the world wants for one last time to use the language of the womb that he will forget so soon. Milia listens and wants to tell him not to be afraid.

Somewhere behind the two nurses' voices coming to her in peremptory tones she sees a shadow-shape wrapped in fog. It's the doctor. No – it's Khawaja Massabki. What has brought him and his two Wadiias here?

Khawaja Massabki stands in front of the glowing stove rubbing his hands together over the flame. He narrows his eyes as if he is the bridegroom while the two women, mother and daughter, stand awaiting his instructions.

She remembers she was sleeping. She remembers her scream, crying out to him, The water! That is when the fog suddenly descended to wrap itself around her. Mansour, I don't want to go to Shtoura! My love, I want to go home.

Carrying a lit candle, Mansour strides ahead of the car. Where did you find the story of the candle? True, I did get out of the car to walk ahead, but does anyone carry a candle in such wind and snow and cold? And then, if I had walked in front of the car, we would not have reached the hotel.

Milia does not feel like talking the story over with this man. She is weary of trying to fix her memories. Memories aren't fixed – you remember things in one way and I in another, and in the end it doesn't really matter. You want me to remember things as you see them. With all due respect, that's not the way it goes. Please, please, tell the driver to hurry! I'm so tired.

She sleeps as the car sways and shudders in the snowstorm that pounds Dahr el-Baydar. The driver is begging her to help him convince this fool of a man that they must turn around and head back to Beirut.

Why do you say that?

The bridegroom is mad, madame! Please help out. Damn this crazy idea. Look, I don't want to make this trip. Can't a person get married without going to Shtoura! Now help me out, please.

What was this man saying?

Lord, where am I? I want to go home. Mansour, where are you?

She knelt in front of the door to the bathroom and heard his hoarse retching. She knocked and begged him to open the door. She said she would ask Khawaja Massabki to get a doctor.

But Mansour refused. From beneath the coughing his voice sounded haltingly, telling her to go back to bed and wait for him. It was the cheese, he said. Don't eat that cheese – it's gone bad. Go on, go to sleep and I will be there. Don't be afraid.

She did not say anything but she was afraid. She was dreaming of a different dream. Marriage, Najib told her, makes a woman soft and warm, just like perfect bread dough. I want to knead you, he said, and put you in the oven and bake you and watch you rise. Come closer.

They were in the garden. The evening shadows bumped against the pair of frangipani trees whose branches arced over the garden entrance.

I love frangipani: flowers of seduction. *Futna . . . fitna*. Do you know why it is called that? Because it is like a woman. It entices you, then seduces you; it twines a man in and makes him lose his mind.

. . .

Because on the outside, the petals, it's white and the center is yellow, and it gives off two scents, one for each color, and when they blend they become seduction and chaos! *Fitna*. What do you think of my explanation?

. . .

Come closer so I can tell you what I think.

She pressed herself against the tree trunk, her back meeting its contours. Her right arm was raised against it and her hand brushed a branch thick with blossoms.

This is what drives me mad, he said pointing to her arm. I just want to put my lips here –

Watch out you don't come any closer! Someone might see us.

I told you, you are like that yellow and white flower. Just one kiss! With one swift movement he grabbed her around her middle and pulled her to him.

Ayyy, she screamed.

Scream if you want to, said the nurse.

Milia opened her eyes to see a white hospital screen. She was choking on the odor, she said. Why did the blossoms smell like this?

Close your eyes and breathe deeply. It's chloroform to take away the pain, said the voice, coming from a direction she could not distinguish.

The whiteness vanished. Little Milia ran through the streets of the night. The voice piercing her nighttime no longer came steadily, and then it broke off and the only echo was a faint moan from the woman's throat. As the sound faded she heard the doctor ordering the two nurses to step back.

Let her get some rest.

Where did the sounds of bells come from? It's labneh in bread, Uncle. Take your hand away from me and let me eat.

Milia knows that her uncle Mitri's story is one that must not be told. The only boy in the family, a brother to two sisters, Mitri died strangulated by the church bell and no one dared take down the corpse, swinging on the long bell rope, until Nakhleh came from the house at a run. He saw his son's body dangling from the bell rope and screamed that they had killed him. He asked the young men of the quarter to help him untie the rope from the boy's neck, which had stretched long and thin like a length of rubber.

Mitri came down from the enormous photograph hanging on the white-washed wall in the home of Nakhleh Shalhoub. Milia saw him come down as though the picture, encased in a gilded wood frame, had suddenly become a window. This uncle in his red tarbush, the white silk abaya that curved over his rotund belly, and a bamboo cane still gripped in his hand, crossed the wooden frame and came into the *dar*. He walked straight over to Milia and hugged her as the aroma of labneh and onions rose. The little girl sensed that this man was taking her far away.

Mitri picks up the small girl and walks back to the picture frame. He sticks his right foot forward and takes a leap as if to cross a stream.

Pay attention, now, dear, watch out you don't fall in the river and drown.

But there's no water, Uncle.

The roar of the water rises to invade her petite ears. Why is the river green? she asks him.

The river is not green. Your eyes are green and so you see everything through a green tint.

Please, take me out, she cries.

She calls out to her brother Musa, but he is standing on the other river-bank, waving both hands at her.

I don't want to go with him.

The girl begins to kick the man but it is no use. Mitri grabs her around the waist and lifts her to perch against his large stomach and walks across the water without sinking.

See how I can walk on the face of the water! If the sons of Zurayq knew who I am, they wouldn't have done to me what they did.

What did they do?

They killed me. Five young men gathered round me in the church court-yard. I heard the bell ringing. They were holding kitchen knives and they attacked me. All I could hear was the bell clanging. It began to ring in my insides, in my eyes and my hands and feet. I realized then what death means. Death is voices and sounds, and it is all a matter of luck and fate. My fate was the church bell.

But how did they kill you?

The bell killed me. To avoid them I held on to the rope and I flew up, and then I was circling and the rope began twisting around my neck as I flew. They stood there below looking like mad dervishes, slicing their knives through the air to scare me – what could scare me about them when I was flying with the bell and the cord was wrapping itself around my neck?

Well, then why did you die?

I died because I died. I still hear the bell ringing, I hear it always, pounding and pounding inside of me, and that's why I tug my tarbush down over my ears. My mother always said to me, Push it up – it should sit higher on your head! What did she know? She had no idea what I was hearing, always hearing, and anyway she wasn't my mother. I called her my mother because that's what she wanted. When my papa married her and she came to the house I said, Welcome, Khala Malakeh. She said, I'm not your aunt and that word *khala* makes the foundations of the house tremble. Call me mother. But how could I do that? Mother?! She was my age, or nearly so. Well, not exactly, maybe ten years older but she looked like a young girl. She married and had children and instead of getting older she got younger. She had my sister Saadeh and then five years later my sister Salma came along. Her belly would grow but she was so small and thin, and pretty too, that she never really looked pregnant. I was fifteen when my father married her. I told him his wife was pretty and, I said, she was awfully young. How can you do it, Papa? I mean . . . with her? He glared at me and said, Get out. He chased me out of the house – well, no, he didn't kick me out permanently but he made me understand that I was not to come anywhere near. So I got on with my life. I built a tree house in the big eucalyptus tree in the garden and I began to sleep there every night. On rainy nights my mother Malakeh would come out of the house to stand beneath the tree telling me to come down and into the house. So I did what she said but as soon as my father saw me he would give me that same look, with his eyes like slits, and I felt strange. Uncomfortable. All my life I lived a stranger in my father's house, and if Malakeh hadn't felt sorry for me and fed me, I would have died of hunger. What a sweet woman she was! I was always angry and upset at the time. My mother had been dead only two months when I started hearing people speaking under their breath. The man should get married, they said, to protect him from evil. *Ya haraam ya* Nasmeh! Her name was Nasmeh, and like her name said, she was as fresh and delicate as a breeze through the trees. She died and I never knew why. She woke up one day and couldn't open her eyes. I heard her saying to my father, over and over, she couldn't . . . she couldn't . . . and she could not see anything and her fever kept rising. She was like that for two days and then she died. She asked for me – everyone said to me, Your mama wants you, and I went to her and I sat on the bed beside her. She took my hand and she held on tight. It felt like holding a block of ice, but I didn't move, and then I heard the women wailing and they said she was dead. I tried to take my hand away but I couldn't. Her hand was like hard wood. I heard the women saying, Look at this boy, how he loves his mama, he's refusing to let go of her hand. A bit later my father came in and said, *Yallah, habibi*, get up. He grabbed me by the shoulders and dragged me and I began to scream, and my mama was dragged along too.

Let go of her hand! my father yelled.

I couldn't talk, it was the crying. The worst thing is when you are crying in the back of your throat. The tears go down there and they sit and then you can't speak because the words can't get by them.

My father grabbed my hand and yanked hard and my mother slipped toward me and the women's moaning got louder. Suddenly, and I don't know where it came from, I heard my voice. Ayy, my hand! He was trying to open her fingers. He began sobbing like a little boy and saying, Wife, forgive me. And then Malakeh came and then she was my mother.

And your hand, how did they get your hand away from hers?

The bell is always ringing in my ears, tell them, Milia, my dear, tell them to stop the sound so I can rest.

All right. So, put me down.

I can't. If I do, you'll die.

I want to die, Milia screamed.

Mansour stood at her bedside. Hearing her, he hurried over to the nurses, who were having a chat in the corridor while they waited for the Italian doctor.

Please, Milia is dying!

The first nurse gave her twin a look and smiled before turning to Mansour and telling him not to worry. They all say that, she said. And then everything goes along just fine.

Mansour could see the heavy sweat beading up on his wife's neck. He took her hand and asked her to open her eyes. She turned toward the source of the voice. Her eyelids parted ever so slightly and she moved her hand indicating that Mansour should go. Her lips moved just enough to whisper one word. *Thirsty.* Mansour hurried out to the nurses and told them his wife was thirsty and he wanted to give her some water.

Not right now, said Nurse II. Give it a few moments for the drug to work so that the doctor can do what he has to do.

He said he was thirsty. Death makes one thirsty, he said. The bell rope had taken him upward suddenly, he said, and so death came as though a long fainting spell. He saw the fearful sight of Mar Ilyas in his chariot of fire. He wanted to go back to the sons of Zurayq and tell them, All right, fellows, let's get over it. Let bygones be bygones and let's go back to being friends.

Nakhleh Shalhoub was alone in the churchyard. He told his wife, Malakeh, he did not see anyone. They all disappeared, he said. On the third day after the burial of his only son he mended things with Abdallah Zurayq and his sons. It was said he received blood money, but he told his wife he hadn't gotten anything.

And so, the story went, Mitri died strangled by the church bell, the first known death since Bishop Massarra had been successful in obtaining a firman from the Sublime Porte that allowed him to put bells in church courtyards. In the past, congregants had rung hand chimes and large church bells came to be installed only with the intervention of the Russian Consul, who persuaded the Ottoman Governor of Beirut to permit the Greek Orthodox to erect bell towers in their churches. At the time many objected, believing this European practice would distance people from prayer and increase the likelihood that church courtyards would become public playgrounds where boys vied to see who could climb highest and swing widest on the bell rope. But it did not occur to anyone that bell ropes would turn into hangman's nooses. So Mitri Shalhoub met the countenance of his Lord strangled on a rope that preserved the tolling of the bell in his ears forever.

Young Mitri was at odds with the sons of Zurayq because of a joke. It began in Beirut harbor, where they all worked as porters. Nakhleh worked with his only son; they were carriers for the agency of Khawaja Jirji el-Jahil, a broadcloth importer. Abdallah Zurayq worked with his four sons for the firm of the Sayyid Muhyi ed-Din ed-Daouq, which specialized in wood imports. The game began with an insult – and everyone knows that Beirut folks are consummate artists when it comes to insults and oaths, to the point where such expressions percolate through every category of conversation and discourse. Beirutis make love with insults, express dislike with curses, become friends and turn into enemies with oaths. And it all means that insults carry no particular meaning. A listener must deduce meanings from the speaker's manner of expression and tone.

The insult that ended Mitri's life was both original and obscure. Samih, Abdallah Zurayq's eldest son, said it as he was carrying a very large and heavy wooden plank on his back. Walking by, Mitri could see that he was tired and he extended a hand to help out, asking, Cracked your back? But the junior Zurayq screamed at him, Hands off the wood! When Mitri persisted in wanting to help, an insult came shooting out of Samih's lips that no one had ever heard before. Take your hand off before I send you back inside your mama's cunt! It seems the lad was delighted with his own on-the-spot curse, for he said it several more times and turned it into a rhythmic chant. Here is where the problem arose. Mitri attacked Samih and began beating him. Samih let the plank slide off his shoulders and instead of defending himself he yelled the insult out so loudly that the workers gathered around the two young men and tried to separate them. Samih would not stop repeating his expression, which crazed Mitri to the point where he said what no one in all of Beirut harbor would ever have dared to say: Get out of here, you son of Laure! May God defend your own mother's Pharaoh-loving cunt!

Mitri told his father he hadn't meant anything by it. He had wanted to respond to the insult with an appropriately similar but innovative one. So he had said the unsayable. Despite their manly swagger, and the bold appearance of their father (famous for his long and carefully twisted moustache), the sons of Zurayq were known as the sons of Laure, because Sitt Laure was the real man of the house. And it was said – and God alone knows – that she was a, well, customer of Khawaja Naji Far'awn, the harbor overseer; and that, furthermore, her husband knew about it but shut his ears and eyes to it. Far'awn-loving, appended to the epithet *son of Laure*, transformed an argument between two boys into an all-out brawl. The five sons of Zurayq were there immediately as if the earth had suddenly parted to reveal them and began to beat everyone in sight. Mitri slipped away, leaving the field of battle to the fighters who soon discovered that he had disappeared. The skirmish broke up but the young men and boys of the quarter heard the Zurayq sons say they would find Mitri and indeed send him back into his mother's cunt.

Mitri was terror stricken. According to Sitt Malakeh, the young man slept for three nights running in the house. He abandoned his tree house and did not show up for work in the harbor. On the fourth morning his father came in to reassure him that everything was resolved. He said he had talked with Abdallah Zurayq and the issue was taken care of and everyone had calmed down. But Mitri was not convinced. He told Malakeh he had seen his own mother in a dream. She had held him close, but he had seen darkness descend and was afraid.

Did he dream about the bell they strangled him with? asked Milia.

No, about his mother, and Lord preserve us, he asked if I could smell his mother's scent. He told me that his father did not even buy a new mattress when he married me. He pulled a fast one on me, that man. He told me he had bought a new bed but the truth is, he repainted the old one and did not even change the mattress. From that day on I couldn't sleep. I started getting up in the night and walking through the house like a ghost. Nakhleh thought I couldn't sleep from grief. A week after the boy died I screamed at my husband. You either get a new bed and change the mattress or I'm going back to my family!

Saadeh would not talk about her dead brother. All she said was that her mother, Malakeh, had borne a lot for his sake. She had stayed in mourning for four years and had decided to do as all bereaved mothers did, staying in black until the end of her life. But her husband ruled against that. It's not your affair, he told her. He was not your son. He was his mother's son. Nakhleh forced her to take off her black mourning clothes.

His mother's son died of strangulation in the end. Samih Zurayq said that he came with his brothers to the churchyard to participate in ringing the bell, and that they had forgotten all about the fight after the apology that Nakhleh Shalhoub offered the Zurayq family on behalf of his son. But no sooner did Mitri see them – and he was already clinging on to the bell rope – than he began to soar upward. They did not understand how he could climb the rope like that, but he went up and up, while the bell pealed as no one had ever heard it ring before. Samih said they saw that boy fly and they did not take in what was happening until the sound of the bell began to deaden and grow faint. When they saw Mitri hanging by his neck and flopping around like a just-slaughtered bird, Samih said they grabbed on to the rope to rescue him but when they reached him it was too late because his neck had already stretched thinner than the rope, and the face at the end of it was bright blue. Nakhleh was not exactly convinced by what they said but there was nothing he could do about it. Starting a war with the sons of Zurayq would mean certain death for him, and revenge would not bring back the boy who had been sent back into his mother's womb, just as they had predicted.

Do you mean that when people die they go back to their mother's womb? Milia asked Grandmama Malakeh.

Girl, what are you talking about! Remember, like I told you, death is a dream. A person stays where he is and journeys at the same time, and comes back only after traveling to the light.

But why did they kill him, Grandmama?

No one killed him, dear. Don't believe what your grandpapa says. He went senile from crying so much. It was his grief that invented this story about the sons of Zurayq hanging the boy on the bell rope. No, the poor boy died of fright. Nothing brings death more than being afraid of death. Your grandpapa is old and feeble. When I married him he was twenty years older than me, and now, look, he seems forty years older, maybe even more, God give me patience with him! I told him not to tell this story to the children but when a person gets old he returns to what he was like as a child and he doesn't know how to talk to anyone but children. Forget the story, my girl. The real story isn't Mitri's, it's mine. I was the stupid one. I don't know how I ever agreed to marry a widow.

Malakeh's marriage was a great surprise: a girl of twenty marrying a widower who had already passed his fortieth birthday. Was it his wealth? True, the story that had imprinted itself in Milia's memory took place when Nakhleh and his only son were working as porters in Beirut harbor. But Nakhleh was not originally a porter and he would not die in poverty. That was the barren patch, as he called that period of time, when the silkworms went as ugly as common worms. Lebanon in the last years of the nineteenth century saw the beginnings of the famine that would devour it during World War I, laying ruin to a third of its population while emigration swallowed up the rest and only those who had no way to leave remained.

Nakhleh had no way to leave and found himself unable to make a living. Sometime around 1890 the man decided to shut his silk goods shop in Abd el-Malik Street, roll up the sleeves of his *qumbaz*, and get to work. That was how he and his son ended up at the port of Beirut. The truth is that it was Mitri who was the porter; his father simply organized and oversaw his son's labor. But things improved. Nakhleh said it was Khawaja Efthymios who paid off his debts and thus he saw his way clear to reopening his little shop – but only after it was too late.

It was too late because Mitri died of hanging, and a lifetime was lost because the man did not dare to demand revenge for his slain son. From that moment – the instant of Mitri's death and discovery – the household was turned completely upside down and Malakeh took over everything.

Why did Milia tell Mansour this story? Was she trying to convince him not to go to Jaffa or was she trying to find a relationship between her grandfather Salim and his Egyptian lover and the dream of her aunt that changed her life? Milia heard the name Efthymios one time only on the tongue of her grandmama. Malakeh was talking with her daughter Saadeh and said something about the moment of release when Efthymios paid Nakhleh. Saadeh asked, Efthymios the very same? Seems Mr. Sergios shows up wherever we are. That sentence stuck in the girl's mind; and now here it was again intermingling with the sound of the bell.

She wanted to say, None of this has anything to do with me. She wanted to say that she was her own person: I am me; I am not my grandmama nor my great-great-grandmama, Lord, how different people become mixed up inside me. I don't know who I am anymore.

He was like that, too, said Tanyous the monk. As he went to the cross he did not feel that he was himself. He felt everyone becoming a part of him. He tried to keep his memories apart but he saw everything together. He became mother and father, the Sitt and the Sayyid, Lady and Lord and lamb. Because he was everything, he could say nothing. If he could have talked, what would he have said? And if he did have things to say, who would have understood him? And if he found someone who did understand, who would believe?

Milia was walking on the road that led down to the Virgin's Wellspring when she heard these words. She sensed the sky opening before her and she had an inkling that she was here to protect Mitri from death. She gave the boy the name Mitri in her mind. No, the truth was that the first name that came into her mind was Issa. She wanted to name the boy Issa, the Messiah's name in Arabic. As a sign and a good omen, she wanted to be called Umm el-Nur, Mother of Light, as the Virgin had been called. But she did not dare announce that, even quietly to her husband. So she named him Mitri out of fear for him. She wanted to protect him from the bell and prevent the sons of Zurayq from slaying him. But her heart filled with fear because his father would take him to Jaffa, and there he would find only war and death waiting for him. She was not afraid of childbirth as her husband believed. She was certain she could lean against the trunk of a palm tree and give birth if need be; she would not even need Sister Milana there to raise the baby and imprint his image on the stark white hospital wall, as the nun had raised her high in the *liwan* of the old Beirut house.

Mansour said his name would be Amin. Suddenly the boy had a different name and Milia felt alone in the world. She was accustomed to talking with him, addressing him by one of his two names. There was the public one which, after a great deal of debate, had been settled on as Ilyas – for this would be auspicious, to name him after the Prophet Ilyas the Ever-Living whose secret Milia had come to know from her visit to him in Maarrat Sidnaya near Damascus where she slept in his grotto and felt the savor of eternity blending with the fragrance of the nectar of local wild figs that she had eaten. And there was his secret name, Mitri, for the sake of her only uncle, whom she had never met except in her dreams. The two names were felled in a single blow when Amin died in Jaffa. In her seventh month of pregnancy she had to get accustomed to a new name and a new child.

When Mansour informed her of the new name, she told him it was out of the question. No one changes a baby's name, she said. It's a very bad omen.

His name was Ilyas, she said, and cried. But Mansour paid no attention to her weeping.

What had happened, and how had this come to be? Normally, when he saw his wife cry, Mansour tried to move heaven and earth. He would beg her not to cry and would reassure her hastily, saying *whatever you want* or *as you like*. He would bend over her wet face and blot her tears one by one with his fingertips. He would calm her with the poetry that ran from his lips like water, putting balsam on her wounds. But Mansour had changed. He had become another man, a stranger. She wanted to tell him that she no longer knew him. But she didn't. Or rather, she did tell him and then she regretted it.

That was the only occasion on which she was sorry to have had a particular dream. Usually she took dreams as they were, for a dream was like fate. Never had she debated her dreams, for they were her windows onto her deepest self: gateways to her spirit and to the souls of others. She dreamed and lived. That is the way she put it to him when he showed how astonishing he found her tendency to speak the language of dreams.

Don't believe your dreams, he said to her.

If I don't believe them, who will I believe?

Believe me.

You, yes of course – but the dreams tell me what will happen.

Dreams are just illusions.

And the poetry you're always chanting to me – isn't that a fistful of illusions?

Poetry is something real and true. The tempo of the words, the music of the meanings – they give sense to things. Do you remember how I spent my time traveling on your account? I would recall a line from one of Ibn Abd Rabbih's poems and I would tell myself, This is me. Listen, Milia.

Body in one land, soul in another
the loneliness of the spirit, the exile of the flesh

Poetry is a dream. I can't imagine a poet except as someone who has a dream and then writes it.

Poetry, she said to him, drops onto poets like revelation because it comes from the same place as dreams. Think about the lives of the prophets and the saints, she said. God addresses Himself to people through dreams. That's how He spoke to Yusuf the Carpenter. He said, Your wife is pregnant. The man was asleep at the time.

But no one came and talked to me like this. You just told me you were pregnant and that was that.

But it was in my dream that I saw I was pregnant – Milia did not finish her sentence. She was afraid that Mansour would believe she was mad. How could she tell him the dream of the child? Even more, how could she say to him that she was absolutely certain that the birth of her child would not occur in Nazareth. No, her husband would be compelled somehow to take her to Bethlehem, exactly as Yusuf had taken his wife.

That night she halted her dream halfway through. Mansour was standing in the kitchen, looking out the window. She saw him from the back and what struck her – and worried her – was his baldness. Mansour's hair had been very thick. There was no history of baldness in his family, he had told her. But now he looked exactly like the driver on the road to Shtoura. In fact, for a startled moment she thought the person she was looking at was the driver. She found herself standing on tiptoes to have a fuller look at his baldness, asking herself in bewilderment what could have brought him here. But then she heard the man's voice and it was Mansour's. He told her that she had changed enormously too. It's as though I don't know you, he said. As if you veil your face. Why?

She said nothing. She felt a shiver of cold run through her and decided to stop this dream. What could the disappearance of her husband's hair mean but death? Anyone who dreams baldness must beg God's protection immediately, because it means death, Grandmama Malakeh had said.

The night Mitri died, her grandmama explained, I dreamed that whole locks of my hair fell out. I was standing in front of the mirror combing my hair and it started falling out, lock by lock, and suddenly I was bald. I screamed and that was the boy's death scream.

She opened her eyes and noticed that she was uncovered. She pulled the wool blanket over her body, told the dream to stop, and went back to sleep. But she saw him again. He was in the same spot. His bald head was scaly with dandruff and she heard his voice. It's as though I don't know you, he said. She reopened her eyes. She knew she must not go back to sleep, for any dream that came to her three times in succession would become reality. She decided to get up and go into the kitchen to make a glass of hot *yansun*. Since childhood she had loved aniseed tea. Every Sunday her father would steep sweetened hot *yansun* and let it go cold. At noon when the family gathered around the table for *kibbeh nayye* he poured himself a glass of arak and, for his children, what he called children's arak, bringing it to them in small glasses filled to the brim with the sweet yellow liquid. They knocked their yellow glasses against his white one, and all took a sip. Much later, when the children discovered that the taste of arak was indeed very like the taste of *yansun*, they began drinking arak made from grape alcohol and aniseed in memory of their father. For the first few days of her marriage Milia tried to have a glass of cold aniseed as her husband drank his arak, but he would not play along. Hey – I drink and you just watch me? No, that's not the way we do it! He was not persuaded of the virtues of *yansun* until after Milia became pregnant and the Italian doctor made certain she knew that alcohol would harm the fetus. Milia went back to children's arak.

That night she went into the kitchen to make hot *yansun*, which was the only drink guaranteed to revive her. Here in Palestine she had learned to drink black tea as if it were coffee. But she still thought of tea as a remedy for chest colds and fever.

How can anyone decide to drink tea instead of Arab coffee? mused Mansour. But that's the way we are. Mansour launched into an explanation of why tea was so popular locally. It was a direct result of British imperialism, he said, and it was the beginning of the end, a sign of inevitable defeat. So we replaced our coffee with their tea! Did you know, Milia, that long ago the Arabs called their wine *qahwa*, as if it were coffee, and then when coffee actually reached them and the habit took root they called it *khamr*, as if it were a kind of alcohol, because it had narcotic effects so they saw it as another kind of spirit. Here, though, we started drinking tea and we grew accustomed to it – so much so that it's seen as a national drink. What a big lie official histories are! Now, arak – did you know that arak is Turkish originally, and not Arab at all? You think that arak is our national drink, across this entire region of Syria and Palestine and Lebanon. We all think that, but no – it isn't even Arab. In all the famous ancient Arabic poetry celebrating *khamr* there's not a single hemistich about arak. *Khamr* means wine or alcohol, but we're so provincial and narrow-minded that we have forgotten this and we talk about arak as if it were our invention.

Going into the kitchen, she did not put on the light because the night itself was bright. She put the little coffeepot on the flame and stood waiting but the water refused to heat up. Everything in the kitchen seemed out of the ordinary: the moonlight shooting through the window to encase the sink in its resplendent silver rays; the cicadas' constant *hass-hass-hass* was almost deafening; the tracery of the tiles sparkling as if giving off their own light, and the *yansun* whose normal yellow had turned bluish. Milia was pressing her hands over her ears to block out the noise when she saw him, a sudden apparition that seemed to enter from nowhere. It was Mansour standing at the window turning his back to her.

I'm making a glass of *yansun*. Would you like one?

Suddenly she saw his baldness and her knees went weak.

And you've changed enormously too, said Mansour.

Milia screamed. *In the name of the blessed cross!* And saw that she was lying in bed wrapped up in the coverlet and there was no light anywhere.

Bells ringing. Where were the bells and why didn't those people take the dead boy down from the bell rope?

Mitri picked her up and carried her inside his photograph as it hung on the wall. He was tall and dark-complexioned and muscular. That is how she had always imagined him. That was what he looked like in the dream of the bamboo cane and the labneh sandwich. But he was not like that at all.

Describing her son, to whom she had not given birth, Malakeh said he was thin and pale-skinned. His red tarbush tipped forward and he was never without his bamboo cane. But here he was large and dark, a brown abaya over his white robe, his right hand grasping the bamboo cane while his left hand encircled the young woman's waist.

Put me down, leave me alone, please, please! Look, I'll bring you *arus el-labneh*, I don't want to go into the picture – one photograph is enough for me.

She screamed, NO! and opened her eyes. She recognized the hospital smell immediately and saw Mansour standing next to her, trying to keep hold of her hand.

You are sweating a lot, he said. Please, please, just calm down, everything is fine. He picked up a small towel and pressed it to her forehead and hands to soak up the beads of sweat.

Milia smiled, seeing him engrossed in his arak and his poetry. It was midsummer and very hot.

How can anyone drink arak in this heat!

Listen, he said. This is the absolutely finest line of the straying king.

You clove the heart in two so half of it is slain
and half is wrapped in chains

Not very beautiful, said Milia. Not very nice at all. I don't like it when death is talked about this way, as if death is a word just like any other that you can toss around. That's not what death is. It's words – it's talking that kills. We shouldn't be so careless about it. And I'm not so fond anymore of these similes and metaphors. A poet imagines and then forgets. You recite the poetry with its proper rhythms and all, and then you go sleep like the dead.

But you're forgetting something very important – before I go to sleep, I'm on fire for –

Isn't there anything in your head except this business! I'm trying to talk about something serious. What I was starting to say is that when you go to sleep, you and these poets of yours forget whatever it is you've been saying and reciting. But I see these things in my dreams and they scare me. Just imagine if all of this poetry stuff became real. If people lived like they were in novels or poems, they would go mad, every one. See – no, it really is not beautiful, this poetry.

You're the beautiful one, gorgeous!

He stood up and walked over to her, a handkerchief ready to wipe off the glistening beads of sweat running down from her bare underarm.

Do you remember? he asked her.

She said she remembered, to make him stop talking and to keep at bay the sea of memories from the days in Beirut when he fell in love and which she knew only through his words. She felt very odd and uncomfortable with these memories of love that Mansour was so insistent on establishing at the heart of their marriage. She told him she believed his memories.

It's like – how should I put this? – like when my mother would tell stories about me as a two-year-old, and she would tell them over and over. What pleased her most was to tell the same story again. Every time, she told the same story but as if she were telling it for the very first time, until in the end she made us believe it was all completely true and we learned to take these as our stories. And now, my dear, you are going to make me believe everything that you remember. When I hear you I feel like it is me who is remembering, not me who is listening.

She was sitting in the shade of the enormous fig tree. The October sun crept through the green leaves to plant splashes of light across her bare fore-arms. Suddenly Mansour appeared. At the time, Milia was living through the period of apprehension that precedes marriage. When she had been with Najib she had decided that marriage would be the moment when she encountered the truth and the reality of life. She would exit the house of woe – the house her mother had made – and would take herself away from the nun's shadow and her family to begin a new story that had no connec-tion to the world of saints. But now she found herself with a man she knew nothing about, really, except that he said he loved her. Was it enough to feel the vibrations of another person's love to fall in love oneself? She loved Mansour's love and she convinced herself that he was her fate. And then came the dream that decided the issue for good. Mansour would be her great dream and she would live her story with him as she had lived all of her earlier stories.

Suddenly Mansour was there. He stood still, watching her. He did not say a word. He was looking at a drop of sweat that was forming slowly on her underarm, its weight about to pull away from her skin.

When did you come? she asked him.

He was silent.

What's the matter with you? Aren't you going to answer?

. . .

She got up to go into the house and heard his voice begging her to stay there, exactly as she was, sitting on the little straw chair she had placed beneath the fig tree.

Allah *yikhalliik*, don't get up. Please!

What is it? she asked.

Stay there, don't move. I want to see where this water drop is going to land. He pointed to the pearl that was rolling slowly onto the underside of her arm.

She looked nervously at the sweat dripping from her underarm. She raised her other hand to wipe it away and heard his voice crying out, Don't!

She stood up, wiped the sweat from her arm, and went toward the house. He followed her, telling her that she did not understand the meaning of love.

What is it, love? she asked.

Love is when I love everything about you, even these pearls.

Don't say pearls – only tears are called that.

She doesn't recall how the rest of that conversation went but now here he was, standing next to her and ready to snatch up the beads of sweat falling from her arm, puffy with pregnancy, repeating a story she has forgotten or perhaps it never happened.

He said, she had wanted to go inside then but he took hold of her forearm. She wriggled away from his hand but lost her balance and fell toward his arms and when he bent over to kiss her arm he could feel her trembling. You were like a little bird, he said.

Don't say that, like a little bird! I told you, I don't like similes, I don't like comparing one thing with another because it's never true. There's nothing that is enough like something else for it to work. That's why I don't under-stand you.

She remembered that he asked her what she was thinking about and she answered, Nothing. But he was insistent and so she had to tell him some story. Whenever she seemed preoccupied he asked her the same thing, and if she did not answer, he was irritated. So she always had to find something, anything, whatever came into her mind to say, to defuse his anxiety.

On that day, she told him about her visit to the grotto of Mar Ilyas. She said she had felt a sense of reassurance when the priest unlocked and opened the metal door protecting the grotto and she stooped double to go in and lie down in the position the Prophet Ilyas adopted as he slept, in flight from Jezebel and her husband, King Achab, after challenging them. There, in a tiny grotto which could hold only one person at a time, Milia came in and lay down while Sister Milana stood outside lighting incense and mumbling her prayers and invocations over and over.

Listening to the story, Mansour remarked that he did not understand any of it. I talk to you about love, he said, and you just go on thinking about saints! It makes no sense.

Why did she go to Maarrat Sidnaya near Damascus and pick her way down those endless stairs to find herself in a rocky hollow stretching all the way from the summit into the wadi, so enormous that it had to have been carved out of bare rock by the Divine hand?

The nun said that she must go there. I made a vow on the girl's behalf, and she must go there. I will take her. Come, Saadeh, come with us.

But Milia's mother was too ill to undertake the long trek to Syria. The nun decided to take Milia and go.

There, on the Damascus Road, Milia had her first sight of Dahr el-Baydar. The nun planned to take Milia to the grotto of Mar Ilyas on the nineteenth of July, the night initiating the feast day of this prophet who mounted to the heavens in a chariot of fire – a day on which believers light fires to express their joy and eat little date cakes and celebrate all night long as a greeting to the greatest of the popular saints in the lands just to the east of the Mediterranean.

Milia was eleven at the time. She was very thin as a result of her long fever. She was very fearful of this prophet whom she would be visiting. The nun told her that Mar Ilyas had saved her life and her future was hostage to this visit. Listen carefully, my girl! When you get there you must talk with him. Your whole life, your entire future, depends on this visit. Mar Ilyas rescued you from death. That's because he is the only saint who never did die. This saint does not like death. God sent him a chariot of fire and carried him up to the heavens and he is there, living with them. He is the only one who still lives.

Isn't he afraid? asked Milia.

What would he be afraid of, girl?

Of the dead. Of living with the dead.

The nun couldn't help but laugh at this clueless girl. She wanted to explain that the prophet lived with the cherubim and seraphim, but how could she make the silly girl understand that these two difficult words were types of angels or that God had let his prophet live for the Messiah's sake so that he would find someone waiting for him at the second coming?

Don't ask such questions, said the nun. These are matters we do not understand. It's more important to believe than to understand. Just get to him and give your heart into his hands.

In Dahr el-Baydar Milia saw fog for the first time in her life, gauzy white clouds that spread across the heights and dipped to brush the earth. She would tell her brother Musa that the prophet's soul made itself into a cloud that touched and surrounded her as she mounted the summit before going to him. When she set foot in Damascus and experienced its bewitching aromas and heard from the nun the story of Paul the messenger who was guided here after his conversion, she yearned to stay. The seven rivers that together are called the Barada roll into the city from every direction, sustaining it like a ship that floats over the fragrance of jasmine. The young girl walked in the nun's shadow and went to Sidnaya, entering the grotto, a chamber lit by candles where the icons seemed to stoop and embrace each other, where sacred images mingled closely with the shadows of the human beings kneeling in silence and darkness. The nun ordered her to prostrate herself and she did. She ordered her to kiss the ancient wooden icon of the Virgin, and she kissed it. The nun told her to recite the Lord's Prayer and she recited in a barely audible voice. The nun gripped her hand tightly and led her out into the monastery courtyard and asked her if she had seen the Lord.

The girl had no idea what she was supposed to have seen. When she entered that low-ceilinged chamber covered in icons, she assumed she had arrived at the grotto of Mar Ilyas and had now fulfilled her vow and could go home. But the nun kept the girl's hand in hers and made her understand that the journey had only begun.

She stood before the rocky slope extending from the summit to the wadi bottom and saw God. The sky was garlanded with beautiful strands of white that looked like bird feathers; the horizon was endless and magnificent, and the grotto awaited her. Milia would remember in sharp detail how she descended the two hundred stone steps, would remember how hard she breathed as she went down, her dizziness, how the *shaykh* with the long beard took her hand and told her to sleep and feel no fear. But she would not remember how she climbed the same number of steps afterward. The nun said she had had to carry Milia because she ran out of breath and began coughing heavily. Milia would not remember.

At the grotto, she watched as a man unlocked the door, saying to Sister

Milana that he would open the grotto only out of respect for her since Monsignor had issued an order that no one should be permitted to enter.

Go on in, said the nun.

The girl's steps were hesitant. She was conscious of having to crouch down to enter, nearly crawling. Inside, she recognized him instantly, by the very long white beard that spread across his lower face to cover his chest. He stood facing her, his figure ringed in fire. She started to step back in terror at the live flames, and she heard the nun's voice commanding her to stay where she was.

Sleep where he slept – lie down on your back.

Milia lies down and turns over carefully onto her back, and almost immediately she sees him turn away, striking his cloak against the rock, and go out. The rock fissures; water gushes forth and puts out the flame. Milia is in the water. A sweet cold gust of wind submerges her and the old man begins to sail upward. She reaches to grip the hem of his robe but, flying in the breeze, the robe slips from her grasp.

The old man disappears. The girl is afraid. She looks toward the door where she entered and sees that it is completely shut. The nun is nowhere to be seen.

Why did you go to sleep in there!? You were meant to pray. Mar Ilyas needed to hear your voice, *yours*, thanking him, once and again. That is why we allowed you inside, into the place where he slept in flight from the king. This very place is where a bird coming out of the heavens alighted to bring him food. And *ya lahwi*!! Instead of praying you slept.

What Milia wanted to say to the nun was that she had not slept for a moment. She wanted to tell her how she had seen the water gushing from the boulder and hundreds of birds spreading their wings to carry the old man aloft. She felt her body perfumed through and through with incense and wondered if now she belonged to another world. Yes, she had closed her eyes but not in sleep. She had closed them for the sake of truly seeing. And she did see. There was one thing she wanted to say to this prophet of flame. She wanted to become a boy – that's what she said. She heard him grumble in despair, and he grunted that all girls wanted the same thing. But it was only because they did not know. If only humans *knew* – then everyone would want to be a woman. He told her about the two Maryams: the Majdaliyya and the Virgin. Every woman can become either one or the other, he told her. And only women can truly feel, and own, the two fullest emotions, love and motherhood. And – he said – both will be fully yours, Milia. Do not worry.

She asked the nun to tell her about Mary Magdalene. Sister Milana averted her face sharply as if she had not heard Milia's question. She carried Milia up the long stone steps, panting and grumbling all the way.

What are you thinking about? Mansour asked her, and she told him the story of her visit to the grotto of Mar Ilyas in Maarrat Sidnaya. She asked him what he thought was the meaning of the words she had heard.

Mar Ilyas told you that you would become the two Maryams? he asked, incredulous.

That's what I heard him say.

Ohhh, God help us! God save us.

From what?

From women.

I don't understand anything, she said.

Me neither, he said.

She didn't understand anything then or now, but here she was, half suspended on a sort of half-bed with Mansour standing beside her.

She said she saw the birds on the church rooftop and the bell that bore the weight of Mitri's distended neck; she saw the bell and Mar Ilyas's birds flocking around it. The birds had carried Mar Ilyas away, she told Saadeh, and the nun was wrong. She *saw* it, she said. Look at the icon, Mama, those are not flames, they are birds.

Where had the birds come from, filling this place with the tolling of bells?

She wanted to say that she did not like to hear bells ringing; and she did not like birds. She wanted to say she longed for some poetry. Why had Mansour stopped reciting poetry to her? She meant to say to him that she thought differently now. She adored metaphors and similes. It was better to listen to words than to be those words.

It was not her fault. He told her he was very tired and could no longer withstand it. She wanted to understand but she could not. It was Asma's fault: Asma, widow of his dead brother, Amin. Well, no, the fault was Amin's. No, not his; it was the mother's fault. His mother had never, ever liked her. His mother believed that Mansour had changed and it was Milia who was to blame. The reality was completely otherwise, of course. Mansour had found Milia because he had already changed. But how could he convince his mother that her son rather than her daughter-in-law had been the agent of change? The mother was blind because she would not see. Mansour had told her that his mother was blind. You have nothing to do with it, he said. But she refuses to see that I have been on the run from her and from Amin as well. Yet Milia also saw how, since Amin's assassination, everything had changed.

The poetry, like the story of Mutanabbi's death as he returned to his city, vanished. He returned because, as the poet fled from the uncle of his sweetheart Dabba who lay in wait for him in the desert, his servant said to him, It is not right that you flee when you have spoken like this.

> *Horses and the night and the desert wastes know me*
> *as do the sword, the lance, the vellum, and the pen*

You mean, his poetry killed him? said Milia.

What was he going to do? asked Mansour.

What an idiot. How can anyone believe his own words? Very stupid, if he did.

When you have come to the end, you have to believe. This is the whole meaning of death. It is the only instant when a person has to face everything with absolute honesty and clarity.

She wanted to ask him why he had disappeared from her nighttime. She did not voice the words but they sounded from her eyes and he heard them. Suddenly the poetry was no longer there and Mansour's desire vanished. He drank his coffee hurriedly and said he was going out but he did not move. Instead, he came closer to her. He laid his hand gently on her cheek and reminded her of the doctor's orders.

The doctor said, seventh month on, that's it.

I don't understand, she said.

It's nothing, he said. I'll be back later.

Tanyous told her that the death of children is the true sign. The monk with his disheveled hair stood in the distance and beckoned her over to him.

God keep you! What are you doing here? Leave! I am going to Jaffa with my husband, and that's the end of it.

What's in Jaffa?

She turned her face away and opened her eyes. She saw Mansour standing there, instructing her to calm down. Take it easy, love, the doctor said we need to give it another hour, and then everything will go smoothly.

Milia looked at him and asked about the baby.

Not yet, my dear, we must wait.

Then she understood it. She said she wanted her mother. She talked about pain. Everything inside was hurting, she said, and she began to shiver and her teeth were chattering.

Mansour ran to the two nurses and brought them into the room. The tall one took one look at the woman on the bed and said she would get the doctor immediately. It's time, she said. The short one came over to Milia, held her hand, and with her other hand found a tissue and mopped the sweat from Milia's forehead, reassuring her all the while.

You – go outside, she said to Mansour. And, you, my dear – speaking to Milia – help me out now and you'll be helping yourself.

The waves of pain began to well up more forcefully. Her body was splitting, splintering, and she wanted to scream and scream. She felt utterly alone.

Mama – come, please come, Mama! Look what they're doing to me, she screamed. Everything was whirling around her and suddenly darkness was everywhere.

He was there, his head bowed. I see the boy, said Tanyous.

Please – no. Please, don't talk about him.

I love children, he said. I love a pregnant woman. The measure of a woman's beauty is pregnancy. Don't believe the stories women tell – they say a woman pregnant with a boy is ugly, and when she's going to have a baby girl she's beautiful. No, that's not how it is. You got pregnant with a baby boy and you have only become more beautiful. A pretty woman becomes truly beautiful once she gets pregnant. Could the Virgin Maryam have possibly grown ugly, pregnant with the Messiah? I said to Mary, the nun, something is not quite right here. Remaining unmarried – for men that's fine and it might even be commended since the Messiah died having never married. All of his women had the same name. He gave them the name Maryam so that he would not get confused over names and could talk to one of them as if he were talking to all. God forgive me – no – well, this is not what I was going to say, but . . . when I saw you standing there, just you, I said to myself, here is the Maryam whom God has sent to me. I will have to go to Jerusalem, and so I said to myself, I will take her – I will take you – with me. But you – no, you will not. Your name isn't even Maryam. I must give you a new name.

She watched as he came closer. No, I don't want to change my name. Please, no.

He instructed the nun on how as a man it was perfectly acceptable to remain unmarried, for the Messiah (peace be upon him) begat no offspring. But women were something else. A woman who does not go through what our sacred Maryam went through – I mean, who does not give birth – will not understand the secret of life.

Milia wanted to ask him about the secret of life. He approached her, coming closer and closer. She wanted to say to him that she was married and this was wrong – and she was pregnant – but here he was next to her in bed.

Why does this monk come to her, and how and from where has this man invaded her night? She wanted to tell him that Mansour was right. You are a madman, she wanted to say. The nuns do not acknowledge you as a monk. Suddenly she was aware that she lay on a narrow bed in a cramped ancient house on the summit of a towering hill. Half asleep, she sensed the monk approach, sensed his drowsiness blending with hers, felt his hot breath mounting her neck. She saw her naked body and tasted the sweet saltiness of the world, and her spirit knew him. She told him this was not right. The doctor told you, Mansour – you told me, *habibi*, that the doctor said – and he silenced her with his black sleeve and she felt her waters swell and pour.

She opened her eyes to find the mattress drenched. She turned to Mansour's bed and saw his form submerged in his deep breathing. She wanted to get out of bed to awaken him but she sensed the water still gushing out and felt too embarrassed to move. She closed her eyes again to go back to sleep and saw him coming to her, and climbing on top of her to lie in all his heaviness on her chest. She cried to him to move off of her – he would kill her son, she cried – and she heard Mansour's worried breathing next to her bed as he asked what was wrong.

The waters, she said. Water all over me.

It's your water sac. We must go to the hospital immediately.

No . . . not today! she said. Tomorrow – I will have the baby tomorrow.

He got her up and told her he was going to get a car.

Today . . . no! she said. It will not be today. And anyway it's raining.

Get dressed, hurry, and get yourself ready. I'm going to bring the car.

Milia was right. The rain was relentless. She knew that her baby would arrive on the night of the twenty-fourth of December. The sign would not be the waters from the water sac, but other waters.

This was what the doctor told them when they reached the Italian Hospital. He told her to go home and asked her to wait for the water.

But the water, doctor – there was a lot of water.

The doctor smiled and told Mansour not to worry. He warned Mansour not to sleep with his wife in her final days of pregnancy.

I swear, I haven't done anything, Mansour protested.

The doctor showed his astonishment and said that the examination he had done indicated that her birth passage and uterus had been active during the previous night. It might have been nothing more than a dream, he said. Pregnancy does give women dreams. No need to be afraid.

She was in bed and already asleep when he came to her and kissed her on her forehead before going to his own bed. He saw her sit up in bed. Light shone from her hair and oil stood on her neck, even spraying the air around her gently.

Come here, come to me, she said.

He found himself getting out of bed and coming to sit down next to her.

Bring some cotton.

He got up and went over to the wardrobe, opened a drawer, took out a roll of cotton and came back to her.

Wipe the oil from my neck with the cotton and then put it away for the boy, she said.

He blotted the oil on her neck but it continued to seep thickly. Soon the entire roll of cotton was heavy with oil.

I'll bring a towel, he said.

No need. But you must remember that this oil is for the boy. Rubbing him with this oil will protect him from sickness.

She saw his shadow figure in the gloom of the Jaffa house. Her mother-in-law had put her foot down; their residence in the family home was to be permanent. It's his father's home, she said. No one abandons his father's home. She told Milia that Amin's widow, Asma, would remain in Amin's room with her children, who would be moved from Mansour's room to their own father's room. Milia and her husband and daughter would live in Mansour's room. There was absolutely no need to build an additional room onto the house.

God's will be done, Milia responded, and then looked her mother-in-law in the eye. A boy, Aunt, it is a boy in my womb, not a girl.

Even before her pregnancy, Milia was certain that her child would be a boy. For his sake she had endured this long voyage of hers. She tried her best to get Mansour to understand that her love for him was her love for the child inside. She tried to make him see that ultimately a woman lives a single love story in her life. Hers was her love for her child, she wanted him to know, because the secret and unfathomable bond that comes into being between a woman and her womb resembles no other tie.

But she sees him, standing in the shadow in the darkened passageway linking the dining room to the kitchen in the Jaffa house. He stands there, still, and Asma is pressed close to him as if he is embracing her. The short dark full figure hangs on to Mansour's neck as if she were scaling his body and Mansour bends down to meet her, burying his face in her neck. She walks toward them. She coughs to let them know she is here and that Mansour must stop. But he does not hear. She is right behind him now and she can see Asma's small open eyes turned upward as if they are traveling to a faraway place. She sees herself float between them as though she were a ghost who could pass through doors and bodies. She turns and gazes toward her life and she dwindles away again, now, just as she did in the dream of Najib when she saw him holding the other woman and understood that this man would leave her.

This was shameful, she told the two of them. The fellow has been dead only a month, aren't you ashamed of yourselves?

They did not hear her or see her, as though they were immersed in a sea of pleasures and secrets. She circled around and stood directly behind Mansour. She put her hands on his shoulders and shook him. Then, in the distance emerged three boys, two as alike as a pair of facing mirrors and the third darker with curly hair and greenish eyes. The three came up to the man embracing the woman and the pair disappeared among the four intertwined legs. Milia ran toward the dark child, who lay sprawled on the floor, blood trickling from his eyes. *Ya waylak min* Allah, she shrieked at Mansour. Don't you see the boy? She leaned down to pick up her son, to flee with him, and then everything went black. She saw herself floating on gelatinous waters while the small child thrashed and panted as though he could not breathe. A tiny fish, its lead-gray skin made to glisten by water and salt, gasps as though it cannot get air it needs. It opens and shuts its eyes as if beseeching help. Milia cups the fish in her hands and swims amidst towering waves. Holding the fish while standing on the rocky shore trying to cover her tiny breasts with her small hands, she sees Mansour swimming. She shouts at her little brother to come. Don't abandon him, brother! This is my son whom I have named Issa, and I am alone, brother. Hurry, hurry before the boy's lungs fill up! Musa has disappeared and the fish swims to Milia, still standing at the water's edge. The fish's skin turns reddish threaded by streaks of white. It rises to the surface and floats on the surface of the water.

Mansour advanced toward them. He took hold of the dead fish and threw it out into the sea. He turned toward Milia and ordered her to come home with him to Jaffa.

But our home is in Nazareth.

Our home is in Jaffa now. Pick up your belongings and follow me.

Milia opened her eyes at the sound of the short nurse's voice. The nurse stood facing her and Milia heard the other nurse's voice behind her, saying that this birth was a difficult one and the doctor must do something.

Step back, said the doctor, and she heard a deep hoarse voice. Do not fear, my daughter, for I am here with you.

The nun appeared. Haajja Milana was old and blind now, and her black gown could not contain her body. In front of her knelt a woman of pure white in a long white robe, her white-blond hair a candle-lit halo. As the woman wept, the nun patted her head, and from her eyes sprinkled pearl drops like the tiny pearls strewn across the stone courtyard at the Church of Our Lady of the Tremblings.

Little Milia appears and stands behind the kneeling woman. She bends over the pearls and tries to pick them up but the pure white beads roll out of her tiny hands.

The nun's voice is rough. Milia, my dear, where is the baby? You should be in the hospital. What are you doing here, girl?

I am in the hospital and you can see how much pain I am in – but what are you doing here and who is this woman kneeling on the floor?

This is the sinning woman who knelt and washed the feet of the Messiah in perfumed water. She is waiting for you, and for your son, too.

She is waiting for me?

The blond woman stands up and approaches Grandfather Salim and takes him into her arms. The nun disappears slowly as if her image is dissolving in the water. The grandfather whom Milia never saw in her life slips out from the arms of his lover and comes to the little girl and takes her in his arms.

Sister Milana is standing erect, and she stretches out her arms as if seeking the guidance of the open air. The white-blond woman draws a black shroud over her body as she steps toward Milia and begins to slap her. She clutches the little girl's short kinky hair – and the hair grows long. Locks of hair fly and scatter across the ground. The girl is certain that the woman means to pull her entire head of hair out with her two bare hands.

Please, Haajja, I don't want to die –

The nun stands impassively watching as little Milia begins to roll across the ground. She hears a raucous laugh issuing from the nun's throat and she screams. Mama, please!

Open your eyes, said the doctor.

Milia opened her eyes to see Tanyous holding her hand, leading her to the wellspring.

Here is the Virgin's Wellspring, he said. Here, drink.

Milia leaned down and drank. She drank deeply but the water did not stem her thirst. She lifted her head from her hands cupped around the water which ran through her fingers and said that she was still thirsty.

Drink, drink as much as you want, but you will still be thirsty. Maryam came here after they crucified her son. She stood where you are standing and wept. From her tears the spring welled up. She bent over it and drank from her tears but her thirst was not quenched. No one can quench their thirst with tears.

The short nurse said the woman was crying so hard that her tears covered her face.

~ 328 ~

She told Tanyous she was not crying. Why would I cry, when I am thirsty and I am drinking. But where does this thirst come from, Father?

It is the thirst of love. Love makes one thirsty. A woman is always thirsty because she can never satisfy her thirst in front of her son. At the cross Maryam the Virgin discovered thirst and for the rest of her life, no matter how much water she drank, her thirst remained. Her thirst was endless because she felt remorse.

Remorse? For what? asked Milia.

She felt remorse because with the death of Yusuf the Carpenter she had thought the difficult time, the time of necessary isolation, had passed and there was no longer any danger. Yusuf had lived on dreams and visions. He told her he was like Ibrahim, peace be upon him, and that he was going to found a new people. It was written in the Syriac gospel I inherited. The truth isn't mine – it is in the Book. I must show you the Book. Tomorrow, come to me in the grotto and I will read it to you.

But I don't know Syriac.

That does not matter, Tanyous answered. What matters is that the Book reads itself. That is how I could read everything that is there. When Yusuf died she rested from her anxieties but the poor woman did not know. At the end she knew, and what was to happen happened.

Milia didn't believe Mansour when he told her the nuns had banished the Lebanese monk from the convent and the church. Look, does it make any sense, woman, for a monk to be living among nuns? After all, nuns never see men except outside the convent.

But he's a saint.

Just like the nun you told me about, who destroyed your mama's life. She is no saint, that one.

She is a holy woman but I do not like her. One isn't forced to love all the saints. God left us free to choose.

The monk is standing next to the hospital birthing bed where a pale-white woman has her legs raised, two nurses and a gray-haired doctor grouped around her. Little Milia stands beside the monk and asks him who this woman is and what is happening to her.

This is you, Milia. When you get to be older you will go to Nazareth and give birth to your only son in the Italian Hospital.

But they want to take me to Jaffa, and I don't want to go.

You are not going to go, don't worry.

And is my son going to stay with me?

May God protect your son!

She saw him. He walked beside his father through the lanes of Nazareth, a boy of twelve whose eyes were consumed by visions. He was trembling with fear as he listened to his father tell him the story of Ibrahim, peace be upon him, and his son Ishaq.

Yusuf the Carpenter explained that God wanted to test his servant Ibrahim, and when the servant obeyed, God rescued the son from death. And me, likewise – God willed that He would test me through you. I heard a voice telling me to kill you. You are not my son and so whose son are you? I wanted to take you to the mountain and offer you as a sacrifice unto God, and then came the dream telling me that the angel blew a divine soul into your mother.

On that day Yasu' the Nazarene was certain he had been saved from the trial that Ishaq had undergone. When he heard the story of Ibrahim and his sacrificial son, the boy would grow weak and upset. He could not truly believe the story as told in the Torah. Deep inside himself he was certain that the father had taken his son to the mountain, bound him, and slaughtered him sacrificially to his god. The Jewish prophets, he felt sure, had rewritten the story to show the boy saved from his father.

Mansour always said that he did not like stories of the Messiah. It tires and bores me to hear the same story over and over again, he said. Look at how different it is with poetry. You can repeat a single line until God knows when, and every time it will transport you into a state of ecstatic bliss. But you can't listen to a story more than two, maybe three times before you are tired of it. For me, stories of Christ become very boring and irritating, but what can I do? I was born a Christian and that's that. When I came to live in Nazareth I didn't even think about it, but I've had enough. No one can live in God's town, and we are going to Jaffa, the city where the Egyptian Prince of Poets, Ahmad Shawqi, came, installing himself in the Manshiyya quarter, where the city fathers flocked around him as he recited his poetry.

But, said Milia, every important ancient Arab poet had – along with his verse – a story that in itself gave him lasting fame. The poetry is not complete without the poet's story, she said. Take Imru'l-Qays. It isn't his poetry that tells us he was a king and son of a king, and that he died because he loved the daughter of the Caesar, and that they called him Abu'l-Quruh, He of the Ulcers. And so on, and so on!

Where do all of these stories come from? How do you know them?

She said she had studied Musa's literature schoolbook so that she could tutor him since he was the family's only hope. He had to succeed, she said. He had to get the baccalaureate so we could eat. Niqula and Abdallah married two sisters from an aristocratic family, the Abu'l-Lamaa, God preserve you from such things! So they had their hands full with these princesses, and there was no one left but Musa. I was with him all the time, memorizing with him, studying with him, until God was merciful and Musa got work in a hotel at Tiberias for a year before he found a real job with Shell in Beirut.

When she told him Musa had worked in Tiberias for an entire year, Mansour blew up. He felt newly deceived – why had Musa not told him about living in Palestine? he demanded to know.

I have no idea, said Milia. All I know is that the boy changed a lot during the time he was working there. When he came back he was very strange. I don't know what the matter with him was. I couldn't even talk to him anymore. He was raging mad with my brother Salim and threatened to never speak to him again in his whole life.

Milia really didn't know what had happened to her brother there. All she knew is that he worked as an account-keeper at the Seaside Inn on Lake Tiberias owned by a Lebanese from the Salhab family. She knew that soon after his return, Sister Milana came to the house to ask him whether he had tasted *musht*, for which Christ had fished with his disciples.

The nun talked about the flavor of *musht*, or Saint Peter's fish as she called it, a fish she had never once tasted. She spoke of the pain of distance and exile lived by a young man of eighteen, and then suddenly she stood up and declared that she smelled the odor of sin. Come to me at the convent, my son, to make penance.

How did the nun know anything about the American girl with whom Musa had fallen in love? Musa said the whole story was invented by the nun. I didn't fall in love with anything or anyone, not really. All it amounts to is that I am just like any other young man.

The story everyone believed was not the true story. Only Milia knew. Musa trusted her with his secret but she had to keep it, and she never did tell anyone. When she heard the story he had lived with Suzanne, the daughter of the priest Yaqub Jamous, she could feel how words become living beings trembling with desire and igniting the strongest emotions.

He mentioned the word *gharam* and she interjected that no, this did not seem a matter of mere desire or infatuation but rather a stronger amalgam, of longing and passion and deep affection. She told him about the poet Jamil ibn Maamar who changed his name so that his beloved's name could become his own second name. He became known as Jamil Buthayna, or Buthayna's Jamil, because he believed that the desire and the passion and the affection he had for her would not die with his death. Its echo would follow his beloved's phantom figure long after the two of them had died.

But I am not that, Musa said. I'm not crazy like this poet of yours. There's something in my heart that's like a fire. After leaving Tiberias I forgot the story, forgot the details. Even the girl's looks I don't remember, really, but the fire is still here. It flames up from my heart to my throat and I feel like I am about to choke.

He described a seventeen-year-old girl with large eyes who came to the Seaside Inn at noon every Sunday for a lunch of fried fish with her clergyman father. The priest wore a red tarbush and over his white shirt he wore a black collar to indicate his rank in the clergy. He drank chilled white wine and seemed always deeply engaged in conversation with his daughter. His gaze never shifted from her deep brown eyes.

Musa was completely taken with her when he saw her for the first time. She wore dresses in shades of brown that outlined her willowy figure and small waist. Her nose was small and slightly sharp and her lips were not overly full. She was always turning this way and that as if searching for someone she expected at any moment.

Yaqub Jamous had been guided to Christianity in America. He belonged to a Jewish family established in Safad since the mid-nineteenth century. Having developed a passion for an American tourist fifteen years older than himself, he followed her to Portland, where he married her in a Protestant church whose congregation espoused the beliefs of the Sabbatarians. He embraced his new faith after devoting himself to studying the divine nature and other theological matters. He worked in commerce while also proselytizing for the faith with his wife Dorothy's brother. After Dorothy's death he returned to his native land, bringing his only daughter, Suzanne, to live with him, the two existing on the subsidies sent by the American missionary wing of the group because he was a clergyman without a congregation or a church. His relatives disclaimed any association with him, and the Arab populace in general was not attracted to a Christian sect that held Saturday sacred as the Jews did. The community of Orthodox Christians in Tiberias who had gone over to Protestantism adhered to the Presbyterian branch of the American missionaries they had known. Presiding over that church in Tiberias was a minister of Syrian origin called Abdallah Sayigh, who was known for his fierce partiality to the Arabs and his aversion to Jewish immigration. Pastor Abdallah led a fierce campaign against Brother Yaqub, accusing him of being a charlatan, and forbade members of his congregation to speak with him because he was not a true Christian; indeed, surely he was a spy for the Zionists, working to fragment and destroy the Palestinian Christian community. Yaqub's only congregation, therefore, was the lovely daughter who spoke no language but English.

It was not in Musa's cards to speak with Suzanne and therefore to discover that she knew no Arabic. He saw her every Sunday and got in the habit of reserving a table that allowed him to sit facing her. He would look long and hard at those brown eyes, and when she lifted her gaze to meet his he would begin a surreptitious and silent dialogue with her. The girl's allure was concentrated in her smile with its slightly distracted air, as if the smile were escaping her lips without her bidding it to do so. When she came back to herself, she would fetch back the smile swiftly, knit her eyebrows, stare at the floor, and stop eating.

Her father was different. This man, cast out from his old environment and ostracized in the new one, did not seem to care, or really to have much awareness of his surroundings. He stuffed his mouth full of Lake Tiberias carp and chatted jovially with everyone. When no one answered him he simply pressed on, his monologue coming to them in his peculiar version of Palestinian speech.

Musa was so in thrall to the girl that he could not feel any concern about the man's somewhat ambiguous reputation or by the accusation of espionage that followed him everywhere. As soon as he heard the light tap of her feet on the floorboards of the restaurant his heart would start to pound hard. Sundays were the anticipated pinnacle of his week, he counted the days and when he reached Saturday night he began to count the hours. He stayed up sleepless in anticipation of seeing her, though if he could avoid insomnia he liked to sleep just so that the morning would come more quickly. When she arrived with her father he became suddenly confused about what he ought to do to claim her attention. He sat facing the two of them and ordered fried Saint Peter's fish accompanied by pancakes with thyme. He sipped a glass of arak as he floated in the girl's eyes and forgot to eat. The days went by, Sunday after Sunday, and still Musa found no way to exchange words with his darling – until Pastor Yaqub hit upon the solution.

One Sunday, having polished off his plate of *musht* followed by a dessert of carob syrup blended with *tahina*, the clergyman turned to the Lebanese youth and asked him why he wasn't eating. He did not listen for an answer before rising from his seat, coming over to Musa's table, picking up a fish, and blessing it, whereupon he ordered the startled young man to eat. Now, son, you can eat as you wish. The food will not run out, for Adonai, peace be upon Him, blessed these waters that are called the Sea of Galilee with His sacred feet. Did you know that Adonai walked on the face of the water but did not drown? He walked and the fish swam with Him. The Messiah walked across the water here, too, bending to bless the fish. That is why the Sea of Galilee has never emptied of fish and never will, until the end of time.

The minister talked, and he ate, and he summoned his daughter to join them at Musa's table. The girl sat down and kept her eyes fixed upward as though she were not of this world. Thus Musa discovered the secret. He told his sister that the girl was not of this world. He said he had met her three times after his brief encounter with her in the restaurant. The first time, he went to her home and stood in front waiting for her. When she came out and began to walk along the street he walked behind her and then caught up and walked next to her. The girl responded to his greeting with a nod of her head. He told her how beautiful she was and asked her if she was ready to come and live with him in Lebanon. He said he had loved her from the very first glance and that he could recognize her merely by the light sound of her feet on the floor. She raised her hand to wish him goodbye and disappeared into a narrow corridor leading to the women's bathhouse. Two days after this meeting and while the girl was sitting at her father's table in the Seaside Inn, Musa summoned the courage to come over to them, holding out his right hand in the pastor's direction. Then he turned to the girl and stuck his hand out, and his whole face went bright red as he asked her what she thought of the Turkish bath where she had gone. Suzanne did not answer but the pastor launched into a lecture about the importance of Arab baths to the formation of Andalusian culture. Jews and Muslim Arabs had frequented the same hammams in Córdoba and Grenada, he said. Tolerance was water, he declared, and so the essence of Christianity is the baptism. But Catholicism did not understand this, which is why the Castilians demolished the bathhouses and burned books when they occupied Andalusia. Pure savagery, my son, said the pastor. Now why don't you come worship in our church?

The three times in total that Musa saw his strange beloved on her own were very alike, and so he did not find much to say about them to his sister. Each time, he followed her, then quickened his pace and walked beside her, speaking but hearing no response before she vanished into the passage leading to the hammam.

And then Suzanne disappeared completely.

Pastor Yaqub began coming alone to the restaurant. Instead of white wine he took to drinking arak. His resonant laugh disappeared and his face was lined with grief and worry. Musa would get up from his own table and go over to greet him but the clergyman would not lift his eyes from the fried fish on his plate. He chewed and swallowed the fish and drank his arak and wrinkled up his eyes as if he were about to cry.

Musa did not dare ask the pastor about his beloved. The girl was gone and standing patiently in front of the house no longer yielded any results. Instead of looking forward to Sunday as a joyous day of reunion, the sight of fried fish began to stir up emotions of distress and aversion in Musa. He stopped eating the Messiah's fish and now he would spend his time sitting in the café at the Seaside Inn staring out at the still waters of Lake Tiberias and feeling lonely.

The pastor told him everything, though. One day he came over to Musa's table and asked if he could sit down. He began to talk. He asked Musa why the young man had not asked about Suzanne, since after all, he loved her. Musa stuttered and did not know what to say. The girl had returned to America, Yaqub Jamous told him, because she could not make herself feel comfortable living in the Holy Land. She refused to learn Arabic, and the Hebrew words she had learned in America were now forgotten. She told her father that when she first set foot in this land she was afraid and that had never changed. All she saw in her dreams, she told him, were nightmarish scenes of death. She hated it here, and she wanted to escape to Portland. The clergyman said he tried every possible argument to convince her to stay on. He had even talked to her about Musa. I told her that you love her and that love is the doorway to life, he said. But the girl was determined to leave, and now I don't know what I will do with my own life here. The Arabs look on me as a Jew and the Jews say I have betrayed the faith of my forefathers. I will follow my daughter; I'll go back.

Musa told his sister that he had been struck dumb, so astonished was he to hear the man asking him to accompany him to Portland. There's plenty of work in America, he had said. You will join our church and our brotherhood, and I will see to it that you marry Suzanne. What do you say?

Musa did not know what to say. He was totally at a loss, hearing this unexpected question. Should he say that he realized now that the girl had not understood a single word he had said to her? And he knew that she had departed without even an inkling of how much he loved her? Or, should he tell the elderly clergyman that he did not like these new religions and that he had had enough religion in the form of the cotton balls soaked in oil that his mother had forced him to swallow when he was little? Or should he admit to the pastor that he did not even like the fish of Lake Tiberias and never had, from the very first bite? He had eaten it entirely for the sake of the pastor and his daughter. For real fish, he thought, you had to try Sultan-Ibrahim, a fish whose hues came from coral, sun, and salt. Nothing could be as good as the catch of saltwater fishermen. This lake which had witnessed the Messiah's story had become a tedious place to be. Should he tell the man now that he intended to return to Beirut, where he could sleep his fill because the fresh moisture of the sea and the salt smells sent him sailing into a true and sound sleep?

Musa said he felt a serious trick had been played on him. He saw himself now as a gullible simpleton whom an American girl had bewitched merely with the fragrance of white skin that shimmered on her arms. He said he tried to look into the clergyman's eyes – closed, as usual, for the man would drop his eyelids when speaking, as if listening to the demons he had summoned and who whispered into his ears. Musa felt betrayed. The pretty girl who had enticed him with the hammam's fresh aroma had been nothing but a figment of his imagination.

Then the priest asked him why he had tried to deflower his daughter.

He said the girl had been in a state of shock after encountering Musa, and that she loved him. She told her father that she had fallen for the young

Lebanese man who stood all day long at the bend waiting for her but never talked to her. It's like he raped me, the girl said to her father. He came to the house. I invited him here. I met him three times. He walked with me to the hammam and sat on the sidewalk waiting for me. When I came out he would bring his face near my hair and sniff the smell as if he were inhaling me. Then he'd go away. The third time, after he sniffed my hair and turned away to go back to the hotel where he works, I took him by the hand and dragged him with me to the house. He seemed afraid. He almost fell down, more than once. But as soon as he came inside and saw that you were not here he fell on me and tried to rip my clothes off. I wanted him anyway so why did he have to do it like this? I felt like he was hurting me and I wanted to cry. He hugged me and then ran out of the house and I didn't understand anything. Then I hated him, and I do *not* want to stay here for another minute.

Me, no! said Musa. No! She made up this story. The pastor began to fuss at the top of his voice, right in the hotel restaurant, and he caused a scandal for me, Musa told Milia.

Musa told only wisps of his story to his sister. It was as though he had lost his memory and the only incident that stood out for him, and that he could talk about, was the fact that he did not know the girl did not speak Arabic. It's her father's fault, he said to Milia. He was sitting with me at the table – he and his daughter – and we were always speaking Arabic. True, she never said anything but she acted as though she understood what we were saying. She would nod her head and laugh whenever her father laughed, as if everything were normal. And when I was walking around with her, she nodded as if she understood what I was saying, even though she never said anything. I just told myself, maybe this is the way she is. These new religious types, these Seventh-day people and all of these religious groups coming to us here from America, maybe in these groups women don't talk to men until they're married. God knows – but I think he was mad. I think the girl needed to escape from him, not flee from me.

The hotel manager, Khawaja Salhab, told me he had decided to ban the man from coming to the restaurant because every Sunday now he was getting drunk and picking arguments with customers. It isn't a pleasant scene – a man of religion and always drunk, I don't want this fellow around, said Khawaja Salhab. But now, tell me – between you and me, what do American girls taste like?

Musa said no one believed his version. They all insisted that they believed him but he could read the envy in their eyes, as if he had indeed slept with the girl. In the end, even he believed the story and in fact he would retell it to his own son Iskandar, who worked as a reporter and editor at the *Ahrar* newspaper in Beirut. When Musa turned seventy, the son asked his father what the truth was about the relationship between Marika and the bishop. And somehow Musa ended up telling him the story of his year at Lake Tiberias, when he was eighteen. He related how he had put his arms around the American girl, who didn't say a word, and then suddenly all he wanted was to run away. It wasn't that he made a decision to leave the place, but he just suddenly left. That was the last thing I expected, he confided to his son. I saw myself – without even quite understanding what was happening – inside her and I was terrified. All I remember is how frightened I was and how alone I felt as I listened to her calling for help.

So, that story was true? asked his son.

I don't know. I do know for certain that the clergyman did not tell the truth. I hadn't yet discovered the way things work. I always refused to go with other young men to Tel Aviv. They said, There you can find bars and women. I didn't go, not once. Later, in Beirut, I learned the way with a girl from Aleppo – I don't remember her name. But that's how the world was in our time. A fellow couldn't do anything outside of the whores' *souq*. That's

~ 340 ~

where we all learned. But the American girl in Tiberias – that really was a love story, and she crossed it off. Maybe it had nothing to do with her. Her father was crazy-mad and he made up the rape and all of that. But the real problem was the nun. The nun announced that she smelled sin. My mother, God have mercy on her, started pressuring me to go to church and confess, and I didn't have anything to confess to. What was I going to say? Anyway, the truly important thing is that the only one who stood with me, and told my mother to leave me alone, was my dear sister, Milia.

Musa looked up at the picture hanging on the wall and tears began to roll down his cheeks.

Why are you crying, Musa, *habibi*! called out Milia.

The woman lying on the birthing bed was moaning and crying. The two nurses stood by and the doctor was grumbling.

This is not going to go smoothly, the doctor said.

Nurse I said there was a problem. Nurse II said the woman's face was turning blue.

The Italian doctor went over to the window, raised the sash, and gulped fresh air. The older nurse asked him what she should do, but instead of answering he turned to the second nurse and said in a low voice that he did not really understand what was happening. The young nurse bent toward him and asked him to repeat what he had said. Nothing, he replied.

The doctor was not Italian, as Mansour had thought. The name et-Talyani stuck to him because he had studied in Italy and had come back to Palestine bringing a very pretty Italian wife who stole the hearts of the Nazareth populace. Rita was considered the epitome of beauty in the small city bursting with monasteries, convents, churches, monks, and nuns. So Ghassan el-Hilw came to be called et-Talyani, after his eccentric wife, who carried a white parasol summer and winter, walking through the Nazareth alleys searching for the wondrous event, hoping to carry a baby. Four years went by without any sign of that longed-for pregnancy, and sometime in their fifth year living in Nazareth she traveled to her country of origin and never came back. But the doctor would not acknowledge the possibility that his wife would not return. He spoke of her as if she had gone on a short visit to her family and would be back in Nazareth next week. He went on expecting her and waiting for her, or so everyone thought. Months passed, and years, and the man went on repeating the same words he had always said whenever he was asked about his Italian wife – who, he said, was on a short visit to her mother, who was ill. The doctor began to walk through the city streets with his wife's white parasol held firmly upright. He mixed Arabic with Italian and he went on practicing as the first gynecologist Nazareth had ever known.

The doctor bent over the young nurse whom Milia had named Wadiia II, his mouth giving off the smell of cigarettes. The nurse averted her face but turned back to the doctor and raised her fingers to her face to remind him that he must stop smoking. But hearing a moan, she bent over the pregnant woman, to hear her say something unclear about crying.

What's the story, doctor? she asked.

Honestly I don't know. It is very strange. Everything looks perfectly normal, but she reacts as though she's afraid.

Yallah, my dear, the nurse said to the moaning woman. We've gotten through a lot of it already – there isn't much more to do.

Milia's eyelashes unraveled and a single tear came out from the corner of her left eye. She told Musa fiercely that he mustn't cry.

Don't cry, *habibi*. It's a dream, that's all. Just open your eyes and everything will go back to the way it was, and then you will see there's nothing to be afraid of.

But Musa did not open his eyes. The little boy tossed and tossed in bed next to his sister, dreams fluttering and beating their wings around his eyes, never leaving him alone. She had seen him coming in the darkness. Little Musa dragged his bare feet across the tiles of the *liwan* and approached his sister's bed. His green striped pajamas shivered and rippled beneath the silvery shadows of the moon creeping in from the window. He moved sluggishly toward his sister. Milia made a place for him next to her in bed, extending her arm so that he could drop his head onto it and fall asleep. But the boy simply climbed heavily into his sister's bed, drew himself into a ball, and dropped immediately into a deep slumber. Milia pulled her arm back, turned onto her left side, closed her eyes, and saw herself stealing into her brother's dream.

Musa sat in the garden exhaling his cigarette smoke and thinking about the story he did not know how to tell anyone. Since his return from Tiberias he no longer knew what he wanted out of this earthly life. His mother, Saadeh, was constantly in pain, or at least she moaned all the time, but after the marriage of her daughter and Milia's move to Nazareth, their mother had had no choice but to take an interest in the house and to do the work necessary to keep a family. Salim had gone to Aleppo, taking Najib with him, staying there with the Aleppan carpenter who got rid of his two daughters in one fell swoop. Niqula and Abdallah had transformed the father's shop into a small coffin-making factory. They had married the two Abu'l-Lamaa sisters and now were wont to act like a pair of fatuous emirs on the sole basis that they were in-laws of a family that had inherited the title of emir sometime in the bygone Ottoman era – even though that family lived in the genteel poverty of the eminent. Musa understood well that the invalid mother would be his lot since all of his brothers had left the house. Musa was convinced that the family had fallen apart because of Salim's idiotic behavior and his mother's underhanded ways. He did not understand that his mother was completely innocent when it came to Salim's plot and its disastrous effect on his sister's anticipated fortune in marriage, when he convinced Najib that their marriages to the two well-off Aleppan sisters was *the* solution to the problem of poverty that there seemed no escaping. When Niqula erupted and said he would kill his brother – that dog! – Musa looked at his mother as if he were accusing her. The mother protested that she had not known anything, but Musa was certain that she had blessed the step taken by her eldest son. In the end, after Musa wedded Adèle Niameh and they moved into the old house, their mother decided to move out, because Adèle could not endure the continuing charade of Saadeh's illnesses, and because Saadeh knew she did not want to end as Hasiba had, breathing in an air of disgust and fear and loss of memory. Musa rented an apartment for his mother near the convent, where she lived alone but also in the company of the saint whose eyes the blue water of glaucoma had begun to consume so that eventually she was swimming in a world of blue incense that gave her to feel that the saints surrounded her on every side.

Saadeh wanted to take Milia's photograph with her to her new home. Musa refused, though. Well, actually, he did not refuse. In resignation he said, *Ya* Mama, anything you wish, and then lifted the framed image down from its place on the wall and handed it to Saadeh. Stooping, she wrapped it in old newspapers. Musa paced in front of the sudden emptiness on the wall and sniffled. His mother stared at him in surprise. Tell me if you can't stand letting go of the picture – sweetheart, I don't want you crying. I don't want the picture, no, no, I don't want it now, not if you're going to get upset like this. The mother bent over the well-wrapped photograph and undid every layer of newsprint. And then she climbed up on the bed to return it to its place.

Mama, come down! yelled Musa. Get down from there! Leave it on the bed.

Saadeh left the photograph lying on the bed and left for her new residence. Musa never told his mother that what made him cry had not been the removal of the photograph or seeing it wrapped in layers of newsprint. He had promised his two daughters that the *liwan* would be theirs. He knew that the two teenaged girls would cover all available wall space with photos of Abdelhalim Hafiz, Dalida, and other singers and actors who had captured wholesale the imaginations of the city's youth who were encountering and embracing a sweep of new habits and understandings daily. As far as he was concerned, it made perfect sense now to remove Milia's likeness from the wall, and when his mother asked to take the photograph with her he was content, even relieved. Taking it down and giving it to his mother was easy enough. But glancing back at the empty white space left by the photograph's removal left him uneasy. He saw the shadow of an image – the image of an image – of his sister traced on the wall. Her almond-shaped eyes were out-lined in the shadows of the light that still emanated from them. Her facial features, though, were now simply grayish strands and contours that inched and curled across the peeling wall.

Her image has stayed on the wall, he wanted to say to his mother. But she would not see it; she did not want to see it. So what more could he say to her?

It's your brother Salim's fault, said Saadeh.

At that, Musa was ready to explode. He wanted to scream in the face of this woman who had transformed his and his wife's lives into a living hell with her insupportable daily devotionals. But he did not scream. He did not argue that it was her fault, and that if it hadn't been for the pressures and burdens she placed on Salim, none of this would have happened. The eldest son of the family was simply not courageous enough to have made the decision on his own; to have left permanently for Aleppo and to have abandoned his precious law studies at the Jesuit university. He would not have done it without his mother's encouragement. Musa had long been absolutely convinced of it.

Ten years after he left the family hearth, Salim came to visit his mother. She declared it high time to forget the past, invoked God's clemency, and summoned all of her children to an immense meal that she had prepared in honor of Salim and his extremely plump wife. Everyone wept as they hugged their elder brother, who had not become a lawyer after all but had returned to his father's craft. All of them, except Niqula, forgave him. Even Musa forgave and asked forgiveness and cried. Only Niqula – red tarbush, respectably corpulent figure, bulging eyes – refused absolutely to kiss his brother in forgiveness.

This was the return of the Prodigal Son, announced their mother. Slaughter the fatted calf, boys, and come to the table of brotherly love.

Salim had not come to Beirut without cause. He was keen to investigate the possibility of returning to work with his brothers Niqula and Abdallah. Business was stagnant in Aleppo, he said, and he was hoping to return to work in his father's carpentry workshop.

You mean, after all of these years you have come back to us to demand a share of what your father left?! *Ya Ayb issh-shom!* Niqula was apoplectic. You shameful man, you ran a knife through us and you destroyed your sister and now you've come to ask this. Get out of here!

Salim did not get out of there. It was Niqula who stood up and left the house. Before doing so, he turned to his mother and said, From the day Milia left we have not had a bite of supper we could swallow, Mama.

Musa was not following their argument over the family business and money matters. He was staring at his older brother, stunned. Salim's features had lengthened and sunk; the white hair of old age had conquered his head, and his lips had lost their fullness. His eyes seemed lost in their sockets. He had become a carbon copy of his father. Anyone who saw him now would believe Yusuf had come back to life. Niqula put a decisive end to the conversation by refusing unconditionally to receive his brother in the shop. Abdallah was confused, as if he did not understand what was unfolding before his eyes, while Musa pondered his eldest brother's shocking transformation into their father's double. But no one could ignore Salim's gravelly voice when he said, It's your fault, Mother – you told me, Go, don't worry about your sister, God will find a solution for Milia.

Silence seized the room, as if Salim's words, though not very loud, had swept a storm through this space where they sat.

You! What exactly did you say to Salim, Mother? asked Musa.

Me! No, not me, I don't remember saying anything.

Yes, you! You turned the girl's life into misery and sent her off to a land that was going up in flames! said Musa.

Saadeh began to cry and the quarrel intensified. Abdallah cursed his mother and his oldest brother. They had destroyed the life of his sister for nothing, he sobbed.

Now, and very promptly, the symptoms of illness made their appearance. Saadeh's face grew florid and she had trouble breathing. Abdallah ran to get the doctor. Musa went into his room and shut the door and decided he would never speak to his mother again.

But these sorts of irrevocable domestic rulings are liable enough to peter out before long. Salim returned to his Aleppan home and once again all news of him ended. And here was Musa helping his mother pack her belongings so that she could move to the house where she would die. Milia's portrait would remain hung on the wall in exactly the same space because the wall refused to give it up.

Come, Musa, *habibi*, come sleep next to me and don't cry.

She could see him. Musa was turning restlessly in his bed and the shadows of his dreams hovered close around his eyes. He sat alone on the shore of Lake Tiberias. Suddenly the waves leapt up to eye level. The Sea of Galilee rose and white froth swallowed the horizon. The waves pushed higher and farther, and the restaurant began to collapse under the fierce pounding of the water. Musa was in a tiny boat, rocked by the waves and the wind. In the distance Milia stood erect. Little Milia walked on the waters of the lake. She strode over the water and stretched out both arms. From this distance she looked like a little bird spreading its wings to fly. But the bird was knocked about in the waves, rising and falling. It appeared and vanished, came nearer and then moved away. Little Milia staggered atop the waves, beads of water washing over her. Mansour grabbed the oars and tried frantically to row with both hands, wanting to reach her. But she moved farther away, the water swallowed her, and Musa's voice could not command the sea to grow quiet. Musa sat alone in the Seaside Inn's restaurant on the deck built of wood planks that extended like a tongue into the lake, allowing restaurant customers to think that they were in a boat lacking only sails. The place was empty, and the only sound was a light crashing of waves beating against the wooden supports that held the restaurant aloft. Musa took a big bite of fish seasoned with lemon and salt and began chewing. His head spun as he saw his teeth fall out. He had felt nothing; he believed at first that he had taken in a mouthful of fish bones. He bent over his plate and spit but his cheeks felt like they were plastered together and his mouth was hollow. Looking down at his plate, Musa saw that all of his teeth had fallen out. He picked up the teeth and began trying to return them to his mouth but it hurt. His mouth was an explosion of pains and he wanted to scream but couldn't. He stared out at the lake, wanting to tell his sister that he was in terrible pain, but the lake was not there. The waves had disappeared and he was in total darkness. Everything was drowned in the darkness of night and the night clung to his body. He tried to open his eyes but could not. They were sealed closed with wax or something like it, and he smelled incense. The man shook himself, made the sign of the cross on his forehead, and started from his bed as he used to do as a small boy, going on tiptoe to sleep next to his sister.

Don't be afraid, love, I'm right here beside you.

She wanted to tell her brother that Father Tanyous had gone away leaving no trace. Was it true that the body of the Lebanese monk had been found near the Virgin's Wellspring? When she asked Mansour what had happened, the man denied any knowledge of it.

But you told me, love.

Me!

Yesterday you told me they found the body and they don't know what they should do with it. The monk was lying there as if he had been crucified. Someone shot him in the mouth and nailed his hands to the ground, and the French nun, the Mother Superior, ordered that it be kept quiet. She had the monk wrapped in a white sheet and said he would be buried in Lebanon, and there would be no more talk about the incident.

Me!

Yes of course, you – do I ever see anyone else in this town?

I told you, let's go, we're going to Jaffa where we have plenty of family. You said you wouldn't move an inch from here before the baby arrives and I'm waiting. So don't complain that you don't see anyone. This is what you wanted!

But that's not what I'm talking about, she said.

She wanted to return to Musa's side to help him put his teeth back in his mouth. Milia knew what this was about. Her grandmama Malakeh had told her of the two dreams that warn of death. Cutting or losing hair and teeth falling out. All other dreams, Malakeh said, are journeys to faraway worlds, because a person's soul cannot endure staying interminably in the body. When the body sleeps, the soul leaves it; when the spirit returns, made lighter and happier by all it has seen, the body metes out a terrible beating. Sleep is like a space of struggle – a battlefield – between soul and body. Milia's grandmother reminded her that when they are awake, people are not conscious of their souls, but when the angel of sleep descends and the soul rises to float above time and place, a person can divine the separate parts of the self united by the will of the Creator. This is the miracle of life; think about it, said Grandmama: how can fire and water meet? A human being is the meeting place of two completely incompatible elements, earth and air. Our bodies are dust to dust, our souls are the air. But the only way we ever become aware of our spirits' abilities to rise above the body is when we dream. When the soul travels, leaving behind the soil that awaits its return, we finally realize what life truly means. But the soul is practicing to abandon the body, and as it does so it discovers its own distinct, unique existence.

You mean, there are two of me, Grandmama? Milia's voice came out timid and breathless.

Of course there are, my dear! Didn't you dream of your aunt Salma before she died? And in your dream, you saw her dreaming – and flying.

I did?

That's why your aunt did not really die. Her soul realized that there was no longer any need for her body. But, you see, the body can't accept this without a struggle. So the body creates problems and causes so much pain that the soul is in agony and gives up hope of leaving the body behind. *Ya haraam*, poor Salma, what agony she went through! Do you remember, Milia, how much your dear aunt suffered?

I don't know, answered the trembling girl. She sensed her soul making preparations to leave her body and it left her in terror. She stared into her own eyes in the mirror offered by the little pond in the garden where she spent most of her time, splashing in the water. She wanted to ask her grandmother if her eyes were part of her body, or whether they belonged to the spirit.

Eyes belong to the human soul, declared the nun. Look at the eyes of Mar Ilyas. See how his eyes gleam with fire? Why, why did you go to sleep, my girl?! I brought you to Mar Ilyas's grotto so that you would see him and he would see you, and then he would remember you always. My daughter, I will die, and I will not be able to intercede for you anymore. Look directly into his eyes and tell him you love him.

The eyes of the prophet who had never died abandoned their sockets to suspend themselves on the sloping arched wall of the grotto. Milia saw their gleam everywhere in this domed grotto, which was large enough only to accommodate one human body lying full length. The prophet would not have been able to stand up straight in his low-ceilinged cave; he would have had to drop to all fours and crawl into the space where he would rest his head. His eyes came out of the red and blue icon set beside the rock that he had made his pillow. Those eyes were everywhere. Milia was afraid, seeing so many eyes. She wanted to thank him because he had rescued her from her illness, and she was on the point of asking him not to forget her when suddenly she saw an eagle in the grotto. How could the eagle have come in here, from the single tiny aperture in the cavern's ceiling? Milia saw him as though her eyes had acquired the ability to pierce walls and spaces and rove the broad and empty firmament. There far above he circled, his great wings spread to catch the thin strands of cloud streaked across the sky like a diaphanous sash. He spiraled across the sky, sharp eyes searching for the grotto's opening. Suddenly the bird folded his wings and began to drop. Milia screamed at him to open out his wings. You will die! Please, please don't do that – who will bring food to poor Mar Ilyas?

But the plummeting eagle did not hear her and she thought he had decided it was time to die. But just above the cavern's opening he suddenly pleated his body until he was no more than an ordinary little bird as compact as any human fist. He sailed into the grotto's interior and only then did he unfurl his tremendous wings, beating them against the cavern walls as if determined to widen the interior space. Milia sat in Mar Ilyas's tiny pit unable to move. She felt herself drawn with irresistible force toward the eagle's talons, which were closing around her, ready to lift her into the open air. The ascent made her dizzy and she could not have been more frightened. She saw her aunt Salma's face appear like a vision in the distant sky. Salma asked her about Ibrahim Hananiya. She was crying.

Auntie, why are you crying? The dead don't cry. They mustn't cry.

Milia did not hear her aunt Salma's answer; the woman had disappeared. The little girl saw herself lying on the wide pavement in front of the Church of the Annunciation in Nazareth. Her belly was swollen and her hands were stretched out cruciform.

And then she saw the two of them, standing exactly opposite. She could not tell them apart. The saintlike nun held Tanyous's hand as if they were a pair of elderly men, their faces attacked so vigorously by wrinkles that it was difficult to tell who they were. She heard a faraway voice instructing her to push. A hand gripped her hard and shook her by the shoulder. Open your eyes, girl, and *push*! *Yallah*, let's finish up here, you have already gone a long distance and there isn't much further to go.

Milia opened her eyes slowly and there was light. A dazzling sun had come out, now that the downpour had stopped, and the brilliance of it pierced every corner. Behind the light stood the aged Italian doctor, telling the woman lying on the birthing bed to help him bring her baby out. My girl, everything is fine and *inshallah* we are almost there but you have to help us out a little.

Milia gave him a little smile. She felt a towelly roughness as one of the nurses swabbed away the cold sweat falling into her eyes, and she asked for Mansour.

Mansour stood next to her. They were in the vast reception hall of the Hotel Massabki, where the photographs were lined up along the wall. He wanted her to stand beneath a photograph of Shaykh Bishara el-Khoury, president of the independent republic of Lebanon, with Jamil Mardam Bey, the prime minister of Syria. This wall of photographs, Mansour explained to her, was a summary of the history of Syria, Lebanon, and Palestine.

Strange, he said, it's as though our history does not exist except on this one wall in a very small city on the Beirut-Damascus road, a wall that is here for the purpose of recording the tale of the Arabs' defeats.

Please – I don't like politics. From the moment we stepped inside this hotel, all you have talked about is King Faisal and the Battle of Maysalun and such things, and it's giving me a headache.

She extricated herself from his grip and turned to another portion of the wall where two framed poems hung side by side.

Mansour went up to them and read out loud.

> *In Massabki we savored what our bodies craved,*
> *and the soft strains of strings and ever a glass!*
> *The place was beauteous, amiable, and so warm*
> *as if hosted by the quaffer Abu Nuwas*

This is by the Egyptians' Prince of Poetry, he said. Ahmad Shawqi always stayed in this hotel. He came with Muhammad Abd el-Wahhab, the musician, carrying his lute. Abd el-Wahhab was forever putting verses of Shawqi's together and setting them to music. Over here is a photograph of Khalil Mutran, who was called the poet of the two lands since he lived in Egypt but was from these parts. He came here, too.

But the Messiah, why bring him into this? And I don't like this poem much. Mansour went up to the second framed poem.

> *Maryam ran frightened, in search of her son*
> *the young Yasua in that vast space*

I called out, Maryam, do not fret and cry
Yasua's at Massabki: calm be your face!

What is the Messiah doing here, in the middle of all of this? No, this isn't real poetry, my dear.

It was on that day – the second day of their marriage – that Mansour realized he would never be able to grasp this woman who had now become his wife. He had told his mother that he had fallen in love with her for her womanliness: her tall and nicely filled-out figure, full hips, small waist – and her clear, soft pale skin, which reminded him of the beautiful pale-white figure, Daad, in *The Orphan Pearl*. The lines of her graceful body inhabited his imagination with the help of ten, twenty, one hundred poems singing the praises of love, in which Arab poets cataloged the innumerable desires and longings and inclinations attaching to the body of the beloved woman.

Where did those longings go? Why had this lethal sense of solitude come over Mansour? Since his brother's death he had lived an unending maelstrom of anxiety, despair, and fear. He was not afraid of Jaffa or of war. He had decided to return to his city because it was what he had to do, and Asma, the young widow, had become his responsibility. He had even dreamed once that he had become husband to two women, Asma and Milia. And why not? He was overpoweringly hungry for it. Milia, in her eighth month of pregnancy, was astonishingly round. As she slept, her long hair flung across the pillow, he sat alone in the sitting room, sipping a cup of tea and smoking. He imagined himself between the two women and felt a quick pulsing through his veins. He was aware of how intensely bodily desire had come to possess him, as if a strong hand had seized his testicles and was squeezing them relentlessly.

Then suddenly he was undressing in the bedroom and was in bed next to Milia. He pressed his hands to her waist and the sleeping woman shifted position, turning her back to him. Her face disappeared beneath the tousled hair strewn across the pillow. He rolled over onto her body to take her. He cupped his hands over her breasts and his lips crept up her neck. And at the instant when he meant to come into her everything in him dwindled to nothing. His desire vanished as if a wave of icy water had choked the flame. Spirit abased, breath throttled, body suffocating, he moved away and lay on his back, humiliated to the core. He was certain that Milia was not asleep, that she had witnessed his collapse; she was watching it. Since the very beginning – ever since their first night at the Massabki – he had never been able to master this business of taking a sleeping woman. It left him uneasy. Yet it was a game he marveled at, as though it freed him and made him lord of the bed, as though Milia would give him what he wanted, when he wanted it, without ever calling him to account. He relished this sport that had charged his very marrow with unquenchable cravings. The woman's restless slumber as he lay close to her had become his greatest pleasure, the source of the poetry he summoned to his lips. But now he was perplexed and his confusion left him in an agony of body and mind. How would he escape this ring of abject defeat into which he had slipped?

He got out of bed, threw on his undergarments and pajamas and heard her voice.

What's wrong, *habibi*?

He didn't answer. He went into the bathroom and closed the door.

Milia got out of bed. She knocked on the bathroom door and asked him if he was ill, and she heard his hoarse voice. It's nothing, my dear. He told her to go back to bed and wait for him.

Mama, where are you? cried the woman lying on her bed of pain in the Italian Hospital in Nazareth. Tanyous the monk stood facing her. He stretched his hands toward her as if they were ready to bring out the new-born.

I don't want to go to Jaffa! I want to take the boy and go to Beirut. Please, Father Tanyous, tell my mother to come and get me. No, no – tell my brother Musa to come and find me so that we can make an escape from here.

The Master, peace be upon Him, Tanyous said, went to his death of his own will. Tanyous opened the book and began to read. Milia did not understand the Syriac words that the Lebanese monk's mouth formed, yet she saw Him, walking through the streets of Jerusalem on the way to Golgotha carrying an enormous wooden cross, soldiers all around him, walking on and on as the whip tore into his back, gazing forward to see only the face of Maryam the Majdaliyya, now so perfectly like his own mother's face. He bent double to shelter the pain through his body, wounded by the implacable whipping. He gazed into the distance and saw Ibrahim the Friend of God walking behind his son, as Ishaq bore on his back the wood his father had gathered for the sacrifice: the son, bent in obedience.

Did he know? Or did the father hide the truth from his son?

That was the question Yasua of Nazareth put to his father Yusuf the Carpenter as they sat together and mended their relationship after the father confessed to his son that he had intended to kill him but that he understood now that this had reflected the will of God.

So, you are just like Ibrahim, said Yasua. You were intending to kill me just like he meant to kill his son and offer him as a sacrifice to his god.

Son, a father does not kill his own son, said Yusuf, grief in his eyes. My eyes were veiled by a black cloud and I hesitated – I did not know what to do. Now it's over. You are my only son – is there anyone who would kill his only son?

And what about him?

I don't know. I expect that Ibrahim did not know about the sheep. He heard Allah's command in his dream. He couldn't act against it, could he?

I'm asking you about Ishaq.

~ 356 ~

No, that was not how the story went. Where did that story come from, the tale of the father's flight? Father Tanyous told her a different version, but then why did she see the son standing before the fire with a knife in his hand? And where had the fire come from? Maryam stood trembling as she faced the Mount of Qafzeh in Nazareth, but she saw no fire. She saw him, and she saw that they wanted to cast him into the steep valley; she stood at the rim of the wadi and trembled. Here, pausing before the courtyard of the church they called Our Lady of the Tremblings, the pregnant woman who has come from Beirut, under the cover of darkness, trembles in the cold air. Father Tanyous asks her why she has come to the church in her nightgown and she replies that she did not realize. I am asleep, Father. I am dreaming. This is all a dream; it has nothing to do with what is happening out there. What has pulled you into my dreaming? Now I am going to open my eyes, find myself in the house, and you will no longer be in front of me.

No, don't open your eyes, says Tanyous, because there's something very important I need to tell you.

The monk reads the story of the merciful Friend Khalil Ibrahim with his son. Do you know why Hebron is called the City of Khalil? His grave is there and his real name is Khalil because he was the friend of Abu Issa.

Abu Issa? But just who is the Father of Issa? she asked.

I see that you don't read books, my girl. Perhaps you do have good reason not to know something in a book that will be written in Beirut fifty years from now. How could you read this book if it is yet to be written?

But you – how can you read something before it's written?

Because I read eyes. And you too, Milia. You will read things before they are written. You will read them in the moment the ancient man stands before your bed in the Italian Hospital and says, Now, Master. The time has come to release Your servant.

You mean, when I have my son you will die?

Not me alone.

No, I don't want my son to die, she cried. Does it make any sense for this to happen? Does it make any sense for a father to kill his own son?

The monk opened the book and began to read.

Ibrahim bound his son in ropes and set him before the pile of kindling. He sat waiting when lo and behold, the sky shone with a light, and Ibrahim saw three angels bearing a white ram that gave off the fragrance of water. They placed him on the pile of wood.

The prophet knelt and his tears ran. He came to his son, untied his fetters, and gently pushed him aside. Ishaq stood and went to the white ram. He put his hand on the animal's head and heard a low moan coming from the belly of the small trembling animal. He ran to cut an armful of green grass to feed the ram. The animal nosed the grass and Ishaq's tears welled. His hands filled with tears. He turned back and saw his father coming, a knife in his hand.

No, Father! shrieked the boy.

Ibrahim shoved his son away, seized the ram by the neck, and slaughtered him with a cry of praise and joy to his Lord. The blood spurted out to fill the wadi, and the boy heard the sound of rushing blood. The sound rang full in his ears. The blood flowed before him in a current that twisted and turned, seeking a channel in the earth, and the screams rose.

When Ibrahim slaughtered the ram, and the man and his son smelled the scent of death, blood-hunger erupted through their bodies. Ibrahim stepped back and gazed upward into the firmament and asked Allah to help him endure this trial. He looked at his son and so the boy bent over the slaughtered ram, who was thrashing about in his blood. He was trying to capture the animal's final heartbeats that pulsed over the white wool spattered with sacrificial red.

He ordered his son to pick up the ram and put him on the pile of wood.

The boy obeyed, carrying the ram to the waiting kindling. He felt the knife blade at his back. The young man smelled his father's scent, a mingling of blood and manure, and was afraid. He threw down the ram and turned back to see the knife blade gleaming in his father's hand, and he fled. The father ran behind his son, entreating him to turn back. But the boy was certain that to return would be to fall under the sharp edge of the knife.

The father tried to catch up with his son but he could not. He retraced his steps to the pile of branches, lit the fire, and offered the slaughtered beast. He sat in the open air, knife in hand. And he remained there, unmoving, awaiting the coming of the true animal.

You mean the Messiah knew he would be killed in sacrifice? asked Milia.

Yes, surely he knew.

So why did he return?

Because the story had to end.

But I don't want the story to end! she exclaimed.

There is no story that does not end.

You're wrong – there isn't a single story that comes to an end. Stories do not end. And I don't believe that the father sat for a thousand years waiting for his son to return so that he could kill him.

Milia said she was tired and wanted to open her eyes.

Don't open your eyes, shrieked the monk. There is still a story I want to tell you.

I'm tired of you and of your stories. The story doesn't go like this. The Messiah knew that there was a sheep. Ibrahim took his son there against his will. He could not rebel against God's command. He took him to the mount, he was suffering terribly but there was nothing else he could do. There he tied him up and lifted his eyes to the heavens and cried out and began to weep. That was the instant when the lamb appeared, and Ibrahim saw it and understood that God was testing him, testing his dedication. He knelt and asked forgiveness. He embraced his son and they wept together. And then they slaughtered the lamb and went home, as if nothing had happened. The Messiah knew this story; he had heard it or read it maybe a thousand times, and that's why when they condemned him to the cross he was not afraid. He knew that his Father, who had sent the animal to save Ishaq from death could not possibly abandon his son.

Then why did He abandon him? asked the monk.

I don't know – you are asking me? You're the one who is supposed to give the answers.

Because, as I told you, he had been waiting for him, all those days he was waiting.

But he did not know – no, don't try to tell me that he knew. He believed there would be a lamb. Otherwise, he would not have gone.

I don't know, said the monk.

She did not want to hear this story again, Milia told him. She was in pain from head to toe. She tried to make a sound but it felt like a hand covered her mouth, and then it enlarged to cover her nose as well, and was throttling her. I am dying, she wanted to say. But she could not say anything. This was death. You die when you can no longer utter these words: I am dying. No! I don't want to die. Who will care for my son, and what if they take him to Jaffa? She wanted to open her eyes and find herself in her own bed. She had told the monk from Lebanon that she could open her eyes whenever she wanted. And then he would have departed her world, because she would be alone in her own bed.

Her eyes parted and the light shattered them. She saw herself in a bed that was not hers, lying on a pile of wood; she sensed the smell of blood. She reached over her belly and at its lowest point she felt blood gathering. She felt water. This is marriage, she whispered, and closed her eyes again.

When she saw him she understood that this bright yellow sun sweeping across her eyes, pressing them closed, beamed from the halo encircling his head. Thus she named him Shams el-Adl, the Sun of Justice. He was the sun and he was justice, walking hand in hand to their death. Yasua walks alone toward Golgotha and remembers his father. He remembers how the story had frightened him – overpowered him – until he was reassured that the true story was the lamb's story: the tale of the lamb coming from the sun's position in the sky to rescue the son from death. The whip lashes him from all directions and he walks on, the smile of victory upon his lips. He sees his face mirrored forever in the eyes of his two Maryams. He feels the pain of the ecstasy of being alive. He walks on and the lamb hovers near. No one sees the lamb but his mother, and when she approaches the gentle beast and puts out her hand to touch its head, she feels emptiness. She looks at her son, wanting to know that what she sees is not an illusion. He averts his gaze and says, Go, woman, for my hour has not yet come.

Blood in the streets. The city has put on a cloak of blood and has bejeweled itself with ruins. Where has the perfume of orange blossoms gone, that scent that had stretched the length of the sparkling shoreline?

One time only Milia had agreed to go to Jaffa with Mansour. He had said, Just come once and have a look. She replied that she had already gone and had seen the city and there was no need to go again. He told her that since she had gone for Amin's funeral she had seen nothing, since at a funeral no one sees anything. She said she hated the city. But Jaffa is the Bride of the Mediterranean! he said. When you say *Jaffa*, he said, you think of the diligences, the sea, the white beaches, the Prophet Ruben, and Daadaa. The tastiest grills and the finest hummus ever, he said – they are right there in Master Daadaa's restaurant on Shabab Street in Jbaileh. He told her he would take her to see the Mosque of Hasan Bey and the famous red hill and the quarter of Rashid, and he would feed her the delicious stewed *fuul* at Fathallah's. He said, he said, he said . . . and she listened to him, wanting to tell him that she was willing to move away from Nazareth but she did not want Jaffa. She wanted Bethlehem.

I know what will happen, she said. They want to take you away from me, and then they will take away my son, and then I don't know what will happen. I smell war and death there. Yesterday, I dreamed –

Please, I beg you – none of those dreams of yours.

He said *none of those dreams of yours* to force her to accompany him. What had happened to the man? She wanted to explain to him that death was not the problem. That the dead are merely sleeping and dreaming, and that their dreams never end. But he was no longer able to grasp what she meant. Had he ever understood any of it? Or did he simply want to swim with her in bed? When he used that word – *sibaha* – he was reciting the poetry of Imru'l-Qays and telling her that the straying king had slept with a woman who was nursing her baby. Tomorrow, he said, that's what I want to do, just like the poet – it must have been something tremendous. She did not answer, and then he told her that when he slept with her he felt like he was swimming.

She went to Jaffa with him. She breathed in the fragrance of oranges. Everyone loved that scent and grew intoxicated on the smell of bitter-orange blossoms. Milia loved this velvety smell as much as they did, but here in Jaffa what she smelled was blood. She told him his city resembled Tripoli in the north of Lebanon.

Jaffa is Tripoli's sister, he said.

She had gone once to Tripoli, she said. Her oldest brother, Salim, took her there when she was seven. She didn't remember much. But she did smell the bitter-orange blossoms. She remembered that.

It's as if I'm in Tripoli, she said. The clock tower square here is like Tell Square there. But she did not like this place, she told him, because she smelled a strange odor here. She saw how Tel Aviv had turned its back to the sea and opened its mouth wide to gobble up Jaffa.

She told Mansour that Jaffa would drown in the sea. They were sitting together on the seafront eating grilled meat. Mansour was drinking arak and Milia stared at the endless blue sky, and she told him that she had dreamed the previous night of the sea sweeping over the city. The Ajami quarter was filled with people speaking Iraqi Arabic, she said, and boats sailed down King Faisal Street. People were gathering in Rashid where seawater had risen in the streets.

Milia is lying back in a car that has come to a stop in the middle of the street while everyone streams by, jostling fiercely, to reach the seafront. Lord! Mansour told me he would not take me to Jaffa before I had the baby. Mansour, what are you doing on the roof of the house in Ajami?

The roar of bombs exploding is everywhere. Asma carries a still-nursing baby and Umm Amin pulls two small children along, as human waves descend toward the harbor. People push each other, rushing forward, peering ahead with eyes that see nothing, for a dense cloud of dust covers everything. Men shove their bodies in amidst the crowds of women and tear off their uniforms as they disappear into the chaos. Mansour crouches on the roof of the house holding an English rifle.

Why are they running away? asks Milia.

They're the Iraqi volunteers. They've tossed away their weapons because their commander has been thrown out and they refuse to take orders from anyone but Hajj Mourad el-Yugoslavi.

I was asking about the children, she said.

Wearing his long heavy coat, Mansour sways and bends in the high winds buffeting the city. She sees him walking along the roof edge holding a lit candle whose flame the fog dulls, and she feels the cold penetrating. The two Wadiias sit beside her in the backseat of the American car. Milia wants to open her eyes but the sun burns everything and she is burning and Mansour is burning. She hears the ship's horn. The Greek ship sitting motionless in

Jaffa harbor is getting ready to sail. Mansour stands beside an old man. The old man says that the Jaffa-Lod detachment has been decimated and the mujahideen who remained have all scattered around the harbor.

Where's Michel Issa? Mansour asks.

A full pale-complexioned face, a black moustache so shaggy it covers his lips, and wet clothes – Michel Issa stood amidst the bombs hurtling down on the city from every direction and felt his voice disappear. When he and Mansour met on the Greek ship, he said he'd realized that he was no longer a general protecting his city once his voice refused to obey him. He knew that the battle was over. The two hundred men who marched here as a relief army to come to their rescue had dispersed among all the rest.

On the deck of the boat, wrapped tightly in his overcoat, Mansour listens to the final blast of the horn before the boat leaves for Beirut.

Asma stands in her black garb in the garden of the Jaffa house and screams to Mansour. Either take me to the Prophet Ruben's festival or divorce me!

When did you marry her, Mansour?

Mansour had never taken anyone to the prophet's festival, which he remembered from his childhood. He remembered the tents and the Sufi's *dhikr* sessions and the white flag on which was written: There is no God but God and Ruben is God's prophet. He remembered the joy erupting from the Great Mosque in the city center and sending its cloud of ecstasy all the way to Ajami. He remembered the women celebrating Ruben on the fifteenth of September but he did not know who this prophet was who had given his name to a small river south of Jaffa. He could not comprehend why the people of Jaffa would spend an entire month in Rubin's tents preparing to welcome in the autumn.

Mansour told her that in the midst of war it was impossible, and he would take her to call out in celebration of Ruben the next year. But the short rotund woman did not understand. She wanted Ruben now.

You must not cry, said the Italian doctor. In a moment, give it another push and before you know it we will be done and everything will be fine.

The ship's horn sounded and the ships of the Companie Gharghour left the harbor. The city was empty now. The sea had taken the people. Where were the people?

A tall man known as the Beiruti, Ataallah Beiruti, stands erect before the British general and an officer from the Haganah, proclaiming Jaffa an open city.

The ship sounds its horn and the Jews are ready to enter the city. The Mosque of Hasan Bey is in their hands. Ajami is in their hands. The city quarters stoop and bow, one against the next. The only sound is the wind knocking against the houses.

Don't forget the key to the house, Milia shouts.

Mansour tosses away his rifle, hurries down from the roof, and runs toward the Greek packet anchored in the harbor. The smoke rises and thickens, the motor growls, and Mansour runs, waving his hands wildly and shouting at the captain to wait for him. He stumbles and falls, stops to shed the overcoat that is slowing his pace, throws it to the ground, and runs.

The ship is on the high sea. Mansour sits on the deck and Jaffa grows distant.

Why did you leave the city? a young Greek sailor asks.

Tents are everywhere.

What is this? asks Milia. Why did you put up the tents here?

They told her that the Prophet Ruben's festival was approaching. They said that Jaffa erects its tents on the south bank of the river and everyone goes there.

Where is Ruben the prophet?

They said he would be sitting alone there, waiting for the people to arrive. The people picked up their tents and went, and all that remained was the smell of blood.

Blood in the streets. Mansour stands before his workshop, which lies in ruins, the machinery soaked in blood and wet with severed limbs. A terrible, lonely silence makes him shiver to the core. Where are you, Milia? Mansour cries out. I am dying, Milia.

Don't cry, *habibi*, I'm here, murmurs the woman lying on the hospital bed.

He walks on, stooping low. Yasua the Nazarene stoops under the heaviness of the cross. He walks through the city's narrow lanes, his body weak with fatigue. This thirty-year-old man has never felt such weariness. In his father's shop he lifted thick tree trunks and never felt this sort of exhaustion. The slim boy with the greenish eyes and the curly black hair and the broad high forehead walked as though his feet did not touch the ground. He worked as though it was not work, as though a strange power nested inside his ribs; and when he tried to tell his story to his father, Yusuf didn't allow him to finish it. No sooner would he start to relate his peculiar dream than his father would snatch the words from his mouth.

The same thing had happened with the fishermen at the Sea of Galilee. No sooner had he walked across the surface of the water and ordered the storm to die down, and then wanted to speak, than the fishermen began to talk, saying they understood the message.

And when he stood on the Mount of Olives addressing them they did not listen to him. They were bewitched by the light that came from his eyes and turned the earth into a never-ending orchard of olive trees.

When he told the people to leave the woman alone as she washed his feet in perfumed water and dried them with her black hair that was long enough to cover her back, they bent over his feet and did not allow him to tell them it was a question of love and the woman's loose hair was the world's pillow.

When he told his mother he was going to Jerusalem and she must not come with him, she did not let him finish what he had to say. She placed her hand on his head and said she was coming because she knew that he was the king.

When they tried him and he found himself alone and in the hands of the executioners, and he wanted to tell them his story, they slapped him with questions that were nothing more than answers.

He smiled at Maryam the Majdaliyya when she asked him why he did not talk. He was the Word, he told her. She asked for an answer to her question.

In truth I tell you that speech is like the grain of wheat in the field. No one owns the word for it is the mere echo of the Word carved into the cross.

He felt the terrible heaviness of the cross they forced him to bear and he was afraid. No, he was not afraid but he was confounded. It was as though his strength had gone, leaving him weak and fragile.

He fasted for forty days and when he called his disciples to supper and gave them the finest of Palestine's wines he took only a single bite of bread. He wanted no food; his longings were for his father.

Amidst weakness and a sense of defeat, whipping, and humiliation, he remembered the lamb and smiled.

Why all of this light? Please, put out the light.

Pain through the eye sockets, and suffering. Why is Hasiba here and why has the clock stopped? White locks of hair are strewn across the pillow. The old woman tries to lift her head but she cannot. Little Milia stands at her grandmother's side. Grandmama says that all the clocks in the house have stopped. She tries to lift her hand from the pillow but it falls before it is even lifted. Milia stands next to her and doesn't know what to do.

The girl runs through the house. The house has turned into a sort of spiral and the girl whirls round and round. All the clocks in the house say that it is three o'clock in the morning.

Wind the clock, Musa, dear.

Musa comes at a run, his clothes covered in mud and blood oozing from his scraped knees.

Why this blood, *habibi*? I told you, the blood dream is no good. Why do you always force me to dream of you covered in blood? I have come from there to Beirut, yes, I traveled even with all of these difficulties. I told my son to wait, to stay in my womb. I told him it would be only a matter of a few hours. I must go to Beirut, I said, your uncle Musa is dreaming and it is a bad dream. I must go to him, and so now I have come to you. And you are here and are covered in blood. Enough blood, God save us from all of this blood! Isn't this what the nun was always calling when she prayed? Remember, how she made us stand in front of the icon, Maryam holding her son, and she called, Almighty God, deliver us from the blood. O God of my salvation, deliver us, that my lips may sing your justice. She ordered us to repeat the prayers after her and we always did. Where is Haajja Milana? Why does she sit all alone with no one to answer when she calls? She said she always sees everything as black, and at the very heart of it was incense. She said she could no longer see human bodies but that she lived with their souls. Why is the nun all alone, and why can she not get out of bed, and where does the smell come from? Is it possible to leave the saint like this, no one taking care of her, no one cleaning and grooming her? Where are you, Saadeh, where are you, Mama?

Saadeh stands next to a metal bed in a darkened room. She puts on a light and the saint orders her to put it out. The light hurts my eyes and I can't see, she moans. Saadeh does not extinguish the light though. She has come to this faraway convent to bathe the nun, she says, and she cannot do it without light. The vapor rises from a copper vessel filled with hot water and the nun shrieks because she does not want a bath. You have come to kill me just as you killed your daughter, Milana screams. Get out, turn out the light and get out!

Shh, Haajja, I've come to bathe you, that's all. Why did they leave you in this state? Why don't you perform a miracle and get up? What's this smell? *Yallah*, let me take off your clothes, I'll just give you a bath and rub your body with cologne and you'll see how much better you are.

Saadeh came close to the nun to help her to remove her clothes. The nun covered her eyes with her hands and began to moan. She sat up straight in bed and screamed that she could smell Satan's stench. You've sent Satan to me, Saadeh! As soon as you came in the smell of incense disappeared. Where is the incense? It runs away from light, and that's why you turned on the light. What do you want with me, I know you've come to kill me! You killed your daughter. I saw her, I saw her – *haraam*, I saw how her whole body went green as if grass had sprouted on it, Lord God, saints preserve us, Lord God! She was sleeping, and dreaming, when the doctor shouted at her to open her eyes. She tried to open them but the light . . . she told them to put out the light but no one heard her. Her body began to shake, like mine is shaking now, and she saw everything. She saw you, Saadeh, and she saw the Devil sitting up there on your right shoulder. Get out – I don't want to die!

Milia tried to open her eyes and she saw him. He was sitting directly beneath her image in the *liwan*, studying the half-erased face and filling the emptinesses in and slipping in words between words in a miniaturistic hand. He was young, his face dark and hair short and curly, and he sat in the red-orange patch of sunlight beaming in from the window. He was writing intensely. She wanted to ask him who he was and why he was sitting beneath her picture. Wearing the longish brown dress that covered her knees and looking up at the high brass bed, she approached him. The little girl gazed at that boy who couldn't have been any more than fourteen years old, as he leaned nearer to the image hanging on the wall and studied an inscription set inside a black frame just beneath it. The inscription, penned in an elegant calligraphic script, was composed of two lines of equal length, between them a white space that the young man sought to fill in with his pen.

She is not dead
but is sleeping

The young woman in the picture has her eyes closed and the boy sitting below her hears the voice of his father summoning him to the table. Musa enters the room, his head entirely gray-white and his eyes shaded by thick white brows. He sits down next to the boy who resembles him. He points to the words written beneath the picture and reads them in a quiet voice. Milia comes nearer and listens to his words but cannot hear them. She tries to read the story the boy is writing between the lines and the curves of the fancy *naskh* script. She cannot read them. She decides that she will open her eyes and leave this dream alone. She will return to the bed in the Italian Hospital where her son awaits her. She reaches down and her hand collides with another hand, this one cupped with water. An unfamiliar hand takes Milia's and raises it, and a voice like that of the nurse says something she does not hear.

She saw the lamb. A lamb rising from the sun, coming toward her, scaling her chest and putting out its tongue. A little lamb standing over her as if to embrace her; she sees tears in its half-closed eyes. She tried to push him away a little and he opened his eyes. Why were they screaming? Tanyous stood in the orange light flooding the room, wearing a muddy black abaya. He came toward the bed, raised his palms high as if in prayer, and opened his mouth. A vapor something like incense wafted out.

Now, Lord, You can release Your servant in peace, as You have said, for mine eyes have seen Your salvation, made ready before the countenances of all peoples, a light announcing Your glory to the nations, and a glory to Your people.

The orange light faded and white light covered everything. Tanyous blended into the whiteness, appeared to step back, and disappeared.

Milia gasped that now she knew the story.

There, when they suspended him on the cross and gave him vinegar to drink; there, when they pierced him with a dagger; there, when his mother and his two Maryams stood waiting, fog veiling their faces; there, he lifted his eyes, looking for the lamb. But the lamb did not come. His eyes searched for his father, and the father did not come. He shut his eyes to remember, but his memory betrayed him. He saw nothing but white.

Musa lifted Milia's image from the wall and wrapped it in white paper and put it in the drawer. Black dots and tracings on the wall formed an image out of dust. The boy with the green eyes and the short curly hair picked up his brush and painted the wall white.

Everything was drawn in white – white over more white, layers of white. Milia tossed in her bed and was suddenly thirsty. Reaching her hand for the water she did not find it. She lifted her arm to rest it on the wall behind her but there was no wall. The lamb crept up her chest. She closed her eyes and saw small, dark Milia leaning over another Milia, the pale young woman lying on the hospital bed groaning in pain. Little Milia leaned over the pregnant woman and kissed her clammy forehead. Little Milia took her hand and whispered, Come with me.

Push! shouts the doctor.

Push again! shouts Nurse I.

Push more! shouts Nurse II.

Milia lifts her arm to shove the lamb away. She hears something like a ululation. The sound of a cry and the word *congratulations*. Doors opening, doors clapping shut, but where is the air? She wants to tell them to open the window. She asks little Milia to help her awaken from this long, long dream.

She hears their voices. What is Mansour doing here, and why is he calling her in a hoarse voice? Where did little Milia go, and why, when she tries to open her eyes, can she not see anything?

I must wake up from this dream.

It's over, she whispered.

She tried to open her eyes.

The little lamb lay on her chest and the photograph turned black.

She tried to open her eyes.

She tried harder.

The little lamb was on her chest and she heard a child crying in the distance.

She tried to open her eyes but the dream would not end.

She tried to open her eyes but could not, and then she knew that she had died.

Translator's Note

This novel is deeply embedded in the spiritual and institutional world of Greek Orthodox Arabs in 1940s Palestine and Lebanon. I therefore have chosen to retain the Arabic names of prophets and saints, and to use Mar – the Orthodox title for saints – interchangeably with Saint. I retain Arabic terms of address at times: Haajja (used as a title of respect for older women, literally one who has gone on the pilgrimage), sitti ("my lady" or "ma'am" but used to address one's grandmother), ustaz (professor, teacher).

I am grateful for the help of several expert colleagues. I want to thank Tony Gorman and Alex Kazamias for aid with Greek Orthodox terminology and practices; Marwa Mouazen for helping with some Levantine colloquial usages; and Richard Todd for checking my poetic flights (and occasional earthly thuds!). And finally I want to thank Jill Schoolman for her patience, cheer, and light and respectful editorial hand.

archipelago books
is a not-for-profit literary press devoted to
promoting cross-cultural exchange through innovative
classic and contemporary international literature
www.archipelagobooks.org